THE FALL OF
DIVINITY

Names:

Title: The Fall of Divinity / Shalyn Elizabeth

Description: First Edition | Series: The fall series ; book one

Identifiers: ISBN 979-8-9935282-0-5 (Paperback)

 Formatted with Vellum

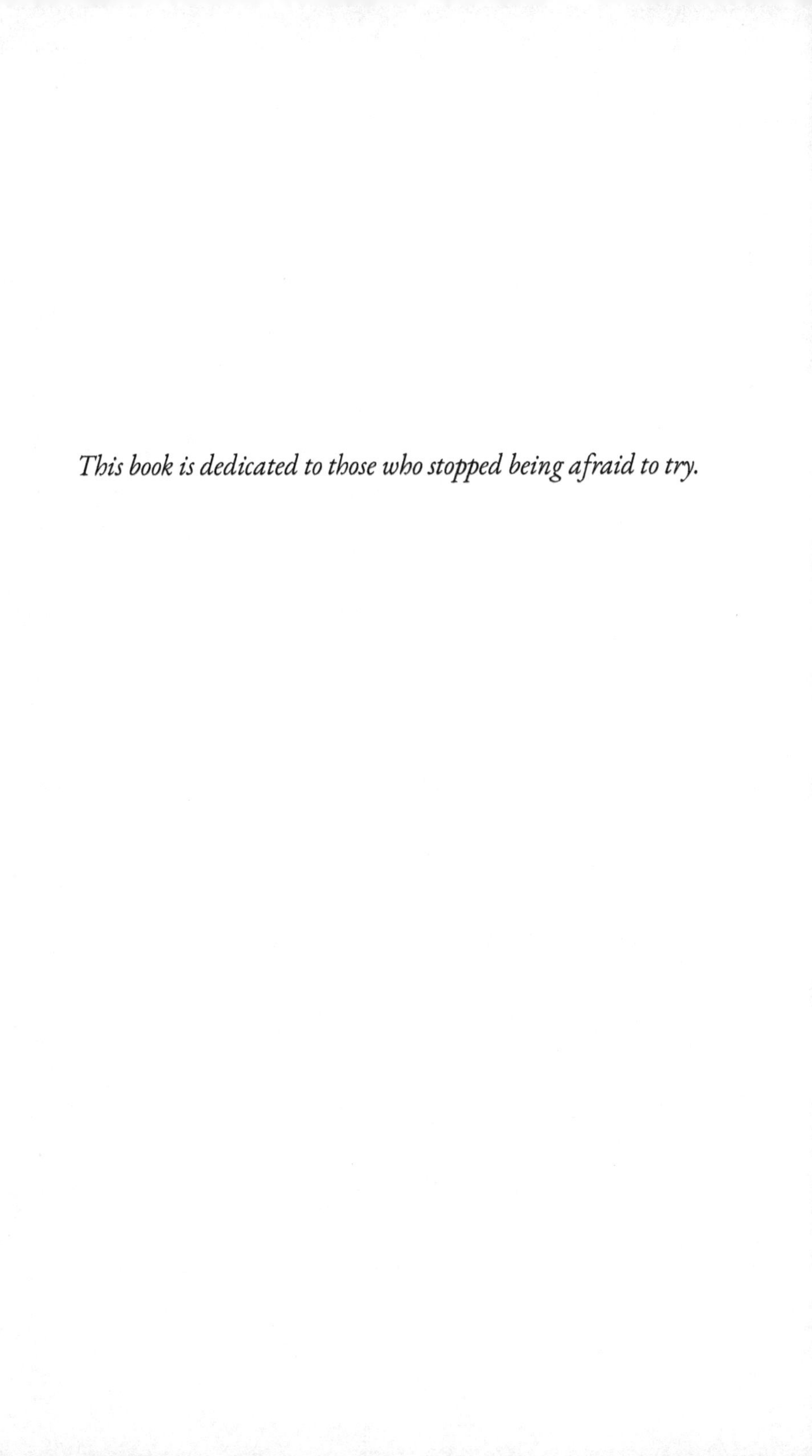

This book is dedicated to those who stopped being afraid to try.

ABOUT THE BOOK

As much as *The Fall of Divinity* is a fantasy romance, it may still contain subject matter that can be triggering to some. Please read responsibly. It will include explicit romance, mature language, violence, sexual assault and other dark and potentially triggering content. It is not intended for anyone under 18 years of age.

THE FALL OF
DIVINITY

PROLOGUE

On this day, two hundred years ago, the final God fell.

I PULLED UP MY SLEEVE AND HELD UP MY RIGHT hand, the needle hovering poignantly above the tip of my middle finger. Its design was thin and sleek, with a point so narrow my eyes struggled to see its true end in the low light. Created with a singular purpose: to cross the threshold of my body's last line of sovereignty.

A sharp scrape of wood-on-wood sliced through the silence of the cathedral walls, echoing down and through the empty pews. The heavy scent of incense loomed like low-flying gossamer clouds. My fingers gripped the opening to the Black Box and my chest expanded, taking in a deep breath as I peered through the haze.

The Box was dimly lit and caught the incense smoke within, creating a soft fog to drift down to the floorboards. The Box offered little, apart from a well-worn velvet seat cushion and an intricate lattice window dividing it into two chambers.

A stifled cough from the Box's neighbor broke the silence.

My head cloaked and my eyes turned down, I peered through the haze at my feet. My shiny satin shoes rubbed against each other in anticipation. The thumping in my chest felt like it would create its own echo if it were any closer to this plane than deep inside my rib cage. A slick layer of sweat started to form on my palms.

"How may I be of assistance to you, my lady?" The Saint offered the customary condolences before a Revelation.

The deep crimson of their robes was unmistakable through the lattice. Unhindered by their veil and my hooded figure, they still knew who I was. With the current herald, I was sure they also knew I was to be wed this evening and were expecting me to make a visit.

"My lady, would you like to begin with the Sacrament?" they asked.

A soft sigh escaped my lips. Readying myself, I held up the needle. I despised needles. A tremor shook me, and the needle threatened to jump from my grip. Taking in a short breath and gritting my teeth together, I took control of my trembling hand, and the sharpened point made swift contact. A rush of heat built at the tip as a small bead of blood formed and threatened to run down to my knuckles. I hurriedly allowed the droplets to fall into the siphon near the divider.

"We thank you for your sacrifice, my lady. What would you like in return for your offering?" asked the Saint.

The feeling of hopelessness settled deep inside my body. I wish I knew; I wish I knew what I could possibly ask them. There was nothing they or I could even do at this point. Clearing my throat, I forced back any hesitant noises threatening to squeak past my lips.

"I need to know if I am doing the right thing," I said in a

hushed tone. The words felt like treason on my tongue. Hot and bitter.

"Do you speak of the marriage? You are to be wed to our King Kairos. It is a blessed union."

A knot in my throat grew at my confirmation of my marriage. "I understand it is a blessed union, but I …"

My fourteenth birthday had passed just last week, and I'd known suitors were propositioning my family but, the King was well into his fortieth year. I had hoped there may be a suitor less … less my senior.

"It is blessed. There is no reason why you are not overjoyed. For his Grace not to have taken a bride yet is a grand undertaking. The honor is high, my lady."

Tucking my chin and nervously biting my lip, tears leaked down my cheeks. I was thankful my hood hung low; it hid the shame that began to crawl over my face.

I tried to compose myself but all I could say in a small, shaky voice was, "Yes, it will be a blessed day."

King Kairos stood before me, cast in the deep red light of the Crimson Moon shining through rose and lancet windows recessed in the walls of the apse. Our hands were joined in front of the altar at the end of the chancel steps of the cathedral.

My pulse thrummed against my temples and I'm sure he felt it rushing through my fingertips. His hands against mine were surprising. Not quite as soft and smooth as any other royals, but with shallow callouses along his palms and fingers. Maybe he was accustomed to a sword or a bow.

The multiple layers of sheer white fabric making up my veil hid any view of him and stifled most other senses aside from touch and hearing, allowing the droning of the Saint's regurgitation of the holy scripts to litter my ears. I had heard them so many times growing up that they ceased to have any further meaning aside from a cacophony of syllables.

Silence reigned, and my heart kicked up into a realm-shattering pace.

Kairos removed his hands from mine and lifted my many veils up and over my face. My eyes tried to focus on him in the dim red light.

He was a handsome king, standing tall, with a proud posture that exuded confidence. His skin was a rich shade of ebony, and his eyes were deep and expressive, with a strength in his features. A defined jawline and a hint of stubble speak of maturity. His hair, coiled and textured, framed his face well.

He looked down at me and his mouth turned up on the ends, giving me a soft smile. It was warm and inviting. Genuine. I joined him as best I could, but feared my smile looked closer to a sneer.

The room was awash of red, the soft glow of the moon's light reflecting off his high cheekbones, giving him an otherworldly look. To be married under the crimson moon was a royal tradition. Its origin had begun long before The Fall. Even if we did not teach or practice its history, the ritualistic wedding still stood.

The red cast lasted for three hours as the moon shifted in the sky. The union would be fully blessed once we were blanketed in darkness.

Searching the faces around me wasn't an option. I knew my mother and brother were here somewhere in the aisles of guests that were not mine. I knew they had their heads high with the white crowns of Egyn standing proud. But my attention must remain at the altar, on my soon-to-be husband.

The exchange of vows took place and the gold and red crowns of the Oriens were placed atop our heads just as the moon waned and a crescent took over the sky, plunging us into darkness. The marriage now complete. Well, almost. A kiss to seal the deal, I guess. Waiting, terrified, my knees trembled beneath me. I sensed Kairos shifting next to me and a hand connecting with my cheek. The breath in my chest hitched and a wave of warmth brushed over my face as a he placed a soft kiss on my forehead.

It was finished.

ONE

10 Years Later

THE SOUND OF MY BARE FEET SLAPPING ACROSS THE long stone hall leading to the East Wing echoed off the walls. I passed through the atrium and met the base of the grand stairwell leading up to my private quarters, picking up the front of my still too long gown and hurrying my pace.

Kairos was back from a ten-month leave, close to the Eastern and Southern borders. The prevalence of demons near the cities was growing stronger. Kairos and his Commander led charges to find out why they were here and to eradicate any they come in contact with. Though the threat of the demons actually making their way inside and past the gates was still unheard of, I carried a prayer for them.

I wasn't expecting Kairos to be back at any particular time, but he'd arrived the day before this year's Crimson Moon festival, which also happened to be our ten-year wedding anniversary. Ten years since I was sent to live off in a faraway kingdom without any family by my side, scared for my life. My mother traveled with me when I'd first arrived and helped me settle in for the first six months or so but over the years her visits came less and less. It was eventually just me and the king for the majority of the decade.

Reaching the end of the stairs, I let loose the trappings of fabric in my skirt and the train rippled behind me, flowing like unkempt wings. I was being fitted for my dress for tomorrow's celebration and alterations were still needed. The bodice was too tight at the bust and the skirts—well—you know about the skirts.

I did feel bad for the seamstress though, the moment I'd heard Kairos was back in the castle, I'd taken off from the riser. The only objection I had from her had been the tugging I felt as I wrenched the gossamer fabrics from her fingers. I'm positive I will be chided for it later.

Turning a corner right before his room, I ran into the firm chest of Commander Bauer. The pressure of the hit threw me off balance and I stepped back onto my train and tripped, falling to the floor.

"Your grace! Are you alright?" he asked, kneeling to help me up, pulling me swiftly by my arm and planting both feet back onto the cold floor. Within the next moment, he pulled me into a hug, squishing my face into his well-adorned jacket, the metal from his little pins poking into my cheek.

This was nice. It'd been so long since I had seen him, I would gladly take a few pin impressions in my cheek to have one of his hugs. He released me after a second, too soon, but kept a firm hand on my shoulders, giving me a once over. My eyes met his face, his mouth lifting into a warm smile.

"I am fine," I said with a light chuckle. "Is Kairos in his study?"

"Where else would I be?" the smokey, deep voice said from

inside the room. My heart swelled at the familiar cadence and the confirmation he was home.

Entering his study, I was greeted with the familiar smell of leather and parchment. Kairos's library was extensive, full of historical tomes, along with his own journals he filled with findings about the demons. He'd filled the walls and shelves to the brim with the collections he'd grown over the years traveling through the kingdoms.

His familiar frame stood in front of the tactical map table in the center of the room, his face full of a familiar warmth as I made my way in. He met me halfway and pulled me into a tight hug. He smelled the same as his room, if I am being honest: leather and parchment. Was that a hint of tobacco? He was supposed to be laying off the stuff.

I pulled away, looking up at him. "Have you been taking to your pipe again?" My voice teasing.

A deep laugh filled his chest, and he looked down at me, his eyes crinkling up at the corners and a soft smile pulling his mouth up to one side. "Nothing gets past your nose, does it?" he said, planting a soft kiss to the top of my head.

We separated and I went to sit on the settee across from the table he was now leaning against. I gathered the fabric from my dress into my lap, holding it against myself and pulling my knees up and under.

While Kairos and the Commander were away, I often found myself in this same spot. I would read the journals or take an afternoon nap. Being surrounded by Kairos's things made me feel less ... less alone.

I knew the traveling was necessary and in the best interest of the kingdom, but as the Queen Consort I had no ruling duties and spent most days closeted in my rooms or wandering the halls. Taking the time to read through his journals brought me closer to him.

"How long will you be staying for this time?" I asked, knowing the answer would inevitably be too short. But the realm needed them. And if what I'd read was true, then it was a miracle he was even here now.

"We will be heading back out at the month's end," the Commander answered as he made his way farther into the study. My teeth bit into my bottom lip nervously. So soon? The end of the month was only twelve days away.

Kairos let out a deep sigh and pushed off from the table, making his way to a high-backed chair near the small fire in the room's hearth. It wasn't the coldest part of the season yet, but the chill of winter was making its way deeper into my bones as the days passed.

A deep crease knitted itself between his brows as he leaned back into the chair. The years had been kind to him, but each time he returned, there was a new silver lock of hair or a few more wrinkles around his mouth. His travels and duties were not easy ones. I'd always felt a little selfish when I wished for him to stay longer, but what he was doing was helping every-one. I couldn't always have my way about things, but I still wanted them. *God, what am I? A child?* I pursed my lips and tilted my head to look him over, trying to give him a knowing look. To show I understood what he was doing wasn't easy.

Commander Bauer stepped farther into the room, his gaze meeting mine. A half-smile crept over his somber face, and I knew this had been hard on him as well. He went to stand behind the high-backed chair and placed his hand on Kairos's shoulder. Kairos, without looking, returned the sentiment by reaching up and giving the Commander's hand a small reas-suring squeeze. He then turned his attention back to me.

"Oh, I had almost forgotten," he said, raising himself from the chair and going to a large trunk on the floor. He opened the heavy lid, fighting through the high pitch squeal from the hinges. A travel trunk like his had surely seen the worst of wear. He rifled through for a moment and pulled out a small viridian green velvet box. He smiled softly before handing it to me.

"Happy Anniversary." He winked; a decade had really come and gone already. I stared at it for a moment, holding the anticipation for as long as I could bear it. I cracked the lid, revealing a black stone nestled in the plumage of fabric within the box. I gnawed on the inside of my cheek, tugging at the soft flesh as I studied the stone. It wasn't smooth or polished; it was raw, like it was just plucked from the earth and connected to a small silver chain.

I held it up to the light, noting the stone was not just black, but full of refracted silver fragments. It wasn't like anything I had ever seen before.

"It's a Legion Stone." Kairos gestured to the necklace and held out his hand. "May I?"

I placed the stone in his palm, and he came around the settee. I moved my hair to one side as he brought the necklace around my throat.

"They are from the South. We came across a peddler near the border. He said it is highly sought after outside of Amaymon."

The moment the stone touched my chest, a sharp sting hit my exposed skin. It wasn't very strong, but the feeling shocked me for a second, drawing a quick inhale through my teeth. I looked up to see the Commander staring at me. His eyes shot up to Kairos. I turned around noting Kairos's face shifting from an intense stare to a grin that wasn't reflected in his eyes. His hands came down and clasped both my shoulders.

"These stones are said to offer protection to those who wear them. The merchant insisted that the wearer keep it on, always." He gave my head a light pat before returning to his own chair.

I didn't like the thoughtful expressions on Kairos and the Commander's faces. "Thank you, it's gorgeous, but ..." I traced inquisitively over the stone again and the same sharp feeling returned. I held up my finger, inspecting it for any physical sign of the pain. Nothing.

I cleared my throat to recenter myself. "I can't accept this; I don't have anything prepared for you. I—I wasn't aware of your return until just a few moments before I came to see you. I'm sorry."

Kairos gave me a low chuckle. "My dear, you have done more than enough. You have supported myself and Commander Bauer for years and watched over our kingdom while I was away. You, Aleda DeLisle, Queen of Oriens, have no need to place a single gift in my hands."

A feeling of pride flowed through me at his compliments. Even though I was technically a Queen Consort and not many knew my face, I was still here in the castle having meetings with our clergymen and leading court when I was needed. *Thankfully, it was rare.*

The King and Commander had been together long before my marriage to Kairos. It was common in alliance marriages for one or both to take a lover or two, but I had never seen a stronger pairing between two people in my short time on this plane.

"You know I will, always." With that, I stood and dismissed myself. I needed to get back to my alterations before this was the end result of my dress for tomorrow night.

Two

Five hundred pin pokes later and the dress was nearly done. I stood atop the riser in my room facing a large three-panel mirror, allowing me to see the gown's soon-to-be-secured silhouette. I tried my best to remain still, but the seamstress was outwardly exhausted of my flinches from her needle pricks. I would jolt each time it would break through the fabric and into the first layer of my skin.

Again. And again.

It would be grounds for a dismissal on most occasions, but this woman was a true master of her craft and nothing short of a goddess when it came to the cuts and shapes she created with her tiny fingers. She was from the North, like me. A true Egyn woman from her white-blonde hairs, now sprinkled with bits of shimmery silver, to her ochre eyes.

I had one of the two main traits. My eyes were the same shade and shape, a slight lift at the ends of them, but still large and round. The one exception was my hair. My hair was an inversion to theirs, a black-brown color that always stood out from the others in Egyn. My mother had said it was passed down from some distant relative and made its way through the family line to me.

The styles the seamstress prepared reminded me so much of home. Long and draping sheer fabrics with a low dipped back ending in a V just above the waist and tied in the middle with secure ribbons holding it together. The long flowing belle sleeves complemented the skirt and the whole piece felt like a dream. If it was in the typical Egyn fashion, the dress would be black as night, but in honor of the Crimson Moon Festival, the seamstress had dyed it in the deepest of reds.

Thankfully, she hadn't held it against me when I'd run off the moment I'd heard of Kairos return. I'd shot through the door like I wasn't connected at the hip by small threads and uncut fabric. There may have been a couple extra pin pokes for good measure, but all in all, the dress was well worth it.

She stood and pulled the train to its longest position, fluffing up the plumes of fabric, allowing them to trace around me and flow just enough off the ground to give me a gorgeous flowing skirt while dancing, fluttering out during spins. It was perfect.

The last pin was placed, and my sweet freedom awaited me.

Finally able to get back into my normal pants and boots, I headed back to the great hall. The stone walls of the castle held very few items aside from the coincidentally deep crimson red of the Orien's banners, bordered with gold and white trimmings. They were a great match for this evening.

I furthered my trek, passing through the atrium where the festival would take place. It was a giant windowed half-dome built off the south side of the castle. The open skylights would allow the red cast from the moon to seep down and ignite the room with a glowing radiance.

Usually, the celebration took place outdoors, but it had been an unusually wet season, and the mud was an uninvited guest. If you found yourself unlucky enough to be greeted by it and fall into a mud pit, we might not find you until you had succumbed to the damp earth's embrace. The local wildlife were the most common casualties of this cruel fate.

The dates surrounding the festival were ones filled with unbalanced emotions on my part. The festivities and the parties were something I thoroughly enjoyed, and the berry wine was always delectable, but the day itself held a deep memory. Ten years had come and gone, though the terror I'd felt that night still lingered. To be married off so young and thrust into a new world with new people was not something that came easily. I had spent the first few months of my marriage holed up in my room, the lady-in-waiting bringing me my meals and tossing me into the tub when I avoided it for too long.

Kairos would visit me once a week for dinners in my room, telling me stories of his travels, reading me his books or offering to play a game of cards. Those soon became my favorite nights. I eventually joined him in the dining halls and met Commander Bauer. He scared me at first, but he soon became just another beloved friend.

When they were home more in the earlier days, I was given free rein of the castle and allowed to go anywhere on the grounds. My favorite spot was above the knight's training lawn. My brother, Thorian, had become a knight while I was still at home in Egyn, and I would watch him train almost every day. Overlooking the lawn was a taste of home. Ten years later, this place had become my home, these rooms were my rooms, and these people were *my* people.

My wandering led me far down into the only hall holding

any historical mementos from before The Fall. The paintings and murals had been left to the aging of time and settling of dust, as they no longer held a value that allowed anyone a need for a visit. Those who resided in the murals were said to date as far back as the creation of the stars themselves, and the celebration of the Crimson Moon was just as old.

The Great Separation was not quite as old, but when those days came, fire may as well have rained from the sky as war razed through the country. The Amaymon kingdom stood with the side of the old ways, of conspiracy and revolt and did not allow for the peace we once knew. Paymon aligned with them through marriage and military not long after and made things a lot more *tense.*

Here in the Oriens and in Egyn, if anything from before The Fall was discovered, it was cast out, and the conspirator sent out to lands beyond Abaddon—the final mountain range ensnaring the farthest southern regions. No one had gone there and returned to speak of it. It was said to be as close to the pits of hell to exist on this plane.

The Fall happened long before I was born, but many still behaved as if it had happened a few weeks ago; a dark cloud weighing heavily on most nations. Even in this sunny kingdom, we have pockets of those who believe the darkness is going to rise and conquer before the year is up.

The Saints took over the teachings soon after and began a simplified turn of praise and offering: *A sacrifice given upon arrival and your words will be heard.* As a young child I would refrain from speaking; the words never found their voice until the day before my wedding. On my trembling lips I prayed for an answer to a question I couldn't ask. Instead, I received my confirmation of the life I now live every day. I still visit the Saints, I still give my sacrifice, I still ask questions I don't seek answers to, for the fear that if I did ask for what I wanted, I would be bereft of any solace.

Facing the worn mural for a moment longer, I tried to make sense of the remaining disfigured pieces. As I turned away, a deep pulling feeling fell over me, unlike anything I've ever felt, and I had stood in these halls and this very spot many times before. My heart trudged to a near halt, my ankles stiffened, and my feet felt like they'd sunk into the floor.

I reached up to my chest and grasped ahold of the Legion Stone, the biting-feeling on my palm pulling me out of the weird daze.

The sound of footsteps coming toward me piqued my attention. I turned and found Ophelia, my ladies' maid.

"Hello, your grace, please pardon my intrusion. The King sent for you. He'd asked for you to return to his chambers after your fitting. I'm sorry if I am late. You see, I checked your chambers first, but I—"

I raised my hand to pause her wordy over-explanation. She was newer, and her nerves got the better of her most of the time.

"Thank you, Ophelia. I'll head to him now." I tried to give her a soft smile, and she stepped down into a deep curtsy, her head bowed low. I placed my hand on her shoulder, "Ophelia, there is no need. I have also given you permission to call me Aleda." Her head peaked up and a blush crept over her cheeks. Yet, she returned her eyes to the floor.

"Yes, yes, you have. Thank you, your—" she cleared her throat. "Thank you, Aleda."

Coming in close to the study, I heard Kairos and the Commander speaking in hushed tones, something tense and dark in his voice. I stood before the door and tried to pick up on any keywords, but their deep voices didn't carry as well as I had hoped. Everything went quiet for a moment, and the commander exited into the hall, finding me standing near the door. My eyes widened, and my breath went still like I'd been caught sneaking into a sweets jar and was about to be reprimanded. *Okay, maybe he did still scare me a little.*

He furrowed his brows and shook his head slightly, disapproving of my eavesdropping. I gave him a half smile and shrugged my shoulders before heading into the study to search out Kairos.

He sat in the same high-back chair, holding a journal in his lap. His head was downturned with his thumb and forefinger pinched at the bridge of his nose. I walked a little farther in and he straightened, bringing forward his finest attempt at a smile, and closing the journal with a small thump.

"Aleda, thank you for joining me. I hope the dress fitting went well. A little less length in the train than before?" he said to me with a toying smile.

"I hope." I would probably be finding pins for the next few days. "But really, it is going to be my favorite dress yet, thank you."

I walked farther into the room to the tactical map table in the center. He'd added new markers in the southern region and a small station just before the midlands. I traced my finger along the borders of the map and the small mountain ranges. We sat at the far east in the Kingdom of Oriens, and our allies were, of course, the north, my country of Egyn. The other two kingdoms, the south being Amaymon and the west, Paymon, were not.

With Kairos being near the borders lately, it always caused a deeper sense of worry than if he was farther north.

My eyes lingered on the northern kingdom and the snow-capped mountains dusted with a white pigment, sitting high above the castle and city. The castle sat perfectly within a valley, the sun would set earlier there, and the rays of the morning light did not cause you to stir until you were already meant to be up. I missed the snow, the chill on the wind, and the way the mountains knit together, forming the passageways from the coast to an outlet near the cathedral.

I had not been back there since the marriage. My family were in good health, and my brother was a Knight in the King's Guard. However, the likelihood of any visit home intertwining with his return was less than probable.

My face fell slightly. Sucking in a deep breath, I asked, "Have you heard from Thorian?" My brother had been on scouting missions for the past two years, entering the heavier saturated demon territories, protecting the small outlier cities and anyone in need, as knights do. He would send word whenever an attack happened, or a demon was sighted. I felt like we were hearing from him weekly. We didn't understand the demons' motives or reasons; we just knew they came after The Fall. Some say it's our penance for causing God to abandon us, to leave those faithless to themselves. That evil now walked amongst us on the physical plane as punishment.

"Not from him specifically, but we came across his company about three months back. It was a bit of a *rushed* encounter. They were heading East at the Northern Queen's request, through the midlands."

"Because of the demons?" A small ping of anxiety crept inside my chest.

He looked at the journal in his hand. "It was. We don't really know what is driving them, but it's getting more centralized."

He paused, tossing me the journal he read through. I went

to sit on the settee, beginning to flip through it, noticing the sketches and drawings.

"What is this?" I ran my fingers along the drawing, and a small tingle formed at the tips of my fingers. After they had traced over the entire design, the feeling built to a hot burning sensation. I pulled my fingers back and stared at the tip. No sign of anything; not even a smudge of charcoal.

I looked up to Kairos. His eyes were wide and watching. I met them, and he relaxed his face, his fingers fidgeting with the large signet ring he wore carrying the royal crest. I'd always thought of it more as a useful tool for sealing correspondence than a piece of fashion, being quite gaudy.

"They are protection sigils from the northern cathedrals. We may start placing them around the grounds here to give us some extra defense against the demons."

Egyn was an old kingdom, only second to Amaymon, and their church went back the deepest; their knowledge of demons was the most advanced. Just recently had other leaders been reaching out to them for more information. However, the threat of conspirators seeking more than just knowledge of the demons could threaten to halt that entirely.

Changing the subject, Kairos took the journal from me and set it on his desk. He turned to face me, crossing his arms over his chest.

"How have you been, my queen? Any revelations on your tryst with the Anders boy?"

A laugh escaped my mouth. "That would warrant a starting point to be able to give an update."

Anders was a member of the knight's patrol and had on occasion given me a token or two, along with some other girls. We had a few walks in the gardens, but he was a two-dimensional being, with only knowledge of knight's histories. I had to refrain from dozing off on far too many occasions in his company until I finally released him from his duty in the castle. He was not fully let go, but he was moved into the maid's court. Reports told me he was having a much better time there.

Taking a seat beside me, he pulled my hand into his, looking over our intertwined fingers. "You cannot spend all your days alone in a forced solitary confinement, Aleda. The maids say you have hardly left the castle grounds in the last two months."

I stood and walked across the study to his desk, inspecting the open scrolls and small maps, sighing against the sturdy wood as my fingers traced over the grain. I longed for a change, not for a walk around the city I'd lived in for the last ten years.

"It's not always the most desirable outing when you have a company of guards and people don't interact with you aside from paying their respects and getting hastily out of your way,"

He knew it had been hard having him and the Commander gone for close to a year. But he at least had his companion with him. I had no one. I felt truly alone in a castle, full of people who didn't get close to me and when they did, it was strictly for titles, gifts or favors. I had learned, the hard way, to be wary of those making their way into my circle. There had been many *friends* come and go once they had the little trinket they were in search of.

"I know," he continued. "But at the moment, there is too much demon activity to have you travel out of the city grounds. Hopefully, soon things will die down and we will find out more about the demons, allowing for safe travel between the lands. We can make a trip to the North, you can pay your family a visit and if we get word to your brother in time, he can meet us there."

My heart sputtered a bit; I would love to go back home to the cool air and the jagged mountain ranges, the most beautiful cathedrals, spotless and shining to the heavens. To see my family. My home.

"That would be amazing! Thank you." I ran to give him a hug, and he just laughed and hugged me back. "It may still be quite a while before it happens, but I promise we will get you back there."

"That's all I need." I gave him one more tight squeeze and headed back to my room.

THREE

The hustle and bustle of the festival happening this evening brought a new life to the castle. The far away guests were arriving early and getting settled into the guest suites. The red tapestries and banners were being cleaned on the lawn and the view out my window was a sea of blanketed reds; vermillion, scarlet, and crimson, flowing and drying in the wind.

It was still early in the day, and breakfast was not to be skipped, so I went to the main dining hall. There, I found Kairos chatting with a visiting Duchess and a few other High Lords and Ladies. The table had not one spare seat, and when Kairos caught my eye and started to summon a servant, I waved him off. I wasn't dressed for this formal of a breakfast, anyway. Wearing only a tunic and pants with my favorite boots. They may have had a hole or two, but they were there for me on all my castle-ground laden adventures.

I popped into the kitchen and grabbed an apple, a few breakfast biscuits and a small jar of honey. Exiting through a maid's corridor to avoid the influx of passersby, I headed to the training grounds. There was a chill in the air, but the breeze flowing through the alcoves and onto the grounds was cool and bright. It was a beautiful day.

Taking a bite of my apple, I leaned against a tall pillar in the shade looking out onto the green.

"Hiding from the riffraff, are we?"

Anders.

My face couldn't hold its composure in any way, and I knew a sneer was front and center. I turned to him over my shoulder, chewing loudly through my half-eaten apple. "Anders," I replied in-between bites.

"Well, don't look so bothered Aleda. I was just giving you a morning greeting."

I took another bite, while he came to stand in front of me. He wore the royal colors: Red and gold. His mantle clean and pressed. Anders's black hair was tied back in neat braids against his scalp, catching many a maid's eye and his height and body filled out his armor well. He was nothing short of handsome and knew it.

"Good morning." I said back dryly.

His mouth pulled into a frown and his brows knitted together. "You're not still mad about the—"

I raised my finger and cut him off. No, he did not get to ruin my day. My so-far-so-good day. I stared at him, opening my mouth like I was going to say something. His brows raised and he shuffled on his feet, as I baited his attention for a little longer, before taking another bite of apple and walking past him towards the training grounds.

With the guests arriving, the grounds were emptied, giving me space to sit against the trunk of a lovely royal poinciana tree at the far east side. The songs of the birds and the breeze settled over me as I took bites of my honeyed biscuits. The sun changed its station, starting to shine right into my eyes. So, I laid back and covered them with my arm. Not long after, the sun was blocked out and the clanking of steel boots disturbed me from my rest. Couldn't this guy take a hint? With my arm still over my face, I spoke out, "Go away, Anders."

"Do most knights have a first name basis with the Queen?"

I lowered my arm and squinted to make out the dark silhouette backlit by the high sun. I was able to make out the Commander standing before me.

"Only the stupid ones," I said, closing my eyes and putting both arms across my face. Fucking Anders. He'd started out charming and chivalrous to only be found under the skirt of my last lady-in-wait.

"I do believe it's time for you to be getting back; you may be needed for the festivities before the sun sets," he said, leaning down, and extending a hand. I grabbed it and lifted myself from the ground, dusting dirt off the seat of my pants.

"That may be so, but I shall not be missed. The Queen Consort rarely is." I leaned down to pick up my jar of honey. The commander gave me an exasperated sigh and rested his hand at the hilt of his sword, his thumb tracing over the pointed steel at the top.

"Have you been training?" he said, gesturing to the training fields before us.

I placed my hands on my hips and leaned back to stretch and loosen my tightened muscles from laying on the ground. "Here and there, not much while you've been away, though."

He looked down and for a moment, a softness to his features traced over him, very different from the typical stern look he'd held for the last decade. For all I knew, he'd come out of the womb with that look on his face.

"I know us being gone has been ... difficult," he said in a softer than normal tone.

He doesn't do this. This is what Kairos did. Kairos was the

soft talker, and the Commander was the strong and stoic one. I placed my hands on his arm and gave him a soft smile. "You are doing what needs to be done for the Kingdom. I'm alright, I promise. I can take care of myself."

He placed his hand over mine and gave it a small, tight squeeze.

"But I had better start getting ready; this hair will not look good all on its own," I said, starting off to my room.

The time had come; my hair was fashioned into long waves with small intricate braiding to lift off some of the weight in the back and give it a cascading look. I painted over my features and colored in my brows to make sure I had a nice contrast when the red glow of the moon shone down on us.

I was all but finished, my dress the last item of clothing, and I'd need at least two maids to help me to ensure my hair didn't fall when I was putting it on.

A knock sounded on my door. "Enter!"

To my surprise, Kairos stepped in, yet to be dressed. He smiled, but it was not the kind of smile that reached his eyes. He walked up behind me and placed his hands on my shoulders, looking into my vanity mirror with me. The longer I looked at him the more I noticed the tax time took. His hair was not only salt and peppered with gray and silver, but the majority had taken over. There were deeper wrinkles near his eyes, and the crease between his brows was now a formal ornament to his face. His deep brown eyes stared back at me a little less bright.

"You have grown into such a beautiful woman, my Queen. It has been a pleasure to have you at my side. You know that don't you?"

I gave him as close to a quizzical look as I could while making sure not to crease my makeup. He placed a kiss on the top of my head.

"Yes, you tell me this every year, Kairos," I said, trying to make light of the conversation. His energy was darker than normal; it felt unnervingly heavy. "Almost word for word. Did you practice in the mirror before you came in here?"

He gave me what felt like a real laugh, not one shrouded in this ambivalent display. "That mind of yours. How you come up with such things escapes me." He patted my shoulders and walked near the door, pulling a small journal from his jacket pocket. "This is for tomorrow, all right?" He placed the journal on my dresser.

I nodded before saying, "I'll be down soon."

FOUR

Entering the Atrium was like visiting a new world. Crimson and scarlet fabrics hung from almost every surface. At the very center was a great opening filled with dancers, swirling their bodies to the lively music. The drink of choice was a berry wine, noted for staining your teeth red after a couple of glasses. Crystal chandeliers hung from the ceiling reflecting the red light of the moon and cascading the room in shining refractions. At the rear of the Atrium were the thrones, giant high-backed chairs with the softest velvet embossed in more crystals.

Sitting alone was King Kairos, his chin resting in his hand and legs extended forward and crossed at the ankles—a picture of a carefree ruler. I made my way over to the seat partnered to his, my train flowing behind me. Thankfully, there was now much less of it.

I saw Anders out of the corner of my eye, making his way to me, and I hurried my steps, only to be stopped intermittently as guests passed by, bowing, curtsying or offering a simple, "Your Grace."

All but one.

A man stood in the center of the floor among the dancers wearing a red bauta mask. Wearing masks wasn't uncommon practice during the Crimson Moon Festival; most of the time they were worn until the moon was hidden and were left off once we were in darkness. It was a rather fun tradition. But he did not offer his respects as the others had. But rather, gave me an exaggerated bow and offered his fingers. I placed my hand in his and he brought it to his mask's lips lying a faux kiss upon my wrist. I couldn't help but let out a small laugh. What an odd exchange. He released my hand and stood to his full height, looking down at me with over a foot of additional height. He gestured to the others dancing, still silent, then reached out his hand to me.

I raised my brows and cocked my head slightly. This was also odd. Yet, there was only an hour left of the festivities, so I obliged the mystery gentlemen. Taking my hand, he led me onto the bustling floor, placing his hand in the middle of my bare back. His hand grazed my flesh and a smarting feeling arose, causing a shiver to work through me.

The music kicked off and we swirled through the droves of other dancers. The fluidity and grace of this mystery man was impeccable. His timing was flawless. He must be of noble stature. But if that were true, why did he neglect to speak to me and call me by my title?

My mind wandered as the music carried us through our steps. Would he be removing his mask once the blood moon had waned? Would he ask me to dance again? Would I want him to?

I came back to my thoughts as the last of the music died out. He released me and I stepped away, feeling dizzy and out of breath. Standing, facing each other, he gave me one last bow, and brought my hand to the mask's mouth once again. With that, he receded and was swept away in the crowd.

I finally made my way over to Kairos and a servant brought me a fresh glass of berry wine. The sweet and sour flavor coated my tongue, and I felt it immediately warm my stomach. Relaxing back into my chair, I looked to my left. Kairos was giving me a studying smirk.

"New dance partner?" he asked, a smile breaking free on his lips.

"I suppose. He was quite interesting. He didn't address me by my title, or actually say *anything* to me. Phenomenal dancer, though." I smiled into my berry wine, feeling a soft blush creep up my face. Thank God this place was cast in a crimson glow, or I'd look like I was close to lighting this room with how red I knew I was becoming. *It's just the wine.*

I played with the long sleeves of my dress and tried to sit back, enjoy the music and watch the rest of the people dancing. It was odd to think that on this day ten years ago I had been standing at the altar to be wed. After the ceremony, Kairos had taken me to his room to talk. He had asked about my brother and in a typical fourteen-year-old fashion I'd talked and talked.

I looked around the room to try and catch another glance of my dance partner, but my search was interrupted by everyone making way to the center of the atrium. The Commander was across the room, near the entrance, looking our way. It was almost time.

I heard someone say, "Oh, it is beginning." The crescent shape was making its way through the room. It grew smaller and smaller, like the light was actually being consumed. We did this every year, and it still brought me such wonder to witness. And just like our wedding day, as soon as the room went black, Kairos would place a single kiss on my forehead.

Finally, the room fell into complete darkness. My eyes

fought to adjust, and I waited a moment for Kairos to rise and find me next to him. A minute ticked by, and then another.

He'd never missed this moment. A small wave of concern ran through me, and I anxiously took another sip of my wine.

One by one, torches were lit, bringing us out of the darkness. Looking to my left, I saw an empty seat. Had he run off to sneak a special moment with the Commander?

Facing the door, I caught sight of Commander Bauer, his eyes wide and his mouth tight. Something was wrong. Panic flared in my chest.

A scream echoed across the room. With only the amber glow of the torches, the atrium became a rough sea of red as the bodies of the nobles and guests ran to the exit; the Commander stuck in the stampede. He shouted at me, but I couldn't hear anything past the blood thundering in my ears. Frozen in place, I spotted a large, dark figure made of shadowy flesh, bent over, his horns tall and curved up like twisted branches, gnarled and wretched.

A demon.

Fear strangled me like thorny tendrils blocking my airway as a scream built in my throat, and I faced it. In the dim torch light, I could vaguely make out the large mass behind the demon. Until. Oh my god. A hand was splayed out on the floor, palm down, and a ring on the index finger. The royal crest.

Kairos.

No, this wasn't happening. My ears rang and all sound turned fuzzy. *This isn't real. I'm dreaming. That's all that this is.* A shake ravaged my body, and I collapsed to my knees. The demon bent forwards, grasping Kairos's neck. His long, talon-like fingers dug into his flesh, and a gurgled breath escaped Kairos's lips. He was still alive! I looked back for the Commander. He was coming closer, sword drawn and ready. I realized I wasn't breathing; I was fading. *Am I going into shock?*

Swinging my head back, I saw the demon rip through Kairos's throat, coating me in a spray of blood. A metallic taste filled my mouth and terror filled my limbs. They were heavy and stuck in place, my eyes locked on the gore before me. I couldn't bring myself to look away.

The demon plunged its dagger-like teeth into his throat, pulling and tearing at his flesh. The sounds of the guests screams were overwhelming and—

A final crunch wrung out and it ripped Kairos's head from his body.

The Commander pushed me behind him, shielding me and raising his sword at the demon. He cried out, heaving his sword across the monster's belly. It screamed in blood-curdling agony. It clawed at the wound, opening it wider, thick sticky black blood spewing across my body. The Commander stepped back, readying his posture like a warrior on the battlefield and cleaved one final blow and the demon's head was severed from its body, tumbling to the floor.

He stilled, dropping his sword to the ground with a clatter. The echoes rippled, finally silencing. The room had emptied and yet felt suffocating.

Tears flooded my eyes, and I let out a wrenched sob. Kairos was kind and wise and took care of me like I was his family. He was my family. He was gone.

Kneeling beside his body, the Commander balled up Kairos's bloodied shirt in his palms and laid his head on Kairos's stomach, his body shaking with sobs. They had been beside each other for over twenty years. A soul-complete mated pair if there ever was one. How will the soul continue once it had found its half then loses it?

Anders burst into the room. "There are more demons! At least seven, Sir."

The Commander stilled, released the tattered shirt, and stood. His face was a hollow mask. He grabbed his sword, returning it to its sheath, then gripped my arm and helped me up. Holding onto my chin and he forced my eyes to meet his.

"There is no time to explain and even less to get you out of here. Go with Anders and get to safety."

I looked down at the lifeless body on the floor and then back to the Commander. Tears sprang free once more. "I'm so sorry." My voice barely came through as a whisper. He gave me a tight nod. Right now, he was a warrior. He would grieve when he was able.

I ran through the halls to my room, holding my gown over my knees so I didn't trip. The high walls felt like they were closing in around me and the hallway was stretching out, longer and longer. Each step didn't feel like it was making any progress, and my heartbeat thrummed in my ears. Reaching the stairs up to the rooms, I paused to throw off my high heels. The last thing I needed on top of all of this was a twisted ankle. Undoing the straps and cuffs, my fingers trembled and fumbled over themselves, unable to get a hold on them. I let out a small cry, "Fucking come on." Tears flooded my vision, making it impossible to get them off.

I stood, trying to take a centering breath and wipe the tears from my face. Inhale, exhale. Finally, I took the damn shoes off and threw them to the side, breaking out into a sprint up the stairs.

My bare feet came to a sliding stop on the smooth stone floor as I neared my room. The door was slightly ajar. I tried to be as stealthy as possible and inched the door open, allowing the light from the hallway to illuminate the dim room. Peeking my head in, it appeared to be untouched. Throwing caution to the wayside, I entered, slammed the door behind me and started to change my clothes, cursing the seamstress and her intricate ribbons and boning. My fingers strained, pulling out and loosening the long silk ribbons.

Finally, working my way free, I grabbed a pair of black riding pants, a grey tunic, and my boots. Rifling through the rest of my armoire, I collected a black summer cloak, rather than the red ones I normally wore. Unfortunately, the light-weight fabric wouldn't offer me much more than concealment. It was dark out, but I needed something to help hide me in the trees. I spotted Kairos's journal on the dresser, swiped it and put it in my bag. Finally, I was ready to leave.

I told Anders to meet me outside the maid's entrance; it was the closest exit on the castle grounds.

I barely made it into the Sylvanmere Forest on foot, and I couldn't catch my breath. Anders ran ahead. The damp forest floor stuck to my shoes like sap and each step got harder and harder to take. I heard a branch snap to my right and swung my head around, freezing. I knew it wasn't Anders; he was too far ahead. Only the sounds of my breathing broke the silence.

I tried to see through the forest, but the moon's faint glow through the dense canopy of leaves wasn't enough. The sounds must be all in my head, exhaustion taking its toll. I took another step forward and my back foot hooked itself onto a stray. I took a sharp tumble down, my palms sinking into the soft soil. I sat back, bringing my weight to my heels and forced my hands out of the deteriorating ground, trying to stand. This time, I landed flat on my back, my bag flung to the side, my feet sunk below the surface. I tried not to struggle, but the pull took me farther down. Panic set in, and I screamed out, "Anders! Help me!" My body kept sinking deeper into the mud. No answer. I managed to free my hand and clung to an exposed root nearby.

I saw a dark shadow in the distance approach me, its body barely visible in the dim light. Footsteps came in closer, and I pulled myself out a little more, my knees still deep below the earth's surface.

"Aleda, here! Grab this." He threw me his mantle to grab onto as he tried to pull me out. My tired fingers hooked into the fabric but after a moment it went limp.

"Anders, why did you stop?" I felt my legs sink deeper again. "Anders, please! Pull me up." The screams were caught in my throat as tears stung my eyes. I clawed at the earth, trying to get a grip on anything. I sucked in one more ragged breath, and turned, searching for the idiot knight. Anders body slammed hard to the ground in front of me. Blood spilled out of this mouth and ragged wet coughs shook him until he finally succumbed. *No.*

A labored breath came from my right, and I froze again. The menacing silhouette of the demon with its twisted horns and black, burnt flesh, emerged from the shroud of trees. It stilled as it entered the slim beam of light filtering through the leaves above. A single moonlit strand to illuminate my end. It let out a shrill scream. I covered my ears and lost any grip I had on Anders's mantel, sinking further.

I cursed as my vision became blurry. I couldn't see the demon, but I knew it was there. It was after my humanity, my soul. Just like Kairos.

I took in a few shallow breaths and closed my eyes, my heart hammering and tears stinging my eyes. I cried out, sheer terror filled my bones, my toes aching as they searched for something solid below me. Nothing. I only fell deeper, and the whimpers of my struggle were my final hymn to the earth.

My body sunk even lower into the mud, until I was up to my ears, gasping to keep my mouth and nose free. I thought I could hear footsteps. Many footsteps. As they got closer, I could feel them shaking the ground, shaking me down to my core. Could it be demons? How many would be hiding here? An entire hoard?

Then I realized, it was a horse. The shaking was hoofbeats. My heart almost stopped. I clung to my last breaths of hope, clawing at the mud, pulling myself up enough to scream, "Help!"

I dipped lower again, my mouth nearly fully covered. I spat out mud and gave my final plea. "Please! I'm getting pulled under!"

The hoofbeats slowed, and I felt a spark of hope in my chest. My head was now stuck with my gaze to the right, and the dark form settled out of my sight.

I heard the stranger dismount and walk carefully over to me. *Not like I might be sucked under at any moment.* Could they pick up the pace?

Nothing happened for a heartbeat. My only airway was my nostrils, and I was millimeters from suffocation.

Finally, a hand plunged into the mud, gripping my shoulder so tightly it felt like it might be bruised by the morning. Then instead of going up, I was pushed down. My eyes widened and I tried to scream, but mud filled my mouth. That spark of hope extinguished. I closed my eyes and prepared for my end.

FIVE

But the end did not come.

Hands wrapped under my armpits, and I was pulled up and out of the mud, thrown onto solid ground.

A thick layer of grime covered my body and I coughed up anything stuck in my airway. I spat out as much as I could, the dirt leaving a coarse layer along my teeth. Disgusting. I tried to wipe it away from my eyes and mouth. All I was really doing was smearing it around at this point. *God, it was in my ears.* I crawled to my bag just a few feet away and slung it over my shoulder attempting to wipe what dirt I could from it.

I took in real, unencumbered air, trying to steady my racing heart. I was hit with the memory of the demon. It was still out there. I looked up to warn my savior and was met with the gargantuan figure before me—a Knight of the Realm. He stood tall, wearing steel armor and a deep red mantle, the color of the royals. I was sure during the red light of the eclipse, it must have looked like he was aflame himself, the shiny steel reflecting the moon's own fire.

He was well aware of what could reside in these woods.

The demons weren't strangers to us, but this was an unnatural amount to see so close together. And it was definitely a more common practice than not to avoid the Sylvanmere Forest at all costs.

The knight stood beside a towering horse with its own armor around its face and ears. He rustled through a saddlebag, adjusting the straps on the rear portion of the saddle. Tightening the last strap, he walked over to me and took my hand in his, the rough leather of his glove slick against mine. He led me over to his horse, his hand still grasping mine.

Finding my voice again, I said, "Thank you for helping me, I—" his grip on my wrist went shockingly tight. My eyes shot up to his helmet—a dark emptiness was all I could see through the small slits that allowed him any vision. I tugged harder, trying to pull my hand free, but his grip only got stronger. In a quick movement, he grasped both my wrists in his and wrapped a rope around them, tying them off.

"What the fuck are you doing?!" It was all happening so fast and before I knew it, I was being dragged along by a fucking horse. "If this is some kind of weird kink that you have, I just want you to know I will *not* be taking part!" I shouted from behind the horse. The asshole hadn't said a goddamn word.

The Knight remained walking as well, but his long stride meant I had to sprint more often than not to keep his pace or be dragged along by the horse.

"Is there any way you can at least tell me where we are going?" Each step felt heavier and heavier. The mud was so thick on my pants, it weighed me down with each movement. I unclasped my mud-covered cloak and dropped it, realizing the knight had ripped it past repair.

"I know there is an ally encampment near here. They'll stop you if they see what you're doing to me." No response. The sun began to rise, little speckles of light peeking through the canopy. I wished I was waking up in my bed from this horrific nightmare.

We reached the edge of the forest, and I started to hear sounds other than the clunking of his steel steps and my ragged breathing. Conversations, metal clanging and deep throaty laughs broke the Knight's silent streak and the monologue I'd had all night. The smell of cooked meats filled the air, and my stomach ached, letting out an audible grumble.

Nearing the entrance of the encampment, the Knight stationed his horse with the others and removed my rope from the saddle. Now the rope was in his hands, and he dragged me through the grounds like some pet. The men we passed stared and muttered amongst themselves. My breath hitched in my throat. I was under no protection of my own and the first person I'd met had strung me to a horse's hindquarters.

Walking through rows of tents, we approached what looked like a command pavilion. The Knight brought the flap of the tent to the side and gestured for me to enter. The inside was large and held a table in the center, a few chairs surrounding it and a good deal of trunks stacked on top of plush rugs.

I looked down at my muddied body, my stomach dropping as I moved my foot to reveal—just what I thought—a mud-filled boot print right on the rug. I shook my head and stood there with my hands clasped together by this stupid rope, waiting for whatever the hell came next.

A moment later, a man walked in after us, coming through

the tent flap with his back to me finishing a conversation with someone outside. "Do you really think quail eggs do the trick? We are rather used to chickens though, aren't we?" As he turned and saw us, he stopped hard in his tracks, looking between me and the Knight until his focus went solely to me. His gaze worked over me, from the top of my head and down until his eyes focused on my feet. I shuffled back a bit and took a hard swallow. He quirked his head to the side and then looked back to the Knight.

"When I said meet me here for breakfast." He paused, a smirk beginning to form on his lips, "this was not what I had in mind." He looked me over once more, and I saw he held a small clutch of quail eggs in his hand. He set the eggs down on the table, his eyes never leaving me. He crept closer, making his way across the space fluidly, each step looking intended and precise. The air in my lungs felt tight and hot, like I had been holding my breath.

Was I holding my breath?

He leaned over me and I felt trapped, as if I was in the snare of a hunter, limbs tangled and doom encroaching with each passing second.

My hands were still bound in front of me. *What the hell am I going to do from here?*

"And who might you be?" He crossed his arms, the sleeve of his white shirt hanging on his forearms like clouds, the center open, revealing a smooth and defined chest.

My mouth went dry, and I tried to open it but nothing wanted to come out. I was stuck staring up at this man and I was kind of fine with that.

He had a close-crop haircut with just enough growth to see a light shadow growing in, but it was very short, and like his chest, his face was smooth. His eyes were a dark shade of grey. He looked like no one I had ever seen before.

I realized I was gawking, and he was patiently waiting for

my response. I drew a blank. My name wasn't well known, but it was easy information to acquire. I suspected this was the same encampment I'd seen in Kairos's study. If so, it was likely someone here knew of me.

Clearing my throat, I said finally, "Evangeline, my name is Evangeline." I'd given my middle name. If these people knew Kairos, then word of his death would travel, and the Queen Consort would become a bargaining piece in anyone game for power. My kingdom may be ravaged, but I wouldn't harm them further with a ransom. I couldn't go back.

"I'm seeking refuge for a short time. I come from the Kingdom of Oriens and there has been an attack. Demons." The words came out short, and much more tense than I had intended.

"Well, Evangeline. I am Ilias, Ilias Terrell." His lips perked up into a tight smile, flashing deep dimples. "We did get word of the attack early this morning; I am happy to see you came away, relatively unscathed. Are you hungry?" he asked with a gentle tone.

"I am, sir. But I feel like a possibility of a bath is far more warranted," I said with a small bow of my head. I didn't know these people or their customs and wanted to show at least a form of respect.

He took a step back, reached for the tiny quail egg, and rolled it around in his palm, looking up to the knight. "Would you mind taking our—" He looks me up and down, "*guest,* Evangeline, here to the bathing area?" The knight nodded and turned back to the entrance of the tent, opening it wide enough for me to slip through next to him. Before the flap closed Ilias yelled out, "And take those restraints off her. She's not an animal."

The knight closed the flap and walked to me. He was so much taller than me, his faceless helmet looking down at me was just cold steel. He gripped my left wrist in his hand and pulled me forward and up, lifting my arms almost above my head, to slide a black stone encrusted dagger between my wrist and the rope. With a slight tug the fibers of the rope spun away from one another. I rubbed my sore wrists, raw and chaffed from the walk last night. He re-sheathed the dagger and headed further into camp.

The bathing area resembled an enclosed horse trough, with a steel tub full of the coldest water imaginable. It was open to elements, the walls surrounding it standing less than a foot above my head. An open sky, barren of clouds and bright with the early morning light was above me.

I pulled a cloth from a stack sitting on a lone stool, dunking it into the water. I started to scrub. The dirt caking my body was dry, and it, along with the frigid water was rough on my sore skin. I hadn't noticed it until now, but my legs shook with exhaustion, and the tips of my fingers were tender and red from when I'd tried to claw my way out of the mud.

A flash of Anders' body filled my mind, and then the vision of Kairos took over. I remembered his limp body on the ground, the screams filling my ears. Then a gust of air blew through the small pace, and the chill on my naked body ate through to my bones. As heat returned to my extremities, I felt dizzy. I squatted and held my knees to my chest and shook. First from the cold, but soon a sob took over. The tears burned my eyes, and the reality that I was in a fucking glorified animal feeder in the middle of the forest hit me at once. I pressed the heels of my palms into my eyes and wiped the tears away. I needed to move. I needed to do something.

Finishing my poor excuse for a bath, I dried off and put on a soft cotton tunic and some trousers someone had left out for me. They weren't the most well-fitting, but it was thoughtful, nonetheless. My hair was still a little damp, so I tied it into a braid for the time being. It was my least favorite hairstyle, but without a brush I was limited on what would appear presentable.

The knight had stood guard over my bathing area the entire time, his back facing me and unmoving. It was like someone had made a statue and left it in his place.

Ready to move on, I stood near the knight, looking up at him. Without glancing my way, he walked forward toward Ilias's tent. I followed. Again.

Reaching the space, I entered the tent, taking a seat near one of the plates containing two eggs with very small yolks—presumably quail—plus a bread roll and some cured meat. My stomach ached at the sight of the food, but a different feeling rose up in my throat. The idea of eating felt shameful. Repulsive. And as I looked closer at the plate, that feeling only grew. The yolk of the egg appeared to have a frost to it and the meat had a layer of congealed fat settled over it, as if it had been sitting out for too long. Gross.

The tent flap opened, and Ilias walked up and around the table quickly; his long legs only needed a few steps before he loomed over me and my untouched meal. He greeted me with a smile, flashing his dimples before taking the seat across from me at the other plate.

"A wash did you well, Miss Evangeline. You're definitely not what I expected to find under all that mud," he said as he broke off a piece of the cured meat, popping it into his mouth. "You look much better like this."

I felt a blush creep up my face. Reaching for my own plate, not wanting to be rude, I did the same with the bit of cured meat. The salty, savory piece was tough, and each bite was filled with a spice unknown to me. I chewed as much as I could and swallowed the piece with a hard gulp, nausea swelling. *No more of whatever that was.*

"Thank you ... for the clothes and the food. It wasn't necessary, but I appreciate it." I looked up from my plate and found his grey eyes locked on me. I felt like a trapped animal, like this man was a predator. He blinked and looked away as he spoke, "It was no problem at all. I only wish we had something more, *feminine,* to offer you. I'm sure those britches are not a tailored fit."

I looked down to the shirt tucked in to the oversized pants and the belt I'd picked up near the bathing area, fastened to its very last notch. "I'm well accustomed to pants; these will be fine." I found myself searching over the room, the large trunks stacked high had locks on them with odd key holes. What could be so important that Ilias and his group carried it with them in such large quantities?

Ilias stretched his back over the chair and dropped something onto the floor. It hit with a loud clang. I jumped back, almost falling out of my chair. My pulse raced and my breathing felt harsh; I was taking in air, but my lungs felt empty. Small gasps came out and I leaned forward, placing a hand over my chest. *Why couldn't I breathe?*

Ilias rushed over and knelt to the floor in front of me, grabbing my face in both of his hands, and guiding me to look up at him.

"Hey, it's okay. Just take a deep breath and hold it for me."

I tried to do as he said but choked.

"Try again and hold it, a deep one."

I sucked in a deep breath and held it, counting to five or

ten or however long before I couldn't hold it any longer. Then another and another. Finally, my heart stopped beating through my chest and I could feel air flowing into my body. Ilias pulled his hands off my cheeks and pushed back a few stray hairs behind my ear. My eyes met his, lingering for what felt like an eternity before I broke the connection and he went back to his seat.

I spoke first. "I'm sorry, I'm still a little shaken up over what happened last night." I bit my lip and felt a burn at the back of my eyes, tears threatening to spring free again.

Ilias reached across the table and placed his hand on mine, giving it a soft squeeze. "You have nothing to apologize for, I can only imagine what you went through." He held his hand on mine for a moment too long and I pulled back, placing both hands in my lap and staring down at my red, raw fingers. His gesture was kind, but I ... I didn't know this man. Or who these people were. It was a lot to process in such a short amount of time. Only a few hours ago I'd been strung along by the knight and his fucking horse.

Looking up from my hands, I saw Ilias lean back in his chair on the rear two legs, his boots propped up on a trunk sitting not too far from the table.

"Ilias," he set his chair back on the ground, his full attention now on me again. "Yes?" he questioned.

"Do you mind telling me who you all are? What this encampment is."

"Well, I told you who I am already." His lips pulled into a smile, and the dimples made another appearance. "As far as my men go, we are of the Midlands. My uncle is the duke, and he has alliances in place with the Oriens."

They were definitely the small settlement I'd seen on Kairos's map. I had suspected but am pleased to have confirmation. The remaining tightness in my chest relaxed but I wanted to continue keeping my identity a secret for now. These people were strangers to me, and alliance or not, Kairos was dead. I did not know where their fealties lie, but I knew it was not with me.

"What about you, Miss Evangeline? What are your plans from here?"

I have no fucking clue. I thought about all the options I had. I can't go back to the Oriens, not now anyway. North? Maybe. Perhaps I could make my way back home and see my family.

"Egyn, I have family back there."

"The North? Up to Egyn? That's quite a trek. Were you meeting someone that can aid you? I'm just assuming that, well, with the state you arrived in that you maybe weren't suited for a journey across the continent."

The tight feeling in my chest returned. It was a stupid idea. How the hell was I going to make my way there? I had no money and no means. Even if I did take every step on my own two feet, I would starve by the halfway point. And that was only if I didn't come across demons.

Ilias spoke breaking me from my thoughts. "How about this?" He leaned over the table, resting his elbows on it, his fingers woven together below his chin. "We leave for the Midlands tonight and that is technically more northern than where we are now. You are welcome to stay with us send any correspondence you need to for your travels and wait for a response from your family."

My heart leapt. Being able to send word to my mother would be all I would need to get myself North. His offer was perfect and easy. And yet, something didn't feel right. He didn't know anything about me and yet he still extended an invitation for a stay of who knows how long? I needed more time to think before I agreed.

"That's very kind of you to offer, and I would be hopeless without it. But can I have a moment to think about it?" I looked up to meet his eyes. He gave me a look that held more concern than offense. There was a soft kindness to his face I hadn't noticed before.

"Of course." He stood from the table and gave me a somber half smile. And then I was alone. Alone for the first time since being rescued from the mud. I felt the visions of Kairos flooding my mind again, creeping up behind my eyelids as I squeezed them shut. I took in a sharp breath and looked around the tent again, spotting my bag underneath a table near the entrance. I went to grab it, and found the poor thing still caked in mud. Reaching inside, I pulled out the journal Kairos had left for me, safe and unsoiled. The book fell open to a letter stuffed in between two pages, Kairos's familiar writing on the envelope, *Aleda, My Queen.*, My heart thumped loud, and my fingers trembled at the lip of the paper. Holding my hand over my mouth, I read his words.

Aleda, my Queen, my greatest joy. I hope this doesn't feel too rushed for you and I know with this being our ten-year anniversary I wanted nothing less than to spend it by your side. Getting to watch you grow into the powerful woman and Queen, I always knew you would be, has filled me with so much happiness and pride. You are so much more special than you will ever understand, and I know you will find someone who sees exactly what you are.

With that, my love, I am so sorry to say that I must leave sooner than I had expected. Word of the demons traveling farther East has made its way to us and we must travel North for reinforcements.

I will make arrangements for you to head North by the end of the month, but we will have to leave tomorrow morning.

I will send for you the moment we have news.

Yours always, Kairos

Tears streamed down my face. He was only at the castle because of me; he shouldn't have come back. Not if all of this could have been avoided. Not if—*fuck*—not if he could still be alive. A sob threatened to break free; my hand the only thing physically blocking the scream from erupting. Dropping to my knees, I held out the letter and read it over again. My tears fell and dripped to the page, soaking into the ink written across on the parchment, the letters blooming and smearing. *No, no, I can't lose this.* I panicked and tried to clean them from the page, making it worse. The black ink transferred to my fingers now and the words lost legibility. I threw my head back in desperation. *Why do I ruin everything?*

After cleaning away my tears and putting Kairos's letter away, I needed to get some fresh air. Being inside this tent felt suffocating. I slung my bag around my shoulder and stepped out past the tent's opening, right into the hard backside of a metal mountain. I fell back and landed on my tailbone. The ground was unforgiving, and the rugs did me no favors here. I sucked in a breath through my teeth and stood. *This fucking guy again.* The knight stepped forward and turned to me, his stature so large it dwarfed me in comparison. I stared up into the emptiness of his helmet's expression and tried to sidestep him.

"Excuse me." The words dripped with as much venom as I could conjure. He stopped me with his outstretched arm. *He wasn't letting me go?* Was I no longer a 'Guest' as Ilias had called me? Anger boiled up inside of me, the sadness taking a backseat to this, this—asshole.

"Let me pass," I gritted out through my teeth.

No movement, yet again. I took a step forward, and he matched me, not letting me pass.

"That's enough, Knight. I'll take over her watch for the time being. Thank you." Ilias came from around the left of the tent and up to meet me. The knight lowered his arms and gave Ilias a nod before walking away. It was just the two of us again.

"I'm sorry if that was a little off putting. I instructed him to keep an eye on you, and he likes to take certain, *liberties,* with his roles," he said scratching a spot on his chest. He looked down to me, "Oh, here, allow me." Ilias pulled a kerchief from his pocket and brought it to my face. I jerked back on instinct, and he paused, offering a soft smile and flashing his dimples at me once again. He moved in, my eyes tracking over the cloth as he wiped it along my cheeks and under my eyes. When he pulled it away, I could see the smudges of black. *The Ink.* I must have smeared it on my face.

I glanced down. My fingers were covered in black ink stains. I'd smeared it all over my face when I tried to clean myself up earlier. He wiped a little more and then folded the kerchief, returning it to his pocket.

"There you are," he said, a calming scent of salt and citrus washed over my face. His eyes bored into mine. I realized I'd never *really* looked at them, they were the loveliest shade of dark grey with a few flecks of blue close to the iris. Such an unnatural color, but they fit well against his light complexion. My cheeks started to burn. He was so close to me.

"Would you care to join me for a walk?" He asked extending a hand. I looked down at it and back up at him. Taking in a deep breath I gave him a short nod before placing my hand in his. He moved quickly to place it into the crook of his arm as he took me out of the company's encampment.

The whole of the forest looked so different when it wasn't cast in darkness. The mud was still prevalent, but nothing like what I'd come across last night. Ilias was quiet for the majority of the walk. It was odd but I felt more comfortable than I'd had expected. This felt like a walk I would have taken through the castle's gardens with a suitor courting me. Of course, there we would have had chaperones and guards around us. This was something I never got to experience. I was thrust into the alliance marriage to Kairos so immediately after coming of age where the taking of suitors wasn't even an option.

We approached a stream, and Ilias released my hand to step to the water's edge. He knelt and scooped a small amount up to his face, rubbing the last of it up and around his neck as if it was a hot summer's day, when in actuality, it was a chilly morning. He stood and faced the water, placing his hands behind his back, and interlocking his fingers.

"I don't mean to be too forward with this." Ilias moved in closer, coming to stand at my side. "Have you made a decision about your travels?" His shoulder brushed against mine and we both looked out past the stream and into the forest. There I would be alone and on foot once again, assuming I survived more than a day. I would be stupid not to take him up on his offer, wouldn't I? He had already shown me a great kindness by feeding and clothing me. Could I burden him further with a stay as well?

A branch snapped behind me and I startled, my heart pounding so loud and the blood rushing through my ears turned from a fuzzy static to a loud ringing. I turned in panic and saw a few birds hop from a branch and fly up over our heads. Nothing was behind me, nothing was wrong, but I couldn't settle the race residing in my rib cage. I squeezed my eyes shut and saw the flashes of Kairos again. His body lay in the pool of red and black blood. I tasted metal on my tongue. Bile rose as I ran to the water's edge. I dipped my hands in the water and splashed it up onto my face. The cold was a shock to my skin. My hair came loose from my braid and fell around me, blanketing me in a shelter of darkness.

I slowed my breathing and focused on the inhale and exhale. A minute or so passed and then I felt fingers reach around my neck and gather my hair. Ilias's warm body knelt beside me as he grabbed for the loose pieces. I turned to him, and he had the saddest look in his eyes. Was it pity? Pity for a lost girl who had gone through two panic attacks? His eyes lowered to my mouth and up to a strand of my hair hanging in front of my eyes. He traced his hand over my cheek as he tucked the stray pieces behind my ear. His fingers traveled down my neck meeting my shoulder. He gave it a squeeze and pulled me to stand. His hands collected both of mine and he looked down at me.

"What will it be, Lady Evangeline?" His fingers tightened around mine. I took a deep breath and looked back into his dark grey eyes.

"I will go with you."

Six

While the camp was being packed and loaded on the horses and wagons, I found one of Ilias's many trunks sitting out by the rest of their cargo and took a seat. The knight had traded his previous blockade for a position behind me, standing as an ominous figure in my peripherals.

I pulled my bag up to my lap, rifled through it just to make sure I still had Kairos's journal and the letter, the only two things I had to remember him by.

Wait, I still had the necklace. I reached up and grasped the black Legion Stone, the familiar sting hitting my skin. I clutched it harder and felt the stone bite into my fingertips. After my last panic attack at the stream, I'd felt emptier than I had before, lost, with just a pit of nothing inside of me. The feeling of this stone, no matter how unpleasant, was a reminder of Kairos and I would cherish it forever.

Ilias walked up just as the sun started to set. *Is this really the best time to travel?* He pulled a tawny-colored horse up with him. Ilias wore leather armor and a sword strapped to his back.

"At the moment, all our horses are occupied. Are you alright with traveling with me?"

Two to a saddle wasn't the most spacious, but I was not in a place to complain. "Yes, I don't mind at all."

"Great. Let me put your things away and we'll be ready to head out."

A tinge of panic hit me as I imagined parting with my bag. Having it on me felt like a sense of security, but traveling, it would possibly fall or swing off my shoulder if I wasn't paying attention.

Removing it from my shoulder, I handed it to him, and he placed it in the left saddlebag. Stepping a foot into the stirrup, I felt two hands secure themselves around my waist. I went rigid. I turned to see Ilias below me and dug my fingers harder into the grips. With a deep breath, I shoved off the ground and with Ilias lifting me, I was able to sit almost effortlessly. He raised himself to sit behind me. His legs bracketed my thighs, and the closeness was something I would need to get used to if we were to ride together for what could be days. I tried my best to keep my back straight and not to lean into him. With a click of his tongue and a snap of the reins, we were on our way to the Midlands.

At the back of the company rode the knight, his larger-than-life black stallion as his mount. His glossy coat shined in the moonlight—a real-life omen. A destroyer of worlds trailing after us like something out of my childhood nightmares. I would turn back to look at them, now and then, the vision never any less intimidating.

At the last turn, Ilias adjusted himself behind me and I felt his abdomen press up against my back and his arms snaked forward to pull me into him. His face moved in towards my ear, his hot breath on my skin. Goosebumps traveled over my arms and I fought not to shiver.

"So, Lady Evangeline, tell me a little about yourself." His words took me by surprise. *Well, for starters I'm a big fat liar.* If I'd known, I'd be traveling with Ilias I did not know if I would have given him a false name. Now, I couldn't tell him, *Hey, by the way, I lied and I'm also the Queen of Oriens sitting on your fucking lap, thanks for taking me on this little trip.* How would that even go over?

"I don't know quite what there is to tell. I may have better responses for catered questions. An autobiography may take a while."

He let out a soft laugh. "A clever girl I see."

I felt a blush creep up my cheeks. *What is the matter with me? Or him?* Was he flirting with me? He leaned back from me, "Hmmm ... alright, let me think. How old are you?"

Nice, an easy one. "I am twenty-four. You?"

"Twenty-nine. What do you do in your free time?"

He really was rapid fire with these questions.

"I like to read, primarily research. I fill my time by looking up facts about the lands and the neighboring kingdoms. Lately it's been on demon-related things. With the amount seemingly increasing, I like to be prepared with whatever I can."

"A fellow bookworm, I do love a good spun story."

Did he not take the risks seriously? We were traveling at night. Was this a part of his own lack of caution and belief? I turned back to look at him.

"A spun story? Do you think that I'm not being factual?"

He tilted his head and smiled, moving in closer, his lips just outside of the shell of me ear. "Would it change how you feel about them if I said no?" My eyes went wide, and I turned back from him to face forward again. He let out a low chuckle and continued, "Well, take it this way—aren't all things written just on an account-by-account basis? A story?"

I paused for a moment, contemplating his response. "I suppose you're right."

He laughed softly, his chest moving against my back.

The chill of the evening came on fast; the cool weather was turning, and while it wasn't freezing yet, keeping my eyes open was the hardest part. As the ride continued, I began to feel myself swaying and nodding off. Ilias wrapped his arms tighter around my waist.

His lips tickled my ear. "If you're tired, you can lean back against me. I won't let you fall. We should be making camp in the morning for a few hours."

I didn't respond but took him up on his offer. I relaxed a little and felt his chest fully meet my back, his arms pulling me closer to him, his chin settling just above my head and his smell enveloping me. He smelled of light, full of salt and citrus, almost familiar. It was nice. I let myself drift off into a light sleep.

I woke up when the horse stepped back, jarring me. Ilias whispered in my ear, "There is some demon activity, keep quiet. Okay?" I nodded against him, my heart rate picking up and anxiety taking hold of my stomach. The knight and other guards accompanying us dismounted and drew their swords. It was still night and a tenebrous darkness snaked through the dense tree canopy. We were off the main roads.

That may have been our first mistake.

Ilias's hold on me tightened, and he drew his own sword. A scream shot through the trees. The knight stayed close to us, but others made their way deeper into the woods. A smaller demon shot out from the tree line to our right, and moving so fast I could barely see him. The knight slashed it almost completely in half with a single cleave of his heavy sword. The black blood splashed its way across the ground and sprayed over the knight. Nausea swelled and I placed a hand over my mouth to hold back all the things that threatened to come from it. The knight moved farther into the wood, and Ilias took the opening, riding off ahead.

After we rode for what must have been an hour, we broke from the canopy and continued under the inky night sky. The moon was waning from the night of the Crimson Moon, but still gifted us with light.

Things were still for a moment, nothing but the sound of the horses' steps crunching over the fallen twigs and leaves on the floor. My head swiveled back and forth while I searched for demons. I knew the last one was small but what if the next one wasn't? What if it was massive and ready to rip my head off just like—

I gulped down my thoughts and tried to physically shake them away.

"Are you all right?" Ilias leaned down to my ear. His voice felt like a soft velvet purr as he tried to stay quiet. His soft citrus smell enveloped me, and I turned to look at him, his face so near to mine. My words were trapped in my throat. His eyes darted forward, and he went rigid before pulling his sword from behind his back. I couldn't see anything in the dark.

Not until, *oh my God.*

A demon revealed itself from the tree line and made its way into the moonlight. The stench of sulfur filled my nostrils. I brought my hand up to cover my nose, growing dizzy. It stepped out farther. Long curved horns reached up to the sky, even with its head slightly bowed forward. Tendrils of smoke came off its flesh, swirling and rising into the atmosphere. With each inhale its body rose and fell.

A scream threatened and I held it back with everything I

had. Ilias dismounted and a whole new fear hit: *I can't have another person die in front of me. Because of me.*

He stood with his sword drawn, protecting me and his horse.

The demon stood, fully showing his size, three feet above Ilias. Its eyes opened to reveal a deep abyss of nothing—stark black against its skin. It took a step forward and the horse let out a scream of fear.

Ilias didn't wait any longer and rushed towards the demon, his sword held overhead, coming down with his first swing. The demon caught the sword in between his hands. Ilias tried to pull it back, but the demon thrust it out of his hands and threw it to the ground, black blood dripping from its hands. Ilias stepped back and pulled two daggers from his boots, slicing at the demon, hitting its wrists and slicing one hand to the ground. It grabbed for its severed limb and threw its head back, screaming a shrill wail into the void.

Viney tendrils of dark smoke leapt from its skin and its body hunched, coiling back like a snake building for a strike. Ilias took the opening and lunged for the sword the demon had knocked from his hands. The moment his fingers gripped the hilt he swung up and split the monster's head from its body. The head hit the ground with a heavy wet thud. Black blood spewed onto the forest floor. The demon's body followed, falling to the floor in a heavy mess.

Ilias straightened. Black blood speckled over his pale skin but that seemed to be the only harm that came to him. A wave of ease washed over me, warming my bones and fighting off the leftover tingles in my skin from fear. I hopped down from the horse, Ilias's dimples flashed as he walked over and placed his hand on my shoulder, looking down at me, his silver-grey eyes shining.

"Are you all right?"

My eyes went wide. Am *I* alright? My body moved on its own and I wrapped my arms around his torso. He went still. I could feel his heart still beating so fast below his leathers. His arms wrapped around me and his chin rested on my head. After a bit, he pulled away and raised his hand to wipe away a tear I hadn't even known I'd let out.

"Let's get on our way," he said, his voice was low and with the now growing familiar velvety tone. I nodded and headed back to the horse. His grip around my waist no longer felt like a foreign object, but a place of security.

We made our way to a small clearing in the woods. It had small green ribbons tied to the trees surrounding us, signifying a previous camp. Ilias told me this is where the company had planned to ride to and make their camp; we were just the first to arrive.

It was still early, enough that we could get a few hours of sleep before we traveled tomorrow. I sat on a large felled tree trunk and watched as Ilias set up a small tent and bed mat. He seemed to struggle a little bit with the initial pitching but got his way around it.

Finally finished, he stood and let out a low grunt. "God, I haven't set up a tent in a while." He walked over to the tree and sat beside me. Taking my hand in his, and pressing his lips to them, he looked over my knuckles. "You can take the tent tonight; I'll keep watch until the rest of the company arrives."

His eyes were bloodshot, and his skin was covered in a layer of sweat and dirt mixing with the speckles of black demon blood.

"Ilias, that's not necessary, I don't have to—" he stopped me, his single index finger wagging in the air. "No, you know that's not even an option. Now please, go get some rest." He pulled me to him and pressed his lips to my hair. I tried for a smile, but it felt labored and heavy; I was so tired. He tried to reciprocate, but it didn't reach his eyes.

I headed into the tent and laid down on the thin sleeping pad, staring up at the seams joining the fabric, counting each stitch, over and over again. I was hoping the counting would tire my brain enough to sleep. I hadn't truly slept since the night before the Crimson Moon Festival. That feels like a different life now. A different world all together. A world where I was a queen, married, and safe. I had nothing now; not even these clothes on my back were mine. I reached up to grasp the stone resting on my chest, feeling the bite into my skin. Inhaling deeply and focusing on a slow exhale, I breathed, trying to find something to cling to, but just dark thoughts bit back at each exertion. I just needed to get North. Once I got back home, everything would be as it should be.

Turning to lie on my side I felt a tear slide down my cheek, hitting the mat below me. I squeezed my eyes shut and wish for sleep.

A loud crack woke me with a jolt. I sat up quickly and headed to the opening of the tent. Darkness was still settled over the forest; I must not have been out for very long. My eyes burned with sleep, and I searched over the camp. I spotted Ilias facing the denser part of the trees. His sword and leathers rested on a log near the tent. His white tunic top was loose from his trousers and flowed in the cool breeze.

I rubbed my hands over my arms to fight the chill off, taking a few steps towards Ilias. It was quiet, but not the same quiet that the demons had walked out from earlier. This was a calm and serene kind of quiet. Ilias's horse didn't seem too bothered by anything, so that settled whatever nerves were prickling up to the surface in my skin.

"Did I wake you?" Ilias's voice was low and gravelly, filled with exhaustion. I took a step back and he turned to me, a deep crease evident between his furrowed brows. His eyes trailed over my body, lingering at the loose edge of my oversized shirt, my bare legs exposed to the elements, and him. I had removed my pants with the hope of a more comfortable sleep, but was now questioning my decision. My mouth went dry, and I couldn't form any words, so I just gave him a nod.

His steps progressed towards me, and I retreated in a matching cadence. One of his brows raised and he tilted his head.

"Is everything all right ... Evangeline?" His voice was that same dark and gravelly tone. It hadn't dawned on me until this moment that we were fully alone. I was at his mercy. He'd just cleaved through a demon and now I stood before him, completely unmatched. My eyes darted to his sword resting near the tent and my heartbeat picked up and I took a step back. I didn't spot his daggers—they must still be strapped to him. His eyes tracked my features, and his face softened. He must have seen the unease veiling my face. He took a deep breath and rested his hands on his hips, stretching his back and twisting his torso.

"Come, let's just sit for a while," he said and walked past me to the felled tree. He patted the space next to him. "I promise, I don't bite; you've been looking at me like I have been known to kick small animals. Did I do something to offend you?"

I stood out by the tree line a little longer. A sinking feeling burrowed its way into my gut. Why did I get this feeling towards Ilias? He had done nothing wrong and only acted with the utmost kindness. I needed to get away from these thoughts, and I was so tired of being afraid.

I sat next to him, looking out and scanning the trees, feeling the space between us grow tense. I felt his eyes on me; they practically burned a hole into my skull. My hands sat in my lap, clenching and unclenching. Closing my eyes, I finally spoke, though the words felt sticky on my tongue. "No, you have done nothing to offend me," I said, meeting his eyes. Eyes I really didn't want to look at right now. The soft grey orbs searched mine, trying to find anything that would help him understand me. "I just, still feel like none of this is really happening. That I am going to wake up from this and be back home." My chest sunk, my heart deflated. I had felt these thoughts this entire time but saying them felt so final. So real.

He took my hand, his thumb tracing small circles over my skin. "I know this is not easy and that we already haven't had a smooth journey, but ... I don't know. I feel like I was supposed to meet you. Somehow, for some reason." He stared at our hands as he spoke, "I just can't believe that it has been all bad, because it hasn't for me." He lifted his chin, his face inches away from mine. His salt and citrus aroma wafted over me and his warm breath tickled over my cheeks. His eyes roamed my skin, like he was trying to commit it to memory, lingering lower until they made their final resting place at my mouth.

I drew in my bottom lip in, my teeth gliding across it, his attention making me fidget. Was he going to *kiss me*? Was I going to *kiss him?* The thoughts bounced around in my head. I could feel as the space between us grew thinner, moving in closer until ...

A water droplet hit my face, awakening me from my daze of what was happening. What almost happened. I wiped it away but as soon as it left, another was in its place. Rain. More and more started to come down and I turned back to the tent.

My hands broke from Ilias's grip, and he stood, heading for the saddlebags, cursing under his breath. The clearing offered little protection from the elements. The tent was small, but I couldn't leave him out here to get soaked. He wasn't planning for me to tag along when they'd packed their things. This tent was meant for him.

"Let's get out of the rain," I said, reaching out to touch his shoulder. He glanced at the tent and gave it an exasperated sigh. "Are you sure?"

I nodded but he shook his head, trying to see what other options he had. A crack of lightning raced over the sky, lighting us for a second. A boom sounded and a heavier rain poured over us.

I crawled into the tent first, getting as close to the edge as possible, and laid on my right side, facing the wall of the tent. I tried not to pay close attention to Ilias's crawling in next to me. To how close he was. He finally settled in, laying on his back. We didn't speak for a while. There were just the sounds of our breathing and the pattering rain hitting the tent. In any other circumstance, I would have been lulled to sleep with its rhythmic pattern hitting the earth, but not tonight. Not with a man I hardly knew so close to me in a forest full of demons. But rather than thinking about the danger, my mind recalled Ilias leaning into me, to his mouth coming in closer to mine. A soft, curling feeling rose in my stomach. His skin on mine had felt comforting and I'd—I'd liked it.

Ilias was the first to break the silence. "Are you asleep?" he asked in a hushed tone.

"No, are you?"

He chuckled low, and I smiled.

"Well since you're not, I just wanted to say thank you for allowing me in. I know these are not the most phenomenal lodgings to be in, but being here, next to you, is comforting in a way I don't really understand."

Heat warmed my cheeks. I turned to face him; his eyes were closed and the furrow in his forehead was gone. "It is, isn't it?" I said. A smile grew on his lips and his dimples imbedded into his cheeks. He turned to face me, his eyes open, staring right back into mine. This was nice, though strange. I didn't know what the future in the Midlands would be like, but this, in this moment, was nice. After a little while he rolled back over.

"Get some rest; we don't have long before we head out again."

I turned back to my side and did as he said. Closing my eyes, I let my brain unravel and allowed myself some sleep.

SEVEN

Bright light beamed into the tent through a small hole in the fabric, right into my eyes. I raised my hand to block it out and stared up at the light shining through my fingers, glowing red seams between each digit. *What time must it be?*

I started to remember everything. Last night, the demons, the rain. My eyes widened and I became all too aware of who was asleep next to me. An arm was draped across my stomach. I turned my head just enough to see Ilias's eyes were still closed, soft puffs of air escaping his lips while he lay against me on his side. Our legs were a tangled mess together. I tried ever so slowly to sneak mine out from in between his by turning to my side and facing away from him.

Ilias's grip on me tightened, and he pulled me closer, the shock of it making me jump. He woke up with a start and sat up instantaneously, his hand still gripping my shirt. His eyes wide and full of sleep, he looked at me and then down to his hand. His fingers released the cloth, and he pushed back as far the tent would allow him to get. A wave of red flashed over his face, and he stumbled over his words.

"Oh god, I am sorry, I—I did I? I'm just going to go," he stammered, rushing out of the tent. I pulled on my pants and followed, noting that the rest of Ilias's company were preparing camp and breakfast. The knight stood directly across the tent's opening, leaning against a tree, his face angled to me. He had to have seen Ilias exit the tent. I wondered what he thought, *no, it doesn't matter what he thought.* My back ached. *God, horseback and sleeping on the ground were not doing me any good.* Twisting and trying to give myself some release I turned to find Ilias, sitting near another guard who passed him a bowl of porridge. The steaming breakfast looked mouthwatering.

Ilias glanced at me and the same red blush blossomed over his cheeks. He collected a second helping, coming over and handing it to me. An audible grumble from my stomach broke the intended silence between me and Ilias. He smiled, his dimples deep with humor.

"Please, eat something. It will be a while before our next break once we get back on the road."

I took the bowl from him, staring into the swirls of steam coming off it and into the chilly morning air. The first bite felt like an answered prayer. I could cry; it was good and hot. The heat traveled down to my toes, warming my soul.

"What *is* this?" I asked, holding back tears; it was so good. *Was that nutmeg? God, I needed to get the recipe.* Ilias let out a soft laugh, patted my shoulder and worked on deconstructing the tent. *Was he just not going to tell me?* I took another bite and, God, it was just as good as the last.

The sound of the spoon scraping on the bottom of the bowl came too soon and all the extras had been eaten. Just about everyone had packed up, and it was time to head on our way again. I walked to meet Ilias at his horse, where he was tightening the final straps on the saddle.

"You ready?" he asked.

"As I'll ever be." I grasped the pommel and slung my foot through the stirrup to swing myself up. This time Ilias didn't help, which made it more difficult. He'd been off all morning.

He climbed on behind me, careful not to touch. His legs still pressed to mine but there was a distance behind me. The cold air without his closeness ate through my tunic shirt like it wasn't even there. I huffed out a breath and the vapor rose before my face. *Why was it so cold here?*

After a few hours, Ilias leaned forward and the heat from his chest felt so good against my back. "Where we are headed is going to get colder; I know after this morning I've kept my distance but, but I hate to see you shivering in front of me. Is it alright if I—" He cleared his throat, as if searching for the right words, "hold you?"

"Yes, please, I'm fucking freezing." I pressed back into him, and he wrapped his arms over me, bringing his cloak forward and over us. The warmth, melted into me with each passing second. His warm breath against my cheek again, he whispered, "You have more of a mouth on you than I expected."

I laughed to myself. *If only he knew.*

"Sorry, that was uh, not my most demure moment."

He pulled me in closer and whispered, "I liked it."

My heart rate picked up—it was, *God,* what was it with us? My mind buzzed and my stomach made a curling feeling. This was nothing like how Anders made me feel, not even a little bit.

After a few more hours, the knight rode past us and made his way to the front of the company, stopping everyone from going further on. One by one, they all started to dismount. The temperature had continued to drop. Once Ilias had stepped down, he helped me off the horse bringing me in under his arm, wrapping his cloak around us. The cold, frigid air was full of our puffy breaths. There wasn't any snow on the ground, but the air chilled me to my bones.

Ilias removed his cloak, keeping it wrapped around me. "I'm going to go and speak to my men. Stay close by, all right?"

I nodded as he turned to go join the ranks of men up ahead, I might as well take advantage of the alone time. Creeping softly back to Ilias's horse, I went through the saddlebag to find my things. I found the familiar strap and pulled it out, digging through it to get my eyes on the journals. The relief I felt having this back in my hands was so strong, I cradled it to my chest. Searching for a ghost of a man among the pages, I opened it. Kairos's familiar writing tore back the shroud again, but I bit back the tears and closed it. I spotted the men still huddled near each other and realized I may have more time than I'd thought.

Dipping just past the tree line, I pulled out the journal in private, giving myself the grace to feel what I needed to, without the others around. I thumbed through a few pages as I stepped farther into the forest. I didn't know everything that was in it, but I didn't want Ilias to see it or me, in another state of disarray. At least not yet.

Sigils filled the pages. The ones for 'protection' were at the front and after that, they became more intricate. The language changed to the old language, the one native to the southern Amaymon Kingdom. He'd spent the last eight months near the border. He must have picked up on it. Odd. It was barely spoken anymore.

My foot caught on a stone, and I tripped forward, dropping the journal. It tumbled across the ground, pages bending and snagging. "Fuck," I cursed under my breath. I crawled forward to grab it, ignoring the pain flaring up in my knees from the fall. As my fingers reached out for it, a huge boot stepped in my way. My eyes traveled up the gargantuan figure and its mirrored armor before me. The knight. And he was in my way to get the journal. I stood, dusting off the dirt and grass covering my pants. He towered over me, just as intimidating as the night he'd pulled me from the mud. His deep red mantle swayed in the breeze, holding a crest I wasn't familiar with on the center. A huge sword rested in the scabbard on his side, ready at a moment's notice. The hilt was fashioned with a black stone. Was it a Legion Stone? Did all of Ilias's men know about them? Or just ... him.

I looked down to my journal in the dirt behind the knight. It laid open to a blank page near the end, and I returned my gaze back to him staring into the small slits in the helmet, searching for any sign of humanity within them. "Excuse me," I said dryly.

He stepped forward, dwarfing me against his stature before he turned around to pick up the journal, closing it with a firm thump before handing it to me.

"Thank you," was all I could say as he walked away. I turned to watch as he went, only to be startled by Ilias suddenly standing before me. I let out a small scream, "God, you scared me."

He laughed and stepped behind me, grabbing the cloak from my neck and wrapping it around himself and me. "I promise that wasn't my intention. Come, let's get back on the road. Being in this high of an altitude is wearing me down. We should make it to the Midlands by tomorrow. It's much warmer there." He pulled me to him, my back flush to his front, his arms wrapped around my shoulders and his chin resting on my head. Was this truly just for warmth? Each touch felt increasingly comfortable. I might actually be enjoying it.

Night had fallen once again; my ass was as sore as it had ever been and the space between my legs was surely rubbed raw. Travel on horseback was definitely not for the weak or wealthy. This time, everyone set up their mats surrounding a small fire. The chill was blistering and ran through me, making me shiver.

I held my fingers as close as my flesh would allow it to the flames, fearful of any rogue spires reaching up to lick and blister my fingertips. My skin was hot, but my bones remained cold. This place felt like cursed land. I had asked Ilias where we were and he'd just said, "Not far." The most *non-answer* answer.

He was still struggling with the damned tent. I would offer to help, but the risk of accidentally snapping off one of my frozen fingers was a bit of a deterrent. One of the guards stood across from the fire, his face covered in a dusting of earth and sweat. There was a sallow sheen on his face, and he was picking at a spot on his arm. I could see the small tear in the fabric. *Did he get that yesterday? When they fought the demons in the woods?*

He turned his arm and that's when I saw it: dark and necrotic tissue. I'd never seen anything like that before, at least not on someone living. He looked to me through the flames, then back to his arm, quickly grabbing a cloth to bind over the wound. I didn't know what that meant, but it couldn't be good.

Ilias broke me from my thoughts. His cadence was lopsided and sluggish, his breaths labored. That tent must have won more rounds than he did. "Ready for bed?"

"More than you know." I got up and followed him the few steps to the tent but paused to look back at the guard. He held his arm near his body, tying off a bandage.

Ilias opened the tent, and I crawled in first, noticing he was lingering near the outside longer than usual. He cleared his throat, and I saw the hint of a blush dance over his cheeks.

"Before presuming anything, I wanted to be sure that our ... interaction this morning, was something you'd prefer to have keep us separate or if you'd still like my company?"

Was he really being bashful? He was holding the tent open and the air flowing through was freezing. I pulled the blanket up and over myself and laid down, facing the tent wall.

"Ilias, get in here before we both freeze."

I felt him enter the space, making shallow impressions into the mat. He laid on top of the blanket, on his side, facing opposite of me. Our backs were inches apart, but I could feel his heat through the blanket. God, it would be so much easier to sleep if he was just a little closer. *Nope,* boundaries, you know better. He'd crossed them already and was trying to be respectful and give me space.

"May I ask you a question?" His voice was soft, not confrontational, but an unnerving feeling bloomed in my gut. I peeked over my shoulder, still turning away. My heart picked up more than it needed to. *A question?* About all my lies?

"Of course," I said, trying to keep my tone under control.

"Did you lose someone? Back in the Oriens? I know you've had a good deal of, well, for lack of a better word, moments, where you look far away. Like you're not here, but in a terrible dream."

His words caught me off guard, so much more than I thought they would.

I took in a deep breath and sat up. I couldn't talk about this lying down. He joined me, the mat crinkling beneath him, and again his brows held their furrowed appearance. Hurriedly he said, "I'm sorry if I upset you, I just—I just wanted to be there for you. If you want to talk about it." He reached for my hands, his soft and firm hands holding mine with grace. It felt intimate in this moment.

"I lost my husband." *The first honest thing I've said to him.*

His hands squeezed mine and his voice was so low, barely above a whisper. "I am so sorry. I feel so stupid, I've been—" His eyes were glassy and grey. "I am sorry for how forward I have been, if I had known I ... I'm sorry."

His words surprised me. The kindness in them felt sincere.

"He was a good man; it was arranged by my parents when I was young. I loved him very much." Ilias's face deepened as he held my words, listening and paying them the attention they needed. "He was ... well he was more of a father figure to me. He was in love with another long before I was ever in the picture. But some marriages they just, they aren't full of *that* kind of love."

His eyes searched over my face, and I felt him stare right through me. They were full of so many questions I was praying he would not ask me. Not yet.

"I'm sure that does not make it any less painful." His fingers squeezed mine. It was comforting. It was what I wanted right now. I wanted him right now. *How?* No fucking clue.

A tear slipped out and traveled down my cheek. His hand reached up to catch it, his fingers swiping over my skin. He moved in closer and tucked back a few stray hairs. His touch lingered like a hot iron, even after it was gone.

"I lost my mother when I was very young," he said, his mouth pulled into a tight line. He shifted and looked away. "She was my favorite person in the entire world and the day she passed, I felt like she took a piece of my soul with her. I haven't been the same since."

My heart broke for him; his eyes were full of so much grief and in that moment, I knew I wasn't alone. It felt like I was with someone who saw me, who knew what I was feeling.

"Time does help, it doesn't ever feel like it, but it will feel better," he said softly.

I nodded and turned from him to look at our tent's opening, the cool air creeping in through the seams. "I hope so."

"We should get some sleep." He gave my hands one last squeeze. The moment his skin left mine, I missed his warmth. He laid on his back with his hands tucked behind his head, closing his eyes and settling his breathing. I watched him, tracing my eyes over his features. He had smooth, light brown eyebrows and sharp angular features. Like those on a hawk, designed to instill fear into its prey. Then my eyes traveled to his lips, maybe for a moment too long. They parted and twitched just for a second. As if he knew I was watching him and held back a smile. I gulped down hard. I wanted to touch him. To be touched by him.

So, for the first time in my lonely life, I hadn't felt like questioning myself. I hadn't felt the shame of others' opinions of me. I was going to do something for myself.

I laid in closer, pulling the blanket up above us both, resting my head on his chest. Hoping, *praying* he reciprocated. Almost on instinct, he pulled me in, brought me into his body and wrapped his arms around me. He turned to lay on his side, facing me. Our bodies were close and connected. Heat filled my blood.

His eyes were heavy lidded, full of sleep, and something ... more. He brought his mouth close, just a hair apart from mine. I didn't protest, holding my breath, worried the moment would fizzle if I moved even an inch. But slowly, his warm lips pressed against mine. He moved gently, wary of my response. But there was no need. Not now.

I reached over and grabbed the back of his neck, and deepening the kiss. He yanked me against his firm chest, the force surprising at first, but I answered with a moan. My leg wrapped over him. I need to be flush against him, to feel him, to feel *alive*. His hands worked their way up my back and into my

hair. He pulled away first, his eyes raking over me and we were both breathless, my lungs fighting to take in air. He craned his head back, swallowing hard, his Adam's apple bobbing. I watched him, unsure of how he felt about everything. My pulse raced. Maybe this wasn't a good idea, maybe I was too—
He let out a soft chuckle and his dimples appeared.

I melted.

He pulled me in down to him, my body still entangled with his. My head found his chest and I fell asleep instantly to the rhythmic thumping below my ear.

Eight

"We made it." Those words could have elicited the same reaction if he would have said we had reached the holy lands of Sunai, or a hot plate of fresh food.

It was sunset. The keep was a well-endowed fortress sitting centralized in the Midlands. The mountains we had just come from almost hid the sun completely from view. But the air here wasn't like those mountains. It was not quite warm, but *warmer* than the last few days of freezing mud and rain.

As we approached the gates, one of the guards' ran up to Ilias and me.

"My Lord, your return has been highly anticipated. May I have you for one moment?"

Ilias nodded at the man. "I will be right back." His warm breath on my neck elicited a very primal reaction low in my belly. He gave me a quick kiss on the cheek. My face heated instantaneously.

I followed along with the rest of the procession until they all dismounted. I lifted my leg to swing off the horse and my ankle caught. My left knee buckled under the weird pressure, and I started to fall, a loud yelp escaping my lips as I tumbled down to the hard ground. But the hard ground I'd expected never came. Instead, I was engulfed by two large arms, catching me around my waist. My feet dangled in the air, a good foot or so. The person set me down and as I found my footing I turned to look, seeing the knight looming over me. The setting sun backlit him, making him look like a monstrous shadow. I took a step back, needing space. He was too close and too— I didn't know. There was an odd feeling to him. I didn't understand it, but every nerve in my body screamed to *run!*

Ilias returned before I actually fled the scene. He reached for my hands and pulled them to his face. His jaw felt rough with the new growth shadowing his cheeks.

"I saw the whole thing; I should have stayed to make sure you were safe. Forgive me?"

He looked to the knight, while pulling me into him, his arms wrapping around me like a blanket of security. "Thank you," he said. The only response was a curt nod before the Knight walked away and started to remove the saddle off his giant black horse.

Turning my attention back to Ilias, I asked, "Why doesn't he speak? Is he mute?"

He chuckled. "No, he is not mute. Knights of the Crimson Cloth take a vow of silence and anonymity. They are not to remove their helmet in the presence of anyone. They are not to marry or bear children so they can be of complete sound body and mind for the cause. My uncle hired him last winter."

I had read of those knights, but I'd thought the practices had since been dissolved. It wasn't deemed necessary by the Saints after The Fall. *Interesting.* I wondered how old he was if he was still employing the lost practices. If he was older, it would explain his lack of *soft.*

Once brought into the keep, I was directed by a handmaiden to my room after Ilias explained he had things to discuss with his uncle. The sense of being alone for the first time in days was much welcomed.

The room was rather ordinary; a simple chair and table, wide dresser, armoire, sideboard and a private bathing chamber, which was a blessing to be had. The bed, though, that was rather different. It was silk sheet-lined with fabric hanging from the ceiling like a gossamer cage. I felt the fabric between my fingers. It was thin, but moved against itself well, shining when the light hit it. It was beautiful. Thin holes within the fabric allowed a breeze to enter.

"It's for the bugs," the handmaiden said. I deflated a bit as the cloth lost a bit of the mystique, but it was still a gorgeous bed.

She brought a pitcher of fresh water and a few glasses, leaving them on the sideboard. Wiping her hands on her apron, she let me know to be ready for dinner in an hour or so.

After cleaning myself from the last few days and picking horsehair out of every crevice, I made my way to the armoire. It held so many lovely dresses, cut and styled in what was presumably the Midland's fashions. All soft blues and greens. Thankfully, there were also a few tunics and pants. If I didn't have to live in a dress, I wouldn't.

I chose a soft cotton dress in a light, spring pear shade of green and let my hair cascade down my back after running a brush through it. It may have lost close to half of its volume with how many knots I brushed out.

Opening my door, I was surprised to find the knight stationed outside it. Before I was even able to close my door, he made his way down the hall. I followed as he likely intended, picking up my pace to keep up with his large gait. Again. It was very reminiscent of our first encounter. I huffed out a breath of air at the memory of being dragged along by his horse after the worst night of my existence.

As we entered the dining room, my eyes fell onto Ilias. He sat at the head of the table, speaking to one of the clergy men, signing some papers. His short, cropped hair was coming in a little bit, casting a darker shadow along his hairline. It was still an indiscernible color, but likely brown since his eyebrows were too.

The knight stayed stationed at the door's threshold as I made my way farther in. The room's walls and floor were made from a tan stone with a rough texture that mimicked the exterior. The light reflecting off the sconces in the walls created a soft glow. The table wasn't the grandest, but it did seat about twelve. Yet, at the moment it appeared just us two would be dining.

As I approached, Ilias urged the man away. He took the papers Ilias had been looking at with him.

"I hope you found your room to your liking." He paused and took a full-bodied look at me as he brought a glass to his mouth. The deep red of his drink clung to his lips. He licked it away with a slow swipe of his tongue, his eyes never leaving me. "The midlands colors look ... immaculate on you." He stood to take my hand, leading me to my chair beside his.

"Thank you, but this is all too much. I know I was only intended to be here until I heard back from my—"

He lifted his hand, stalling me. "You can stay as long as is intended. You never know how long the post takes, and to get all the way to Egyn? It could be quite some time. I want you to be comfortable here." His hand reached over to rest on the top of my thigh. Heat grew in my cheeks, and I reached forward for the stem of my glass, praying it was a form of alcohol. I took a sip and had to hide a smile. It was a gorgeous wine.

I cleared my throat and said, "Either way, thank you."

He was beaming, with the type of smile that made you feel like you needed to smile back. His dimples were proud against his cheeks.

I took a bite of my food; it had an interesting *flavor*. I was starving, but this was not the best rendition of cuisine I had seen yet. It was lacking salt and other basic herbs, and unfortunately, tough. It was some kind of white meat, a type of bird, I assumed. Nothing I am familiar with. I took another sip of my wine to wash it down and my head began to feel a bit lighter on my shoulders.

"Oh! I almost forgot." Ilias's jarring exclamation made me jump. "Once we're done eating and of course, if you'd care to join, I would love to show you the gardens. Even in the moonlight, it is a sight."

<hr>

After dinner, I excused myself to my room and to my surprise, found a brand-new cloak laid out for me. It was dark black and had a nice heavy weight to it. This would be perfect for the garden. I was curious how Ilias had this plotted out; we'd only been separated for a few minutes. I wrapped it around my shoulders and tied it off; it was the perfect length.

A gentle rapping at my door pulled my attention away. Ilias leaned against the door frame, his mouth quirked up into a half smile, showing off one of his devilish dimples. He was dressed the same as before in a long-sleeved dark navy tunic. It complimented his eyes and his skin, but the fabric did him a world of favors around his torso. He was so lean and toned.

"A picture of grace, yet again." He came in, taking a few

steps towards me, grabbing my face in both of his hands. His salty citrus aroma cascaded over me. With the mixture of him and the wine, I was starting to feel fully intoxicated.

"You're too kind. You didn't have to do all this."

He pulled away, tilting his head to the side and giving me a quizzical look. He reached down to the cloak, pulling the fabric between his fingers, his brows knitting together.

"Yes ... but I don't do these things because I have to. I like to. Evangeline, you—" he paused, "I like you very much, and I like to do things for those I like. Please. Now, shall we?" He laced his fingers between mine, leading me from the room and down the long hallways to the far east side of the keep.

It was a good walk, but the night air was perfect. The trees grew in dense clusters close to the edge and a very small bank held a waterway surrounded by reeds and tall grass; it was too small to be considered a true lake but looked deep enough to enjoy on a warm day. A few large citrus trees were just starting their cool weather blossoms. The wind blew through and cast ripples on the water's surface. To jump in and float for hours would be a dream.

Ilias reached down and grabbed my hand in his. His skin was pleasantly warm against the growing chill on mine. He began to circle his thumb on the back of my hand.

"This was one of my mother's favorite places to visit," he finally said, breaking the silence. "She would find a soft patch of grass and sit in the sun, letting the rays toast her skin for hours. She was always happy here."

His face grew still, and he stared intently at the water. A sense of peace came over him and it was like looking at a different person. A person without regal ties and duties, and the court persona. They were washed away. And he was just a man speaking about his mother, about a cherished memory. I was growing to like this side of him.

A few silent moments passed between us, and he pulled me in closer. His hand went up to my hair, pulling little wind-whipped strands and tucking them neatly behind my ear. His fingers were so soft and delicate. He studied my face and settled on my mouth. His eyes darkened and his face moved in closer. The distance between us grew smaller and smaller. Our inhales and exhalations were the same breath now.

My pulse thrummed in my ears. I needed this distance to close. My body was lit with electricity where we'd touched, and he was still so far away. *Ilias I am begging you to—*

The gap closed and his lips finally met mine, in a single perfect kiss. It was sweet and soft with no expectations of any kind.

He pulled away and I shortened the space further to wrap my arms around his torso. I leaned my head on his chest and felt his heart beating against my ear. Closing my eyes, I let myself enjoy this.

The next morning, I joined Ilias for breakfast. The table was filled with choices: fruit, eggs, and meats, but they had these sweet breads. *Oh my god, they were delicious.* Soft and fluffy with a dusting of cardamom and sugar. I probably had three to myself.

Ilias was reading over letters and would on occasion bring his hand down to my thigh and run his fingers along my leg, or toy with my hair while he read. It was always sweet gestures with him. At one point, he told me he'd have to go away for a few days, but he'd have a party when he got back for his birthday. "It'll be a grand celebration," he said.

He spent the day working, and I walked the grounds with my steel shadow following. The knight wasn't the worst company on account of he didn't speak and, in that manner, didn't complain. It really was more so the fact that I had no privacy aside from confining myself to my room. And even with that, he would stand outside my door for the entire day.

After dinner, Ilias showed up to my door wearing a cloak and said he had a surprise for me, pulling a bottle of wine out from behind his back.

We walked the gardens again, taking long languid sips from the bottle. Its tart juice filled my stomach and made me feel light and dizzy in the most splendid way. We stayed closer to flowers on this walk, and along the roses and well-trimmed bushes. A gazebo at the end of the path. It was a bit old and needed refinishing, but in the moonlight, it softly glowed.

There was a small bench inside, and he sat, taking another swig from the bottle. He held it up to see how little was left; just a few meager sips sloshing around at the bottom.

"Here, you take the rest," he said handing the bottle over. He spread his limbs out long and relaxed back into the bench, his arms stretched out behind his head. I tilted the bottle back, finishing the last dregs. Just like that, we were out of booze.

"Take a seat, I'm sure your footing is a bit wobbly yet." He patted the seat next to him.

In my buzzing haze, I shook my head, declining his offer. His face dropped slightly, and his shoulders slumped.

"You see, I have a different seat in mind," I said with a coy smile.

His brows raised and I came to stand in front of him. He shot me a devilish smile. "And which seat would that be, Lady Evangeline?"

My false name on his lips felt like a sin, but I fought through it, staying in the moment. He reached out a hand and placed it high on my thigh. He pulled me into him, staring up at me, eyes full of heat. I lowered my face to his, our lips hovering just millimeters apart, and felt his warm breath come across my face. With a jerk, he pulled me upon his lap. His thighs were hard beneath mine and my dress hiked up, exposing my legs. His hands reached behind me and cradled my lower back. I finally closed the space between us fully. My lips settled over his and a spark ignited through me.

But his mouth barely moved against mine. I must have done something wrong. Been too forward. I pulled back, looking away, not feeling strong enough to see whatever emotion blanketed his features. He grasped my chin and forced me to face him.

"I think this may be the best seat in the house," he says.

My heart sputtered and my cheeks heated, anticipation growing deep in my lower stomach. Thank God he's not one to make me wait.

His frenzied lips crashed into mine. My mouth moved in tandem with his, and that spark traveled through my skin and down my spine, sending a shiver to wrack over me.

It felt like he couldn't get enough of me. He tasted like salt and citrus, so bright and full of life. Moving his hands lower, he grabbed my ass, pulling me flush to his lap. A gasp escaped my lips, and he started to trace kisses down my jaw to my neck. I threw my head back, swimming with the wine and his kiss still hanging on my lips. He drew his mouth down my chest, leaving a trail to the swell of my breasts. He paused to inhale my scent. I felt heat growing in my core and pressed down on him. His was so hard against me, even through his constricting pants, I could feel how much he wanted me. I ground myself on him, the heat in my core increasing. A low curling feeling grew stronger, and he let out an exasperated sigh into my breasts. He said something but it was too muffled to understand.

Taking my lips back in his, he returned his hands to my back and placed his forehead against my chest, panting.

"I think I have a new reason to make the garden my favorite place." His voice was deep and soft like velvet.

"It is a lovely garden," I said, smiling at him.

Taking a deep breath and feeling the wine start to wane, I asked to go back to my room; my liquid courage had run out. Leaving me at my door, Ilias leaned down and gave me a kiss goodnight. Before closing it, I saw the knight take his post for the evening. Before he reached the door, I slammed it shut. *Never a moment alone.*

NINE

THE NEXT MORNING, I SLEPT IN LATER THAN USUAL. I would've kept sleeping if not for the handmaiden Ami, making her way into the room and opening the blinds to let in the late morning rays of the sun. I groaned and shielded my eyes under the covers.

"What time is it?" I asked, speaking out through the pillows and blankets, my muffled voice still loud enough for Ami to hear.

"A quarter past eleven, my lady," her soft voice said, almost trilling on each syllable.

God, I've wasted the entire morning. I sat up and drew the blankets back, trying to open my eyes and focus on the room, but they burned. My head ached from the wine last night. I threw myself back down and extended my arms out, my fingers landing on something, *crunchy?*

No, it was a letter. I flipped it over in my hands a few times, examining the thing. No sign of a name-address; just a blank envelope. I opened it. The first line was absolutely from Ilias. My cheeks heated immediately.

I looked up to see Ami hovering nearby. I pulled the note to my chest.

"Ami! This is private." My voice was shrill.

She laughed it off and said, "Oh yes, very much so. Would you like me to start you a cool bath? Or ..."

"I can draw my own bath, thank you," I said, kicking off the covers and heading to the bathing chamber. I began to fill the tub with *warm* water and looked back to the letter. Ilias had ended it by saying he would be back in a few days and requested upon his arrival, '*Another night like in the garden.*'

My cheeks flushed again, reading it over and over. God, what did I even do? I was absolutely drunk, and drunk me and *me*, me. Well, we were not of the same mind and body. Putting the note away I stepped into the bath. I had the rest of whatever this day held ahead of me. I might as well take the opportunity to explore.

Because I had now missed breakfast and lunch, I decided to search for something to eat. The Great Hall was more active here at this hour, probably because Ilias or the duke weren't around and liked them more privacy. It was nice, in a way. I was able to get a better understanding what the duke was like as a ruler, hearing it from the mouths of his people.

It was unfortunately hard to keep a low profile, having my shadow following me everywhere. He gave me a wide berth, settling back near the entrance, but his station was fixed on me. Always. If he walked around the room or in between tables. I felt his eyes on me, boring into the back of my head.

I eavesdropped on a few of the ladies-in-waiting at a table not too far from me. Normally, I would have avoided it, but they had no notion of wanting to maintain a tactful conversation.

"Did you know that the Crimson Cloth Knight had slain over forty demons in the last year?" one of them whispered.

"I heard he single-handedly ran through Poliemonte and left no survivors. Women, children, all gone," another said. "Did you know he killed his best friend in the Cerulean Games?"

"I wonder why he's on guard dog duty for the *Lady* that Lord Ilias picked up. Probably some whore he snagged off the streets. Do you remember what happened to the last one?"

My cheeks burned.

They kept snickering to themselves, and I was thankful my back faced them. My fists clenched under the tablecloth, rage and embarrassment filling my veins. It was going to take everything I had inside of me not to turn around and cause a scene.

A loud crash rang through the hall. As I turned along with everyone else, I noted a silver platter rolling on the floor near my feet, the remains of teacups still glittering in pools of tea. My jaw fell open, and I fought against a smile.

The culprit was the hilt of the knight's sword. It had wrapped itself around the tablecloth at the ladies-in-waiting's table, spilling their lunch and tea to the floor. The knight bowed in apology, untangled the hilt of his sword and walked back to the room's entrance.

The ladies' chatter was so cacophonous I couldn't discern a single syllable, just frazzled little birds squawking.

I turned away and sat back in my chair, bringing my teacup to my lips, trying my hardest to hold back the smile I knew shined through. Who was I kidding, *I was fucking beaming.* I turned back to the knight and gave him a small knowing nod. Maybe my shadow wasn't *all bad.*

The next place I felt compelled to visit was the cathedral. Most major areas had them: the Midlands, Oriens, and Egyn, all had their own cathedrals filled with the Saints. Their red-veiled figures lived and breathed within these halls and honored the scriptures. But my favorite part was the undercroft, where old things went to die. There I could find works, if I was lucky, on things that were before The Fall. They should have all been destroyed but I'd had success previously finding a book, or a clipping holding the banned information back in the Oriens Cathedral.

The undercroft also had specific records areas; sometimes they held collections of demon attacks, when they happened and the severity. It wouldn't hurt to take a peek now, would it?

My latest information regarding them was the journal Kairos gave me. I was only able to get so far into it before he started to write in old Amaymon. I knew a few words but was rusty. Amaymon was the oldest kingdom. It was also the most southern, bordering the wastelands of Abaddon. Amaymon and Paymon were still known to have cathedrals, but my knowledge of their involvement with the Saints was unknown. With their alliance, it had limited most inter-kingdom travel to only those with crossing papers. And those were not easy to get.

Walking in, my knight and I were welcomed by the familiar incense and smell of settled dust. It was late afternoon, and the sun moved over the mountains, casting the most amazing colors in the cathedral walls through the stained glass rose windows.

Immediately below the windows was the empty altar space. All altars had been removed after The Fall. No deity or God to worship but we still needed a sense of hope with the demons running rampant. The God's name escapes me as I stared up to its placeholder, a Saint standing before us, pacing slowly in the chancel, waiting for the next Sacrament.

I made my admission and grabbed for one of the many needles laid out. Unwrapping it from its cover, I held it to the light. This small, smooth piece of steel had haunted me from my first visit as a child.

Trying to hold as steady as possible, I brought the needle to my middle finger, taking a deep breath in through my nose and letting it out slowly from my mouth as I sunk it into my soft flesh.

"*Fuck.*"

The word escaped my mouth no louder than a whisper, but, *oh my god.* I looked around and saw the Saint looking down at me, arms crossed and through the thickly veiled face, felt the daggers burrow into my flesh.

My heart racing, I dripped the droplets into the siphon, bow, and leave the place of offering as quickly as my feet would allow me. I stepped back to the knight and gestured for him to move in and make his Sacrament. A Knight of the Crimson Cloth was connected with the cathedrals and Saints. He would have to make one as well, right?

But he just stood there.

I huffed past him; I was already embarrassed by my outburst and now he didn't leave a Sacrament.

What is this world coming to?

Eventually I moved on. The undercroft was massive. Rows and rows of boxes and shelves filled with city records, books on local wildlife, and lots of *junk.* It was like someone grabbed all the non-useful things from the entire Midlands and tossed it down here. Finding anything was going to be near impossible.

I started at the singular desk sitting alone with no chair, and removed all the dusty records from it, using it as my reference pile. One by one, I started to stack books on it: A local landmarks guide, an old Amaymon reference dictionary, a tome of stones and igneous rocks to name a few.

Hours passed, and the candles hit the low light glimmer. My stomach was starting to speak out, and I realized I had no clue how late it really was. There was no daylight and no clocks, down here. It was like a tomb to time.

I looked down at my pants and cloak, covered in a nice caking of dust and whatever clung to the walls—something sticky that gave off the smell of damp air.

I spotted my shadow, the knight seated, his legs propped up on a stool and leaning back. The large, armored figure may as well have been asleep for all I knew.

Did I dare wake him? Or try and sneak out and let him figure where I might have gone?

Turning away, I took one last look over the shelf I was working away at. I wanted to make sure I had all I could get before I left.

That's when I saw it. High up on a shelf, was a book with a small red ribbon hanging over the ledge. I didn't know what it was about the ribbon, but it must mark something of value.

The thing was up quite high, and I wouldn't dare ask the sleeping giant for a favor, but he may have something on him I could use. I walked over and snatched the stool his legs were resting on, dropping his feet to the floor. His body flew forward in a jerk. *He was so asleep.*

I brought the stool over to the shelf and reached up as high as I could, only to find I was just shy of it. *Goddamn it.*

Reaching up on my toes, I tilted the stool so it went up on half its legs; just *a little farther.* Finally, my fingers wrapped around the ribbon, and I pulled the book from its rest.

"Got it!" I exclaimed, pulling the book to my chest. But the stool settled back to its forelegs too hard and the back one crumbled. I fell back and landed hard on the floor of the under-croft. My teeth bit against each other and my spine felt like it was compressed.

The knight walked over and helped me up. I winced when he pulled me up by my arms; my tailbone felt fractured, but my fingers still clung to the book.

I wiped away the thick layer of dirt on the cover to see the symbol. A very familiar symbol. I looked up to the knight, who was snuffing out the candles. His mantel held the same symbol. I knew so little about the Knights of the Crimson Cloth; this may help me understand why my guard didn't speak but just lurked around me.

I shoved the book into my bag instead of placing it on my pile on the desk. I just couldn't leave it behind. The Saints were not keen on lending out books; I had learned that lesson back home. I would have to ask for forgiveness later.

As we made our way back to the main body of the cathedral, the halls were swarming with Saints and guests for the evening service. The pews were filling up and patrons donned their most righteous cassocks like it was a celestial holiday. This place was, *interesting*.

I stood in the back, watching the faces of the people here. All ages and races gathered under one roof to sit beneath an empty altar. The Midlands offered the joining borders of many king-doms, and that was one thing I really did take notice of. Back in the Oriens, the vast majority of people looked like Kairos with their dark skin and coiled hair. They often had the most intricate braided hair designs. The men would wear it tight and close to their scalp. The Oriens were a gorgeous people. Outsiders, like me, stood out.

Here, the Midlands seemed to act as a crucible, a true melting pot of people.

I slipped out, seemingly undetected, with the book in my

bag hidden away for a reading at a later time. Even if I was only *borrowing* it.

The walk to the keep felt so much longer on the way back. My stomach grumbled every few steps and my energy waned. The knight walked so far ahead of me with so few, I swore he was making them wider somehow.

The moon shone bright in the sky, casting us in a little light, but the dark alleys we passed felt like they held infamous creatures in their shadows.

I hurried closer to the knight, my quick steps alerting him, and he turned, stopping in his tracks. His fingers slowly wrapped around the hilt of his sword. The black stone encrusted in the top sat just above his hold.

I gulped down hard, "What's going on ..."

He drew the blade from its sheath, and my eyes traced over the dark and menacing honed steel. I saw my reflection staring back at me in it and shivered. The knight stepped towards me, and I froze. I couldn't look away. Why couldn't I move? Why was he brandishing his sword in the first place?

A loud clatter came from the dark alley immediately to our right. We turned in unison to the noise and he took a few steps towards it. My pulse raced and my breath hitched in my throat. Could it be a demon? Within the city walls? I choked out a ragged sounding breath, and put a hand to my chest, trying calm myself. It was fine. The big scary knight guy was here to —to—

The culprit revealed itself. One step at a time, it leached from the darkness into the pale moonlight. Its eyes were wide and stared straight into my soul from its inky, black body. Its jaw opened showing razor sharp teeth, the only noise escaping ...

"Meow."

My jaw dropped to the floor as the little guy sauntered up to the knight whose sword was drawn and ready to slay. It was fearless. The cat rubbed itself along the knight's armored shin, rubbing and curling its tail in a happy little twirl.

I dropped to the ground and scratched his little head. The purrs flowed out of it like a symphony.

It was so cute!

He crawled into my lap and rubbed its face on my chin, purrs running wild. *I think a pet could be nice.* I looked over to the knight, standing over us. He slowly shook his head from side-to-side. I stood, holding the cat to face him. His little legs swung in the air and his tail curled as it let out a soft meow.

"How can you say *No?*"

The knight gave another hard and stern shake. I rolled my eyes, "Fine," I said, and set the little guy down. He ran back up to the knight, did one more twirl around his shins, and slunk back into the shadows.

"You are no fun. What if I just wanted some company? Am I not allowed that?"

He returned his sword to its sheath and continued his walk back to the keep.

It felt like another eternity passed and yet we still had so much farther to walk, the knight pacing ten steps in front of me. I just wanted food and sleep. Eventually, we came upon a tavern on our right, *The Middle Maid*, the words carved haphazardly into a plank of wood sitting above an open window, glowing with life. The smell of hot food and ale flooded into the small courtyard of the tavern and my stomach grumbled. It was quite late, and I was sure there was no way of collecting dinner once we got back.

I decided to make a detour to the tavern. *I'll just see him back in my room later.*

I pushed open the door and was hit with the discordance of music and shouts, laughter and cheers. It was an energy I had never felt before.

A middle-aged woman with a low-cut brassiere came up to greet me. Her eyes searched over me, head to toe. This place may be more a *locals only* spot, but I was champing at the bit for whatever they were serving inside.

"Table for uh ... two?" she asked. I quirked my head and turned. *God, how did he get here already?*

She was now eyeing the knight, up and down.

"Yes ... Thank you."

She nodded and brought us back through the overcrowded tavern. Men shouted and drank, and women dressed in similar clothes to our host sat on their laps, with grins as wide as can be.

We were brought over to a table in the back near a window. A cool breeze settled in around us; we were now a good deal away from the hearth heating the livelier area. But I thought I'd enjoy this more. I was more of a *spectator.*

"Anything you need at the moment?"

"An ale please," I asked, scooting into a long bench seat.

"I'll bring two. Be back straight away."

I raised my hand to correct her but before I could say that won't be necessary, she ran off to get them. I sat back against the dividing wall in-between the tables. It was made of a hard worn leather with small pieces missing near the edges, exposing the inner stuffings. I tapped my fingers on the table and looked out the window.

I wondered if the little kitty belonged to anyone; it wasn't very skinny, and its coat was nice. I still couldn't believe he'd said '*No*'. The big hunk of steel was on the other side of the table, and he seemed equally bemused, his attentions on the interior of the inn, watching over the people here. They were a lively bunch, but no one I cared to really converse with. I looked back to the knight and once again, thrummed my fingers on the table, looking intently at his helmet.

He reached over and flattened out my hand, ceasing my tapping. I frowned and pulled my hand out from under his steel gauntlet. I'd noticed he only seemed to wear them when he wasn't riding. Then he wore leather gloves. *Would it make sense to have multiple suits of armor?*

Breaking the forever silence, I asked, "You're not going to drink, are you? You know, on account of the—" I pointed to my head.

He looked down to me, interlocking his fingers and resting them on the table.

"Thought so."

The maiden brought back the two ales and set one in front of each of us, the foaming head spilling over onto the table. *Perfect.*

"Anything else?"

"I'll take a stew, please. Just one." I said, holding up a single finger and flashing her a smile. She nodded and left us once again. I reached over and slid the knight's ale across the table. "More for me."

Taking my first sip of the foaming, lukewarm alcohol, I felt the buzz in my stomach immediately. It'd been quite a while since lunch. I prayed the stew came with a bread roll.

Getting close to the bottom of my first ale, my head was nice and light. I caught myself staring up at the knight again and sunk into my seat, lowering my eyelids and glaring at him.

"I don't like you."

He let out a slight movement from his chest. I can only

assume it was the start to a chuckle. Or my drunken eyes were playing tricks on me.

The stew finally came, and I was overjoyed; a bread roll did accompany the meal. *I could cry.* Thanking the lady, I took my first bite. *Oh,* this was good. Far better than anything the keep had whipped up. Scarfing down a few spoonfuls with another sip of ale, I peered up once more. The knight stared out the window.

"You don't like me either," I said as I bit into the bread roll. *It was still warm.* He turned to face me, and I stared up into the reflective emptiness of his helmet. He paused for a moment, then unfolded a cloth napkin at the table, extending it out to me. I snatched it and leaned forward, over the table. In the reflection of his helmet, I saw bits of stew scattered around my mouth. *Lovely.* I wiped my face and tossed the napkins back to him, hitting him on the visor, leaving a messy streak on the polished steel.

"*That* was for not letting me keep the cat." I drank down the last few drops of my ale, slamming it down on the table and making the foam go flying. The men in the tavern threw up their tankards in unison and shouted, what I assumed was the Midlands word for *cheers.* I laughed and repeated it to them. A warm, comfortable feeling settled into my chest. Even though I had a security detail at all times, this meal felt freeing. A sense of normal I never had back home. Here, I wasn't queen consort, I was just a girl having a meal and a drink. *Maybe one day it will be with better company.* For now, this would do.

After becoming full on both alcohol and stew, *God it was good,* we finally left for the keep. The knight tossed a few coins to the table, and the well-endowed woman wished us a 'Good Evening.'

When I took my first steps through the overly filled tavern,

I had to do a lot of maneuvering to get past the now very inebriated patrons. It didn't help that I was one too.

Looking down at my boots, being wary of each step around the feet that belonged to seated bodies, one cuts in front of me and almost knocked me back on my ass. I peeked my head up and saw a man with a swollen nose and cheeks deeply flushed from drinking. His eyes traveled down my body, and sick bile rose in my throat. His mouth pulled into a smirk and his deep yellow teeth shone through the opening in his lips. I wasn't fit to handle this right now. I tried to shove past him, saying, "Excuse me."

He hooked a finger around the loop of my bag and almost pulled it from my shoulder. My eyes widened, and I turned to look at him, my heart hammering in my chest.

"Not so fast, sweetling. Stay awhile; I just got here." His breath was overwhelmingly hot and humid, and the scent of sour malt smacked me in the face. *He did not just get here.*

Before I could respond, my Knight moved. His steel gauntlet met the man's throat, a loud grunt moving past his putrid lips. My Knight shoved him back to slam into the table closest to us. Food and drink hit the floor and smacked into the surrounding patrons. *The Middle Maid* had become so unsettlingly quiet, you could hear a pin drop. All eyes were on me and my knight. His fingers were still wrapped around the man's throat and only a few grunts and gurgles broke through the quiet.

My knight loosened his hold, the man's red and watery eyes searched franticly for someone to help him. The woman who served us stepped in, her hands clad to each hip, and looked from my knight, to me, to the man, shaking her head.

"Boris, you fucking idiot—what did you do?" It seemed like this was not Boris's first infraction. His head shook, and he tried to grab at my knight's hand around his throat. His legs flailed off the table.

"Fucking *apologize* and the nice man may let you get back to yer dinner."

My knight's grip remained around his throat for one more tight squeeze before he released him. A choked gasp escaped Boris' mouth.

"*Sorry!* I'm sorry." He looked at my knight and then my knight turned to me. Boris' eyes followed, boring into mine. The terror behind them was palpable. He slid off the table and bent to his knees in front of me. "I am *so* sorry." His voice trembled as he spoke. His sour, putrid smell wafted over me again, causing a sick feeling in the back of my throat. *I've got to get out of here before I let up all the stew.*

"Apology accepted." I turned to my knight, "Let's *go*," I said, through my teeth. Rushing now through the rest of the way, all eyes tracked us until we left.

The cool breeze from the outside hit my face, and I took my first step out onto the uneven road. *Was it always this uneven?* Another step, then another. This is fine, just one foot in front of the other. That was until the tip of my boot caught on something and I flew forward.

My eyes squeezed shut, and I waited for the hard, grinding little pebbles and rocks to dig into my chin. But it never came. I slowly opened my eyes, one lid at a time, the ground just inches away from my nose, but we didn't meet.

My knight had caught me with an arm around my middle and pulled me to my feet. He stood me up and pulled my cloak straight and dusted off my shoulders.

"Thanks," I grumbled passively. I turned from him with another attempt at walking. A step, then another ... then the same arm came around and half lifted, and half led me the rest of the way to the keep. I would have complained but it didn't seem like I was going to make it on my own two feet for much longer.

It was a very long trek back before I was finally at my bedroom door. My knight opened it, and I made my way in, overjoyed the walking was about to stop. He reached to close the door, and I turned and stopped him, my face peeking out through the sliver of an opening.

The words were held hostage in my mouth, but I knew, *I* knew, I was a lot to handle. I blew out a long exhale and said, "Thank you ... I may not, *not* like you after all."

He stood for a second and then pulled the door closed the rest of the way.

TEN

A few days passed, and Ilias was set to be back today. In the days leading up to his return, the keep was transformed into a place fit for a grand party. Tapestries and gourmand fabrics sealed every crack in the Grand Hall and main rooms. The colors were of the midlands, soft blues and greens. It was all so elaborate, and it felt like it should be a happy time, but I couldn't forget the Crimson Moon Festival.

I pushed back those thoughts; we were moving forward. Ilias sent word back that I was to meet with the seamstress in town. I made my way there with my shadow. Upon my arrival, I discovered she had prepared a gown already. It was in the northern color, the darkest black fabrics available with a high neck collar, the chest exposed, scooping down to a corseted middle and a long trailing skirt. It had a wrist bustle for dancing and shimmering crystals all over the gown. It reminded me of a night sky.

Standing before the mirrors, my hair pulled up and the gorgeous gown draped on my body, a wave hit me. This girl looking back at me, *was me*, for all intents and purposes, but as

I looked closer, I could see the dark circles under her eyes, and the pallid skin connected to bone was of a stranger.

Being here was a distraction, a distraction to a much larger problem. I was running away from my old life. I still hadn't sent those letters to my mother, I still hadn't opened Kairos's journal since the first day. Even the book I stole, the one from the cathedral, was left untouched.

I was tired of the demons; I was tired of being afraid of another attack, and yet the feeling of the impending doom gnawed at the back of my skull, behind the eyes staring back at me. I was becoming a cast of my old self, and I knew it. This facade would catch up with me if I kept it going.

I had to go. I had to get North.

I paced in my room. Ilias should be back by now. I'd waited in my room for him to summon me, but I'd heard nothing. Becoming impatient, I took leeway within the hall of the keep and headed towards the drawing room to see if I might catch word of his arrival.

I told my knight I wasn't leaving the keep's walls so he could stand vigil elsewhere or even just use the bathroom. I didn't know, but I wanted him to do something not involving me for once.

As I approached Ilias's drawing room, I saw the door was slightly open, and voices spilled out through the crack. One of them was definitely Ilias and the other, the other sounded different—familiar—but different.

I pressed back against the wall, flattening out. Who was he talking to? I knew the voice—it was like a distant memory, but I couldn't quite place it.

Moving in closer, I peered through the crack in the door,

scanning over the room with my sliver of sight. The only thing visible to me was Ilias's backside. His shoulders were forward and tense. As I watched, he pressed his palms onto a table and leaned into them. His voice grew lower and sharper. I bent in just a little more—the silence was shattered by loud footsteps coming down the hall from behind me. Ilias must have heard. He turned, his eyes searching over the doorway. I pulled back and slunk away from the door. Then it was closed with a hard slam. I jumped at his pure aggression and turned to see who had caught me eavesdropping.

My knight stood in the center of the large hall, taking up all the space for absolutely no reason, his arms full of bags. *What could he be shopping for?* Without a word I walked past him and headed back to my room. Ilias would come and see me when he was available. Maybe he was speaking with his uncle. If it was his uncle maybe he'd been to the Oriens Court before and I had heard him speak then?

Ami assisted me with my hair for the party, twisting it into a complex knot due to my dress having a high neck, held together with too many pins to count. When I looked in the mirror, I realized she was right. It accented my cheekbones and created a lift to my face. She applied a light-colored powder under my eyes to help with the shadows and then lined them with kohl for contrast. Her final touch was a rouge for my cheeks and lips.

She helped me into my dress and while she was tightening the laces in the corset, my mind wandered. There was still no word from Ilias, and I couldn't get that conversation out of my head. He was so consumed in what was obviously a private moment. Could something have happened while he was away?

The last tight cinch of the corset sprung me loose from my thoughts. The air rushed out of my lungs, and I turned to her, "I think it's tight enough. If I am still to breathe this shouldn't be any tighter." I said, placing a hand over my abdomen, taking in shallow inhales.

She gave me a soft smile and tied it off.

"You'll be fine, my dear." With that, she took her leave, and I turned back to the mirror. The gossamer fabric glittered around me, and one small movement made the whole thing shimmer. The mirror showed me a queen ... or a girl befitting a queen once.

It was time to go.

I opened my door to find my knight standing in his usual place, but not in his usual fittings. He was still encased head to toe in mirrored steel, but was draped in sashes, and his mantle was longer with a more intricate insignia. That must have been inside those bags he was carrying.

Instead of him taking the lead and walking ahead, he stood next to me, extending his elbow. I quirked a brow up at him.

"Really?"

He stood, unmoving and still holding out the extended elbow. I shook my head and took his arm. I guess he was my escort for the evening.

We made our way down the halls. The music echoed from the party and the sounds stirred something in me; I could feel it bubbling back to the surface, Kairos, the Crimson Moon Festival, the demons. My arm tightened around the cool steel and my knight turned to look down at me. I kept my eyes forward, feeling his gaze boring into me from behind his helmet. I raised my chin and shook my head, dismissing any concern.

Thankfully, he continued walking. I couldn't let this take over me. Not now, not tonight.

We found the room filled with many voices and music,

guests dancing and eating. We took the first few steps down to the floor below. The moment my dress caught the light through the doorway, it lit up like stars. The room quieted, and step by step all eyes turned to us. My chin held high, I took each step like how I had for the last decade.

We made our way down and through the symphony of whispers as we came to the center of the room. Ilias stood in the opening of the partygoers in a deep navy jacket and pants with a matching mask. He walked up, taking my arm from my knight. He pulled me close, resting his cheek against mine.

"God, I've missed you." His breath was warm on the shell of my ear. A wave of heat danced over my skin. I pulled away and smiled up at him. Only the top half of his face was hidden behind the mask, the bottom half left his coy smile and dimples in full view. He leaned in closer, connecting our bodies. His lips came down to mine in a soft caress against my own.

My mind swam with the idea of how public this was and how those ladies-in-waiting had called me, *"some whore."* Their words hit me like a hammer to an anvil, and the memory was just as tenacious. *Was that how everyone saw me with him?*

Ilias led me to the dance floor. The other guests were already kicked up into the steps. Luckily it was a familiar tune if you'd ever been to court before. Ilias led me through the dance flawlessly, like he had been dancing for half a century. Even though I'd done the same dance for years, he still blew me away.

As the music settled into a lull, he looked around the room, his eyes scanning over the faces. I wondered if he'd seen me after all when I was eavesdropping outside his drawing room. I opened my mouth, but he turned to me at the very same moment, his eyes shining into mine and my brain went blank, "Uhhmm ... drink, can I have a drink?" *Stupid.* I shook my head and started over.

"The dancing has made me quite parched; can you show me where I can get a refreshment?" *Like a good and proper lady, geez.*

Ilias gave me an answering nod. His hand found the small of my back as he guided me over to a server with a tray in hand, a deep ruby beverage glinting in the candlelight. He grabbed a long-stemmed glass and handed it to me, taking one for himself. The moment the drink hit my lips I tasted the tart sweetness of berry wine. The same berry wine I'd drank the night Kairos was slaughtered like a fucking animal by that monster. That, *that, demon.*

The wine caught on its way down, making me cough. I felt my pulse in my temples and my heart hammered against my rib cage. I knew going to a grand party might make me feel some kind of way, but this, *this is the fucking icing on the cake.* I took in a deep breath and tried to steady my exhale, slow and controlled. *Calm yourself.*

I set the glass back on the tray and looked around the room at the partygoers, trying to distract myself. I noticed Ilias appeared to be doing the same. His eyes went over the room, watching the night unfold. But his attention remained elsewhere as he brought the drink back up to his lips, the florid stain of the berry wine blooming along his soft pout. Ilias's tongue swiped over them to collect any loose dew drops of alcohol. If I got there first, would I feel the same dizzying effect of the wine without the memories? Maybe. *Maybe.*

I moved into him, placing my hand on his chest and he turned to me, a smile brimming his lips. He set his glass down and pulled me in. I moved my hand up to his neck, angling him down to me. Closing the space, he brought his lips to mine. His mouth was greedier than before, less hesitant. He moved his hands to my hair and his fingers pressed into my scalp, deepening the kiss. I opened my mouth against him, and he indulged my motivations, his tongue moving in and working against mine. That's when I tasted it, the tart sweetness I was afraid of, but there was more. Something else. The salty, citrusy taste of him transformed the wine into a new intoxication. A new flavor to drink in.

His hands moved to my hips, and he pushed us apart. The space between us grew, and the rift in my chest grew as well. His hands grabbed for my shoulders, and he leaned down to look at me, his eyes boring into mine.

"I have to go make a toast; I will be *right* back." His right hand cupped my cheek and his thumb swiped softly over my skin. I nodded against it. He centered himself in the room, a glass in hand.

I slunk back to a far wall, watching him smile and speak about how grateful he was to his guests. He toasted to a healthy and bountiful harvest and said all the expected things a man in power would say.

My breath stilled and out of the corner of my eye I saw a black figure. My blood ran cold and the hairs on the back of my neck stood straight up. A cold sweat broke out on my palms. Images of Kairos flashed in my mind again: *his body in the pool of red and black blood.*

Ilias raised his glass, and the attendees shouted out, but I couldn't hear what they were saying.

His hand lying on the floor, moving with the cadence of the demon ripping into this throat.

A deep ringing built in my ears, and I grew dizzy. I was petrified to speak out, but even more so to not.

The snapping and squealing of his head being ripped from his body, the spray of blood painting me. The taste of it hitting my tongue and filling my nostrils with the putrid scent of death and decay.

A loud bang set me off. I turned to look for the black

figure and spied it standing behind Ilias. Its arms were raised and in their hands were ... fireworks? Shots of sparklers raised up high over Ilias's head and the room erupted into an uproar of cheers.

My face was cold and clammy with the post-panic frenzy of nerves coursing through me. I took off, running down the halls, giving a silent apology to Ilias as I fled. I spied my knight and ran into the door next to him—a small bathing chamber for guests, and slammed the door, locking him and anyone else out.

I tried to gulp down air, but this corset was suffocating and the pins in my hair felt like they were pulling every strand to its breaking point. I needed to get everything off me. I began to rip at the ribbons of the corset and pulled each pin out of my hair, throwing them onto the ground. My hair tumbled over my shoulders. The fucking corset was loose, but I couldn't get the damn thing off by myself.

Bracing my hands on the sink, my knuckles turned white. I squeezed my eyes closed, but all I could see was Kairos, his body. Then Anders' body flashed into my head. Then the way I'd sunk below the surface of the mud. My own death had been so fucking close. I remembered how the Commander was wracked with grief and had to push it down to protect me. Their screams echoed in my ears. I turned my back against the wall and slid down, forcing the heels of my palms into my eyes. I let out a strangled sob.

A few silent moments passed and then a small knock at the door broke me from my memories. I didn't want anyone to see me like this.

"Go away." Another knock came. "I said *go away.*"

"Yes, I heard you the first time. Would it be too much trouble to ask you to reconsider?" Ilias was at the door.

I inhaled and pushed myself up off the ground. Making my

way to the door, I unlocked it. He ripped it open. I rushed to lock it behind him while he grabbed my face in his hands.

"What happened out there? Are you okay?" His eyes were full of worry as they searched mine. His hands practically shook as he held me. *God, he was so worried.* This wasn't supposed to happen. My mouth started to quiver, and a tear slipped down my cheek.

"I'm so sorry, I—" The words caught, and I couldn't say anything else. Nothing came out.

"Stop. What do you have to be sorry for?" His brows furrowed as he wiped the tear away.

"I ruined the party. I made a scene and just—"

"No, no, you didn't."

He pulled me into him, wrapping his arms around me, my head on his chest. He ran his hand down my hair.

"All you did was save everyone from an hour of long, boring words that no one actually means. After you left, I excused us all, and they went on their way. Everything is fine, I promise."

I nodded into his chest and pulled away. *I just need a little space.* Walking over to a wall opposite him, I leaned back against it.

"Evangeline, what *did* happen tonight?"

I flinched at the sound of the false name I gave him. I didn't want to look at him. I couldn't, not with a lie hanging still so far in between us. Just further confirming my guilt. I took a centering breath before I spoke.

"The attack, the one that happened the night before I was brought to you, it was during the Crimson Moon Festival. It was just too soon to be around all—" I threw my hands out. "This."

He remained silent and did not protest me or my reasons. He let me be me.

I spied my face in the mirror, no longer looking like the girl I'd been at the beginning of the party. Kohl was smeared down my cheeks, and my hair was a mess from how I'd pulled out the pins. I closed my eyes and responded, "I was fine for most of the night; I had a wonderful time. It was just like a wave crashed into me. It took me out and washed me into a sea of memories and I needed a moment."

He came up behind me and wrapped his arms around my waist, pulling me back into him. I turned in his arms and faced him, placing my hands on his chest and moving them up to his shoulders.

"Ilias, can I ask you something?"

"Of course,"

"Do you like me?"

"You know I like you, I—"

I placed a finger on his lips, silencing him from saying anything else.

"No, do you *like* me?"

He cocked his head to the side and gave me a half smile.

"Yes, I *like* you, very much." He took my hands in his and held them to his chest. "But I don't think now is the best time to discuss this."

The feeling of rejection hit me like a rock in the gut. He hadn't come and seen me when he got home like I'd thought he would. He was distant at the party and now this. *What was I even doing here?* I needed to send word home. I was an idiot for staying here and not sending out a single letter.

I freed my hands and went for the door, unlocking it and walking hastily back to my room. My knight stood a few feet ahead of me and opened the door swiftly, allowing me in, and closing it behind me.

I felt so stupid. I looked like a mess and had just ruined his party and then after he'd wiped away my tears, I tried to *come* on to him. Of course, he wouldn't take that bait. *Who would*? As soon as the door shut fully, I went to my bed, grabbed a nearby pillow and screamed into it. Eventually, I fell back onto my bed, trying to take deep breaths but my damn corset strangled me. Lying down, my hands worked the front, trying get any of the hooks free. Once I had the front undone, I made my way to the wardrobe and used the mirrors to help undo the back.

The doors to my room flung open and I jumped and turned with a fright.

"Who the hell just barges in?" My voice stilled as I saw Ilias in the doorway, his eyes dark and heavy.

He closed the door behind him and stalked over to me. His steps were quick, and he was on me in moments. He wrapped his hand in my tangled mess of hair and forced me to him, my mouth on his. Hard and fast. His mouth enveloped mine, ravenous, and I tried to keep up. Both of us were breathless when he pulled away. His hand was still tight in my hair as he bared my neck, his lips devouring the sensitive skin. There was a small sliver available to him with the high neck of the dress, but he still sent shivers down my spine. He worked his way up to my ears, his breath wet and hot.

"Oh love, I more than *like you*. I *want you*, more than I can ever put into words." His lips crashed even harder into mine. Taking me by surprise, I opened my mouth with a small gasp, and he took full liberty to explore me. I ran my hand over his short hair, and the tiny hairs tickled my palm. He released my mouth and spun me to face away from him.

His voice low, he said, "Let me finish taking this off for you, yeah?" He pulled my hair to one side and threw it over a shoulder, getting it out of the way of the laces. His fingers worked fast and efficient. In moments the corset dropped to ground, then the outer layer of the dress, dropping in a heap of fabric at my feet, leaving me in just my slip. His arms wrapped around me again, pulling my back into his firm chest. He forced my chin up and my head rested on his shoulder. His mouth found my neck and the freedom he now had with the collar out of the way gave him full access to roam over my skin. His lips were hot and he sucked deeply on the crook of my neck. I let out a soft gasp.

He answered with a low rumble in his chest. His hands reached over and grabbed at my breasts through the slip, massaging me and searching my body. My want for him grew, the muscles in my lower stomach tightening. His hand felt so good; I wanted them over every inch of me. Like he could read my thoughts, his hands headed further south, pulling up my slip and traveling to the bare skin of my thighs.

His fingers traced the soft lip of my undergarments, just barely slipping beneath them. I started to push further into his hand, but he retreated, and a disappointed groan slipped from my mouth. He let out a soft chuckle next to my ear and shushed me. Salt and citrus rushed over my face. He reached further and cups my center fully, holding me in his hand. "Do you want more?" he whispered against my skin. Words had left me and all I could do was nod, leaning my body heavier into his. He moved my undergarments to the side and his warm fingers met the soft skin. His fingers slipped between my wet folds and traced over me gently. I reached down to hold his hand in place and grinded into his fingers. His lips found the soft spot on my neck again and sucked just a little more. I felt the tension building in between my thighs, and I reached my free hand up to his face, pulling him over to kiss me.

I wanted to taste him and feel how good his hand felt against me at the same time. My grinding picked up, and he slipped a finger inside of me. I gasped into his mouth, and he responded by sinking a second finger inside. The pressure of his palm against my clit and the feeling of both fingers drew me to the edge.

I released, then tightened against him. Wave after wave took me and I whimpered my last moans into his mouth. My body went limp, and he guided me back to my bed.

I laid down on it sideways with my legs still hanging off, and he joined me, his body settling into the plush mattress. He moved in next to me on his side, his head resting on his hand. Looking into his eyes, I reached over and traced a shape on his cheek. He closed his eyes. I let my fingers linger down his chest and then lower towards the top of his trousers. I found the top, but he stopped me, holding my hand in his.

"Later," he said. "There is plenty of time for that. This was about you. Not saying I didn't also enjoy myself." He reached down and adjusted himself in his pants. "Get some sleep. I'll see you in the morning." He leaned over and kissed my cheek, his soft lips holding there for a long time.

Eleven

Ilias's aforementioned '*Later,*' was not quite as far into the future as I had originally anticipated.

I sat in Ilias's room the next day in a chair facing the outside through his balcony door, a soft and chilly breeze carrying through the room. The chair was large and plush, with intricate brocade fabric. My legs intertwined with his as we both sat at either end of the chair. He was looking out through the doors, and his eyes searched the skies. He wore nothing but a loose and open white shirt and trousers and seemed calm, wearing a face I had never seen before. His fingers lazily traced over the designs woven through the cushion's fabric, and his breathing was slow and controlled.

I was supposed to be reading through the small table side book of the midlands bird species I'd snagged from next to Ilias's bed but watching him was much more tantalizing.

His fingers stilled, and he peered over to me, his eyes catching mine. He smirked, dimples revealing themselves against his smooth and freshly shaven cheeks. How can I dare look away?

"Enjoying your book, love?"

"You know, not as much as I would have thought." I sat up a little straighter, "I keep getting *distracted*."

Ilias quirked up his brow, sitting straighter himself, pulling his legs out from our entanglement. He leaned over my legs and placed a hand on the back of the couch, holding his weight there as he pulled the book up from my fingers, closing it and tossing it to the floor. It landed with a hard slam. My eyes followed it, but he grabbed my cheeks, holding them firm in his grip.

His face was only a few inches away from mine and that salty citrus scent of his filled all my airways. The closeness brought a heat to my face, and traveled down, deep through my stomach and to the now throbbing feeling between my legs.

Oh god he was so— His mouth closed in around mine and before I could even finish the thought; he was making me forget how to construct a sentence. He kissed me fast and hard, intention behind every swipe of his tongue. When he bit my lip, I couldn't help but smile against him.

His hand released from my cheeks and worked its way into my hair. I tried to reach my arms up to wrap around his neck, but he stops me. Pulling away and breaking the kiss, he sat back onto his heals. His shirt was open and exposed his hard and defined chest.

He reached down and grabbed for my thighs, pulling hard enough to scoot me down the chair to him. His fingers worked the laces at the closure of my pants, and he swiftly removed them, sliding them down my legs. My heart was beating through my chest as he took me in, the daylight through the open doors shining bright on us. I was on full display to this man.

I watched his chest expand with a deep breath as he lowered to me. His mouth found mine once more, his fingers drifting low on my bodice, playing with the strings holding the top fabric together.

He pulled them loose and let my cleavage show. Then he leaned over, traveling little kisses down to my ear and working his way to my shoulder, leaving little bites in his wake. He pulled soft gasps from my mouth. His hands roamed, stroking along my breast, and finding my now peaked nipple. He pinched it between his thumb and forefinger making my core ache.

He settled himself onto the floor in front of the chair. His hands slid up my thighs and his thumbs dug softly into my sensitive skin, forcing me to spread my legs wider. Bringing his mouth to the soft skin of my heated core, he placed a kiss at my entrance. A shiver raced up my spine. He leaned back from me, his eyes dark and heavy-lidded. Full of desire and—and was he *smirking* at me?

He leaned his head down for another kiss. I pressed back into the chair, closing my eyes and trying to control my breathing.

His tongue traced up my center and I gasped. He caught me off guard. Delving deep into me, he feasted. His tongue and lips worked me into a tight coil. His teeth grazed across my sensitive clit, and I let out an uncontrollable jerk. He began to focus on that very spot. I squeezed my fingers into the chair and reached to grasp at his shoulders as I feel myself about to, about to—

A knock at the door breaks the cusp of my orgasm.

It was right there!

Ilias lifted his head, his mouth swollen and glossy. He wiped his mouth and made his way to the door. A growing bulge was visible in his trousers. I threw my head back into the chair. That was impeccable timing.

Still reeling from my *almost* orgasm, I made my way back to my room. Ilias had to go and take care of whatever came to break our *engagement* at the door. Reaching the comfort of my fortress of a bed, I laid on my plush pillows and untied my pants, shimmying them down my legs.

My fingers glided over the still damp and sensitive skin. The aching feeling of being so close and denied the release I craved was building back in moments. My fingers moved down and circled the tender bud, building and bringing me back to the crescendo I was craving.

I thought of Ilias and that chair and the pulse in my ears grew louder. I was almost there; my breathing was speeding up and—

My door *OPENED,* to reveal Ami, carrying fresh linens in her arms. She stopped in her tracks and stared at me, the panic rising on her face as it registered what she'd just walked in on.

"My lady! I am so sorry, please excuse my intrusion." She backed away from the door and into the hallway. But looming behind her was the ever-present suit of armor. He faced into the room, not turning away from me. Heat flushed over my whole body, and I snapped my legs together, reaching for the blankets.

"Close the door!" I shout at him.

He slowly reaches for the knob and gently closes the door.

"What the fuck ..." I groaned out, throwing my head back into the pillows.

Hours passed and pacing my room was beginning to feel unhealthy. There were only so many times I could walk between these four walls. I spied the bag stuffed under the bed and remembered the book I had *borrowed* from the cathedral. I had done the damn deed of swiping it; the least I could do was take a look.

Pulling the bag out, my fingers traced over the two books' spines. I wasn't ready to open Kairos's journal, so I reached for the Crimson Cloth Knight's journal with it's dark, worn leather. The insignia debossed into it looked like it was hand-carved with small imperfections.

Flipping through the pages, it struck me how similar it was to Kairos's journal, but this one was fully written out in old Amaymon. I should have grabbed that reference dictionary, though taking one book was already enough.

Continuing through the pages I noted sigils and diagrams drawn in random margins, some familiar to me and some of tools or shapes I didn't recognize.

The farther into the book, the more hurried the words became, letters jumbling into each other to the point where they did not look like letters at all. I knew few words or phrases in old Amaymon, but they were mostly curse words, nothing that would help at all right now.

Oh wait.

There was one word, out of the hundred I couldn't make out. It was next to a drawing of what looked like a sacrament needle.

Sangyl.

Blood.

My eyes widened as I looked at the depictions and diagrams. The following pages held crude images of black beings with horns rising from their crowns. *Demons.* An unnerving feeling came over me. I flipped to the next page and staring back at me were the dead eyes of a creature that belonged in Abaddon. Its eyes were empty and yet felt as if they could bore right into my soul. I couldn't look away. I couldn't blink. My eyes began to sting with the dryness of the air, and my breath stuck in my throat.

All I saw was blood and ash, burning buildings and screaming people. Death and darkness. I tried to move, to force my eyes to blink or my lungs to take in air, but nothing came. I was petrified in this spot.

I have been waiting for you …

I heard the words in my mind as clear as any conversation. The voice rang out and I felt it trying to work its way deeper into my mind. A scream built in my throat but never came. I clung to my will and pushed the voice from my skull.

I resist—

I resist you—

Let me go!

The words screamed through my head. Louder and louder.

A rough gale burst through the room and the pages of the book flipped over. The feeling of being stuck left, and I slammed the book closed. Taking in gulps of air, I placed my face in my hands. A sheer feeling of terror imbedded deeper within me. I pulled my hands away and saw them covered in deep red blood. I tried to wipe away on my pants, but it smeared everywhere. I got up and ran to the bathing chamber, running my hands under the cool water in the sink, but —*What?*

Finding the closest mirror and I looked to see—nothing. No blood on my hands. There was nothing there.

I needed to get out of this room. Now.

Reaching for the door handle and I paused, my fingers hovering. I wanted out of this room, but *my knight* for sure was going to be out there. But staying here any longer made the chill return to my skin.

Fuck this.

I shot out of my room far too fast and just ran. To the stables I went, why not?

My knight followed and much too quickly did his strides match mine. We made our way there with me looking like a maniac, walking too quickly, and almost out of breath by the time I got to the covered stables.

The smell of feed and feces overwhelmed me, and I had to stop. Flies zipped by my ears, the ground was wet with, *something*.

My knight moved past me, pulling out his black stallion. The giant beast towered over me. He also grabbed a couple of brushes and a bag of sugar cubes that sat near the entrance of the stall and gestured for me to follow him.

We made our way to a small open area far enough away from the smell of animals that I no longer had the over-whelming urge to bring my tunic top up and over my face to try to block out the stench.

He brought his horse to a stop and set down the items next to an empty bucket he picked up and turned upside down, wiping off any grass or dirt. My knight motioned for me to go to the bucket, and I quirked a brow at him. *Did he make me a place to sit?*

If not, that is what I ended up doing anyway. I took a seat and glanced out to the low, setting sun casting the sky into a soft swirl of tangerine and gold. The color of the sunset reflected off the shiny steel plates of his armor. He looked as if he caught all the radiance of the daytime star and brought it down to the earth's soil.

It was lovely.

Lovely? What the fuck was I thinking?

I must have been looking a little too long because he stopped brushing his horse to look back at me. I swallowed hard and fought the urge to turn away. He tossed the brush to me.

I caught it and tilted my head. "You want me to do it?" He nodded and pointed down to the other brush. I grabbed it and walked towards him and the black steed. He took the new brush from my hand and went to work on the backside of the horse, near the rear legs. I was sure the horse would kick me if I got too close.

I'd brushed my own horses back home, but this one was intimidating, looking like he could knock me over and trample me in a moment. I shook my head free of my irrational thoughts and brought the brush to his pelt. His skin twitched under my touch, but he seemed to relax the more I ran the bristles over his coat. I seemed to relax too.

For a moment, my mind was free of almost everything. All I thought about was the horse's hair patterns and the way they felt under my skin. After a little while, I stopped using the brush and was running my hands over his velvety black hairs, feeling his life-force beneath my fingertips. He was beautiful.

The knight was finished with his brushing task as well. He was just *watching* me. I furrowed my brows at him. "What?" I said accusingly. He shook his head and came over to me. Taking my brush from me, he placed it back down by the bucket and reached for the sugar cube bag.

Coming up to the horse's face, he pulled off his gloves and put them into the crook of his arm. This was the first piece of his skin that I had ever seen beneath his omnipresent armor.

As he ran a hand down his mount's snout, the horse nudged him, urging him for the treat. The knight reached into the bag, pulling out a sugar cube and holding it out to the horse with a flat, outstretched hand. The horse's lips came down and snatched it from him. He plunged another hand into the bag and offered me a cube. I waved my hand at him. "I'm okay."

He walked to me, grabbed my wrist, and pulled me to the front of the horse. I thought about causing a struggle but decided to just succumb to whatever he was doing. The horse's ears went forward in warning, and I felt a spike in my blood pressure. This horse did *not* like me. My knight placed his hands on my shoulders, gave them a small squeeze, and then reached his hand past me to the horse with the sugar cube.

As the horse came in to grab it, my knight grabbed my hand in his free one and brought it to the horse's snout. My palm was open and shaking. What if the horse bit off my finger realizing we'd switched our hands?

But he didn't. Its lips tickled my palm as it took the cube, crunching it and searching eagerly for more. I let out a soft chuckle as it nudged my hand for another. It's ears relaxed, and so did I.

My shoulders dropped and I took a deep breath, I hadn't even realized I was holding. My knight handed me another sugar cube and guided my hand over with his beneath mine.

His hand was so warm, and I felt his callouses against my knuckles. The horse snatched the sugar cube from my palm. I jumped slightly but was thankful the horse had interrupted my thoughts of how my knight's skin felt.

A sinking feeling crept in as I remembered what he'd walked in on only a few hours ago. My face grew hot. I noticed how close he was behind me. My body was almost pressed up against his. *I needed to leave.*

I took off back to the stables, going in through the stalls and kept moving deeper, letting the smells surround me again just to get my mind off the damn knight seeing me so—I gulped hard—*exposed.*

The deeper I got into the stables, the darker it became. The sun was setting and cast little light. The few lanterns left to light the place were set up at the entrance. The shadows started to grow taller, and an eerie feeling came over me. I normally hated the dark, but this felt *bad*.

A chill wind burst through the front of the stables, knocking into the doors and throwing a few tools off the walls. I reached up to grab for the Legion Stone around my neck. My fingers grasped it, and the familiar bite ate into my flesh, pulling me from the anxious feeling crawling through me.

Then I heard something shuffling through the last stall. This far into the stable there were no other horses, so what could it be? A rodent maybe? *I hope.*

Stepping carefully to avoid startling whatever I may find, I tiptoed to the gate of the stall. I peered over the edge, but the gate shifted under my pressure, and swung open, letting out a high-pitch squeal as it worked on its hinges.

The sun fully set, and the stall was cast in full darkness. I tried to step in to get a better look and—out of the darkest corner of the stall a figure stood, much straighter and much more human-like than I'd been expecting. It was visibly shaking and having trouble remaining upright. Its arm moved forward, grasping onto the gate and shoving it closed.

I was pushed back from the force and fell to the ground, the air knocked from my lungs. I landed hard on my back, hitting my head on something on the stable floor.

I tried to sit up and allow my eyes to adjust in the dark. Decaying fingers latched onto the top of the gate, five, then ten. It looked like it was pulling itself up, like it couldn't stand on its own.

The door opened, and a scream started in my throat. I threw my hand over my mouth to hold it in. My eyes widened with horror.

I scrambled up to run to the stable's exit. I knew there were tools and horse trappings laying around, but in the dark I couldn't see them. One foot hooked onto something, and I stumbled forward, bracing my fall on my knees. I was able to kick whatever tripped me off. Risking a look behind me, I turned, the shape was coming closer. I stood on wobbly legs, rushed to the entrance, my arms pumping at my sides and my lungs fighting the air trying to fill them. I was so close. The light from a weak lantern near the doors illuminated the space.

Finally, I could see it.

It was a man. He had no shirt on, only a loose and tattered pair of trousers and bare feet covered in a layer of muck. His body was not right, though. His skin was pale, and there were black protruding veins leaching up from the waist of his pants and over his abdomen and face. His eyes were dark black and empty, like a glossy and bottomless pit. There were no irises or emotion.

He staggered forward, in slow uncertain steps, tripping over the same obstruction I had and falling to the ground in a hard, wet slump. I couldn't see his chest falling and rising. *Was he dead?*

I spied my knight standing at the entrance of the stable. His statuesque appearance only lasted a moment as I stood fully, my heart racing and unsure of anything that had just *fucking* happened.

He ran over and knelt next to the body of the man, grabbing him and flipping him over onto his back. The man was familiar, his face was—*oh my god!*

This was one of the guards who had traveled with us back from the encampment outside of the Oriens. The one who had the cut on his arm. *What could have happened to do this?* He wasn't a demon, not really. He was a man, but just, different. Nausea swelled the longer I looked at the black veins enlarged in his skin and the sallow tint of his flesh.

I ran into a stall and released whatever sat at the bottom of my belly. I heard a body being dragged along the stable floor, my knight's heavy metal steps and the uneasy wet sound it made as he moved him. I didn't even want to think about what just happened. I shoved the heel of my palms into my eyes —hard.

What the fuck was that?

Ami rounded the corner in her regular clothes with a basket in hand and stopped in her tracks as she honed-in on me. Her eyes widened as her gaze raked over the scene before her. She looked deep into the dark stable at the body dragged on the floor by my knight and visibly shook.

"Lady Evangeline, please—please come with me." She walked in closer, extending a shaking hand to me. I reached out and held on tight finding her fingers slick and clammy.

She led me back to my room and as the door shut behind her, dropped her basket and frantically reached for me. She gripped at my tunic sleeve, pulling it up and examining every inch of my skin.

"Ami, what are you—"

She lifted the tunic over my back and pulled the fabric up. I face her, grabbing at her wrists to still her for just a moment.

"Ami, stop. What is going on?"

"Did he scratch you? A bite? Anything?" Her voice was shaky and barely coming out. She turned back to my hands, flipping my palm over. I spied a small red patch of skin in the center. *That wasn't there earlier.*

"No, no, he didn't touch me. I tripped and fell, that's why I look like, well, *this*." I gestured down to my filthy clothes covered in straw and mud. God, who knows what would have happened if he hadn't expired on his own.

A strong exhale passed her lips, and her shoulders relaxed and lowered.

"If you're all right, I must be going then, I—"

"What? No, you can't leave until you tell me what this examination was all about."

Ami's eyes darted back and forth, avoiding my gaze as she chewed on her bottom lip. I reached for her hand and took it into my own. "Ami, what are you not telling me?"

She took a deep inhale and finally pulled her eyes to mine. Her soft brown eyes shone bright behind a glossy layer of panic. "The man, he was what my people call a Caenum."

I furrowed my brows. I'd never heard that term before. "I am going to need you to elaborate a little bit for me, Ami," I said crossing my arms over my chest. She was hiding more than I'd thought.

"It means cursed. Those who are unlucky enough to be touched by a demon and live, well, they never truly survive. They are Caenum. Cursed to live in agony for days. If they are lucky, it comes fast. Three days for most. If not, it starts to break down your body and soul until you are nothing left. A husk. Like that man."

She walked to the door and opened it, turning back to me for a moment. Her face was full of uncertainty.

"If he wasn't a demon, and he was this, *Caenum*, then why were you looking to see if he had touched me?"

"I would rather be safe than sorry, my lady. I don't know everything. I only have heard stories and conversations from my childhood in Amaymon. I just want you to stay safe."

Amaymon? My thoughts swam in my head as I weighed the options of asking her about Old Amaymon and risk ratting myself out about the journals. I let out a sigh. I had no other valid options.

"You're from Amaymon?"

"Yes, my lady. I am. I have been under Lord Ilias's hire for the last seven years or so. Before that I was in Amaymon."

"Do you ... by chance, know Old Amaymon?"

Her eyes turned cautious, and she stared at the floor. "My lady, Old Amaymon isn't common tongue."

"That's not what I am asking, Ami."

She let out an exasperated sigh and nodded.

"Great, now I need you to help me with something."

TWELVE

A KNOCK AT MY DOOR WOKE ME. ILIAS STEPPED IN before I could respond. He looked like a spring chicken, bright and beaming. "Good morning, Love."

I responded with a much less enthusiastic, "Morning."

He came and sat at the edge of the bed, pulling the blankets away from my face and scooting in closer to me. I shot him a sleepy smile.

"What time is it?" I rubbed my eyes and realized the room was still dark.

"It is about an hour before sunrise." He walked to the closed curtains and parted them, revealing the still inky black night sky. There wasn't a single ray of sunshine to break through into the room.

I'd been up for hours with Ami last night translating the Knight's journal. We'd started at the beginning, and the vast majority was nothing too riveting. A lot of battle plans, a few sonnets, and a letter to home that was never sent. The only thing that piqued my interest was the remaining portion of the Sangyl quote. It read *'The Only True Rebirth is Bathed in the*

Blood of the Fallen.' After that I'd let her get on with the rest of her evening.

As I wiped the last of the sleep from my eyes, I took a closer look at Ilias and asked, "Why are you up so early? And looking like *this?*" I gestured at his pressed and always perfectly fitted outfit and clean presentation.

Giving me a soft laugh, he leaned down to place a kiss on my cheek. His fingers moved to my hair and stayed for a moment. I smiled as his cool scent of citrus and salt lingered on my face like a caress.

He stood and walked over to my sideboard and poured himself a glass of water. Taking a sip, he lowered the glass and said, "I heard about your run in with the deranged man living in the stables." He took a deep breath, pausing slightly before he continued, "Have you ever thought about self-defense?"

God, it was way too early for this, wasn't it? The *man* was not something I wanted to revisit, especially not at this hour. If that was what he was. Ami had referred to him as a Caenum. I still needed to do some digging on that word.

"Not particularly no, I was trained back—back home."

He circled the glass of water in the air, his mouth pulling to one side. "Even so, I think it would do you good to have a refresher. I'll have someone bring you up some training leathers. Meet me in the training room in twenty minutes."

This was much less a request and very much a demand. I sighed and gave him a sleepy nod.

"Wonderful, I'll see you shortly." he said, exiting the room.

I let out a grunt and rolled onto my back. "Five more minutes," I whispered to myself. There was another knock and in came Ami with my new outfit. She was uncharacteristically short; only a quick greeting before dropping the clothes and leaving. I wasn't going to push her. If she felt uncomfortable after what happened last night, I'd let her do what she needed to.

***

I would give Ilias this; the outfit fit me perfectly, like it had been tailored. The soft curves of my body were held in, and it made me look and feel like I could do some damage.

On exiting my room, I glared up at my knight and closed my door with a tight slam. I hadn't seen him last night. It had been a different knight standing guard. The thought of an unknown man outside my door had made me uneasy so I'd just stayed in my room the rest of the night after Ami left.

My knight led me to the training room where Ilias wore matching leathers. My mouth grew dry. He was tall and made of lean muscle and the leathers left it all out for display. I felt a soft heat bloom in my lower stomach and an ache start in my chest. *God, he was a sight.*

He took me through a few practice stances with a short sword, but I struggled with his teaching method. I had been training with Commander Bauer on and off for the last ten years, and this was nothing like that. Ilias was very critical and when he knocked me onto my back for the umpteen time, I told him it was time to retire.

The rest of the day was a tired haze. Ilias speaking through dinner felt like a song of incomprehensible warbles, and I couldn't latch on to a single syllable all night. I felt myself nodding off and though I tried my hardest to keep up with the conversation, it was hopeless. My eyes kept drifting shut.

Blink.

I held up my fork to bring a bite of food to my mouth, slowly chewing at it.

Blink.

I forced down a dry swallow, bringing the heavy glass to my lips.

Blink.

"I will be leaving again tomorrow, I have arranged ..." Ilias's voice sounded far away.

Blink.

I shook my head, trying to force myself to focus. I looked up to him, his eyes searching my face.

"How does that sound?" he said with a soft smile on his lips.

Not knowing entirely what he'd said, but I didn't want to him to realize just how little I'd heard of the entire dinner conversation. I gave him my best *'I wasn't just dozing off'* smile.

"That sounds great." Though I wasn't sure what I may have just agreed to.

The next day Ilias did leave; I remembered hearing that part of the conversation, but whatever else came after was a fuzzy blur of consonants and vowels.

His trips were short, but I typically enjoyed being left to my own devices. I'd been alone quite often in the Oriens, and Kairos's explorations were for months at a time. A few days here or there was manageable. I thought that leaving the grounds too often wouldn't be smart; the Midlands weren't far from the west, so the chance of recognition was heightened the more I explored outside the inner walls of the keep.

I still didn't find the food served for the meals quite good, so when Ilias wasn't joining me, I tried my best to skip it. But today, my stomach was not happy with me, so I went searching for something edible.

In the kitchen a few of the servants gossiped like hens. My

intrusion went unnoticed, and they gabbed on. I reached the cellar door and combed through the dry goods. The one thing I had enjoyed was a delicate sweet dessert bread I now knew the Midlands were famous for. Picking and prodding, it seemed like we were out of it. My stomach was even more angry and was starting to speak out against the lack of food. I placed a hand over it, heading back into the kitchen.

The ladies stopped their gabbing and looked at me, clutching my stomach. "My lady ... are you in *need* of something?" They stared at my hand's placement. I pulled it away abruptly.

"I was just looking for a snack. I slept through breakfast." Not true, but I didn't want them to spit in my supper if they found out I didn't like their food.

"Just a snack? Well, we do have a shipment of the bread coming in, but not until tomorrow." The woman who spoke still eyed my stomach. She turned to look at one of the ladies.

"Are you in need of anything *else?*" she pressed.

I frowned, unsure of their meaning.

"What *else* could I be searching for?" I mimicked her tone.

She looked a little nervous now. "Well, if you are in *need,* we do have a tea that could *help.*" She was still leering at my mid-section.

My eyes widened.

"I am not pregnant! I'm, I'm ... not." The exact opposite, actually.

Her face tightened at my outburst.

The accusation was off-putting, to say the least. She came over to me, placing her hand on my shoulder, trying to calm me.

"I see, my lady. Please do not take it as anything more than a solution to a possible implication. I meant no harm."

My face softened, and my shoulders relaxed a bit.

"But if you are trying to avoid such an occurrence, we do have something for that as well."

My face grew hot. Ilias and I had hardly done much of anything, least of all that. But was it coming in the near future? This was not the right time to have a child. I wasn't even telling this man my actual name, for god's sake. Looking up into her well lived-in eyes and soft down turned mouth, I knew she wasn't being malicious.

"Perhaps that would be something I'd eventually need," I said feeling the blush on my cheeks deepen.

Her mouth softened. "Let me gather it for you."

I toyed with my skirt and bounced my knee against the chair I sat on as the time stretched on. Was she gathering these items fresh? My goodness.

She returned after another five minutes and handed me a few sachets.

"This is good for six months use or so. The first time, it may upset your stomach, but it will keep any *surprises* at bay. You take one, steep it in cold water for ten minutes the day of your first bleed and it will keep you barren until the following. It must be done on the first day each time."

That would be today. Grasping them from her, I said, "Thank you." She gave me a soft smile. "I'll bring you some bread when it arrives."

Walking from the kitchen I was met with my knight looming in the doorway. I was looking intently at the sachets and then raised my head to look up the helmet. I blushed at the thought of him possibly knowing what they were and closed them tightly in my fists. "*Excuse me.*" I said as I pushed past him in the doorway.

I made it back to my room and put all but one of the sachets in my bag. I didn't know who would tamper with them or possibly throw them away, but they needed to be out of reach to anyone but me.

Pulling up a glass, I placed the little bag inside and filled with the cool water. Allowing it to steep, the color of the water slowly got darker and darker. This tea looked close to black as the tenth minute approached. Picking up the glass, I brought it to my nose. The smell was similar to rancid licorice. I pulled it back and gagged. *How the fuck was I supposed to drink this?*

Taking a deep breath, I plugged my nose and brought the glass to my mouth, swallowing its entire contents in a few gulps. I set the cup down and brought a hand to my mouth. Another gag rose in my throat. I ran to the bathing chamber and settled my face just above the cool lip of the tub. The feeling in my stomach calmed, but my head started to swirl. I glanced at my hands and let out a moan. My fingers were elongating and twisting in unnatural movements. I stood to see my face in the mirror; it wasn't right. My facial features were contorting and wobbling. I stumbled into my room and flung myself on the mattress. The pillars housing the canopy swallowed me whole as blackness invaded my vision.

A heaviness fell upon my chest, but my head still felt light, like it was floating away from my body. Going up higher and higher.

There you are ...

"Where am I?"

There you are, my queen ...

"How do you know who I am?"

My queen ... you were made for me ... I will always know who you are.

"Who are you?"

You will know me again soon ... don't worry

"Tell me who you are."

I am you, and you are me. We are one and the same, my queen.

"Who are you?"

Silence came again.

I woke finally to what felt like deep into the night, my body in a pool of sweat and my clothes drenched. *Why was I so hot?* Every day had been growing increasingly brisk but now, now I couldn't get free from a heat burning through my body.

I splashed some cool water on my face, and it helped for the moment, but I needed more. I threw open my windows and the chilly air broke into the room. I felt it hit the surface of my skin, but it couldn't penetrate deep enough to give me any true relief.

A flash of a memory hit me; the pool of water Ilias took me to. It wasn't far; I thought I could make it there off memory. I pulled at the sweat-soaked collar of my shirt. God it was getting stronger, I could feel the heat building.

There was no way I would want to go there with my shadow tagging along, even if he let me go at this hour. I looked down from the second story and saw a thick ledge, probably a foot and a half wide. Plenty of space. There was a tree farther down the way that had grown very close to the walls. There was my way down. Developing my plan, I started to pack a bag.

Throwing it around my shoulders, I looked down over the balcony at the ledge. *It's fine, I'm fine. It's not that far up.* I brought my leg over the railing and that first touch onto the solid stone filled me with the hope that this plan wasn't an absolute catastrophe waiting to happen. I got my footing and shimmied along the ledge to make it to the slightly overgrown tree. Thankfully, it allowed for an easier way down.

I tested my weight on a branch, and it bowed slightly under my foot. *It should be fine.* I climbed over, finding my footing from one branch to another. Nice and slow. I looked down and my eyes felt like they were going crossed. Two floors felt much higher now than it had a moment ago.

I steadied myself and climbed down farther. Finally reaching the lowest branch, I stepped down. A loud *Crack* broke the silence of the night. I fell close to five feet and landed flat on my back, the wind knocked out of me.

After a minute, I struggled to stand and force air back into my lungs. I got down. That was all that mattered. I made my way to the lake at the far end of the keep. It was only a ten-minute walk or so, but in the dark of the night it felt so much farther.

There it was. Shiny moonlight danced across the rippling surface like a sea of stars. Perfect.

I took off my sweat-soaked clothes, leaving only my Legion Stone hanging from my neck and grabbed my towel, keeping it close to the water's edge. I dipped my toes into the water, making ripples of light flash around me. The water was cool and bit at my skin in the most delightful way. Finally wading up to my chest, I leaned back and let the water come over me. It rushed in over my ears and settled into a dark and quiet blackness. Opening my eyes, beneath the water, I saw the faint glow of the moon high in the sky.

Coming back to the surface, I floated for a while, my body relaxing for the first time in a very long time. I took in a deep, centering breath and a gust of wind blew through the trees. A storm of blossoms fell from above, littering across the water's surface, casting me in a pool of swirling petals. Closing my eyes I let the bliss take me. I dunked below the surface and came up, my overly warmed skin with the cool water was the perfect mix. The serene sounds of the wildlife in the night were a symphony of chirps, croaks, and the wind whooshing gently through the trees.

After a while, my skin felt more like a prune than not, and I knew I should be getting back. Reaching for the towel, I dried my hair and face. Reaching down to dry my legs, I found I was not alone and let out a loud scream of surprise.

My knight. Standing no more than ten feet away from me and just outside of the tree line. My eyes were heated, and I was pissed off.

"What the fuck! Why did you have to sneak up on me!? Couldn't you have made yourself known, *somehow?*" I said as I hurriedly wrapped the towel around my bare body and marched over to my clothes. Muttering curses at him under my breath, I gathered my things in my arms and looked up at him. He stood unmoving as usual, and his lack of *fucking anything* was driving me crazy. I pulled out my clothes and started to dress, seeing him still turned in my direction.

"Turn around!"

He lazily crossed his arms and turned away. Not taking any more chances, so did I. Throwing back on my loose tunic and pants, I stomped into my boots and made my way past him. How had he even known I was a gone? Did he do a nightly check that had somehow gone unnoticed? Ugh. A chill raced up my spine at the idea that he might be watching me sleep.

Storming back through to the keep, I made it to my bedroom and slammed the door in his face. Fucking asshole. His seeing my little bits the other day wasn't enough? He had to get an eye on the whole package? I was fuming. I crossed my arms and tapped my foot. Turning towards the door, I opened it hard and fast and got in front of his face; or as much as I could. The fucker was tall.

"I don't know where you get off on seeing me in compromising positions, but it stops here." I pointed my finger up at his helmet.

He just stared down at me. I was talking to a fucking display set of armor for all I ever got from him.

I let out an upset grunt and went back into my room, slamming the door as hard as I could. God, he made me feel like a child.

THIRTEEN

The next day, I chose to stay in my room for as long as I could handle without going completely insane. Which turned out to be close to sunset. Luckily, I made it through without needing to leave for meals as the woman from the kitchen held true to her word and brought me up some sweet bread.

I pulled apart the soft pillowy roll and a plume of warm steam erupted into the air. I swear I tried to savor the thing but devoured it almost immediately.

Trying to keep myself occupied, I chose to finally look further into Kairos's journal. I still wasn't privy to Old Amaymon, but Ami's help the other night did help me pick through a passage about Legion Stones. Their black color was unlike the other black rocks that came from deep in the earth or near a larger sulfur deposit, like a volcano. Legion Stones had a rough texture no matter how much it was processed to be smooth, and as far as it could be seen, no one could break them to make smaller chunks. They were incredibly strong and always remained the same size and shape they were pulled from the earth.

I held my stone to the diagram in the journal. It seemed to be the same one he'd depicted.

It was noted in next to it, "*Do not remove once worn.*" I took a hard swallow; I didn't plan on removing it, but there was no further explanation or reason given.

Almost on cue, my stomach let out a rumble so ferocious it required a response immediately. I crossed my arms over it and prayed it didn't find anything vital scrumptious enough to devour. I needed to eat a real meal. The probability of my knight being stuck at his post was also high; they almost never changed guard. He would eat when I would.

The bastard deserved a little hunger strike after how much he'd seemed drawn to seeing me in so many *less than modest* positions.

My face heated at the memories. First the time Ami burst into my room and now a full view at the lake. The old fuck could skip a few meals.

Stepping out from my room, I made my way to the dining hall. I paid him no attention and just made my way down trying to appear as unbothered as possible. *God, he gets to me so much and doesn't even say anything.* That made me feel almost worse. Just his presence brought this out of me.

I took a seat in my usual chair and lifted my wine-filled glass to my lips. The sickly-sweet juice filled my stomach making me dizzy. I should've eaten first. I looked across the table and saw him sitting inhumanly still, his helmet aimed right at me. My eyes bored into the small, dark depths of the slits where he would have any vision. He could be staring back or avoiding my gaze all together. I'd never fucking know.

A letter from Ilias had come for me. The small wax seal held the Midlands crest and was still unbroken. At least I knew they didn't tamper with the post. I had sent word to my mother the other day and Ilias promised that the curriers were the best in all the five nations.

I unfolded Ilias's letter, it said he would be back as soon as he could make it and, in the meantime, he'd arranged another training session, this time with my knight. I felt my eyes roll deep into my skull. My fucking knight training me? *I was surely going to perish*. With a sigh, I folded the letter and placed it back on the table.

The food came out shortly after. It was a type of small game bird local to the area and bundle of loose peas and a bread roll. I smiled the best faux smile I could afford. Not a single morsel of salt on the plate. I took my first bite—the meal was the same as the rest. Bland and flavorless.

Avoiding another bite, I pushed the peas around and looked up across from me. My knight was not going to remove his helmet to consume a meal in front of me. He had to leave and go to a private dining area. The only time under his watch I was free.

The freedom I'd felt at the lake was blissful, but I knew I was alone in the darkness in a place I was not familiar with. I could have been hurt. Besides, just the knowledge of the Caenum and how close I had one get to me should have been enough to scare me into never leaving his side. I sighed to myself. Those things escaped me last night and trying to sneak away from my knight was stupid.

I leaned back into my chair. I hated this. I hated that I was feeling *guilty*? Guilty for sneaking out and then being upset when I put myself in compromising positions over and over again.

My fingers gripped my fork, knuckles turning white, and my teeth grinded as my stomach rumbled louder. The plate before me was inedible, and I thought back to the meal I had at

The Middle Maid. The stew and the ale had been such a wonderful pairing when they had hit my taste buds.

My stomach let out another growl. I raised my fork and took another wary bite of my dinner. God, I really didn't want to be that much of a brat, but these cooks did not have any heart in their food.

My knight was given his meal and as he stood to go into the private area, I made the quick decision to stop him. I stood, running in front of him, blocking the entrance with my body and outstretched arms.

"How about a white flag?"

He tilted his head at me. His plate of food looked just as unappetizing as my own.

"Meet me outside the keep gate in ten minutes."

He stood straight, holding the platter in both hands, and looked down. I gave him a half smile, knowing he'd have to follow and said, "Great, see you then."

Without looking back, I headed upstairs to grab my cloak.

I made it outside two minutes past the time I'd said and was gulping air. I'd run up and down those stairs and was still late. Looking to my left and right, I saw no knight in my field of vision.

"It was only two minutes," I said out loud.

Did he really just go back inside?

Then, from the corner of my eye, he appeared on his large black stallion. I dove my teeth into my bottom lip to keep from smiling as he came up next to me and reached his arm down. I grabbed it and climbed up behind him.

"To the tavern" I shouted, my arm pointing to the large iron gate. He shook his head, but we were on our way.

The familiar smells of roasted meat, and warm ale hit me before I saw the tavern come into view. As we approached, I almost threw myself off the back of the horse, making my way to the door as my knight tied up the black beast and headed in behind me.

The maid recognized us, though I sensed a northern girl with a walking suit of armor might be hard to forget. She began to take us to a table but before we made our way down, I stopped her. "Is there a place more private we may be able to go?"

She tilted her head and placed a hand on her hip. "There is, but you gotta pay for a private *meal*."

I looked between her and my knight. "That's fine. I can pay for it."

She brought us to a small room on the second floor; it had a bed and a small table with one chair and a tiny bathing chamber. I nearly laughed. My knight standing larger than life around the petite furniture was almost comical. But he needed to try this food. After the tasteless meals from the keep, it was a necessity.

I ordered us two stews and one ale. I wasn't sure if he was a drinker, but with the many other vows he'd taken, I doubted drinking was on the table if celibacy wasn't.

The thought of celibacy and my knight caught me more than it should have. Looking at the man sitting on the bed of a too small room I realized I'd paid for a room only used for those who do not practice celibacy. The silence stretched on. Light chatter and voices bled in through the walls, but we didn't say a word to each other. Which was normal, but right now; it just felt different. And I, of course, had put us in this situation.

I sat at the table and fidgeted with the skin on my fingernails, avoiding looking in his direction. A knock came a moment later, making me jump, but thankfully pulled me from my spiraling thoughts.

"Enter," I called.

The maiden came in with the stew. The spicy, flavorful aroma wafted in with her and I started to salivate. I took a few bites while it was still hot and washed it down with my ale before the maiden could even leave.

"Okay, so my idea is," I said between a mouthful of stew. "I'll go wait in the bathing chamber and you eat the stew out here. You can use the chair and table to—"

He crossed his arms and shook his head.

"Please, I did this whole thing so you could try it. All the meals at the keep are terrible; I'm sure even you can taste that."

He didn't move a muscle. I let out a hard sigh and lifted my bowl from the table.

"Just eat it quickly. I'll be having mine sitting near the chamber pot." He stood and stopped me, taking the bowl from my hands and setting it down on the table. He picked his up and went into the small excuse of a bathing chamber, closing the door and leaving me alone.

I rested my ear to the hard wood of the door and listened to see if he was going to eat it or throw it out and pretend to eat. There was only silence on the other side of the door. *He's going to let it get cold.*

"I swear it's not poisoned ..."

Stupid, of course it's not poisoned. Why would I even say that?

I heard what sounded to be the creaking of metal and something placed on a hard surface. Then there were a few scrapes of the spoon on the bowl. A smile grew on my face, followed by a blush. I was excited for him to try a dumb stew. Why?

I sat down and went back to mine. It had cooled a good

deal but was absolutely delicious. Today's bowl had potatoes and a spicy sausage. It was, dare I say it, better than the last. I needed to turn the cooks in the keep onto whoever was making miracles in this kitchen.

A few minutes passed and I started to feel full and cozy. I nestled into the chair and placed the heels of my boots onto the bed, letting my eyes close for a second.

The creaking of the bathroom door startled me from my rest and my knight came out, with his helmet back on, I don't know what I was expecting—but! His bowl was empty.

He walked behind me and placed the bowl on the table. I took my feet down from the bed and turned in the chair, my arms crossed over the top rail and my chin rested on them.

"It was good, wasn't it?"

He walked to me and patted my head with his gloved hand like I was a small child. *I knew it. He was an old guy.*

We made our way back to the keep, my belly full of good food and good ale. This was the best ending to this day.

Tomorrow morning came too soon, and my training leathers were washed and brought up for me. My knight and I entered the training room. It looked untouched from the last time Ilias and I were here. I gave a mental eye roll remembering his over-corrective instructions.

I got into the stances Commander Bauer had showed me at the very beginning of my training back home, long before the Ilias's *teachings*.

My knight took his opposing position. There was no way I would beat him with sheer strength alone. If I could use speed and out-maneuver the metal beast, I may have a chance.

Drawing my short sword out I looked up into the shadow

of his helmet—cold iron stared back. He drew a training sword, and I fought not to snicker. It was dwarfed in comparison to his large frame and armored body, so different than the one he typically brandished along his belt.

I took the first few steps forward and threw a few tested moves to see just how fast his reflexes were compared to mine. Like last time, I was fluidly countered, every strike thrown back at me, forcing my arm to jerk painfully. I stood and swung my arm, jostling my shoulder back, trying to ease the tension growing in my joints.

I thought back to what those girls had said in the dining room. How he'd killed his best friend. If he was able to do that, would I be in any actual danger here? My heart started to beat harder, and I began to pant; air wasn't making its way through me. I needed to calm myself.

I stood and faced him again, making the first move and running at him with my sword raised. I swung, and he easily backed out of the way. The force of my swing mixed with my poor footing spun me off balance, and he took the opportunity to sneak his foot beneath mine, tripping me. I fell backwards, my sword skittering across the mat. I landed with a hard thump as all the air left my lungs. When I could breathe again, I muttered a curse and rolled back over onto my stomach, forcing my body up on my tired arms. I kept my back to him, which in battle was not smart, but I didn't care.

I walked over to my fallen sword, gripping it tightly and swung again, and again. The only thing you could hear was the clanging steel of our practice swords. There were no words; there were never any words with him.

Stalking forward, I lunged, sweat building along my brow. My hair clung to my face. I swung again, coming up through the right and got caught with his hilt a little too close. My hair fell into my eyes.

He pushed both swords down and kicked me back, landing the blow right into my sternum. I fell hard, out of breath and coughing. I squeezed my eyes shut, feeling the straining in my rib cage. Each inhale hurt so bad. Tears threatened to make their way to the surface.

I was fucking useless. I couldn't stop anything from happening to me, to Kairos, to anyone. I couldn't protect anyone. I was helpless.

God, my chest hurts. A tear slipped out, traveling down my face. The near silent droplet slapped to the mat. I reached my hands up and wiped hard at any additional tears searching to join in the rebellion.

I felt so stupid. My knight and I had seemed to have come to a more common ground lately, but I wouldn't have called us *friends.* This training session felt like none of that had happened. Like he was angry with me for some reason.

The unamused look of his helmet angled down at me. My vision was fuzzy around the edges, and I remained on the ground. My knight came closer, looming over me, and stretched out his hand. Like he was offering some sign of truce. But no, this was just getting me more pissed off. I smacked it away. Too full of pride, I sat up and pressed my hands into my knees to further my rise. I walked to my thrown sword and got into position once again.

He didn't advance at all; only let me get close enough to swing in his direction before a well-angled hit threw my sword from my hand again and spun me to fall onto my hands and knees. Sweat dripped down my back and I couldn't catch my breath again.

The floor bit into my knees and my shoulder throbbed. He walked past me and in the direction of my sword, kneeling to pick it up. His back was to me. *No fucking way.* I paused for only a moment, weighing out my options.

Racing for his crouched body, I lunged forward and gripped his neck from behind and reached my fingers underneath the lip of his helmet, using all my speed to rip it from his shoulder and throw it onto the ground.

He shook me off, and I landed on to my back. Hard.

I raised myself up on my elbows and spied the helmet just out of arm's reach. I returned my gaze forward and realized I was looking straight into my sword, aimed at my throat. My breath grew fast and uncontrolled. I knew I'd crossed a line, but there was no going back.

I allowed my eyes to follow up the length of the sword, up into the armored fist shaking with anger. I dared to look higher. From the base of the neck of the armored chest plate rose into a black cloth face covering his neck up over his nose and around the majority of his head.

But nothing covered his eyes. They were the most intense dark brown sitting in a tan-olive complexion. They stared at me, filled with shock and anger, his heavy dark brow furrowed in place and met with a few stray waves of dark hair, slick to his forehead with sweat.

His eyes met mine and for a moment they hardened more than I'd thought possible. His gaze shook me to my core, and heat crept up my face. Not from exertion or exercise, but of surprise. From what was visible of his face, all half of it, was beautiful. His face could challenge the statues in the garden, or the paintings of knights lining halls in the western kingdom. The knight that stood before me, my knight was breathtaking.

Only a few breaths passed before he lowered the sword, dropping it to the ground in a loud clatter. He walked past me, his mantle grazing my knees and leaned down to grab his helmet. He placed it back into its usual spot, shoulders squared as his back faced me. He was gone again beneath the steel helmet. Only a few seconds passed as he stood there, unmoving and statuesque, but God, they felt like an eternity. He finally moved, heading straight for the door, and walked out. Leaving me there on the floor.

My heart was still racing as I collected my thoughts. He was definitely not old. And not like anything I thought he was. I sat up, my legs crossed on the floor below me, and all the interactions we'd had ran through my head in a flash. The peek through the door, the lake. *Oh my god.* A hot flush overtook my face. I shoved my head in my hands and groaned. *Why couldn't he be old and gross?*

I gathered myself, putting back the practice swords, and walked out into the hallway. I looked to my right as I always did. He stood there. Ominous and strong. Acting as if nothing had happened. Maybe that would make things easier for the both of us. To forget. I began my walk back to my room, but this time, *this time*, I was all too aware of how close he was.

FOURTEEN

I ran into Ami on my way back to my room. She said Ilias had returned while we were in the training room and was expecting me for dinner.

My chest ached from the fucking kick, rattling every breath I took, and now Ilias returning was almost bittersweet. I wanted nothing more to see him, but my body was fighting the urge to collapse with every step I took.

Once behind the safety of my bedroom door, I pressed my back against it, hardly feeling like I could be kept upright on my own.

A sour scent worked its way up to my nostrils and I tugged at the collar of my training clothes. The sweat-dampened leather reeked. *God, I needed a bath before Ilias comes anywhere near me.*

I headed to my bathing chambers and ran a quick bath with some relaxing salts. My muscles ached and there was nothing I wanted more than to soak and rest them.

Leaning back into the water, I let myself drift off for just a moment. Images bounced into my mind behind my eyelids:

Droplets of sweat racing down from a head of dark loose curls to a pair of eyes that looked straight through me. I gulped hard and adjusted in the tub. My skin felt hot in the tepid water. Even with just a half-visible face I couldn't get him out of my head. Out of all my imaginings of what he could possibly be under that helmet, it was never something so—so, ugh; I couldn't.

I had to let this go. He'd held a sword to my goddamn throat. He was not anything I anticipated, and that made his presence all the more volatile. I reiterated the fact that I knew absolutely nothing about this man.

Hell, I'd probably never see his face again, especially with the cheap shot I'd taken. It was unsportsmanlike and while I knew he was only training with me, I'd been harsh. But fuck that kick threw me over the edge. I'd been angry, and had never thought in a million years I would succeed in removing his helmet. I'd thought at this point it was practically fused to his head. For all I knew, he'd been a shell of armor with a spell cast to allow it to follow me around. I would have expected that more than what I saw. What he was.

Fully refreshed, I looked at my beaten-up body. My shoulder was a little swollen and now I had some matching bruises on my knees. Thankfully, my sternum was fully intact with no ruptured blood vessels, and I could still wear my dress.

Ami had laid it out for me this morning; all black, the dress had long sleeves with a bell at the end and a deep V down the center ending just above my bellybutton. The skirt hung with a loose and flyaway fabric just above my ankles.

I heard a knock at my door just as I was fixing my hair, puffing a mouthful of air through my lips. I opened the door to find Ilias—his usual glimmering eyes and strong face smiling down at me, visibly happy to see me.

"Can I come in?" He asked with a tilt to his head. My lack of immediate invitation must have thrown him off.

"Of course, I was just surprised to see you. I wasn't expecting you until at least dinner."

"It's past dinner, my love, we missed it. I was at the table waiting for you and thought you may have fallen asleep. I see you were merely holding me hostage until you were ready to punish me. You don't know how hard it would have been to sit across from you looking like this." He looked down at me with such longing and hunger. It had only been a few days.

As he moved in closer, he reached out and cradled my elbows in his hands, bringing my arms to him, wrapping them around his back and closing the space. He placed a welcoming kiss against my lips, and a smile formed. He leaned in closer, deepening our kiss and he wrapped his arms around my waist. I moved my arms up around his shoulders and brushed up against his freshly cropped hair. His mouth moving against mine was something I'd missed desperately.

He pulled away first and leaned closer to my ear, and in a soft whisper to ask "So should we have dinner in your room? Or mine?"

His breath was soft and warm against the shell of my ear, sending a shiver down my spine. I shook in his arms slightly, and he let out a soft chuckle. I looked up into his grey eyes; they were as crisp and bright as shards of ice.

"I think I'm fine with having a meal up here if you are," I smirked. I don't want to seem too eager to have him all to myself.

"Then your room it is." He clasped my cheeks in his palms and planted one more kiss before departing. "I'm going to get cleaned up, then. Do you mind if I use your bathing chamber?"

I shook my head slightly, while he disappeared into the small chamber.

Walking over to my bed I lightly toyed with the curtains to my canopy. At some point, someone had added long crimson fabrics that reminded me of the Saints in their flowing veils cascading over their heads into a train as they headed into the cathedrals.

Ilias exited the bathing chambers shirtless, his smooth chest and stomach showing off his fit physique. Loose fitting pants highlighted his delightful V lines, just barely hanging on to any decency he had left in his current outfit.

I brought my eyes back to his face and saw his smile grow, showing off those dimples I'd missed so much. His bright eyes shined with so much desire; I felt my face heat up. The thin piece of canopy was the only true barrier hiding the growing blush on my cheeks.

He stalked over to me with such direction and poise that I felt like I was going to crumble under his gaze. He reached the bed and gently pulled the fabric back from my view, tucking it behind the bedpost. He looked down at me and brought his hand close to the collar of my dress, traveling down the V, across the swell of my breast and onto the apex above my navel. My skin tightened and pimpled at his touch, my nipples hardening and shining through the sheer fabric.

His eyes followed his fingers and then with a small movement he dipped his index finger into the V, tugging the fabric just enough for me to follow along.

I was so close to him now that I felt his warmth against my exposed skin. The smell of his familiar citrus and salt waft over me. He slipped another finger into the dress, and then his left hand reached up to join the right. Four fingers were now at the very center of the slit. He paused and glanced at my lips, licking his with anticipation, and leaned down to meet mine. His kiss was more indulgent this time, soft and warm, like he was pulling my soul into him, like he needed me completely or might wither away.

Once he pulled away, drunk from our kiss, he said, "I hope you weren't too fond of this."

He ripped the bodice wide open, revealing my breasts to the cool air of the room. I gasped. He took the moment of surprise and entered my mouth with his tongue, kissing me desperately, reaching up to cup my right breast. I leaned into him. Wanting more. He took my already sensitive nipple between his thumb and forefinger and sensation fired through me. I moaned into his mouth. He let out a responding growl. I could hardly handle the ache growing in my lower abdomen.

He reached down and grabbed my ass to lift me to him. I brought my legs around his torso and molded my lips even more to him. We hadn't come up for air in what felt like forever, and I was floating so high on this moment. His touch was like a spark on my skin, sending little lightning strikes across my body. I felt him against me, how much he wanted me, how he was ready for me.

I grinded against him to try to fill the ache, but I needed more. There was too much fabric between us, and I couldn't take it anymore. I was pooling and coiling deep inside from this friction, and I knew he wouldn't let me feel that way much longer.

He leaned us over and draped me across the mattress, still letting me hold him tight between my legs. Still so full of need.

He freed his lips from mine and made his was down my body, leaving a trail of kisses down my jaw, over my neck, my collarbones, and stopping at the peak of my nipple. Just a soft breath over it and my skin contracted for him. He pulled me into his mouth, sucking so deeply I let out another gasp.

He moved his hands down my exposed stomach and lifted

the rest of my dress out of the way. I eagerly grasped for it and held it above my waist, clinging to it. He let out a soft chuckle. His fingers hooked around my underwear and with a little tug, I raised my hips. He pulled them down, his hands gliding over my skin, all the way to my toes.

He saw me for everything that I was and looked at me like I was everything he'd ever needed. The hunger in his eyes bored into me and I was sure he could see how much I wanted him too. If there wasn't already a puddle beneath me, there would be one soon.

He sucked in a deep breath and lowered to his knees. His hands warmed my thighs and slowly spread me just a little bit wider. My cheeks heated even more, and I placed a hand over my mouth and looked up to the ceiling.

"You're so beautiful," he said softly tracing his hand along my slit. Gathering moisture along his fingers, he brought them up to tease the soft bud near my core. I writhed under the softness, craving more.

He stood up and lowered his trousers to bring out his cock, gliding his fingers down his length and up to the tip. His head was thrown back and a soft growl escaped his lips. He leaned down and placed a hungry kiss to the apex of my thigh, so close to my center. He met my gaze.

"This is what you do to me." He stroked himself more for me. I leaned up onto my elbows and scooted closer, placing a kiss on his chest. He moved to meet my lips. I reached out to grasp him. He shuddered at my touch, then relaxed once I started pumping him. I slid off the bed and kneeled before him.

Still stroking him gently, I felt him twitch in my palm. The small bead of pre-cum sat like a pearl along his tip. I leaned in and licked it off. Ilias gasped and shuddered under my touch. He placed his hands on my shoulders for a moment to steady himself. I licked my lips and took him into my mouth, swirling my tongue over his tip and sucking gently at first.

His grip on my shoulders tightened, and he let out a soft "fuck" under his breath. I started to pick up the pace taking him in as far as I could, almost gagging as he hit the back of my throat. His size surprised me and the closer he got, I felt him swell even more. He gripped my hair and forced me to take him just a little deeper; just a little faster. I started to drool and drip saliva onto my lap as I worked him more. His grip on my hair tightened as he released. Salty, warm come slid down onto my tongue. He slowly pulled himself out of my mouth, a rouge drop making its way down my face.

He cupped my chin between his fingers and wiped me clean. I closed my mouth and swallowed what was left, and he leaned in for another hungry kiss, his tongue exploring my mouth and tasting himself in me. He was salty and sweet.

"Get back on the bed for me, Evangeline."

My face shifted into a mask immediately. The sound of my false name on his lips boiled up all the guilt I'd been burying beneath the surface.

He didn't seem to take notice as he gripped my thighs and forced me to the edge of the bed, my hips straddling him. And to my surprise, he was hard again, twitching near my very exposed and very available sex.

Temptation reared its head, regrettably, as he pulled up his pants, tucking himself away.

He leaned down to kiss up my thigh, lowering back to his knees. This time it was a lot less slow and sweet as his lips connect with my hot, sensitive flesh. He took me into his mouth, the force of his tongue already sweeping my folds and devouring me whole. I cried out with surprise, and he responded with a harder swipe of his tongue inside of me. *God, this felt like too much stimulation.* He turned his focus to the soft nub at the top and I squealed out a moan reaching forward to grab at his shaved head, the tiny hairs tickling my fingers. *I spoke too soon.* I was almost wishing I had something a little more to pull on.

He reached his left arm up and started to stroke my nipples, and taking the pebbled flesh into his fingers, pinching lightly, causing me to writhe again underneath him. With his right hand, he worked a finger inside of me. A second soon joined and my breath caught in my throat. My release built inside of me, and I was having trouble focusing on anything else than what's happening in my body, but my eyes widen and take in my surroundings, my fingers gripped into the sheets, and I stared at the canopy above me. Everywhere I turned was soft billowing fabrics, the cool feeling of them against my bare skin, I was reeling within my inner world. This had to be a dream.

I was brought back to reality by the stronger thrusts of his fingers, curling up to help bring me to my end. The tension burst through my body, my legs trembling. Ilias was still feeding into me and sucking on my now too sensitive clit. "Ilias ... God ... Please." I all but kicked him away, my walls clamping down so hard on his fingers that the feeling of them being pulled out left me empty inside. I was relaxed and in a bliss-filled post orgasm haze. But empty.

A knock at the door startled me and I laid farther into my bed, letting the fabric around me settle in like a dark cave. I pretended I was not in a ripped dress and looking thoroughly like I had been fucked.

Ilias got up and went to see what caused the intrusion. It was a clergyman, letting him know he was needed in the war room. The door opened wide enough for me to see my knight at his post to the right of the door.

Had he heard much? Heard me? A wave of guilt started to

rise, and I didn't know why. Why should I feel guilty about experiencing pleasure with the man I—I knew that I liked him very much but more feels so ... I shook my head like it would rearrange my thoughts and got whatever was running rampant cast from my brain with the force of it.

Ilias ran back and placed a quick kiss on my cheek apologizing for having to leave.

"I'll try to be back soon, okay?"

I nodded, and he closed the door behind him. I got up from the bed and made my way to the bathing chambers once again.

I drew a steaming hot bath and set out all the various oils and salts once again, lifting the lids, one by one, and seeing which would be the most relaxing. There was a lavender, a smokey woodsy scent, and a jasmine, but the one I settled on was a sandalwood with peppermint aroma.

Dripping a few drops into the hot water, it brought billowing clouds of the deep scent up into my nostrils. This one reminded me of back home.

Letting out a long sigh, I felt the weight of reality squeeze in through the cracks in my mind. I'd been here for a while now and things with Ilias had been good, but the plan for going North still needed to happen. I still had to go home.

Do I take Ilias with me and introduce him to my family?

I settled in and relaxed against the smooth tub. The cold stone against my back was a welcome feeling to the hot temperature of the bath water. This time, I truly allowed myself to soak. A moan of relief escaped my lips, and I started to feel my eyelids drift closed.

The stairs went for so long; my short legs were hardly able to keep up to the speed attached to the hand holding me, pulling me along.

As we descended the steps, we passed three, four, five sets of the Saints, dressed in the traditional red drapes and cloaks. Their faces were fully covered by the sheer cloth; no facial expressions could be offered.

Finally reaching the bottom, we entered the undercroft, not as deep as the catacombs but still deep under the cathedral. This room was dark and stale, built up with the dark stones of our city and only a few wall sconces for light. There was a circle in a middle with markings along and around it. They were meant to be for safety and protection but were more like a cage. The protections were for us, but if you were in that circle, there was no getting out.

At least no one had yet.

In the center of the circle was a black silhouette of a man, facing away from us, crouched over and breathing heavily. I could see the expansion of his rib cage through his spine. He held his head between his knees. A chain connected to his neck, locked onto a pole standing in the center of the protection circle. I felt like I had to look away but couldn't. Something pulled me. My eyes widened and watered from the dry air down here. But I feared if I blinked, I'd miss something.

My mother released my hand and crouched to my eye level speaking softly, but I couldn't make out any of the words; they felt like another language or a jumble of vowels. She started to shake me. I couldn't understand so I didn't respond. A scream was trapped in my throat, and I kept trying to push it away. She shook me harder and harder until—

Waking with a jolt; my eyes adjusted to the light around me, and I realized I was still in my bathing chambers. I wasn't with my mother, but I also wasn't alone. My knight held his weight over the tub, his hands on each of my shoulders, his leather gloved fingers biting into my flesh.

He paused, assessing me, and *not letting go.* I was staring up at him, stuck in his grasp but not sure why he was in here in the first place. I was all too aware that I was naked in the bath, and he was very, very close to falling into the tub with me. "Knight …" I rasped.

He let go of me, and stood up, staggering as he took a few steps away. I brought my arms up to cover myself as much as possible turning away from him. A hot blush coursed through my whole body and every cell inside of me wanted to order him to leave, but I was so captivated by the way his posture was so unsteady.

Had I been making noises from my nightmare? *Had I been screaming out loud and not just in my dream?*

These kinds of nightmares had haunted me for a long time, but they'd felt worse after Kairos's death. This one was so vivid.

My knight straightened, his body stiff and started for the door leading to the rest of my room. His large frame squeezed past the slender doorframe of the bathing chambers. I felt guilty about earlier in the training room.

I shouldn't have removed his helmet. I'd reacted poorly. I knew that. He just got under my skin, so deep and fast.

Before he got too far into my room, I shouted for him. "Wait! Knight!"

He stopped, standing past the doorway, objecting to have to squeeze a suit of amour back through. I stared up into the small opening in his helmet, little black slits feeding into my view. "I wanted to say I was sorry. For earlier. I shouldn't have removed your helmet. I know—I'm sorry."

He responded by placing a fisted hand over his chest and bowing. He straightened and closed the door to the chamber.

Fifteen

The next morning, I met Ilias in the dining hall for breakfast. He was seated already with a plate of toast smeared with what looks to be a red fruit spread. He held a letter only inches away from his face, his grey iris' bouncing left to right as they traced over every word.

He reached down to his toast without looking, his thumb going right into the fruit spread. Still without looking away from the paper, he brought it up to his supple lips and licked it off, locking eyes with me across the table. A smile crept up across his face, and he flashed me his perfect white teeth.

"What are you doing all the way over there?" His tone was playful but still questioning.

"I didn't want to impose on your *workspace*," I answered and gestured to the many letters and papers stretched all along the side of the table he was on.

He folded the letter he'd been reading and put it into a pocket on the inside of his jacket. His attention once again back on me.

"Come over here," he said, sterner.

I did as instructed getting up from my seat and standing before him on the other side of the table. The moment I stood in front of him, he reached down and swiped his arm over the table, skittering and tossing all the papers and whatever else was on the table. They tumbled to the floor. My mouth dropped open. In that same breath, he reached for me, wrenching me to him. His lips crashed into mine and he tugged me even closer, lifting me from the ground and placing me to sit on the table. My body was now occupying the workspace. His lips worked against mine and I couldn't help but smile into him.

He pulled away first, his eyes looking deep into mine, searching my face. "Don't ever think you are less important than any bit of work on my table." He kissed me again, pulling my chest flush to his body. "I will *always* take you over, or *on top* of my work." His fingers slid lower and grasped the tops of my thighs, his thumbs working closer to the soft skin between them, igniting a flame in me just inches away. He moved back in and kissed along my jawline. I exposed more of my neck, giving him access. Whatever he wanted from me, he could fucking take it.

He made his way down to my exposed collar and his mouth traced over my throat. I felt my pulse thrumming in my veins as his lips settled. I was sure he could feel how fast my heart was beating right now. My breaths were shallow, and my bosom was just a breath away from heaving.

He pulled back and placed his forehead to mine. His eyes were closed, and a tension riddled his features. I reached up and placed a hand to his cheek. He leaned into it.

"Is everything okay?"

Abruptly, he stood and took a few steps away, facing the other direction. He then placed both hands on the back of his head.

I slid off the dining table, waiting for Ilias. He pulled the letter back out from his jacket as if contemplating a great decision. It was still too far away for me to see what it said.

When he turned back, the tension in his face was stronger, a deep crease forming between his brows. His silence made my heart race in a whole new way than before. Was it a letter from my family? *Would he open it and read it?*

I couldn't take it anymore. "Ilias, tell me what's wrong." My voice came out hard.

H cleared his throat and lowered the letter.

"It seems our request for aid from the Kingdom of Paymon has finally been accepted."

I couldn't read his expression. Was he joyous or concerned?

"That's good?" I said warily.

He nodded and smiled up at me. "It's very good." He inhaled deeply and stepped closer, grabbing my hands in his.

"Will you come with me?" His eyes searched mine, likely seeing only shock.

"Come with you? To Paymon?" Paymon was the western kingdom in alliance with Amaymon. My throat felt tight. As the Queen Consort of the Oriens, I would never step foot in their lands but as Evangeline, a girl on the run and wanting to head North, I had no qualms with them, right? If I did, it would be alarming, wouldn't it?

Ilias's eyes bored into me, waiting for my answer. Against the alarms blaring in my head, I answered him. "Yes, I'll go."

He grabbed my face and placed a soft kiss. "Wonderful." He stood and dusted off his pants.

"I have to go make preparations for our travels. We will leave tonight."

"Tonight?"

After my morning with Ilias, I found myself on the second story of the keep in a hall with large open windows facing out to the outdoor training grounds. My steps echoed off the stone floors and a chill breeze along with the sound of steel clanging on steel, rushed in through the opening.

Following the sound further down, I peeked over an open ledge. Down below, I could see the full figures of two knights, one very familiar.

My knight's towering figure was almost matched by his training partner. After a few blows, my knight completely disarmed the other and held his sword to his neck. Just like he'd done to mine.

I took a big gulp of air, remembering the way his dark eyes had bored into mine. All the other times we interacted raced through my head. The first night I'd been covered in mud and he'd dragged me along by his horse. Then I remembered how he'd caught me as I lost my handling on the horse. His hands were so large, and they'd held me effortlessly, setting me onto the ground.

I chewed hard on my bottom lip as more memories raced into my mind's eyes. The vast number of times he'd seen me *naked*. It came close, if not the same amount, to how much Ilias had seen of me.

I started to feel dizzy.

Confused.

I turned to leave, not paying attention to where I was going, and forcefully bumped into a maid walking by. She carried a tray with freshly polished candlesticks, and they wobbled angrily on the tray. I reached to stop them from falling but was only able to grasp two before rest fell to the floor with a clatter. The noise echoed through the stone hallways, ringing through the courtyard.

The knights looked up from the training area and I felt my

knight staring at me. I bent quickly to help the woman pick up the fallen candlesticks and heard a loud grunt. Looking back over the ledge, I saw my momentary distraction had allowed for the other knight to knock my knight off his feet.

I turned and leaned against a pillar in between two windows, smiling to myself. Hurriedly, I made my way back to my room to prepare for the trip. I grabbed a few changes of clothes, a nice dress for court, and some hairpins, placing them into a small sack. Kairos journal sat on a table, and I contemplated bringing it with me. Flipping through the pages, I stopped at one of the sigils, tracing over it. A tingle rose up my arm. "I better not lose this." I said to myself as I shoved it in my bag along with the knight's journal from the cathedral.

As the night fell over the ridge, I made my way to the stables. Horses nickered and whinnied, the rest of the company silent. Ilias stepped out from around his horse, and I saw his hands working to fasten the straps and clasps.

I wrapped my arms around his middle, placing my cheek on his back and closing my eyes, taking in the salty citrus scent of him and how pleasant he felt in my arms.

He turned to face me and pulled me in closer, resting his chin on the top of my head. He felt like a newfound piece of home in this weird, fucked up situation.

"Are you ready?" His voice softly vibrated his chest, and I nodded against him.

We rode together on his horse again; he sat behind me and held me close to him. A cloak was wrapped tight around each of our shoulders, but still the night air was freezing and ate into my bones. The closeness of his body behind me brought me little warmth and comfort as we rode on in silence; the only sounds were the clopping steps of the horses and any distant chirps or low wails from animals hiding deeper in the forest.

The threat of demons hung heavy as we chose another evening to start this long travel to Paymon. Ilias assured me he'd sent a scouting mission into the forest surrounding the keep as soon as he'd received the letter of acceptance, and we were safe. Even then, I felt a nervous chill race along my skin every time I heard the unnatural noises hiding in the darkness.

My body grew stiff, but my fingers took the brunt of the cold. Moving them was painful as the temperature declined through the night. There were seven of us total, Ilias, myself, my knight, and four more men. Looking to be royal guards. I was surprised they weren't knights as well. *Just guards?*

I was sure there was a reason for the small party, and it was not my place to question Ilias's tactics, but it felt like a long way to go with such few men.

Hours must have passed, and yet the early morning sun still hadn't threatened to break up the night sky. We let the horses take a break, giving them food and water. The dark canopy of trees above us offered very little visible moonlight. We were in a such a deep darkness, it reminded me of the first night in the woods.

I looked out into the vast emptiness deep within the trees. The chill somehow burrowed deeper into my core, and I shook, unable to keep back a wash of memories until it was all I could see.

The forest disappeared and I was back in the atrium, the crimson light invading my vision and screams filling my ears. It was so loud. I covered my ears. A scream tore through every part of me. A burning feeling started in my throat, and I realized it was me screaming, screaming at Kairos's body lying on the ground in a pool of black and red blood. I leaned down and touched his face. He was hidden in shadows and as I moved closer, I saw it was Anders face now, showing a permanent look of terror. I tried to turn away but couldn't. My eyes were locked onto his face.

My breathing grew hard and heavy, spots appearing in my vision and I felt the edges grow dim. A voice in the distance got louder and louder.

"Evangeline! Get down!"

An arrow flew right past me, embedding itself into the tree at my side. I snapped around, eyes wide. A dark figure stood in the tree line. I couldn't see much else, but the familiar sound of a bowstring stretching sent panic down my throat. I ducked immediately and the arrow passed right where my head would have been.

My knight rushed in front of me and created a barricade with his shield from the barrage of quills. The loud bangs of them hitting off the hard steel sounded like a thunderstorm.

I searched through the rest of the company and saw two of the other guards with their swords drawn, fighting against two large and well-equipped bandits. One bandit fell, but the guard left himself open. A blade pierced through the side of his thin armor plates, dragging it along his belly. Blood and entrails poured from the guard's wound. The smell of iron and earth hit me, and I started to shake uncontrollably. I raised a weak hand to my mouth, my eyes wide in horror. The guard's body collapsed into the mess with a wet thud. I bent over and heaved, my guts threatening to join his.

Where was Ilias?

I stayed shrunken behind the large body of my knight as he fought any oncoming men. His huge sword raked through them almost effortlessly. Swing after swing, they went down.

One man fell right in front of me, coughing up blood and spit. His eyes met mine, the life leaving them, as he released one last rasp and gurgle from his dirty gaping maw.

Kairos's face swam through my memories. I wanted to let the screams build up through me and yell them into the world as terror filled me but now would not be the time for that. I remembered the way Commander Bauer stood over Kairos. The way he separated his duty from his grief in the moment it was necessary. One breath. Two. I needed to move. I couldn't stay here.

I left my knight, starting to race through the trees, getting farther and farther from the discordance of swords and shouts. Throughout the trees to my right, I saw a flash of light.

ILIAS!

It was him. He was on a horse and running from a bandit also on horseback. I ran towards him. And the bandit.

I came closer to them, and waved my hands at Ilias, trying to get his attention. His eyes met mine for a second, his gaze panicked. The bandit swiped at him with his blade, the saddle bags dropping to the forest floor. Ilias let out a yell and spurred his horse. I stared in shock as his figure shrunk, disappearing into the darkness. The bandit rode off after him, leaving me alone. I went to examine the fallen saddle bags. The leather bags were banged up and dirty, but inside was my momentary glory. The journals were intact. I held them tight to my chest and took the first deep breath I was able to hold onto.

The hairs on my body stood straight as a familiar stretching sound rang through in the air. My eyes went wide, and I stared right into a drawn arrow. I took a gulp of air; it might be my last. I closed my eyes, knowing there was nowhere for me to run. I was crouched down on my knees in the dark cold dirt, the tiny pebbles eating into my shins and the thin skin of my knees.

I would take my end.

But my end did not come.

A loud grunt brought my attention back. In front of me stood my knight, his body working once again as a human shield. This time though, the arrow shot true and hit the separation between the chest plate and the waist of his armor, sinking itself into his left hip.

He reached down grabbing a small dagger from his side and threw it, hitting the archer square in the chest, knocking him back to the ground.

Pressing off the ground to stand, I felt a rope encircle my neck. I reached up but before I could do anything, it tightened and pulled me back, dropping me hard to the ground. My head hit the forest floor, stars tangling in my vision. My fingers gripped at the rope as it tightened around my throat, the rough fibers cut into my skin. The rope went taut and tugged me deeper into the forest. I flailed my legs, trying to scream but no air was getting in.

Once I was pulled far enough out, a bandit approached me, pulling the rope from my neck. He spotted my Legion Stone. His eyes widened and he grabbed it, his nails scratching at my skin as he ripped the chain apart. He stared down at his hand, lowering his sword.

I kicked out and hit him square in the chest. His fingers loosened around his weapon. I lunged for it, missing, but managing to knock it away. The sword skittered across the ground. I fell hard on my hip, a low grunt leaving my lips as pain burned up my side. I crawled to the sword. My fingers gripped the hilt just as he grabbed onto my ankle. I pulled the sword flush to my body and his nails burrowed into my skin. I cried out. He pulled me down, crawling up my body to the sword. I made space, I braced my forearm against his neck and managed to roll over, thrusting the sword into the small space where his collarbone met his neck. Blood spurted, raining all over my face.

The taste of copper seeped into my mouth. His hands reached for my throat, trying to get a hold on me. I screamed as I thrusted once more into his side, trying to make a serious injury, but it was hard from this angle. I was so tired.

He stopped moving, his body slumping on top of me. I panted, catching my breath before squirming out from under him, and tossing his body to the side.

I spat out the blood and whatever else had made its way into my mouth. I reached up to wipe my face and felt the damage done to my skin. My neck was raw and chewed up.

The sound of heavy footsteps sent me into another wave of panic, and I reached down to grab the short sword, holding it ready for whoever was going to—

A familiar shape came into view, and I dropped the sword. My knight. I fell to my knees. I didn't want to stand or speak or exist in this moment.

"Is it over?" The words hardly made their way out.

His response was a firm grasp on my bicep, pulling me up off the ground. The pressure wasn't bad, but the feeling of it on my raw and angry skin made me wince.

Sixteen

I COULD SEE THE LIGHT BREAKING THROUGH THE canopy of leaves after walking for what felt like forever. Just a little farther and I would be out of these forsaken woods.

Once we passed the tree line it was like entering into a new realm; there was waist high grass flowing in the early morning breeze. The rolling hills could be seen until it met on the horizon line to the clear blue sky. It would have been a beautiful day in any other scenario. No towers, no houses; just green luscious grass swaying in a soft dance as my fingers waved over them.

The sunlight brought with it a sense of security, to my flagging energy. The bright light warmed my face, and I closed my eyes, the rays starting to tingle on my skin. I took a few more steps and collapsed onto my knees in the tall grass, dropping the journals next to me; my arms too tired to carry them any longer.

I looked down at my hands caked in dirt. Dried blood congealed under my fingernails and along the scratches on my knuckles. I turned my arms over to look at the back of my bicep; the cuts ran deeper there. I hoped these didn't get infected.

The ambush had come out of nowhere. I reached my fingers up to touch the raw skin of my throat. The rope had rubbed off layer after layer when it had dragged me deeper into the forest.

Could they have known who I was? *Was this some kind of ransom seeking exercise for them?* I guessed they could have if they were given the right information, but right now they weren't around to ask. No one was fucking around.

Ilias had taken off and I was left with the least interactive person on the planet. I should get used to my own inner monologue because that was the only thing to keep me company now.

As loud footsteps broke the peace of the moment, my knight walked past me, heading toward a rogue boulder not much farther ahead. The arrow in his hip was still lodged there but it looked like he'd cut it down so it wouldn't stick out and cause even more discomfort.

He sat down hard, the loud clang of his armor against the stone was jarring. He let out a sigh, his entire chest rising and falling. We'd escaped by the skin of our teeth, and he knew that.

He reached up, gripping the sides of his helmet, and lifted it from his shoulders. His face was still half covered by the black cloth—only his eyes exposed—but just from them I could see his sullen expression. He stared into his muddy reflection on the once mirror polished steel. Taking in one more deep breath, he stood and threw the helmet into the middle of the clearing.

I looked at him, stunned. How—how did he just ... just *throw it?*

He'd never taken it off and now it was tossed onto the dirt like a piece of garbage. He pulled down his facial covering and revealed everything.

My already ragged breathing stalled in my throat. The half of his face I saw in the training room was nothing more than a tease to this, to him.

He had strong angled cheek bones that were fixed to a square prominent jaw. His lips were full and plump, more than mine were and the bridge of his nose was pristine. Most men in a warrior's position would have had their nose broken at least once in training, if not more in battle.

He sat back down and ran a hand through his hair, a few defiant strands making their way back to hang over his forehead and kiss his dark brows. Slowly, he turned to me. I couldn't look away. The contact was so direct and so stifling, I'd forgotten who was in front of me. He sneered pressing his tongue to his cheek and turned back, facing forward. I watched as the muscles in his jaw ticked.

He took a deep breath and lifted his chin to the sky, and said, "Do you have a fucking death wish?"

I felt paralyzed. What *was happening?*

"I ... I ..." I had never heard his voice before. He'd never once spoken to me. Wasn't supposed to speak to me. His voice was so deep and dark, well-worn in, and with an accent I can just barely place as Amaymon, similar to Ami.

My jaw went slack, and I forced it closed. I had to physically collect my thoughts to put any remnants of a sentence together.

My mind ran back to all the times I'd been indecently exposed *in front of him.*

The pond, the bathtub, the day in my room. My face heated and I flung myself back into the tall grass, staring up at the bright blue sky of the early morning. The grass would be my cover from him, he could stay there with his helmet off the whole time if he wished, but I'd stay down here. In my nice new grass bed.

Closing my eyes, I tried to settle my breathing. I had hardly noticed it had kicked up. Just *why?* Why couldn't he be old or ugly or anything but absolutely—

Hearing the metal armor scrape off the rock, I sat up slightly. He got up and walked over to the helmet, lifting it with his left hand and using the end of his red mantle, to dust off the dirt and clean the blood.

Still not looking at me, he said, "Next time don't fucking run off when I had things under control."

My heart sputtered for a second.

Under control.

Under control?

I shot up in the grass to see if this guy was fucking serious.

"What part of that did you have under control, exactly?"

He turned to glare at me.

I laid back down in the grass, the memories of Kairos flooding back, the time in his study and the day he gave me my tenth anniversary gift. I raised a hand to where my Legion Stone once sat, the vacant hole in my chest growing larger. The sting of its edges had become a comfort after his death.

"Get up," was his only response.

He brought his fingers up to his lips and let out a high-pitched whistle. Then he put his helmet back over his head. My knight left his boulder and walked over to me his silhouette eating into the sunshine that I was enjoying. He reached down with a gloved hand. Rejecting it, I found my footing and lifted myself up to meet him.

"I can walk," I replied shortly. I'm still unsure of this whole *speaking to me* thing.

He gave me a curt nod and turned to the forest as the large black stallion rode out from the shadows. He'd blended in so well I hadn't seen him until he was out past the tree line.

My knight greeted the horse, removing his gloves and

running his fingers over its velvety black snout. He assessed the bags and fixed the straps before turning my way.

"Are you going to get on, or did you want to follow along behind us again?"

Our first encounter circled my mind, when he'd tied me up and had forced me to walk through the night on the worst day of my entire existence. No way was I letting that happen again. I pushed past him, staring at how high the stirrups hung in front of me.

My sore limbs barely made it up, but I was able to throw my leg over and seat myself. My knight lifted himself with more difficulty than usual; I was sure the arrowhead embedded in his side was not the most comfortable.

A wave of guilt hit me. The only reason he even got hurt was because I'd run off. I'd made it worse. *God, I made everything fucking worse.*

After a few hours, I started to see a mountain range coming into view. The Southern gate of Relion? Its three peaks were known all across the lands, bordering the southern kingdom of Amaymon. *What the hell were we doing all the way down here?*

"Aren't we supposed to be going to meet up with Ilias? It's east and we're headed south."

"That was before we lost the convoy, and the guards, and Ilias."

I shifted nervously on the horse; my portion of the seat was so small, and my legs were going numb. I moved slightly and my knight let out a loud grunt going rigid behind me.

"Watch your fucking ass, you just jammed the arrow." His words were hard and short, like they came out through gritted teeth.

"I'm sorry ..." Silence was my only response again. We rode into the night with nothing but hoofbeats and breathing to break up the quiet of the approaching night.

I can't fucking take this anymore. "Tell me what's South then," I demanded.

I could hear the pause in his breathing as he tried to adjust himself on the seat before answering.

"South is a trades town with an allied outpost. There is that one and one more before we make it to Paymon. Our best bet to meet up with Ilias is to start there."

His breathing was shallow. The arrow must be more than an annoying prick.

"We won't get there until tomorrow, so we will head as far as we can and then make camp."

The rest of the ride could be summed up into one word, *bridled.*

We found our way into a less dense part of the forest. It offered some protection from the sun, and the demons typically didn't head this close to the edge. My biggest fear was another ambush. Hopefully, just the two of us would draw less attention. Then again, I was walking with a close to seven-foot-tall suit of armor with a bright crimson cape. He was a beacon for all those around us.

The sun went down fast over the high mountain ridge and the chill came on strong. My knight was able to make a small fire out of the limited brush around, but it was small and didn't offer much heat.

I was tired, hungry, and cold. The only positive thing in all of this was the fact that I was so worn out that sleep took me as soon as I made my arm into a pillow on the ground.

SEVENTEEN

Something shifted in the brush nearby waking me from my dreamless sleep. It was still very dark out, so I must not have been resting for that long. I sat up and felt my blanket fall around me. My blanket? I looked over my body in the glow of the fire and saw a red fabric had been placed over me while I slept.

It held the emblem of the knights on the center. My knight's mantle.

I searched for him and as my eyes adjusted in the darkness, I saw a pile of metal leaning against a tree. There was more rustling towards a small creek we'd passed by earlier.

Using the darkness as my camouflage, I rose, refusing to stay put, and made my way towards the sounds. Turning around the side of a tree, I stopped in my tracks.

A large, shadowed figure was before me. He was crouched over, but his size was still something to revel at. His back was all I saw so far, and it had glossy crisscross marks going from the shoulder blades to above the hip bones. At least a dozen crosshatched their way along the spine. Sucking in a steady breath, I tried to take a slightly closer look.

As I took my step forward, he stood. His build was large and had thick corded muscles all along his body. His armor had given nothing away in the slightest.

Ilias was very lean; he still had a lot of defined muscles, but this was— *God, stop comparing them. There's no comparing to be had.*

All he was wearing were trousers, and they were rolled up to meet his knees and pulled down to just below his waistline. He had a cloth tied around his waist; he must have removed the arrow.

My skin crawled thinking about what that must have felt like.

He took a step into the creek, then another. It must be freezing even during the day, and he waded in until it was at his waist. His hands skimmed along the water, making little ripples of moonlight. He leaned down and brought water to his face, scrubbing to remove the days' worth of sweat and grime. Then his hair, his soft waves, bounced back into place and glistened with each little movement. God, I was gawking. But I couldn't bring myself to look away.

I hadn't realized how far I had stepped out of the tree line, but I was no longer lingering beside the trunk. I was in full view of him. One tilt of his head and he could see me watching him.

Did I want him to see me watching him? Why did it matter? People bathe. Knights need to bathe. He stood looking like an otherworldly being in the light of the moon, standing in a pool of reflective silver. All the world fell away. There were no more sounds from the creek or the leaves rustling in a nighttime breeze.

Finally, he turned to me. But he was not looking at me, he was looking through me. No eye contact or acknowledgment. His exposed chest had the same shiny marks as his back and was covered in a layer of hair. His chest and stomach had soft curls that made their way down to the lip of his pants, in a very uhm—pointed direction.

He walked through the water, his feet meeting the soft bank of land, dripping puddles with every step as he made his way towards me. My breathing hitched and my mouth went dry, but I couldn't bring myself to look away. Then he reached me. His skin was only inches from mine and an electric charge built through me.

His eyes still weren't catching my gaze. He leaned forward, his breath hot on my shoulder. A scent of smokey musk and pine washed over me as he moved in closer. Nerves in my stomach curled. *Too close, he was too close and too near-naked.*

He inhaled deeply through his nose and made his way closer to my ear. I pressed my body farther into the tree behind me, the bark eating into my fingers, holding me in place.

With his voice even deeper than before, he whispered, "You stink." My mouth hung open, and I let out a choked laugh. He raised his hand, placing a single finger under my chin and forced it shut. "Wash before we head out tomorrow." His accent dripped off the last word, thick and syrupy like honey.

A hot blush crept over my face. We had just traveled for two days, were ambushed and had slept on the ground. Even if I didn't smell the best, he didn't have to be so crass.

I shoved him back, my hands meeting his bare chest but I ended up pushing myself back more than I pushed him away. He was like a wall of stone. *God, he was infuriating.*

As I stumbled back from my *exertions,* and he let out a soft chuckle, walking past me and heading back to the camp.

Once he was out of sight I lifted my torn shirt to my nose. It really did smell bad. But I had nothing else to wear while these dried. I took a few steps further and tripped over a small bundle of fabric.

Leaning down, I picked up a piece, holding it out in front of me. It was a fresh shirt and some oversized black linen pants. Did he leave these for me? How did he know I would come snooping?

He was right. I did need to bathe and now with a fresh pair of clothes, I didn't have any other excuses.

I headed towards the creek and started to undress, my shirt sticking to my body with the blood of one of the attackers. After peeling it off my skin and pulling off my trousers, I was soon as bare as the day I was born.

I took my first hesitant step towards the small body of water. The closer I got I noticed the wispy clouds of vapor rising from it. I dipped my foot in. It was quite warm. Almost hot. I climbed down and fully saturated my body in the warm water. I dunked my head and came to the surface, letting my body float near the water's edge. I closed my eyes and let myself forget for a moment. It was refreshing after the day we had.

A shiver ran down my spine even in the warm water and I opened my eyes to find my knight dressed in a similar outfit to the one left out for me, leaning carelessly against a tree trunk, not entirely looking in my direction.

I touched my toes to the ground and the shallow creek reached just below my collarbones, the dark water covering me enough to not feel fully exposed.

"How long have you been there?"

"Long enough," he replied with a smirk. He stepped away from the tree and walked towards the clothes near the water's edge.

"These are for you." He bent down and lifted the clothes, holding up a shirt that was obviously from his personal collection. "They may not fit well, but they won't smell like death like your other ones did."

Heat rose on my cheeks, and I moved deeper into the water, up to my chin. I blamed it on the warm water, not the fact that every time he spoke, my chest felt a little tighter than before.

"Thank you," was all I replied with. I don't even know what to say. *Thanks for sharing your clothes with me. I'm sure being fully enveloped in your—* STOP.

What the hell was wrong with me? As far as he knew I was *with* Ilias.

With.

Was I with him? What even *were* we? He'd so obviously left me to fend for myself out here after I'd seen him in the woods. He hadn't even *tried.* I clenched my fists together as a new emotion welled up inside me. Anger. I was angry at Ilias. He left me to the possibility of fucking death and rode off?

The realization made my blood boil. This hot water was only perpetuating my internal heat. God, it was so hot now. I wanted to get out, but not with the ever-watching eyes of my *protector.*

I gulped back the thoughts fighting to the surface. The one that hit me over the head was the fact that—that he'd come back for me. He'd *saved* me. I looked over at him once more. He was standing near, leaning on a tree trunk, face angled to the sky, allowing for a clear view of the hard-set angles of his jaw and strong neck. His eyes reflected the glow from the moon and looked like orbs of pure white. He turned and looked right into my eyes. Our gaze was locked in a battle of wills, and I gave way first, moving my body slightly higher in the water. *It was so fucking hot.*

"Why is it so warm in here? It's not this warm in the lakes back home, even in the Summer."

He turned away from me and walked to the edge of the tree line.

"Geothermal pools."

Then he slunk into the darkness, leaving me to get dressed in private.

This wasn't my first time in a man's clothes, but this fabric was unusually rough and too big in every place imaginable. Yet I was grateful to have them as an option over my own clothes in their current state.

As the fabric went over my face, I took in his smokey musk and pine scent. The shirt was drenched in it. I held the fabric to my nose and inhaled deeply. There was a hint of something familiar. I couldn't place it but—

A loud crunching in darkness deep into the denser tree shook me from my thoughts and a chill ran up my spine.

I am out of here.

The small fire was still useless in our little camp, but the light from the moon broke fully from behind the black clouds above. Its silver light lit up the area enough to inspect the damage done to the journals.

The two-book pile was a mix of shredded pages pulled from their spines, and leather covers scratched and gouged. Kairos's journal was the worse of the two, the first few pages missing completely. Thumbing through them quickly, I saw something reflective as the paper fluttered past. I flipped back a few pages and landed on a blank space in the dead center of the book. I didn't remember seeing this when I'd read through before.

I moved the book up closer to my face and tilted the book away to catch the moonlight. It happened again, a light, reflective shine against the pages. I tilted it more and into the full moonlight.

At the top it read *Sorsloc Cruor*.

The page crinkled as I tried to read farther down, and it slipped from my grasp, the edge of the paper slicing into my finger. I pulled back abruptly, but a small drop of blood fell onto the seemingly empty page.

In an instant, the page erupted with heat as the trails of light lit a sigil in the center. Each intricate swoop and interlinking line came forth before my eyes.

I traced a finger over the mark, a sharp shock making me wrench my finger away. I shook it out—that was a stronger sting than I'd ever felt before. The book fell from my lap, and I stared at my now-pristine finger.

"What did you do?" my knight said flatly. He sat on the ground, leaning against a tree with his head propped back and eyes closed.

"Nothing," I responded in the same monotonous voice.

He angled his head down, opening his eyes and pushed off the ground to cross the narrow campground in a step and a half.

Panic rose in me, and I jumped up, clutching the books to my chest and stepping away from him until my back hit a tree.

In a moment, he was in front of me. He leaned in closer, one arm extending to meet the tree at my back. He angled his body down, trapping me to this very spot. His smokey pine scent filled my lungs, his eyes in the overcast light from the moon were empty voids of darkness.

I swallowed hard.

"Give it to me," he said in a low voice, extending his free hand out to me.

I shook my head and held them tighter, trying to take a step away from him. He brought his other arm down, connecting with the tree on both sides of me.

"Uh, uh, uh, hand it over."

"No."

"I'll give you two options. You can give me the book since I asked nicely, or it will end up as kindling for the next fire. Your choice."

My mouth opened but the fear of him using my last cherished item from Kairos as a fire starter won this battle. I shoved the books into his chest and pushed past his left side, making sure to bump him on the way out.

I heard the grunt escape his lips as I made contact with the sore side of his body.

The asshole deserved it.

Sitting back down on my spot in the dirt, I stared into the empty void of the forest. Treacherous thoughts fought their way in. I pressed my hands into my eyes and braced for them, a wave of misery flooding my mind.

How did I get here? I recounted all my life choices. Where had I gone wrong to be stuck out here with the worst possible option available?

What sin was I being punished for?

Adultery? My *husband* was dead. Murder? That was self-defense. Why was I here? Was I not a good person? Was I not a good queen to my people?

Liar...

Liar.

You're a worthless liar. You hated your life. You're happy Kairos is dead. You still haven't told the man who took you in who you really are. You're ashamed of who you are. YOU ARE A LIAR!

Silent tears wet my cheeks as the words in my head

screeched out into the night. I hated myself. I hated what I'd become. I hated who I was.

My knight flipped through the journals behind me. The sounds echoed, filling me with rage as pages slid against another, and another. I was so angry, so fucking angry.

My fists balled, and the remnants of my nails dug into the soft flesh. They weren't nearly long enough to draw blood, but they still hurt. I raised my hand to my throat and felt the raw skin, still sore and growing chapped in the cold, dry air.

"What are you doing with books written in old Amaymon?" he asked, breaking my moment of torment.

"One was a gift and the other one I stole from the Midlands Cathedral." I didn't care anymore, bare my sins to the world. Add thief to the goddamned list.

"Move over," he said, and I shuffled on the dirt, making room near the fire. He sat down, his legs crossed, his knee leaning against mine. He was so uncomfortably close.

He aimed a page of the book in my direction. "Do you know what this means?" His finger pointed to a word in Old Amaymon.

I glanced over to it, seeing the unfamiliar language again. It was in Kairos's frantic handwriting near the end of the journal.

"No." My tone was dry and short.

He closed the book and set it in front of me, getting up to go back to his tree again. He sat back down and leaned against it but didn't stop watching me. "It's from the old book. It means Soul Tie, like from when the old God ruled. People would offer their souls in exchange for—well anything they could imagine."

I met his eyes.

"How do you know all this? How can you *read* this?"

"The history of Amaymon and the Knights of the Crimson Cloth are deeply linked. It's not just a hierarchy."

My notion was correct when I'd heard him speak initially; he was from the South. But no matter where you were from, you were not supposed to talk about this stuff, about anything from the old book or the old world. It was forbidden.

I didn't say anything else. I laid back down and faced away from him. I just wanted tonight to be over. Please.

EIGHTEEN

Garrison Avesta. The name was like a beacon of hope. We had been riding for hours. My oversized clothes were doing very little to keep my bones insulated. Every gust of wind pushed right through any weaves in the fabrics and my body would break out in goosebumps.

We grabbed a few pieces of food from a local stand and headed toward the city's only inn. It was a warm red color and two levels high. The roof sloped a little to the right; I assumed from water damage.

Upon entering, it didn't seem the most populous structure. No one sat at the tables filling the small area and the only soul in the place was a pre-pubescent boy behind the bar cleaning glasses with a questionably clean cloth.

I walked up to the bar and waited for the kid to look my way, but he seemed quite occupied with those glasses. He also seemed to be in a too big tunic with one shoulder sloppily exposed and a belt tightened far past its last notch.

"Excuse me ..."

The young boy shot up and almost dropped the glass he

was working on. He had bright blue eyes and flaxen hair, cropped short and low to his scalp.

"Oh sorry, ma'm. I didn't see ya. How can I help you?" he said with an endearing smile, taking me off guard.

"Well, uhm, I'd like a room, please."

"Right on ya, ma'm. We have four rooms, and they are all available at the moment. You can go take your pick, then take the key from the door. They're all in there already."

"Thank you, I'll do that ..." Interesting system, but again, there was a child in charge.

My heart skipped a beat at the notion of four rooms to pick from. To be alone and sleep in a bed that wasn't made of a thin straw mat, or just plain dirt, was enough to make me cry.

Until we got to them.

Room number 1 - No mattress of any kind; it was just a wood frame near a window.

Room number 2 - Oh this one *had* a mattress alright; it was also covered in a slurry of blood and/or vomit. No.

Room number 3 - Seemingly harmless. I made my way to the bathing chamber to be ransacked by a plethora of rodents. Did I scream? Yes.

Room number 4 - It had to be better, right? It was the *last* option. There was a mattress, the bathroom wasn't filled with rodents, and no bloodied vomit. Was it pristine? Absolutely not.

Rain started to pour outside the windows and a leak in the roof left a single drop to fall in the middle of a small round table in the room. It was accompanied by an equally small chair. The wood-framed bed was a larger size than expected against the dwarfed dining furniture. There was a small hearth that was near its last few embers, so the room was, at the very least, warm.

I went to the bed and sat on the mattress; the cushion all but collapsed under my weight. Looking at my knight standing in the doorway of the room was just as silly a sight as the view had been of him in *The Middle Maid*. His already large stature seemed that much bigger in the small room.

I let a puff of air past my lips and set my foot to rest on my knee, grabbing at the fraying strands of leather. Pulling off my tattered boot, my feet roared out in protest. The heels were almost gone, and I was a few steps away from having my sock poke through the bottom. There had to be a shop with a suitable replacement nearby. Maybe some better fitting clothes, too.

"Can I go buy some new clothes?"

Silence. I looked at him and he just stared back.

"Haven't we come far enough past this?" I dropped my arms to my sides in an exasperated attempt to show my displeasure. I walked to the bag my knight had brought in with us. It contained some money and my journals. I rifled through it and plucked out a few coins, dropping a couple in my haste. They landed in a clatter, and one rolled under the small table.

My knight reached down and grabbed my wrist, holding up a single finger to his helmet. Silencing me and he slowly pointed to the door.

My eyes followed his direction and my breathing hitched in my chest. There was a shadow beneath the door to our room, blocking the light from the hall. Was someone listening to us? If they saw him and knew about the knights of the Crimson Cloth, they would know he had taken a vow of silence. Speaking could give them reason to call for treason.

He jangled my wrist, and the coins plopped into his hand.

He took them and left out the door, closing it quietly behind him.

It felt like hours passed and any form of pacing wasn't attainable in such a small room. Plus, I was starting to get hungry. They looked to have some kind of kitchen downstairs; I thought it would be fine to wander around.

Looking down under the table, I spied the rogue coin and slipped it into my oversized trouser pocket as I headed down to the lower portion of the inn.

The young boy from earlier was still working behind the bar. He noticed me this time around and came over, leaning his body over the counter space between us.

"What'll ya be having ma'm?"

I cocked my head a little and raised a brow at him. "I'm looking for some food. Can I get that here?"

He gave me a quick nod. "Yes ma'm, we have dinner. Will it be just one?"

Should I ask what dinner entailed or wait and see what came out? Either way, I was starving.

"Yes, just one. Thank you." He gave another nod and ran off into the kitchen.

Finding a seat at the bar, I noticed the way the place had filled in with more patrons. Women sat on men's laps with large, painted-on smiles, laughing at their not so funny jokes.

A loud clunking stirred me from my viewing, and a drunken couple made their way down the stairs from the rooms. They must have picked one of the other options available. I couldn't imagine which one they would have chosen.

The woman had rich bouncing dark curls and deep brown skin, and her partner was of similar complexion, but he was quite short and wore Oriens guard's colors. His hand was gripping her waist and working its way down to grab at her bottom. She let out a sharp giggle and smacked at him, grabbing his hand and pulling him the rest of the way down the stairs.

They pulled up two chairs right next to me. Her perfume was heavy with fresh orange blossoms, a bright, luscious scent. They must be from the West. I wondered what had brought them here.

I was still waiting for my food when a band of three guards walked in, wearing similar fashion to the knight, but no red cape. They removed their helmets and sat across from me. They had a hodgepodge of features and didn't look like they were from anywhere in particular.

One of them tried desperately to make eye contact, and I made the conscious effort to keep my gaze to the bottles infront of me, my hands searching for something to keep me busy. I reached for my napkin, anxiously twisting it to oblivion.

Thankfully, they took their attention off me and started to talk amongst themselves, speaking low enough to where I couldn't make out much of the conversation. They say it's rude to listen in on others, but I wanted to know why they would they be in this run-down inn?

Something didn't feel right about them. I'd grown up around royal guards my entire life and they just didn't give off the right type of persona.

"Demon activity tonight..."

My ears perked up at the only words I could discern.

"Where?" I asked.

The one who tried to make eye contact earlier paused, tilting his head to the side and looking me up and down. "Here," he said, licking his lips. "They were seen inside the gates."

"They? More than one?" *Are you kidding me?*

"Yeah, they've been seen in groups of three lately. Getting smarter." He pointed a finger at his temple, tapping it lightly.

My food was served in the nick of time, and I dropped a coin on the bar and headed up to my room. When I passed by the guards, one of them reached out and pulled on my bicep, stalling me for a moment. My stomach rolled over as I looked into his beady, dark eyes.

"If for any reason they make their way into this place, I want you to know that we'll be keeping an eye out for you." He licked his tongue over his lip again.

My body went cold. The thought of being anywhere near this man again, raised every alarm in my head.

My knight was still gone when I'd returned and with the table being too small to eat at, I sat on the bed. I crossed my legs, leaning forward and removing the lid from the covered tray of food. A heavy scent of warm meat and herbs filled the room. A slab of lightly cooked red meat, a small potato stew and a bread roll sat on the tray. My mouth watered.

All too soon, I found myself scraping the bottom of the bowl after eating every single drop of soup. It was the best thing I could have tasted after the trek we had. Looking over to a small clock in the room and saw the time ticking by. It was getting later and later. My knight still hadn't returned.

The rain had stopped, and the incessant dripping onto the table ceased with it. I saw the last few glimpses of the sunset outside. I wanted out of this stale, stuffy room.

Outside, the smell of freshly dampened earth filled the air. I stayed close to the inn, being careful not to wander too far with the possibility of demons nearby.

I was free to pace to my heart's contentment, but each step I took, I felt the bottom of my boot separating farther and farther apart, to the point where little pebbles lodged between my sock and boot.

Leaning against a nearby post, I tried to pluck out the annoying pebbles, removing the boot and dumping it upside down. A women's scream made me jolt upright.

"Stop! Please!"

My heart raced as I looked around, seeing only empty streets darkening with each passing minute. No one was out right now, and I wondered *fucking* why? It was just me and some other broad, stupid enough to be out at this time with demons on the loose.

"Please— Stop!" The sounds of her cries ate at my chest; I couldn't let her die.

I took off running in the direction of the screams. I didn't know what I would do when I got there but I couldn't stand on the sideline while someone died again. I would not be able to live with myself.

I raced around a building and saw the dead end in a dark alley, the screams echoing off the buildings encasing the dark street. Her wails grew weaker and weaker, more hopeless with each passing breath.

I spied her, pressed up against the wall, surrounded by three black figures. These weren't the monsters I'd been expecting. They held a blade to her throat, her silent whimpers passing her lips as they pulled her skirts up and cut away at her stockings.

Everything I'd been keeping bottled up exploded out of me. I raced forward, not caring that I was unarmed. I couldn't let them do this.

"Stop! Leave her the fuck alone!" I screamed as I rammed my body as hard as I could into one of them. He fell into the one holding the blade on the woman and pulled back for a moment, allowing her enough room to get away from the knife.

She backed away and ran away, crying, racing down the alley. I turned back for a second and one man came up behind me and wrenched my arms back. I planted my feet into the ground and pulled away, screaming and tugging at their grip on me. My chest grew tight and tears of fear and anger started to pool in my eyes, blurring my vision.

"Let me go!" I screamed, gulping down breaths. The main one, the one with beady eyes, came over and placed a hand over my mouth, bringing his face inches away from mine. He was so close I could smell the putrid sour breath waft over me.

"Shhhhhhh ... this will be over fast if you're a good little minx."

Bile burned the back of my throat. It was the same fucking guard from the inn. I knew there was something off about this piece of shit. I rolled forward and head-butted him in the nose. He pulled back, shouting, and deep red blood gushed down to his mouth. He swore with red-stained teeth.

"Fucking bitch! Lay her down, she gets it NOW."

The other man came around and grabbed one of my arms while the other started to pull at my pants. I thrashed and screamed for them to stop. I kicked at one and he pulled my ankle hard, ripping my boot in the process and reached for the waist of my pants. These stupid fucking too big trousers slid down easily in his repulsive grasp.

Once they were down around my ankles and only my underwear was left as the only barrier to their filthy intentions, the main one pulled down his own britches, fisting himself and smiling at me with those red blood-stained teeth. If I had not already seen a demon, I would have said this man was an embodiment of evil. His soulless, dark eyes held no remorse.

I kicked and flailed as hard as I could, my muscles screaming out at me, but I still tried. I shrunk into myself, pulling my legs up as far as they'll go, but the other man's grip on me ground into my already wounded ankle from when we were ambushed.

As he got a grip on my knees and took out a knife to cut away at my underwear. I kept fighting and his knife cut into the soft flesh of my thigh as he struggled to hold me down.

"No! Stop! Please!" Tears streamed down my face and blood rushed in my ears. I prayed that I would pass out before any of this continued. I prayed to whoever would listen. The old gods, the new, anyone. Please—

A choked sound escaped my assailant and the arms around me stilled.

A sword had been shoved into my attackers back, the blade almost reaching me. My eyes trailed up, finding the familiar form standing over me.

My knight pulled the sword out and the man slumped, blood spilling onto the dirt. He grabbed at my attacker's hair for a handhold and threw his body to the side. The other two men dropped me to the ground and tried to run away. I fell hard, scraping the still healing, tender skin on the back of my arms on the coarse dirt.

My knight grabbed one of the men just above his collar and squeezed. I heard small crunching noises as his throat collapsed. He lifted the attacker off the ground and shoved him back onto an exposed hook standing out in the alleyway, letting him hang while he reached back for his sword. He held the sword to his gut, saying, "You should never have laid a finger on what is mine." My knight slowly shoved the blade in between his ribs and dragged it across his abdomen. A waterfall of dark red blood and entrails flowed onto the alley floor.

My breathing was erratic, and I tried to bring myself to the present, to the now and not force my way into the darkness. Stay here. Stay alive.

I reached down to pull up my pants and my legs collapsed beneath me. The alley walls felt like they were closing in on me. My ears rang, and a heave made its way up my throat.

My knight knelt in front of me. His presence alone was a beacon of hope for me. *Where the hell had he been?*

His gloved hand moved under my chin, gently forcing my face up to meet his. Tears burned my face and the cuts between my thighs were on fire, but I felt none of it. I felt for the first time in a long time like someone was there for me.

I lunged forward, wrapping my arms around his neck and shoving my head into the crook of the armor. He stilled for a moment and then wrapped his arms around me. He was hard and cold, but it was the comfort I needed.

We stayed like that for a moment until he shifted his weight and pulled away from me. He unhooked and wrapped his red mantel around my shoulders. He settled against me and put an arm under my knees and behind my back. Lifting me to his chest as he walked us back to the inn.

NINETEEN

Back in the room of the inn, I felt like a visitor in my own body. My head was foggy, and my limbs were numb and lifeless. It could be the pure exhaustion of the struggle on my body or the mental fatigue of these continuous exchanges of dread that had made themselves home in my life.

I needed to remind myself of what was real and happening to me, or I would implode. I focused on things I knew for sure —I was back in the too small room with the weird table and chair. I was whole and intact. I was alive. I was—safe.

The thoughts struggled to still, but as I looked at the steel man in front of me, I did know this last one was true. I am safe.

My fingers held tight to the crimson fabric wrapped around me, and I pulled it tighter against my cheeks, inhaling my knight's smokey musk and pine scent.

As my knight came out of the bathing chambers, he was no longer in a suit of armor but in soft linen pants and a loose-fitting tunic. It was so weird to see *him*.

He knelt to my eye level and his lazy curls sat softly against his dark brows. His face held very little emotion, but in his dark eyes I saw sympathy as he reached for the mantle, my fingers still, tightly holding it. His rough, calloused hands met mine and he loosened my grip enough to pull it away.

He stood and laid the mantle over the foot of the bed.

"The water won't be warm for long."

Still a man of few words.

I stood before the foggy mirror and examined my bruised and tattered body. I hadn't looked at myself in days. Scrapes and bruises covered my legs and abdomen. The softer, more shadowy parts of me were now less soft and less shadowy. I was losing myself by the day. From the mud and dirt caking my skin, to the deep dark circles under my eyes, I barely recognized the person staring back at me. I was a million miles away from being a queen. From being me.

Silent streams of tears streaked down my cheeks. I braced myself against the counter and my shoulders shook. A sob broke free, and the cold cut of the stone counter ate into the rough skin on my hands.

A knock broke my attention, and I wiped away the remaining tears staining my face.

"Are you alright?"

"I'm fine." I could barely get the words out.

Finally, I made my way to the tub in the center of the chamber and waded into the lukewarm water; it stung the cuts on my body and offered me very little comfort. I couldn't bring myself to wash. Just sitting there, my skin crawled. I could still feel their hands on me. The way their fingers dug into my arms and my thighs.

I pressed the palms of my hands into my eyes to stop the

burning tears from breaking through again. No more tears. I couldn't.

I let my hands fall away from me and settled deeper into the water, disturbing the suds. The dirt and soap clouds mixed and swirled along the surface of the water. It was hypnotic watching them chase each other in an endless whirl.

Another knock at the door broke me from my trance.

The door opened slightly, and I pulled my legs into my chest, resting my chin on my knees and looking to my left. Avoiding the mirror and the knight in the doorway.

"Are you okay?" His tone was low but filled with actual concern.

The only response I could offer is a nod, still avoiding his gaze.

He walked further into the room and pulled a stool up next to the tub. The legs scratched on the floor as he tried to scoot in closer. In my peripheral vision, I could see just how disproportionally big he was on the small chair.

"You know the goal of a bath is to clean yourself. You almost look dirtier than before you got in." He said in a teasing tone.

Still avoiding him, I didn't respond. I couldn't bring myself to say anything.

He sighed and grabbed a cloth and soap dunking it into the water, disturbing my swirls, and lathering it up as he reached over to take one of my hands in his. He carefully started to scrub at my palms and my fingers, paying extra attention to my nails, wiping away the built-up dirt and whatever else had made its way under them until they were clean for the first time in days.

He worked his way up my arm until he got to my shoulder, then moved the stool to the other side to repeat the cleaning.

Once he was done, he moved to behind the tub, gently

gathering my hair into his hands and laying it along my back. He grabbed a small cup sitting near the tub and poured water from my neck down. The water coated my back and cleaned the dirt away.

"Slide down for me." His voice was calm, and soft this time.

I obliged. Leaning back, I dipped my head below the surface, the water coming up and over my face. I didn't care that my naked body was before him. I was numb and cold. The last thing I needed was to feel more shame over myself.

It was fine for a moment, holding my breath beneath the few inches of water, then panic built in my chest. I was suffocating. I flung myself forward, my arms gripping the sides of the tub until my knuckles turned white. I gulped down air and still felt like I couldn't breathe. My chest heaved.

My knight reached a hand onto my shoulder and said, "You're alright, it's just some soap. I know it's not your favorite, but it won't hurt."

I let out a dry laugh, closing my eyes and coming back to the present. I took a deep breath and sat back near the edge again.

He worked soap into my hair. His large fingers were not the most graceful and he caught a few knots that wrenched my head back. But the kindness was welcomed and much appreciated. Once he finished lathering, he dunked his hands in the water, rinsing them clean of soap.

Coming over to the side of the tub, I felt his eyes bore into my face, but I couldn't bring myself to meet him.

He grabbed my chin between his fingers and forced me to look into his eyes. They were dark and cool and so very much not what I would have imagined hiding under that helmet.

"We have to rinse this now. You can hold my hand and if it becomes too much, just pull and I will lift you up. Okay?"

Tears threatened to break free again, and I blinked them away. I let out a soft "okay," but didn't know if anything audible escaped my lips.

He released my chin and reached his hand in front of me. I placed my hand in his and let him envelop mine. It was strong and calloused. Safe.

I took in a deep breath and dipped below the surface once again. This time, I could feel his other hand working through my hair. Then, before I knew it, he was the one to pull me up.

He leaned in a little closer and whispered, "good girl." A tight feeling in my chest grew at his praise. My hand was still in his as I turned to face him. My eyes searched over his face and landed back on his own.

"Thank you." This thank you wasn't just for this sad excuse for a sponge bath, but for everything. I would be dead or worse, in the clutches of multiple evil souls doing things I couldn't even begin to imagine.

He looked down at me through his thick lashes, and his mouth pulled to one side, giving me a somber smile.

"You're welcome, Lady Evangeline." His voice was low and husky. A wave of guilt welled up inside of me. He stood and made his way to the door.

As he reached the threshold, I let out a whispered, "Aleda."

"What was that?" He turned back to face me and leaned his wide frame against the doorframe.

"My name is Aleda."

He gave me a slight tilt of his head, furrowing his brow. His lips tightened into a straight line. He looked confused and rightly so.

Who would have two names and above all, why did I say anything? I looked away at this point. The scrutiny of his gaze was eating into me.

His towering figure stood in the doorway for a moment longer until he leaned down into a bow, "Lady Aleda."

Now dry from what was the most interesting bath of my life, I found a nicely folded garment on the counter. Holding it up in the dim light of the room, I saw that it was a sleep shift. Its soft, silky fabric was very much welcomed over the scratchy tunic I'd had for the past few days.

I pulled it over my head, and it slid on, fitting perfectly. I looked at myself once again in the cloudy mirror. The shift was the color of a moonbeam; the silver-white fabric made my skin look like it was glowing. For a moment, I didn't see the bruises on my body or the raw, chapped skin on my throat. Instead, I saw the soft swells of my breasts through the opalescent sheer shift, the pink peaks of my nipples cutting into it like little stones.

The thought of exiting the room solely in this was —confusing.

There was a short robe hanging on the back of the door. I grabbed it and wrapped it around myself. The scratchy fabric irritated the torn skin on the backs of my arms.

Entering back into the room, I saw my knight reclined back in the single chair with his feet propped up on the small table and a stronger fire blazing in the small hearth. The chill of this town wasn't at its peak, but the warmth filling the room was a pleasure I was grateful for. I stood near the active licking flames for a moment, letting the heat work itself through my bones.

My knight didn't stir from his spot as I made my way to the bed, his eyes fixed on the fire.

I faced the bed, leaving my back to the rest of the room as I hurriedly removed the robe and climbed under the blanket.

Why was I feeling so uneasy? He had seen me in every type of compromising position. He was no stranger to a woman in a night shift, I was sure.

He was a knight of the crimson cloth, and depending on when he began that title, he may or may not have seen a woman in a night shift—he doesn't do *that.* God, even in my own head, I felt shameful imagining him—nope, this stopped here. I tugged the covers tight to my chin and forced my eyes closed.

Twenty

"She mustn't know, not yet." A hushed whisper broke the silence.

"She will have to find out eventually; they all will. There isn't much time."

My mother, holding my hand, bent down to me, her face wet with tears. She held a hand out and pulled a lock of white hair forward from my head and twirled it around her finger before tucking it behind my ear.

"My love, you know it will only hurt for a second. No matter what, just know that it will be over quickly. You are strong. So much stronger than you think. Will you be brave for me?"

I nodded, and she gave me her best attempt at a smile, pulling me into a hug. Her familiar smell of narcissus fell over me, enveloping my senses. She always loved those flowers.

My mother pulled away from me and to my right was a familiar man, standing tall and strong. But his face was like a dark void with no color or facial features. Just emptiness.

I was pulled farther from the dark corner of the room and

into the center, near the sigils on the floor. I spied a dark shadowy figure. Its eyes were closed, its face somber. Their arms were spread open by chains on each side, and it stood upright, the horns twisting and curling to the sky. A demon.

I walked closer. A few timid steps and I placed my small foot on a sigil. A shock wave shot through me, and the demon opened its eyes. The most intense red color looked back at me.

A scream was forming on my lips, but my mouth wouldn't open. Nothing would come out. I thrashed out of my mother's reach and ran as far as I could. The man with the void face caught me, shaking my shoulders and saying nothing. There was no noise. Just my own crying screams.

"Aleda!"

My name was called out in a whisper that may as well have been a shout. Someone was gripping my arms, shaking me awake. I opened my eyes. In my groggy sleep state, I saw my knight above me. The dim light of the fire barely allowed me to make out the features of his face, but I knew it was him. The smokey musk and pine scent was not one I would soon forget.

I watched as his eyes fell to my lips and my breath caught. I ran my teeth along my bottom lip, feeling unsettled by his closeness. My heartbeat picked up. With his grip on me I was sure he must have felt just how rapid it was beating.

He let go and stood back up. "You were shouting in your sleep. We can't wake the whole inn." His voice was tense, but I sensed concern in his tone. He reached up and ran his fingers thoughtfully through the mess of waves on his head. They immediately sprung forward again.

The coils were dense and dark, like he had exited the bath moments before waking me. He walked to the hearth and rested his hand on the mantle, leaning his head forward, his shoulder high and tense.

"Do you get those a lot?" His voice was low and tired.

I sat up. My nightmares had always been a problem, but no one had ever been close enough to notice them, to wake me from them.

"I've had them for as long as I can remember."

He pushed off the mantle and stood at the edge of the bed. "Move to the other side."

I furrowed my brows and looked at him. He wasn't really—

"Don't just look at me, move to the other side of the bed. We can't risk you calling any more attention to us." Without any time to protest, my knight lifted the blanket and slid his large frame onto the already too small mattress. With a low huff, I turned to my right and faced the wall, trying to make as much space between us as humanly possible.

I could feel his side of the bed shift and drop under his weight. He settled down into his space and under the blanket. His legs stretched out and lightly brushed against mine. The coarse hair of his shin grazed against my calf, and I instinctually pulled my knees up closer to myself.

He shifted a few more times before he finally stilled, and we were left with just the sounds of our breathing and the crackling from the dying fire.

Minutes passed. I couldn't believe I'd told him my real name. A cold unease made a pit in my stomach. Would he mention it to Ilias when we finally met up with him? *Please, God. No.*

Still facing the wall, I broke the silence, "Can you promise that you won't tell anyone my name?" I inhaled deep breaths through my nose, trying to calm my nerves. And after a moment, he finally gifted me with his response.

"I suppose so. I don't see a reason to tell anyone at the moment."

At the moment? I shot up, turning to look at him and resting on my left arm. His eyes were focused on the ceiling, and he had both arms resting under his head.

My arm was now sinking into the bed, and I felt the thin strap from my shift drop off my shoulder, but was too distracted by his lack of exuberance to my request.

"No. I need you to promise me." My words were almost shaky as they fought through my true fear of being found out a liar.

He let out a huff of a breath and turned to face me, his head resting in his right hand, his other arm draped across his abdomen. I found myself tracing over his features again. Trying to commit him to memory, like I didn't know if this would be the last time I'd see him unmasked. Especially after we met back up with everyone. I was most positive these cameos would come to a halt.

I started at the bottom and worked my way up: the small bits of stubble growing in over his chin and along his cheeks, drawing higher to his full lips. The bottom one slightly bigger than the top, up to his strong nose. He had a small dusting of freckles just below his eyes— His eyes were dark and deep, like pools of onyx in the low light, housed in thick dark lashes. He had small fine lines curved up next to them—maybe the remnants of a youth full of sunshine and laughing.

He stared back at me, his eyes meeting mine for a moment, and then they swept over my bare shoulder. His stare burned a hole through me. I was staring just as intently, but under his scrutiny I felt like a trapped animal. Nowhere to run; a doe stuck in a hunter's snare.

He reached across the empty space between us and placed his index finger just below the fallen strap. Alarms went off in my head. His eyes followed his finger drawing it back into place. He left a scorching fire on my skin while at the same time a shiver crept up my body and goosebumps littered my flesh.

Pausing for a moment at the top of my shoulder, his eyes returned to mine and he said, "I promise." His accent was heavy on the two words.

He rolled onto his back once more, hands under his head, and closed his eyes.

I was stunned. *Was my jaw still connected to my head?* Still unmoving and in a small state of shock, I finally laid back down on my side and faced the wall, scooting as far to the edge of the bed as I could manage.

My head swam, and it felt like I was never going to be able to get to sleep.

The wind whipped through my hair as I held close to the balcony. The pages of a book titled *The Most Beautiful Birds in the Midlands* flipped carelessly with each passing gust.

A hand came up around my waist and pulled me back to a hard, muscular chest. I turned and saw the familiar dimples and short cropped hair, a smile building on my lips as Ilias pulled me in. His lips moved to mine and just like an internal instinct, we moved together like a true pairing.

He sat me down on the plush settee and knelt before me. His fingers moved up from my ankles to the hem of my skirt and higher, billowing the fabric around my torso.

I laid my head back and ground my fingers into the cushions as he lowered himself to my soft flesh. He started out slow like he always did, trailing kisses on the sensitive skin of my thigh until he finally met my core. A slick, wet tongue swiped over me.

A loud pleasure-induced moan tumbled from my lips as he worked me further. Nipping at the sensitive bud of nerves causing me to grow so close to a— He pulled away, and my ache grew stronger.

"Look at you, you're so ready for me." The words came out deep and rough.

I lifted my head and was met by his onyx pools. My breath caught in my throat as I saw the way his lips glistened in the light, covered in me. He stared into my eyes as he slowly swiped his tongue over them.

My brows raised at the realization of those eyes. It was not Ilias but I—I wanted him and not— He stood and angled himself to me. There was a pressure against my entrance, so much pressure ... my head fell back, and my eyes rolled into the back of my head ... oh my god—

A tickle on my nose brought me out of my dream, my eyes were still closed as I let out an exasperated breath. *Why did dreams always end at the good part?* Good part? What the hell was I thinking? He isn't, I wouldn't—

I must have gotten hot in the middle of the night; the blanket was wadded up against my chest. The heat was still radiating into my body as I opened my eyes, let out a sleepy stretch and found the source of the tickling.

My knight's hair was spilling into my face. Examining further, I realized my blanket was nowhere to be found, my head was resting on his chest with my arm and leg draped over his sleeping body.

Panic welled up in my chest. *Oh my god.* And just after my *dream.* My heart pounded erratically in my chest and a heat bloomed between my thighs. *Stop this, treacherous body of mine.*

My shift was raised, revealing the swell of my butt as my leg fell over his torso and his arm was very, very close. His fingers were just inches away from my bare skin.

I dared to look up and saw his face was turned away from me. His features were so soft and almost angelic now, the dark waves blanketing his forehead and cheeks. His lips had looked so good when they were covered in my— *Stop!*

I needed to separate myself from him, from this situation. I lifted my leg, and he shuffled slightly, pulling his knee up and rubbing me right in between my legs. I bit my lip to hold back any sound, but my eyes wanted to roll back into their skull.

Much less gracefully, I tumbled off him and rolled back to my side facing the wall as deeply as I could allow. Hoping, *praying,* he was a deep sleeper.

A few minutes passed in pure agony as I waited for any change.

How did *he* not push me off if I was seemingly trying to climb him like a goddamned tree? How long was I like that for? Where the hell was the blanket?

His breathing changed and he let out a strangled sounding noise as his body stretched out on the bed. His weight shifted more and jostled me slightly. I tensed all my muscles to stay turned on my side as I felt heat building up against my back. Warm breath danced over my cheeks and moved my stray hairs to tickle my nose. It took everything in me not to move and brush them away.

"How did you sleep? Doesn't seem like you had any other *nightmares.*"

I didn't respond. I just wanted him to think I was asleep and leave.

"It was so weird though, you kept making all these *noises*, and when I tried to wake you, you just crawled on top of me."

My eyes flew open, pure terror shredding through me.

"I tried to push you off, but you were very ..." He paused thoughtfully, *"persistent."*

My blood couldn't decide whether to run cold or build to a boil. A storm of emotion built inside of me, though, that was for certain.

"What a role reversal we have here. I am speaking to you in droves, and you can't seem to even give me one of your ... *little noises.*" His voice was dark and heady.

Deep in-between my legs, a throb began. I wanted to fight it, to tell myself it wasn't happening, but I felt him press in closer to me, his arm sinking into the bed behind my head as his mouth hovered just above my ear.

The smokey musk and pine scent surrounded me, making my head spin. It was almost intoxicating.

"A-led-a ..."

I shivered at his breath and the way he drew out every syllable. I needed a little fucking space.

I tried to catch him off guard, push his arm out from underneath him and throw him off the bed, but I only half succeeded. When his arm went down, he fell on top of me, and God he was heavy. His legs fell between mine and he lifted himself back up, both arms on each side of my head.

He looked down at me. The light in the early morning shined through the window, casting his rogue sleep-strewn hairs into a golden halo around his head. His eyes had more of a golden amber color than the deep, almost black onyx of the evening light.

He looked like a golden god. I swallowed hard and my breath caught. He saw me go tense and rigid against his body. His eyes searched mine and then traveled down my chest. My nipples were peaked and felt like they could cut through the thin fabric of my shift.

Every part of me was hypersensitive to his touch. Every contact point was noted, and I felt a fluttering beat in my chest. His pelvis rested between my legs, and my shift rode up to reveal the tops of my thighs. I looked down between us. His shirt had pulled up and the deep olive skin on his belly contrasted with my pale skin. I looked back up, his eyes staring into mine. His face was only inches away. He parted his lips like he was going to speak, but we sat in silence for what felt like an eternity.

Between my legs, I felt a pressure growing against me.

God smite me right now; I beg of you.

I bit my lip and looked away, trying to just separate myself from what was happening and how I was reacting to him. And him to me?

He took a deep, steadying breath and lifted off me, leaving the bed and heading straight for the bathing chamber.

Now alone, I needed to get out of this bed and out of this shift. On the table was a pile of clothes. I rifled through them and saw they were women's clothes, and about my size.

Is this what he was doing when he was gone yesterday?

On the floor was a new pair of boots as well. He got all of this for me ...

I didn't know how much time I had alone, so I quickly got dressed and headed down the stairs of the inn. I wanted just a little space and time to myself after this morning. And last night.

But when I sat in the same spot in the bar, the events from last night flooded back into my mind. The way the guards were so close to—*stop*—it hadn't. *It hadn't happened.* I repeated the words as much as I could to myself. I was fine and they were stopped.

But fuck, why? Why couldn't I catch a fucking break?

The young boy behind the bar had been replaced with a presumably older sibling. They had the same flaxen hair and soft features. He served me breakfast. I tried to swallow the meal down, but each bite tasted like ash. Not from lack of seasoning or effort, but from me. The anxiety riddling my body invaded my mind and my tongue.

The sound of the clunking steps of my knight as he made his way down the stairs were enough to right the train of thought beginning to circle around the ever-widening pit of self-deprecation. He came to sit across from me, back in his full suit of armor, the saddlebags in his arms. He reclined in his chair as much as it would go and waited for me to finish. Not being able to stomach another bite, I stood. He did the same and headed for the door.

Twenty-One

WE RODE FOR ANOTHER HALF A DAY BEFORE THE next town came into view. It was the last stop before the second outpost just outside of the Paymon lands.

Both of us sharing this ride on horseback, got cramped at times. Intermittently, when we would stop for water, my knight would walk alongside the midnight steed, and I would get the whole seat to myself. You would assume I would enjoy that more than having my legs encased by two steel covered ones the size of tree trunks, but I—I think I preferred the feeling of him. The closeness was an assured blanket of safety surrounding me.

He wasn't far away when he would walk alongside the horse and me, but it wasn't quite the same.

All these feelings had been so confusing, after everything that had happened with Ilias. The idea of going all this way to meet him felt like the last place I wanted to be headed, but I knew he was my only ticket to get North and get home. Not meeting him meant I could lose out on any correspondence from my mother.

The cobblestone streets of the town echoed off the walls with each passing clop. It was nearly sunset, and the warm sun-dappled clouds reflected off my knight's armor a little less lustrously than the last time I'd taken notice. God, that felt like an eternity ago. Our days of travel coated thick layers of dirt and grime, not just to my clothes but his armor was far from having its usually polished finish.

At the center of the town was a familiar building, holding spires and cones reaching to the sky as other cathedrals did within the larger cities, but this one was a fraction of the scale. I supposed for a small town they hadn't found the egregious places of worship a necessity.

A low humming bell rang out and almost immediately the double doors to the building were opened, revealing the towns-people exiting from an evening service.

Surprised gasps fled through the group as the patrons noticed us. Among the concerned faces, was a man who held back the others at the threshold, stopping them from leaving, his eyes latched onto us like a hawk. He was not quite middle-aged and had the early streaks of salt and pepper intertwining with his beard and long hair worn pulled back from his face. He approached us while keeping his hand raised to the people behind him.

"What brings you two *travelers,* to our community?" His mouth was tight and brow furrowed as he kept a sharp eye on my knight standing next to me.

Did we appear that menacing?

"We're just passing through, hoping to find an inn for the night." I tried to keep my voice strong and steady. There was no lie in my words to waver me.

His features didn't soften. The black stallion beneath us tremored and stepped anxiously in place, letting out a grunt.

"We don't have an inn, ma'am. We don't get many *visitors,* so we don't have so much a need for one."

My heart sank, and almost like an omen in itself, a blisteringly cold gale shot through the town square. Teeth-shattering cold knifed into my bones and I curled my fingers into my chest to keep them warm.

The man's face softened, it was subtle—but there. He inhaled deeply, turning back to the group of people still standing in the structure's doorway. A woman came forward.

She was pale and tall with a wealth of golden curls traveling down her back, the wind whipping them violently around her like an aura of light dancing as the final rays of sun met the wavering locks. Her eyes never left the man before us. He reached his hand out as she approached, and she met it with her own.

We waited as he spoke to her in a low voice, soft enough to where we couldn't make out a sound. Her eyes darted back and forth from him to us. Finally, she nodded her head, and he nodded with her.

He turned back to us, his face still stern, but a bit softer than when we first arrived.

"Like I said, we don't have an inn here, but you are welcome to stay in the church. With this weather we also bring in the young livestock, so you won't be without neighbors, but it's out of the elements."

I almost jumped from my seat with excitement. Anything was going to be better than walking all night or sleeping on the ground again.

"Thank you so much, I can pay you—"

He cut me off, raising his hand. "Enough of that, let's head inside." He turned and walked back to the *church.* Before The Fall there had been private places of worship called churches, but I hadn't ever heard of them existing after the Saints took over the cathedrals.

Making my way off the saddle and into the small building, I saw very little furniture, aside from rows and rows of pews leading up to face an—an altar.

In the center of the domed end of the building sat a warn mural depicting a man, his face hidden from all. In his hands as he carried two objects, one circular in his left and one larger, like a sword maybe, in his right. Most of the depiction was bleached from age. I mean, it had to be over two hundred years old if it was from before The Fall.

This place was lost in time to the new world and the Saint's teachings. Tomes of Old Amaymon lined a back wall, the spines dusty and tattered. I ran my fingers across them and felt the soft, worn leather give under my touch.

"Do you know the teachings?" the man from before asked.

I faced him. "I know *of* the teachings, but where I'm from they are, well, they are not mentioned."

"Ahh yes, our old teaching rival the Saints now, don't they?"

Rival? I'd never heard of it as any kind of rivalry. More of a right versus wrong, bad versus good, evolution versus ... the past.

"My name is Cartier, the woman who was gracious enough to let you stay here is my wife, Marigold." He looked to her across the room, his eyes soft and caring as they watched her.

"Thank you for letting us stay. My name is Evangeline." The false name came off my tongue a little too easily now.

They set up a small section on the floor with mats stacked up and a few thick blankets, and just like they'd said, let the young animals in as well: about three baby goats, a piglet and a sow, and one bright white lamb. The lamb's knobby legs were still unsure of each step, like it had just been born this week.

As I sat down on the built-up bed, the little lamb stumbled over, nestled up to me and it laid its head in my lap. I touched its soft baby wool, warm under my fingertips.

I looked over to my knight and saw him standing before the altar, his hand atop his sheathed sword as he stood, staring up into the face of the mural. He was unmoving, like he had been so many times in the midlands keep, again like a statue. It was so different from who I had grown to know, all those days we'd spent side by side. I had no clue who was under there.

We had been left alone in the church for a little over an hour now and he was still in his full suit of armor. I doubted he'd remove it with the possibility of anyone coming to check on us. But with that, I was sure he wasn't going to talk to me either. It didn't matter too much, I guessed. He already wasn't the most engaging conversationalist, but it was still something nice to have. To not talk into the void.

I saw the familiar Box in the far corner of the church. Maybe not everything had been changed by the Saint's. I doubted they had anyone sitting in the companion side to take a Revelation. Even so, I went to examine the Box, its walls worn with chipped paint along the edges, exposing through to the wood it was built from. I wondered how old those trees had been and what the world must have been like at that time. Had it been constructed before or after the Fall?

Inside was a cushioned bench seat and a thin, sheer curtain hanging in the middle, dividing the small chamber into two. The lattice window was missing.

The Box was sealed off from the world to allow for as much privacy as possible. The lack of light made my eyes strain, and I could barely make out shapes in the ever-dark compartment. I closed my eyes and rested my head back, collecting each steady breath within my lungs, focusing on each expanse and how the air floated past my lips on the exhale.

A creak from the other end of the Box stirred my attention. A steady flow of silver light bled into the small space until a form stood in front of it, blocking out the rest of the world.

The silence of the small space grew from a sense of comforting escape to a feeling of static energy working its way into my skin. Minutes passed and the quiet of the night still rang out before us.

If he wasn't going to say anything, what was the point of coming in here in the first place?

I pulled back the sheer dividing curtain. "Why—"

It wasn't my knight, and it wasn't Cartier. I saw the sharp outlines of the bauta mask. His face was turned straight, not taking notice of me. My heart rate picked up, and a chill crept over my skin, finding station at the base of my spine.

Almost painfully slow, he turned to me, his hands clasped in his lap until he fully faced my direction. Then he extended an outstretched hand to me, like he had at the Crimson Moon Festival.

Unsure if this was the smartest thing to do, I met his hand with mine. And just like before, his fingers clasped mine, and he brought them up to the mouth of his mask, holding them there for a moment.

This time, the engagement held much more dread. My blood grew cold as he lowered our fingers from his mask's mouth and brought his other hand to join ours. I could feel him place something in mine, the feeling of it sharp against my skin in an almost familiar sensation. He drew his hands back and kept my fingers closed around whatever he had given me.

I looked down to my closed fingers, gently opening them to reveal the gift. In my hand was a black Legion Stone. It was tied to the same chain that Kairos had given me right before the chaos that had become my life had begun.

I lifted my eyes back to him and the moment they met his masked face, he flung the sheer curtain closed. I rushed to pull it back, seeking answers as to where he came from and who he was and how he—

A wave of energy hit me flinging me back into the vast darkness of the void, floating in space as a small trickle of light broke through the emptiness. Then another and another. Small shooting stars built across the night sky.

One by one they clustered together, spinning, twining, and bringing forth one giant star floating before me. The heat burned my skin, but I didn't pull away. I forced my fingers to reach for it. To meet the star. To become the star.

Its light engulfed and burned me alive. I felt—

Wet.

I forced my eyes open to the burning brightness of the morning light. The little lamb rubbed its wet nose against my cheek, pressing harder into me, seeking attention.

I looked around, remembering we were in the church we'd taken sanctuary in for the night. My knight was nowhere to be found as I turned my head around to see each corner of the small building. It was empty aside from the lamb lying next to me. Despite the fuzzy feeling in my head and the burning behind my eyes, I moved to stand and felt something sharp under my back. Turning on the pile of blankets, I spied the source of the discomfort.

My breath caught in my throat as I held it up to the light— the Legion Stone from my dream. But it couldn't have been a dream, could it? I looked toward the black Box, and felt the same unnerving feeling build up through my body. Ignoring it, I stood, dusting my clothes off, and placed the Legion Stone back around my neck, pulling out my collar to allow the stone to hit against my bare chest, welcoming the familiar sting.

The small head of the lamb pressed into my calves, still so desperate for attention. I looked down to her, admiring her pure, white wool covered face and deep dark eyes. Her soft bleats finally beat me down enough to where I reached down and picked up her tiny body. She immediately calmed and rested her head against me.

I stepped through the doorway and outside the church's walls, looking over the town in shock. This town couldn't be the same one. It was bustling with life and people, with an energy that hadn't been there the night before. Ahead of me, in the soft morning rays peeking past the clouds, was my knight. He was checking the stallion's saddle, pulling against various straps and checking through the saddlebags, but he wasn't alone.

A group of seven or so young children were crowded around him, watching him work. They kept a distance and whispered to themselves, but there was a seemingly invisible barrier they had yet to cross.

Just then, he looked at me. His large, armored figure held my gaze.The lamb grew restless in my arms. I lowered it down to the ground and it ran to the children. Its wobbly legs were still barely keeping its body upright. I couldn't help but let out a little laugh.

Turning my attention back to my knight, I noticed he was still watching me. He took a few steps but was stopped short by the smallest of the children, a young girl with the same billowy blonde curls as Marigold. She stood before him, facing away from me so I couldn't quite make out what she was asking.

My knight picked her up by her middle and placed her on top of the horse's saddle. Her giddy squeals echoed out through the small-town square. He grabbed the horse by the reins and walked them in a small circle.

One by one the children asked to join in, leaving him with a line a half dozen long.

Just then Marigold came up beside me, her blonde curls tied up in a neat bun at the top of her head and she wore a much sturdier outfit.

"What actually brings you two all the way out here?" Her words themselves were pressing, but her tone was calm and gentle.

Still not looking away from the scene before me, I answered back. "We are headed to Paymon; our company was attacked by bandits, and we've been trying to make our way ever since then."

I felt her eyes traveling over my face, making a very noticeable station at the healing skin around my neck. "Come with me," she said, and without argument, I followed.

She took me to her home, not too far from where we were. The front of the house was overtaken with ivy and inside was a large hearth near a few cushioned chairs and a large dining table with a well-fashioned kitchen full of medicinal herbs and other plants I recognized from my books.

She sat me near the dining table and brought over a few jars of varying liquids, a cloth and a mortar and pestle. In the first jar was a strong-smelling liquid that gave off an earthy botanical aroma with notes of spices. She dampened the cloth and brought it to my neck.

"Can you pull this down a tad for me, dear."

I nodded and pulled my collar far enough below my neck so she could reach my healing, chapped skin. The Legion Stone peeked out, and she stopped in her tracks.

"Why do you have that?" Her eyes grew wide.

"It was a gift," I said, not wanting to fill her in on the details that I wasn't sure about.

"A gift ..." The words were drawn out, but she went back to dabbing the cloth against my neck. After the astringent, she used the mortar and pestle to grind up a yellow root that she mixed with the salve and rubbed it gently on the still healing skin. *That rope really did a number on me.*

After she was finished, I tucked the stone back beneath my collar. She went back to the pantry; the door was left slightly ajar. I saw more jars lining the shelves through the opening. These ones were also filled to the brim, but instead of her earthy-toned elixirs, these were all filled with an inky black substance.

"The men who did that to your throat, they were after the stone?"

Her question shouldn't have caused a visceral reaction, but my body tensed. She was unaware that they succeeded in taking it from my neck and this one, well ...

I opened my mouth to answer her question, but she stopped me, grabbing my arms in a tight grip.

"This *gift*," she said as she reached into my shirt and pulled out the Legion Stone, holding it in her hands, not appearing to feel the stinging sharp ache that came each time I held it. "is not one to take lightly. Do not let anyone know that you have this. You may not survive the next time a greedy man seeks you out for it."

She placed the stone back under my shirt and reached a hand up to touch my cheek. Her eyes softened, and she pulled me into a hug. My arms hesitated for a moment, but her body was warm and pressed hard, she reminded me of my mother, with her soft yet strong disposition. I finally reached up and wrapped my arms, reciprocating. This kindness had not ever been shown to me by a stranger. She didn't know me, but she and her people had done more than I could ever repay.

My mouth pressed up against her shoulder and, I fought back a wave of emotion, pulling back the shakiness building in my throat to let out a single, "Thank you."

Twenty-Two

Midnight approached, the moon was still high in the sky and the sweet salvation of the Kingdom of Paymon's lantern-lit outer wall came into view. The city occupied the flattest lands in the area, the walls were the only form of exterior protection with two smaller inner walls, the grand castle secure in the center.

The closer we got to the outer wall, the livelier the night became. Travelers from all over had settlements and caravans lining the exterior. Makeshift taverns made of large tents and small tables were all filled with patrons.

A group seemed to be forming around one tavern in particular. We dismounted, and I finally stretched my aching body, gaining feeling back into my numb toes. The shouts grew louder at the center of the group and my curiosity got the better of me. I wanted to see what could be so enthralling.

I worked my way through the crowd and up to the source. To my surprise, it was a very inebriated Ilias. He was sitting atop a table, waving his hands as he described a grand tale. I huffed a breath past my lips as he brought his glass to his lips, downing the rest of whatever he was drinking. As he finished, he brought his hand up to his mouth to wipe away the moisture and slammed the glass down to the table, foam flying.

His eyes searched the faces in the crowd until they fell to me, and I saw his expression change immediately. It went from shock to something else, ending up on a bright smile, pulling his cheeks up and showcasing his embedded dimples. He jumped up from his spot and raced over to me, his arms pulling me to him roughly, jerking me.

"I'm so happy you made it alright; I've been so worried." His hand came up to my cheek, his touch hard and tugging on my skin. I pulled back on instinct, and his mouth turned down at the corners. My attempt to make up for my lack of enthusiasm resulted in my placing a hand on his chest.

My mouth opened to respond to him, but he crashed his own down to mine. The feeling was so foreign and odd, when just days ago it was the one I had craved.

He pulled back and the residue of the kiss and whatever he was drinking clung to me with a sour taste on my tongue. Ilias swayed and pulled me closer. My feeling of unease grew. Though our reunion was only a few breaths long, I craved space dearly.

I scanned the space for a familiar face in the crowd and came back empty-handed; my knight nowhere to be seen.

"Is it okay if I go and get cleaned up?"

His light grey eyes bored into me, no more glaze to them, like he'd been snapped out of a trance. Then in a moment they went back to their soft look, small lines crinkling near his eyes as he gave another too big smile.

"Yes, of course. Let me show you to our room."

Our room.

Hearing that we would be sharing a space made my stomach flip and I didn't know why.

No, I did know why.

He brought me within one of the walls that sat on the outermost part of the eastern kingdom, and to a small inn. The rooms were on the outside of the building in a long line, like small single dwellings. It was a fair-sized room with a large settee, a fireplace and plush rugs, and a large table in the center. And a bed, one single bed that I would have to share with Ilias.

He crossed the room and went for the bathing chamber, leaving the door cracked. I could hear the loud splashing as he relieved himself.

He spoke out from the room to me, "When you're all finished, there is a play happening in the town square. I think you would like it. It's a band of traveling actors who perform at all hours. Once you're ready, come down, and we can head out."

The last thing I wanted was to go anywhere after the traveling we'd endured to make it to the city's outer wall. I wanted to climb into that bed and hide away for days. To rot and let my blisters dry up and heal, let my chapped skin regain its lost moisture. I needed rest. Not entertainment.

I pulled my things out and strewed them carelessly across the bed. The glossy sheer white shift stood out against the rest of the mismatched too-big clothes. Holding it between my fingers the feel of the soft silk on my skin brought me back to when my partner in bed was not Ilias. It was someone I—I took a deep gulp and stashed the shift in the bottom of the bag. The last thing I wanted was for Ilias thinking it would be an item I'd wear for him.

As if on cue, he exited the bathing chamber and walked up behind me, snaking an arm around my middle and pulling me to him, nuzzling his face into the crook of my neck and placing a soft kiss on the sensitive skin. "I missed you," he whispered against my neck.

A tinge of guilt hit my gut, and I pressed back into him a little. I turned in his arms to reciprocate his affections. I wrapped my arms around his body, but my brows knitted together as I leaned into his chest.

What was I doing here? Why was I all the way in the fucking Paymon kingdom in the first place with the duke of the Midland's nephew on a diplomatic meeting? I had no place here. Not like this.

Just a little longer, I said to myself in a silent prayer.

"I missed you too." The words were a lie, but I needed my lie to last just a *little longer.*

He pulled away, looking at me, scanning my face. "Go get cleaned up and we'll leave, yeah?"

I nodded and headed to the bathing chamber.

The play was beginning as we walked up, taking our seats in the back to avoid disrupting what had already started. Ilias grabbed for my hand as we sat, and his soft fingers traced lazy lines on my skin. He leaned in to say something to me, but I didn't hear him, caught off guard by the heavy liquor scent coming off him.

I gestured to the actors ahead, showing that I wanted to pay attention.

The curtain closed on the scene and as it reopened a small girl came on stage, her steps short as she paced to the center, standing before an empty altar, like the ones in the cathedrals. She was crying and sat on her knees in front of it. A red light cast over them, drenching the stage and the girl in deep crimson. A large figure walked from the shadows and stood behind the altar.

After a moment, he faced the girl, stretching out his hand and lifting her from the floor. All light extinguished, and blackness filled the stage. Then in a flash, the red was back, and a new third figure was present. A circle of flames emitted from the floor, holding all three within its circumference.

This new figure stood between them, standing taller and towering over them both. Atop its head were large, twisted horns reaching to the sky and long knife-like claws outstretched from its fingers. A demon.

The flames grew higher, and flashes of light illuminated its face. It's cracked and calloused features looked even more grotesque, filled with light and shadows.

My heart picked up in a frenzy and I went to stand. But Ilias's hand tightened around my wrist, and he pulled me back to my seat.

"It's just getting good. What are you doing?" His voice was tight and clipped.

I turned to face the actors again, my face growing hot. "Nothing ... I'm sorry."

His hand was like a vice around my wrist, keeping me in place. I reached down to pry his fingers away. He finally relaxed them against me and roughly laced his fingers with mine. This action of closeness made me even more uncomfortable.

A loud scream came from the girl on stage as the man beside her was thrown back by the demon. A new man entered the stage and helped her to her feet, telling her she needed to run away, to get as far away as she could from this place.

She sprinted from the stage, and the man attacked the demon himself. Loud screams and blood-curdling cries fill the space around me. I swallowed, my throat feeling rough and raw.

Before I knew it, I was standing on my feet, a scream coming from my own mouth. All eyes were on me. I looked around franticly and saw that even the actors on the stage had stopped to see who the crazy woman screaming in the audience was.

Without a second thought, I took off running, not caring that I left Ilias behind or that I had no fucking idea where I was going. I just needed out of there.

I reached the first sturdy wall of a building and clung to the cool stone, pressing my back against it, my skull making rough contact with the wall. I winced and reached up to rub the sore spot, turning to look down the alley.

No more than ten feet down, I spied the young girl actor smoking something acrid in a rolled paper. She was a small woman, but definitely not as young as she appeared on the stage. How did they know? How did they have a story so similar to what had happened to me the night of the Crimson Moon Festival? Did they know the nightmare my life had become since then?

Feeling a pull in my chest, I went up to her. "Hey! Can I speak to you?"

"Sorry, no autographs until the play is over."

"I don't want an autograph. I wanted to know how you came up with that story."

She dropped whatever she was smoking and snuffed it out into the dirt under her shoe.

"Oh, a fan, are we? Well, an artist never reveals their secrets," she said as she began to brush me off and turn away. I reached out and grabbed her cloak. She fell to the ground, exclaiming, "Hey what the fu—"

I stood over her, my face lit with the torches lining the street.

"Oh my god." She stared at me, eyes widening. "You're her."

I leaned down and grabbed her collar. In a hard whisper, I said, "And *who* is that?"

She gulped and started to shout. "Someone help! She's attacking me!"

A couple of men came around the corner. "Hey! Leave her alone!"

"Shit," I said under my breath and took off running to my room. It was only a few buildings away, but as soon as the door closed, I quickly latched it behind me. I kicked my shoes off and made my way towards the settee, grabbing a blanket. The last place I wanted to be when Ilias finally came back was in a bed with him, so willing to join me.

Laying down, I brought my knees up to my chest to fit snuggly into the small space and covered myself with the blanket.

The sound of the door opening stirred me from any sleep I was able to find. Unsteady steps made their way through the threshold into the room. It was Ilias, stumbling on his own feet. He found his center of gravity after a moment and righted himself. Noticing I was not in the bed, he looked over at me, confused.

"What are you doing down there?" he said with a slight slur, but his tone was hard and heavy. I started to respond but he cut me off. "You were so fucking rude out there, you know that?" His words were sharp and short, not indicating a need for a response from me, but I spoke out anyway.

"I wasn't trying to be rude I—"

He raised his hand, stopping me. He brought his hand up

to his brow and leaned onto the table in the middle of the room.

My temper surged in my blood, rage reaching my fingers, and I clenched my hands into fists at my sides. He had so much to say but wouldn't let me get a goddamned word in. I stood and stepped away from the settee, moving a fraction closer to him. I started again, "I am sorry if my leaving seemed rude, I didn't intend to—"

He turned to me in that moment, his eyes dark and heavy. Not the eyes of the Ilias I knew. "You didn't intend to *embarrass* me? To scream in the middle of the fucking play and then cause a scene as you ran out?" he said, turning away from me.

My eyes filled with tears and I fucking *hated* that they were. I wasn't sad. I wasn't anything but furious with him, but my traitorous emotions welled up and filled my eyes. I needed to stand up for myself, to face him and say that I would not be treated this way.

"Will you please look at me?" I choke out.

Nothing.

I forced myself to move my feet and made my way across the plush rug lining the hardwood floors.

"Ilias," I whispered, reaching up to his face. But before I could touch him, he slapped me. Hard and forcibly. I turned away in shock, my foot tangling on the rug, and I fell, slamming my face into the edge of the table. My brow and mouth felt like they had been split open.

I crumpled to the floor, my face stinging. Shock set in and my hands grew shaky as they reached up to palm the battered skin. A buzzing feeling filled my skull, and my vision blurred momentarily. Tears welled as I looked up to him. His figure was tight, and shoulders held high and tense as he took in deep inhales through his barred teeth.

He looked more like a wild animal than the man who'd

showed me kindness when I was just a stranger to him. I turned away, unable to hold his predatory gaze any longer. Tears poured from my eyes, streaking down the warming skin of my cheek.

I stood. Still facing away from him I wiped my face clean. The hairs on the back of my neck rose as I sensed his body moving closer to me. I went rigid, honing my body for whatever would come my way next.

Gentle fingers wrapped around the back of my bicep and pulled me to turn around. As I faced him, the man who stood above me, who had just hit me fully across the face, was missing and the tender eyes of Ilias had returned.

His soft fingertips reached for my cheek, and I jerked from him.

"Don't fucking touch me." I spat out the words, filling them with venom.

His grip on me tightened, and he searched my face with eyes that looked confused and sad.

"Evangeline, I'm so sorry I—"

I wrenched out of his grasp and shoved him back, heading to the door and grabbing a large black cloak hanging on a stand. I needed to get the fuck out of there.

In my rush, I neglected to grab goddamned shoes. My bare feet paced on the soft, packed dirt of the streets. I tightened the cloak around my body with the hood pulled down far enough to hide my growing bruise and identity from Ilias or anyone who came looking for me.

I passed through the now docile alleys of merchants closing their carts. The wine merchant was carrying cases back to his covered trailer, his hands full and his back turned as I slunk behind him and snagged anything within reach, hiding it beneath my cloak.

My quick barefoot steps must have been an accomplice to my success, but I still turned left down two more alleys to get ahead of the merchant on the off chance he took notice.

Finally, I came across an empty table. I climbed on top and rested my dusty feet on the bench seat. I pulled the bottle out, giving it a good first look.

The spirit was in an unlabeled bottle, but as I removed the cork, the familiar scent of pine and mint erupted from it.

Gin.

Gross.

But I brought the bottle to my lips and took a long, hard pull. The liquor burned my throat, but I welcomed it. I needed it to numb my aching face and equally damaged heart. I didn't *love* Ilias, not even close, but ... I sighed to myself. To be treated as I had been by someone who said they would help me made me feel lost. I felt—a lot of things.

Heat crept up over my cheeks and I knew the liquor was working its magic as my mind wandered. And boy, did it wander.

It wandered back to the bed I'd shared with a large and bronzed man with two perfect lips that I couldn't stop thinking about and— My thoughts were interrupted by two feet coming into view of my hooded figure.

Only up to the ankles was visible, but I knew who they belonged to. And so did other parts of me.

A tight curling feeling built in my lower stomach. I was just about to admit to myself that I couldn't stop thinking about this man, and just like a fucking gift sent from above, he appeared before me.

He shuffled slightly and in an instant my hood was ripped

back from my head. I turned away from him, hiding the shame and the mark placed upon me by Ilias.

Rough fingers gripped my chin and forced me to look up into the cold steel helmet. A distorted reflection of my marred skin looked back at me. My eyes stung with unshed tears. The fingers around my chin loosened, and I pulled myself fully free, bringing the bottle back up to my lips and chugging down as much of the vile liquid as I could. I was halfway through when it was pulled away from my grasp all together.

My knight held it out and flipped it upside down, spilling the remaining contents into the dirt, splashing mud and liquor onto my bare feet.

"That wasn't very nice, you know," I said. My tongue felt heavy. The words were difficult to get out past my lips. He shrugged and walked away, tossing a loud object onto the table behind me. I turned to see what it was, but my vision had to catch up with my head, the act making me dizzy.

My eyes finally focused and before me was ... I squinted.

Boots.

Following my knight through the city at night was a new, yet familiar experience. Everywhere and everyone were in their own worlds, living life passing by bodies reflecting on themselves in routines unique, yet so similar as they moved throughout the day.

My goal was to pass through unnoticed, like a shape in a dream or a shadow lingering in peripheral vision.

The hood of my cloak was pulled low over my head, draping down past my chin as I kept my head angled to the floor. The blooming bruises on my face felt hot and hard as the swelling increased. I fucking hated this; hiding my face because of the ill-perpetrated rage of a man. A man who was my only source and means of protection.

We wouldn't get word of any reciprocated letters from my mother or any news regarding my return home out here. I had to just get through these last few days—maybe a week at the longest. I needed to get away from him.

My eyes never left the heels of my knight. I had no sense of awareness in my hood other than the crunching dirt below me and the two feet leading me. Leading me where? No clue.

I let out a rough gust of air as I made a hard connection with cold steel, bouncing back slightly.

I lifted my hood to see why we stopped so abruptly. Craning my neck to my left, I spied a larger-than-life building; a glass house with glossy spires reaching to the heavens. *The Eastern Cathedral of Paymon.* Its reputation carried through the kingdoms and it—it was beyond words. A true house of glass and stained windows. It was dark now, but I could only imagine how it must have looked just a few hours ago as the sun was setting. I was a little sad I had missed it.

I had read historical tomes in Kairos's study on every cathedral, and this one was by far my favorite. I let out a sigh, thinking back to the smell of leather and parchment ... and tobacco that always filled that room and comforted me while they were away. Being there was my connection to him, and being here, felt like a sliver of that.

My knight continued, walking into the crystal cathedral. We entered and the layout was very similar to most others. Its empty altar sat beneath an ornate flag with the Amaymon flag hanging behind it.

Without stopping, my knight continued his stride through the cathedral, passing through the pews and making his way to an open hallway. This area was all constructed the same as any other cathedral: wood and stone as the primary building materials. The crystal windows were designated to the rooms of worship.

At the end of the hallway sat two Saints, their crimson veils pulled over their faces and soft words moving past their lips to one another. As we approached, they stiffened and stood a little straighter. My knight moved swiftly past them with no more than a nod exchanged. *No questioning?*

Not that I was all too familiar with what questions they would ask a man who made a vow to not speak.

The way he spoke to me that first day still rang out in my ears from time to time. I often felt myself reach to speak to him. Almost too often since then. A tinge of an emotion I didn't quite know how to place filled my chest. It wasn't quite sadness, but a sense of loss like the way you feel when you miss someone you hadn't seen in a long time. Even though he was standing next to me, he wore head-to-toe steel with the red mantle flowing behind him, making him a different person than the one I'd spent days riding with.

I ... I missed him.

A set of stairs met us now, and of course he chose to descend them. The stairwell was lit with torches every ten steps or so, leaving us in a constant state of shadows as we made our way down. We passed a few more Saints, but they also paid us no mind.

After a few more minutes, we came up to a large, arched entrance in an unlit tunnel. There were two torches on each side, giving the illusion it wasn't complete blackness down there. He reached up and took one, giving me even less light. He stepped into the tunnel, and a chill crept up my spine. I took a step back, hoping to find where the stairs started.

"Uhh, I'll just wait for you up there, okay." I turned to take another step, but my hood got gently pulled back and I'm turned back to face the tunnel. I let out a deep breath and followed behind him. The torch was doing a fine job of lighting the way, which helped—slightly. The farther we walked into the tunnel, markings on the walls became more visible. Then more and more until legible words surrounded us. He kept walking. If we weren't going to stop and read, then what was the point of traveling down here? Was he following orders Ilias made and sending me to my death? *Was he going to murder me?*

My eyes flew to the sword fashioned at his hip and the dagger on his breastplate scouring over the rest of him to see if I could find any other weapons hidden on his person.

He stopped and turned to me. I leapt back a few steps as he held out the torch.

"Hold this," my knight said dryly. The sound of his voice after so much silence warmed me in a way I didn't understand.

He passed the torch off to me, the flame low as the heat brushed over my skin. He reached both hands up and lifted his helmet from his shoulders tucking it beneath one arm. His free hand reached up and pushed his soft dark waves from his face. The thicker pieces clung together and cascaded down to the nape of his neck.

He turned to me, and in the firelight, the reflection in his eyes created its own type of flame igniting in me. I was afraid; of him, of who I had become, and I couldn't trust myself with the feeblest of things. Least of all, emotions when it came to— *God, why can't I stop this?*

Because when I looked at him and felt him really looking back, it was like a mirror. I wasn't ready to face my reflection. I took in a shaky breath, but didn't cower in his presence, I didn't run. I stared at him and I didn't *want* to look away yet.

His eyes were dark and deep and vast. His gaze matched mine and for a moment we were caught in a game of wills until

I saw his eyes rake over me, landing on the broken and bruised skin.

A new kind of fire leapt behind his eyes. Palpable rage. I could feel it light up the air around us. He turned and looked over the wall before him, his hand tracing over the stone. His chest expanded with a deep breath, and he blew it out slow and controlled through his lips. He set the helmet down, pulled his gloves off and crouched to the floor, picking up what looked to be chalk.

Silently, I watched him, soaking in as much of him as possible. I never thought I would ever, in a million years, be standing here with him and not want to call him out for being an ass and just—just look at him. All of him. The tan-olive skin, his perfect fucking nose, and his lips. God, when did I start thinking so much about his lips?

His eyes never left the wall, but his lips lifted at the corners. "Enjoying the view?" he said with a soft chuckle.

I smiled and turned to face my own wall. "Maybe I am." The soft confirmation left my mouth in a shaky breath.

"I can take that back now," he said, reaching for the torch.

I pulled it out of reach. "Not so fast ... I think I rather like holding it."

He raised a hand in submission.

"Where are we?" I asked.

"We are in the undercroft."

"Yes, I am familiar with cathedral foundations, but this is not just any undercroft."

He turned to face me. "A lot of the townspeople have come to call this place the *Vas Cordis.*"

I met his dark eyes once again. "What does that mean?"

He seemed so much closer then. Like we had been pulled in by an invisible force. He stood behind me and I felt the pressure of his presence grow thick against me.

"It means fallen heart. It's where people come to leave the names of their loved ones, to honor those who have passed or those who wish to make a proclamation. The youth find their way down here and write their sweetheart's names to show how serious they are about them. *Not quite a proposal*, but a promise."

All those markings and words, all names. All people who cared so deeply about someone else that they loved and wanted to immortalize them. It was inspiring.

"Is this only for the people from this place?"

"Not entirely. I suppose the majority of them are, but only because it's not well known to outsiders."

I was stuck thinking about the people I had lost; Kairos was gone, and my father had passed away when I was young, and my brother, Thorian, was out there, hopefully alive and well, but ... God, you never know. It would be only right to honor those who had passed on into the next realm.

"Can I—can I write some names?" The words came out heavier than I'd intended.

He placed the chalk into my hand, his fingers lingering for just a moment too long, and goosebumps ravaged my skin. He was very, very close.

"Of course." He took the torch from my other hand, and I stepped forward, holding out the thin piece of chalk to the stone wall.

The first name was the hardest to write, then one by one all those I had lost were now looking back at me. A single tear escaped and ran down my sore cheek. I reached up to wipe it and winced.

Still looking at the wall, I said, "Do you have any names you wish to write?"

He grabbed the chalk from me. His body, once again, was so very close. Reaching over my shoulder, he touched the chalk to the wall, pausing for a moment and he slowly and carefully started to write A-l-e-d-a.

My lips parted and my breathing hitched at my name. My real name.

Remaining silent, he lowered the chalk back into my hand. Looking down at the little stick of white in my palm, my heart swelled. This object seemed too small to cause the onslaught of emotions I was feeling. But knowing I was seen. I wasn't the Queen Consort, or Evangeline, or *some whore*. I was Aleda.

I pressed the chalk against the wall; this pull of reciprocation filling me. My eyes widened. I didn't—I didn't know his name. A huff of air rushed past my lips. He had always just been "My knight." This whole time I had been such a stuck-up snob. All this time we'd spent together and not once, not one time did I ever think to ask. A wave of guilt hit me like a tidal wave. The knowledge of him being there behind me, waiting. Waiting for me to write something he knows I do not know.

My hand started to shake, and the tip of the chalk broke off on the wall. A small, sad sigh escaped my mouth and then in a moment his hand closed over mine. The touch of his callouses were rough against my soft knuckles. A fire filled my blood.

He slowly moved my hand against the wall and spelled
G-i-d-e-o-n.

Gideon.

He released my hand and leaned down close to my right ear and said, "A promise for a promise."

I turned to face him, his towering figure looking down at me; I was like a fly caught in a web, stuck in place between his body, the wall and his heavy gaze. His deep onyx eyes searched mine, catching glints of the torch light. A halo of gold found their way into them. His eyes finally fixed on my mouth.

My lips were now too dry, and I slid my tongue over them, trying to add a slim amount of moisture. He found my gaze and I stared back, not wanting to miss a moment of this. Of looking at him, unbridled and in front of me.

My breathing sped up and I'd started to feel a bit light-headed. His free hand reached up and cupped my chin. My heart was fully in my stomach now and my lungs had shriveled in on themselves.

He leaned down and placed a single whisper of a kiss on my forehead, the only place that didn't hurt on my ravaged face. He stayed for a long moment, and I closed my eyes, letting myself feel like I was floating.

"Gideon ..." His name felt foreign on my lips.

He pulled away, looking at me through deeply hooded eyes.

"Aleda?" he said raising a brow.

I bit my lip slightly, avoiding looking at him. His body was too close. The space in here was too tight. He was touching me. I looked up and found his eyes still on me.

"Will you kiss me?"

A soft smile pulled up on his lips. "I just did."

His breath wafted over me, bringing once again the intoxicating smokey musk and pine.

My mouth hung open slightly at his comment. *God, he was insufferable.* I took a deep breath in. "Yes, I guess you did."

He leaned down next to my ear, my skin vibrating with tension as he let out two words that I clung to like a hymn. "So impatient ..."

The buzzing feeling in my head grew stronger and I felt heavy. Blackness invaded my vision, and I fell into darkness.

Twenty-Three

Something cool against my cheek stirred me. Little droplets of water trickled down into my hair, tickling my skin. I heard a voice in the room, quickly hushed and the worry lining it was palpable. It grew more frantic with each passing word until the volume built to where I could finally make out his words.

"She fell, she got her foot stuck in these fucking rugs, I swear I would never lay a finger on her ..." Ilias. His voice traveled, like he couldn't even keep up with the story he was spinning.

I finally opened my eyes, moved the wet cloth from my face, and sat up. My cheek was still sore, but it did feel better. My lip on the other hand. I ran my tongue over the split skin and tasted a tart herbal flavor, the fragrance familiar. It must be the salve from Marigold.

The room went quiet as I sat up, my eyes sweeping the room. I saw Ilias near the entrance to the room speaking to a concerned-looking man peering through the door at me. He must have been who Ilias was lying to.

Then to my left I saw my knight seated in a chair close to the bed. Back in his full armor, helmet, and gloves back in place and next to the roaring fire. Everything was starting to come back to me, the cathedral, the tunnel, the names ... his name. God, his name.

Gideon.

Gideon.

I looked at him, the words hanging on the tip of my tongue. I wanted to speak them more than anything. To make sure it wasn't a dream. That it was real. That I had asked him to kiss me—oh, God.

A wave of embarrassment rippled over me, and my cheeks grew fiery hot to the touch. Then to only *black out*. I was going to pass away from the mere shame of it.

Trying to stand, I noticed I was still in my same clothes, but my boots were missing, and my feet were clean. I noticed Gideon looking in my direction. I glanced back to my feet, not wanting to hold the gaze of anyone in this room.

"You didn't have to do that," I said in just above a whisper to him.

Ilias closed the door on the man and walked over to me, placing his hands on the foot of the bed.

"You're awake, how are you feeling?" His eyes were red and puffy and the look of apology on his face seemed sincere. He came closer to me on the bed, kneeling and grabbing my hands in his.

"I am so sorry. I—I was drinking and not acting like myself. You deserved none of that." He reached his hand to my face, and I turned away on instinct. His touch was one I'd craved and yearned for, but now, I only felt disdain and disgust. Tears stung the back of my throat, but I refused to let them loose over this.

Over him.

His hand shrunk back. "I understand. I *will* make this up to you."

I looked toward Gideon. His fists were balled up and he looked away to the door. Ilias followed my line of sight. He stood, facing Gideon. "You're free to go," he said in a low voice.

Gideon turned his head toward me, not moving from his seat.

Ilias took a deep breath, his shoulders raising and tightening. "I said—you can go," he said in a clipped tone.

Gideon didn't move. Ilias's shoulders were almost up to his ears, his neck growing red; his patience was wearing thin, and the boiling point was almost here once again.

"Get the fuck out before I remove your status." The words leaked out through his tight, gritted teeth. The threat ate into my own chest. I couldn't let that happen. To be stuck with just Ilias would be torture.

I stood and placed a hand on Ilias's shoulder, moving past him to get in between him and Gideon.

"Thank you, Knight. I will be needing more rest now." I turned from him and back to Ilias, whose eyes were filled with intense emotions, his face stiff and pinched.

Gideon stood from the chair, giving me a bow and made his way to the door. He left it open, and Ilias walked over, separating from me for a blessed moment and slammed it shut.

He extinguished all the lights aside from the fireplace, crawling into bed. Without choice, I laid down, facing away from him. I hoped, prayed he left me alone after everything that had happened.

All too soon I felt his hands travel over my stomach. He pulled me into him. His erection was already against my back, and I felt bile well up inside of me. I used to want nothing more than him, and now it just felt wrong. His hands roamed over me, following the curves of my body and clasping my breasts. He nuzzled in close to me and his breath teased the baby hairs on my neck.

I tapped his hand, "Hey, I um, can't, my monthly."

Just like that, he pulled his hand away, almost too quickly. He sat up and took a deep breath.

"Well, then I may just go and take care of this myself then." He headed into the bathing chamber. After a few minutes, he stepped back out and crawled back into bed. He leaned over and kissed my cheek before saying goodnight.

I stared into the dwindling fireplace for what felt like hours before finally getting up to sit in the large chair my knight, Gideon, had sat in. I realized how much his size had filled the chair as I pulled my legs up and reclined with ample space. My mind wandered as the low licking flames created a hypnotizing trance. It was almost like they too were breathing, in and out, matching my own rhythm.

The mural in the church floated into my mind's eye. The bleached and tattered appearance held similarities to the ones in the forgotten hall of the Oriens castle. How had we come so far in just a couple hundred years? How was it all forgotten? If it was truly where we began, then why did we deny it so? Deny its power and very existence to the point of claiming perjury and banishment to Abaddon?

Unable to stay seated any longer, I went to leave this forsaken room and my bedmate. I wrapped myself in a cloak and turned the handle as slowly and gently as possible, closing it with the same care.

Once outside, I settled back against the door next to Gideon, in his usual post. This inn was a small step up from where we'd stayed the other night, but not by much.

My mind wandered back to that night. I wanted nothing more than to go back there, to just a couple of days in the past. Back to a different person sharing my bed.

A soft heat bloomed in my lower stomach as I remembered how his body on top of mine had felt, how warm his skin was as it rubbed up against me. I closed my eyes and leaned my head against the door.

"Thank you, for earlier. I know that you are meant to work for Ilias but—"

"I am meant to protect you," he cut me off in a dark hushed tone.

"Getting a little brave now, are we?"

"Why aren't you asleep?" he asked, instead of acknowledging my comment.

"I can't, not the most comfortable bedmate, if I'm being honest." I sighed again and a long pause stretched out between us.

He turned to me and said, "And you've had more comfortable bedmates then?"

There it went again—that fucking hot blush crawling up and over my skin. *I felt like I was on fucking fire.* Even through the little slits in his helmet, he must have seen just how ridiculous I looked, glowing red with a beaten and bruised face.

"If I said no?"

He leaned in closer, almost close enough to touch his helmet to my overheated skin, and let me tell you, that cool steel would feel like a branding iron with how hot I was becoming.

"Then I would say you're a better liar than I thought."

My mouth dropped open and he moved back, turning the knob and pushing the door open.

"Go," he said as he gestured into the room like some child that's out past their bedtime.

I sighed deeply and heeded his instructions. As I was just about to fully slink through the door, I heard a whisper next to my ear, "good girl."

A shock shot through me and went straight to my core. I turned to look at him, but he was facing straight and back in his post. I peeked through the small opening in the door. Ilias was still passed out in bed. The last thing I wanted to do was lie next to that man, so I curled up on the settee and closed my eyes to prepare for what may come tomorrow.

TWENTY-FOUR

THE NEXT MORNING, I WOKE UP WITH ILIAS MISSING from the bed, having left it in a mess of quilts and pillows lining the floor and half strewn from the bed.

My face felt better, and I traced over my still sore lip, but it seemed that the skin had knitted closed overnight with the help of the salve.

I sighed; today was the day we'd meet the Queen of Paymon. I knew very little about her from my time in the Oriens, but what I did remember from Kairos and the Commander was that she had deep ties with Amaymon, the kingdom of the south. The amount of influence involved with her was unknown to me.

Getting up from the settee I gathered my things. If we were to meet her today, I didn't want to be the reason for the lack of punctuality.

I ventured out into the hallway. There was no knight or guard at the door and still no sign of Ilias. I walked to the area with the horses, and everyone but me was already ready to leave. Ilias came from behind and lifted me up into a spin, making a scene of his strong affections. I all but rolled my eyes after what had happened last night.

Ilias took my face in his hands and pulled me into a kiss. His lips traveled down to my ear, and I felt his hot breath on me. I couldn't take it. I pulled away slightly, not trying to bring any unnecessary attention to my discomfort, but I needed space.

"How long until we arrive?" I asked, giving him my best smile.

He grabbed my hand in his and walked me to a horse. "We will enter by this evening. Once we make it through each gate, we will be allowed entrance." He took my things from me and placed them in a saddlebag, turning back to me.

"Each gate is a checkpoint. Our things will require inspection and then once we are fully cleared, we will be allowed entrance into the castle. Probably just before nightfall."

Nightfall? It was still so early; it would take that long to get through the gates? At least we would be entering in the veil of darkness; my bruised skin would be better hidden then.

He gave me a hoist up onto my horse and rubbed one of my thighs, giving it a squeeze. His public forced affections were making me sick to my stomach.

Finally heading off to his horse, he left me be. Gideon rode up next to me on his same large black steed, looking powerful and domineering. He went to ride next to me, tilting his head to the side. I gave him a half smile and led my horse onward, keeping far to the back and pulling my cloak's hood over my face.

We made it through the final checkpoint by sunset. The golden colors cascaded along the sky and reflected off the crystal cathedral not too far away from us; its spires lit up like torches in the amber lights.

As the castle made its way into view, our company was greeted by the clergymen, but no queen, which for most would be considered a slight, but we were quite late compared to our expected time.

Being led to a place to dismount our horses, I was the last to arrive. Most of the men had already taken off their bags and made their way up into the castle. Ilias had made his way inside first, of course; he had to keep the best face.

Holding back a bit, I rode up next to Gideon. He had removed his gloves and was reaching into a pocket to give his black stallion a few sugar cubes as a treat. Once we entered, I was sure they would be taken to the stables and given a much more fitting meal.

Coming to a full stop, I began my dismount and felt two hands come up to my waist to help me down from my horse. My feet touched the solid ground, and I quickly turned to face the only person it could be. Gideon stood tall, looming over me, his hands staying on my waist for a moment longer. Probably too long. He lowered them to his sides, and I reached out. Just for a second I let my hands graze over his knuckles.

The sugar crystals on them transferred to my fingertips. I brought one up to my mouth and wrapped my lips around it, cleaning it of the crystals and savoring the sweet flavor.

He reached forward, grabbing my hand, yanking it out my mouth. I felt a blush coming up over my cheeks. *God, that was not subtle at all.* He grabbed my things from my saddlebag and walked in ahead of me. I followed, my head lowered.

Inside, we were directed to the great receiving hall. The walls contained more murals than I had ever seen, each wall decorated in a visual history with floor to ceiling depictions of the people here, pre and post-fall. I'd never seen anything like this before.

The scene before me was that of the old god Zaphon. He had long black hair and pale white skin, and a crown atop his head made of shiny, black crystals. He sat on a large black throne. Under the depiction it said something in the old Amaymon. But Zaphon's face was empty, though. Painted over. A shiver rode up my spine.

Being escorted further into the grounds, we crossed a bridge and entered into the garden. There were fruit trees that held such luscious bounties they weighed down the branches, and rows and rows of flowers, their blooms closed under the night sky. Farther in we passed a maze. It took up a good chunk of the land here and had walls twice as tall as any of the patrons entering inside.

As we crossed fully through, servants brought us to the guest apartments. It was a large block of buildings with a grand stone hall between the two sides of rooms; there must have been over a dozen here complete with stairs leading up to a second level.

My room was on the second story, with a balcony over-looking the garden and a perfect view into the maze. Its tall hedges and intricate shapes were hypnotic to my tired eyes.

A young woman was showing me around the space: there was a closet of dresses available to pick from, a sideboard with glasses and a pitcher of water, a private bathing chamber and a hearth with two plush chairs sitting across from the bed.

Ilias stepped through the doors and into the room, his steps were confident, and self-assured with echoes coming from each hard sole of his boot filling the room.

"These guest apartments are quite large, not what I was expecting. But then, should I expect much less from the gracious Queen of Paymon?"

He walked to the bed and stroked his fingers along the intricate duvet, "I'll be back after my conversation with the Queen, not sure when I'll be done, so don't wait up for me."

The young woman who brought me in visibly stiffened at his comment. Her eyes darted back and forth between us, taking careful note of our hands. Mostly the left one.

"I am sorry, Sir, but the Queen does not allow unmarried guests to share quarters. You will be staying in your own apartment down the hall and Lady Evangeline will remain here."

My heart soared across the room to the heavens at her words. Thank God for this girl and thank God for the Queen's morals.

Ilias, to my surprise, didn't seem upset by her proclamation. He just stood for a moment, his mouth open slightly, like there were words wanting to come out. Thankfully they did not.

A royal guard stood in the doorway, calling our attention to him. "The Queen is ready to speak with you now, Lord Terrell."

Ilias took heed of his words and exited the room, as did the young woman who'd shown me around. As the door was closing behind them, I spied the all-too-familiar figure standing outside.

My heart kicked up at just the sight of him, and I didn't even know what to think about all of this. About him. I knew I couldn't stay here or even stay with Ilias at this rate. I needed to get word North. I needed to get the fuck out of here.

My eyes traveled back to the door to my room. The only thing that would give me any inclination to stay was the very person hired to look after me. Was there more to that? Was that even something viable to seek after? Was I just being a stupid girl and falling for anyone who gave me the fucking time of day?

I sat on the plush mattress and lay back, throwing my hands over my face. I breathed in deep through my nose and released a controlled exhale out of my mouth.

Everything is fine. I'm fine, I thought as I pushed up off the bed, walking to finally take in the view from my balcony. I had the most perfect view of the maze just past the floral garden. Its intricate crosses and patterns were expertly cut out. Small lanterns gave a faint glow in the waning light showed pathways through the dense hedges. What it would be like to get stuck out there?

TWENTY-FIVE

A FEW HOURS LATER, A MEAL WAS BROUGHT UP. IT consisted of a large flat fish, a medley of roasted vegetables, and some light-colored grain. The flavors were very foreign to me, but I enjoyed them, tasting hints of spice and a tangy vinegar.

After finishing, I walked the perimeter of my room. A few times. Being alone was a godsend, but it was also increasingly boring. I could rummage through my journals but most of the language was still written in old Amaymon and without a reference book or a key, it was close to useless information.

I paused, stilling my stride. This place must have a library, or if not a library, a room of records with an Amaymon reference book. This place was allied with them. There had to be people who spoke it.

The young girl who brought me here, God, I wished I had asked for her name; she might know where I could find it. If it were any other circumstance other than in a reigning Queen's home, I would have wandered out to do my own searching, but I didn't know the level of freedom she allowed her guests, if any, and I didn't want to draw any unwanted attention to myself.

I decided to ask whoever brought me my next meal what the rules were for guests. But until then—I let out a sigh—I was stuck in here.

I eyed the water pitcher on the sideboard. As refreshing as it may be, I was in the mood for something a bit more ... *enthusiastic.*

Promptly, I started to rummage through all the cabinets below, seeking out a more exuberant spirit. I began to lose hope until I reached the final cabinet of the sideboard, moved a few tall glasses out of the way, and saw the clear decanter nestled at the very back. Pulling it out and taking a closer look at the bottle, I noticed it was clearly old and had a thick layer of dust on it. The label was long worn off. Who knew how long this had been aging back there?

I pulled out the cork with some resistance and took a sniff of the bottle's contents; it was thick and smoky with a heavy citrus influence and something else I couldn't exactly place. Jasmine maybe?

Standing, I grabbed a glass and poured myself a heavy help-ing. *Fuck it, it's not like I'm going to be leaving this room for the night.*

I took in the deep, heady scent one more time before bringing it to my lips. The feeling of warmth immediately met my tongue with a welcomed burn.

My balcony door was still wide open, and chill winds blew into the room, filling it with fresh air and life. I had felt suffo-cated for so long with Ilias that even the near blistering cold on my skin felt like a release.

I walked once more to the ledge, placing my glass on the smooth stone. Closing my eyes and breathing in deep, the liquor was coursing through me, and I felt a light feeling in my head already. The aging of this drink must really amplify the effects.

I took another stiff sip and set it down, spinning the base in small circles, growing entranced by the small rings of moisture it left behind.

My head started to swim, and the dizziness from yesterday came back full force. I reached up and gripped my fingers around my Legion Stone, feeling the sting eat into my palm, stronger than it had ever been before. Jerking my hand away, I knocked my glass to the floor in front of me. Shards of it riddled across the tile.

The door to my room flung open and in walked two knights. Or one. Or two. My vision was going double until they finally melded and met in the middle to form the steel giant standing in the entrance of my room.

I took a step forward and then the next, my toe catching on the threshold of the balcony. I fell into the mess of glass. Tiny shards embedded themselves into my palms, but I could hardly feel it. My body felt like it no longer belonged to me, and I was just a visitor watching things unfold behind my eyes.

I held up my hands seeing the deep red bead to the surface of my palms and trickle down my arms. Then I finally registered what happened. Blood, so much blood. His blood, the black swirling blood of the demons. Screams and red. So much red.

My hearing started to go fuzzy, and my heart thrummed deep in my chest. I could feel it. See it. My hands were numb, and my heart was too. So much fucking blood.

Gideon dropped to his knees in front of me, throwing off his gloves and reaching out for a piece of fabric hanging on one of the plush chairs. He gripped my hands in his and wrapped the cloth around my palms to staunch the blood. Holding them firm.

I heard mumbles, whispers, but couldn't make them out.

"*... couldn't ...*"

"*... I couldn't ...*"

"*I couldn't save them ...*"

Tears flooded my vision, and words broke through. I realized they were coming from me. I was saying them as the tears ran down my cheeks. My body shook. No, I was being shaken. I looked up and focused my eyes.

Gideon sat before me, his helmet removed, his eyes filled with a different emotion than I had seen before. It was his steady hands on my shoulders, shaking me, speaking to me and trying to get my attention.

"Aleda, did you take something? What did you eat? Aleda, please, speak to me." His tone was hushed but forceful.

I tried to force my tongue to move, but it wasn't cooperating anymore. His hands reached under my arms, and he lifted me to my feet, pulling me into the bathing chamber and setting me on top of the counter near the faucet, my body sliding against the cold stone wall behind me. He started to run the water, and I fought to keep my eyes open.

Cold water was splashed over my face and my chest, the shock making me shoot up and take in a deep and sharp inhale. "Fuck!" I shouted, finally able to get control of my voice again.

He held a glass of water to my mouth, and I drunk it down as fast as I could, finally breathing in a steadier rhythm.

He gripped my chin in his fingers and pulled my face to look at him, to stare into his pretty dark brown eyes—no, not brown, they were a deep honey. Golden. So beautiful. So very beautiful.

He paused, his brows knitting together, and his eyes exploring my face.

"Beautiful?" he questioned.

I could feel my eyes grow wide, why would he say that?

"What?"

"You just called me beautiful."

"No, I didn't I—"

"Don't lie to me," he said, cutting me off as he moves to unwrap my hands, "Look away if the blood is going to bother you."

I didn't. I couldn't bring myself to. My palms were still a mess. It was not something that required stitches, but all the glass needed to get taken out.

He kneeled in front of me, still tall enough to get a good look at my palms even though I sat all the way up on the counter. Using his fingers, he started to pull out the shards of glass, placing each tiny piece in a pile. The glass coated in my blood sat on the wood, glossy and crimson.

His right hand cradled mine while the left plucked at my torn flesh. The feel of his bare skin on mine was all that I kept my focus on. Not on the blood or the twinges of pain with the removal, but how his hands were so rough and so gentle all at the same time.

It had been just last night since our time in the underground tunnel in the cathedral and that was the last time he'd removed his helmet in front of me. The last time I had seen his face and when he told me his name and—*nope*, not going there.

My head was still swimming from the liquor, and I needed to leave those thoughts in the past. Those memories were only going to get me in trouble right now.

But he was kneeling before me covered in my blood, how could I possibly—not look at how thick and dense his lashes were, or the way just a few strands of his dark wavy hair fell forward, connecting to his strong brows? Or how he had a perfectly sculpted nose that sat above two very kissable lips? *Stop! Stop, brain. We can't do this.* We, as in me and my brain.

He looked at me, eyes dark and boring into me.

"And what is *this?*"

No, he's not a mind reader, he can't be. Was I saying that *out loud?*

"Yes, you are."

My heartrate picked up. Was I saying *everything* out loud?

"Yes," he said dryly, but I could see his lips picking up into a smile and God, that sent a shockwave to my core. He had the most beautiful smile.

"Thank you."

Finally taking control of my tongue, I asked, "Am I saying every thought that pops into my fucking head?"

This time the smile was gone, his mouth in a tight line. "What did you drink?"

"I'm not sure, I—I found a bottle of liquor in the cabinets. I thought it may be a type of aged whiskey."

He let go of my hands, unlocked the door, and brought the decanter back into the bathroom. He poured a little into the sink basin and watched it swirl. The smokey citrus smell wafted into the room. His eyes widened and a huge smile came over his face. He laughed so hard I swore tears formed in his eyes.

"This is *not* liquor, Amri."

My heart beat faster at the sound of a nickname.

"Then what is it?"

"It's Labra Laxa. It's a kind of truth serum. It works by inebriating the consumer and shortening the brain to mouth connection." He set it down on the counter behind me.

"That's fucking stupid ... why would it be in my room in the first place?"

My tongue still felt so heavy as I spoke, each word a struggle to pass my lips. I threw my hand over my mouth, not wanting to let out anymore unwanted proclamations. "Ouch!" The force shoved a glass piece deeper into my palm.

He put the decanter down on the counter behind me and

knelt before me, examining my hands again. He was silent at work, whereas I just had my mind running in circles. Why would that drink be in my room? Could I ask him to stay in the room while I slept as extra security?

My room. At night. Sleeping ... images from my dream the night we shared the bed in the inn flooded me, the way he looked all covered in my— I looked down and felt the words making their way from my brain to my goddamn treacherous tongue.

My legs were spread apart, and he was kneeling between them just like my dream ...

I physically bit my lip to keep from any other words from escaping.

His eyes shot up; brows raised, in true surprise as a smile crept across his face, showing me his teeth and revealing deep long smile lines in his cheeks and little crinkles near his eyes.

"Ahh ... the same dream where you were making all those *little noises?*"

My face turned bright red. I could feel it burning down to my toes.

He pulled out a particularly poignant shard, and a sharp gasp escaped my lips.

"Kind of like that," he said, still intent on taking the shards from my palm. It hurt, and thankfully so because it distracted me from anymore unwelcome thoughts.

Once he finished, he brought over a wet cloth to clean up the blood and wash out the cuts. Then he wrapped my hands in a little fabric to keep the cuts dry. Finally, he got up and went back to his helmet and gloves. My stomach dropped. He was going back to being the knight, not Gideon.

I stood, examining my new, mummified hands, still feeling the buzz from the truth serum. A pulling feeling rippled through my chest, the kind where I knew I was going to deeply regret what I said next.

"I like when you touch me." I paused briefly. "If I can think of one positive thing out of all the pain I have experienced these last few days, it would be that you were there every time." I ran my teeth over my bottom lip, knowing I'd just said too much. It was stupid and immature and just supposed to be a thought kept inside my brain and now it hung in the dead air between us.

I threw my head back, letting out an exasperated sigh. "I am so incredibly over this Labra Labra shit."

Standing straighter, I looked over at him. He stared at me, his eyes dark and heavy, with another new look decorating his face. He stalked over to me. Standing too close, but still torturously too far away. My skin felt like it was stretching to close the gap between us.

His towering figure was hard and serious as he reached out his right arm. My skin hummed, wanting any form of contact. But it never came.

Instead, he reached past me, grabbed the decanter and said, "Labra *Laxa,*" and brought it to his lips. He took a long swig. Small droplets raced down his chin. He dropped the decanter onto the counter next to me with a clatter. His hands gripped the counter on each side of me, his knuckles turning white. This man had ensnared me, pulling me out of the mud as I'd thought I had given my final breath to the earth, who took an arrow for me and fought for me.

There was a storm brewing behind his eyes, and I was caught at the epicenter.

He reached down, lifting my chin to stare into my eyes. His mouth was only a few inches from mine now.

"Touching you is like torture for me."

I winced at his words, trying to pull away, and he grabbed

my chin harder, forcing me to look at him. He moved in closer, speaking in just above a whisper.

"Every time my skin brushes yours, I know just how fleeting that moment will be. How quickly it will end. I long to feel every inch of you, Amri. To taste you." His voice dropped lower, and he moved his hand down now to my lower back, pressing me flush to him.

"I wish to hold you in my arms and have you calling out *my* name, *not his*. Mine. I long for you more than you can ever imagine."

Knowing what he meant almost broke me in half. The way I had been with Ilias in the Midlands, before he'd showed me what kind of man he truly was.

He leaned his forehead down to press against mine, "The feeling of my skin on yours tears open whatever wall I had just spent so long building back up from the last time. Every brick, I lay over, and over again, crumbles to the earth. I have dreamt of you every night since then." His breath was heavy brushing past my face, smelling of the smoke and citrus from the serum.

There was no lie in his words. There couldn't be. I knew firsthand just how potent it was and how quickly just a few sips had loosened my tongue.

Our mouths inched closer, and I felt the veil from the truth serum fading away. His lips hovered over mine. I closed my eyes and waited for the press of his to finally meet mine, but it never came.

I opened my eyes. His were closed, his two brows once again knit together in a hard line.

"Goodnight, Aleda."

My breath hitched and all I could get out was a curt, "Goodnight."

He released me, grabbing his things and walked out the door.

Twenty-Six

Gideon

Closing her door behind me, I made my way down the halls. I reached for a young guard and wrenched him by his collar, getting his attention roughly, but effectively, as his eyes widened. I could see he was young and still wet behind the ears.

I brought him to face me and then pointed to Aleda's door. He understood my silent order and nodded, "Yes, sir. I'll stay up here."

Shoving him off, I made my way outside. I needed air. I needed to get some distance between me and anyone else before I ended up saying anything.

Stalking through the gardens, I found a small, well-hidden alcove. And I leaned into it, pulling off my helmet and facing the cold wall of the castle. I leaned my forehead on it and took a deep breath. The moment the exhale passed my lips, thoughts of her flooded me. Like they always did. She snuck in, uninvited and made herself home, burrowing deep inside my fucking head.

I punched my gloved hand into the wall. A small piece of stone crumbled beneath it and the soft, throbbing pain brought me back to earth.

Why did she have to be so fucking clumsy? If she could just sit and do nothing like any other woman in the realm, then none of this would have even been a goddamn issue.

The moment I broke my vow to speak to her, I knew it was over. I knew she had gotten so deep inside of me that I couldn't move through the rest of my time with her and not speak out.

"Do you have a fucking death wish?"

The fear that gripped me the moment I saw her run back into that man's clutches. Right into her possible death. And she always did the same self-assured rogue behaviors. Climbing down a keep wall at midnight to sneak out to a lake, *alone.* She could have been— God.

I rubbed my hand roughly down my face, pressing my thumb and forefinger into my eyes and breathing as the serum worked through me.

—But she'd looked so beautiful then. So free, going into the water naked and glowing in the moonlight. She'd swam across the water with petals falling around her, like an actual goddess. She was ethereal. She was mesmerizing.

This wasn't supposed to happen. She wasn't supposed to be this way.

Leaning my head back I let out an exasperated laugh, because I couldn't believe I'd told her all of that. The serum was fucking fast acting.

When I was kneeling before her, and she'd looked down at me and said that, I could have fucking taken her right there. I could have taken her back at the inn, when it was just us two.

When she crawled onto me in the middle of the night. I could have pushed her off. I should have.

But the way she'd felt against me was like a flame had ignited on my skin and through my body. She pulled me into her atmosphere, and I was stuck, this other worldly draw I had never felt before. I didn't understand it. I'd fought against it for so long. Keeping my distance, being unkind. And she had too; she'd fought me on everything. She'd even slammed doors in my face. I wanted her to hate me. Because if she could stay away from me, then she would be better.

I was the weak one. I'd broken long before she ever had.

I leaned my head against the wall and brought my hand up to the collar of my chest plate. It was so tight and heavy. I tried to take some centering breaths, squeezing my eyes shut one more time. My mind was a whirlwind of memories and visions of her. Of how her body felt beneath me. When her nightgown rode up against my legs and I was flush with her very center and only a couple pieces of fabric had held me back from her.

My cock had strained against my pants in that room, and she'd felt it. I saw the look on her face. She knew I wanted her then. Just the thought of her now, of filling her and hearing my name on her lips. I couldn't stand it. I'm reined in by my breaches, but if she saw. If she saw what she does to me.

Fucking enough.

I replaced my helmet and headed for the maze. I needed to distract myself. Getting lost in a maze at night sounded like a big enough distraction.

Twenty-Seven

Please tell me how I was supposed to just sit in my room after whatever that was? This man had just told me the most intimate things I'd ever heard in my life and left. Left me to stew and sit there alone.

I pulled out my journals to find something to occupy my thoughts. They were so shrouded in Gideon. Choosing to look further through Kairos's journal, I flipped through the pages, and a flash of red caught my eye. I flipped back to find it, a red circle with an intricate sigil stood out on the yellowing paper. Gideon's cloak had the same symbol: The Crimson Cloth Knights.

The surrounding words were in Old Amaymon, so all the information was useless, but I found myself tracing over the intricate loops and crossing lines. God why ... Why was he *everywhere?* The stingy feeling I felt when I'd last crossed over the sigils was now a complacent hum against my fingertips.

A woman laughing down below the balcony caught my attention. Her high-pitched giggles and chirps broke through the silence of the growing evening. Becoming restless and still alone, I made my way back to the balcony, curious to see what was going on below. Each step reverberated through my body as the buzz from the truth serum wore off. My hands stung and my brain was a mess. I wanted nothing more than an actual stiff drink.

Beneath me, a pretty, young maiden was making herself very familiar with a young man in a cloak. I knew leering at people from above was not considered the most proper, but I didn't care in that moment. I'd claim insanity before telling anyone what had happened tonight between Gideon and myself.

She twirled in his arm, dancing under the moonlit night sky. As she was pulled back against his body, the hood of his cloak was flung back from his head, revealing a cropped head of hair. My throat caught as his face came more into view. Ilias. It was Ilias with the young girl. He was dancing with her. I watched as he leaned forward and kissed her. Intimately. Passionately. His hands fumbled beneath her skirts, and she giggled.

I slunk back in the shadows, stepping back until I hit a wall and slumped to the ground. He'd been in here no more than a few hours ago and the handmaiden was well aware of our *status*. Even though I wanted nothing to do with him, embarrassment blazed through me. I was supposed to be his and now he was rifling through another girl's skirts right below my fucking window.

The realization hit me. He was just *in my roo*m. He knows I'm up here and was doing it anyway. Rage bubbled through me. How dare he treat me so carelessly last night, then kiss me publicly, then now, grab at a girl right below my fucking window?

I took a deep breath, calming myself, and stood. This was enough. I would not allow myself to be treated this way. To be humiliated. I was the Queen of the Kingdom of Oriens. I was a strong and powerful woman. The maid's giggles began to fade. I glanced out the window, seeing them head into the maze.

<hr>

I opened my door a crack and noticed a new guard stationed there. Feeling a sense of relief and uncertainty at the same time, I made my way out.

"Can I help you, my lady?" he said, stopping me in my tracks.

"Oh yes, I am quite interested in a midnight snack. Would you be able to point me in the direction of the kitchen?"

He looked at me with a puzzled expression.

"We can have something brought up for you if you'd like."

"That's alright, I couldn't trouble anyone for my little peckishness. I can make my way through. Is there a servant's entrance available?"

"Of course, continue down the stairs and take the immediate left through the slim door."

"Thank you. What was your name?"

"Godrick, my lady."

"Thank you, Godrick." I gave him a sly wink.

I started off the way he directed, made my way down the stairs heading straight for the maze. But there were two royal guards chatting right outside of it, dressed head to toe in the vibrant colors of the Paymon royals. It was more of an elaborate costume than utility.

Pressing my back to the wall nearest to them, I kept myself out of view hoping to hear what they were saying.

"Have you received any news back about—"

The guard's question was cut off by the other tossing an

elbow into his gut. A soft grunt was all I could hear, until the other one spoke in a more hushed tone.

"Not *here*. You know full well that idiot is in there and if he catches wind of any of this, it'll be our heads."

Idiot?

Ilias.

I pushed my fingers into my face, realizing I was the only person in the whole realm that didn't know of Ilias and his reputation. Either way, I needed to get past them. I wracked my brain for any possible thing I could say as to why I wanted to go in. But other than to get lost and never come back, I had nothing to tell them.

I snuck to the corner of the wall I was hiding behind and tried to peek at the guards. Both stood at attention, no longer speaking. I heard footsteps coming from the opposite end of the hall.

A woman with olive tan skin and a mass of dark brown curly hair was making her way down to the two guards. Their posture stiffened immediately, and they bowed as she stopped in front of them. She said something unintelligible, and they saluted, leaving the area. *Odd*. I turned the corner farther and realized she was no longer there either.

The entrance to the maze was wide open, and I closed the distance quickly, entering. The atmosphere was ominous and looming. The lanterns at each corner did very little, and I was cast into darkness beneath its high walls until I made it beyond the eerie glow.

I thought I'd done a well enough job memorizing what I could see from my balcony, but I was at a loss. The first turn was a dead end, and then the next.

Panic rose at the thought of not only confronting Ilias but also being stuck in here for the night until someone came to look for me.

Godrick thought I was down in the kitchen. How long would it take for him to scout over into the maze? Maybe once enough time had passed, I could shout, call out for help and see if they could follow my voice.

Some shuffling came from just up ahead—the sound of footsteps on the dry dirt. Ilias was so close; I could feel it. I wanted to catch him in the fucking act and tell him that he was just like the other scum I had seen my whole life in the courts.

My pace matched the blustering tempo of my heart. Under the lantern in the corner, I turned and slammed headfirst into a steel wall. I bounced back and a hand grasped around my wrist, yanking me into solid arms that wrapped around my middle. My breath felt like it had been knocked from my chest.

As I forced air back into my lungs, the familiar notes of smoke, musk, and pine surrounded me.

"Gideon," I breathed out, half in surprise, half from the way my lungs had emptied after I'd slammed into him.

He leaned down, his helmet pressing against my cheek.

"Hmm." The sound was like a low growl, rumbling deep from his chest. "Have I ever told you how good my name sounds coming from your lips ... *Aleda.*" His gravelly voice drew out every syllable.

My throat bobbed and a rush of heat headed straight for my core. *Why now?*

His cold steel helmet pressed harder into me, and I gave way, allowing him to press into my neck. His hands spread across my back, lifting me and pulling me flush against his armored chest.

The way my body craved to feel his skin on mine drove me to a point where I could lose myself in my need for him. I pulled at his straps trying to get an opening so I could touch his skin. Then it dawned on me. The forwardness. Was he still feeling the effects of the serum? It would make sense why he was in here. Looking for a solitary place to let it run its course. Little did he know, it was about to get a whole lot busier in here.

I pushed him away from me. He didn't protest, and I stared up into the small slits of openings in his helmet. My mouth opened to tell him why I was here just as the sound of soft slapping made its way over to us. It sounded like it was just a few rows over. "Getting into voyeurism now, are we?" he whispered.

I let out a scoff. He was one to talk after all the times he'd viewed me undressed and in the most inappropriate settings. I faced the direction of the noise. "In a most unfortunate way," I retorted, my mouth pulling into a smirk.

He quirked his head and listened. The sound grew louder and the rhythm of the slapping rings out in the silence. His aura changed and the air around us felt almost menacing. The way it felt whenever he was fighting. After a moment, he took off in the direction. *Shit! No, this wasn't about him. This was about Ilias and me.*

"Wait! You don't have to go out there!"

It was impossible to keep up behind him as he weaved through the maze's intricate walls. Gideon rounded the corner much faster than me.

While I was still making my way to the clearing, I heard Ilias exclaim in frustration at the interruption. "What the fuck do you want?" he said, to Gideon as I came from behind the hedge. He spotted me as I stepped closer. His eyes burned with rage, and he whipped back to Gideon. "Did you do this? Did you fucking bring her here?!"

The girl with him was leaning against a raised fountain bench, rushing to lower her skirts as her eyes bounced back and forth between Ilias and us. The concerned look on her face grew until she made the smart decision to run off.

Ilias finally moved, walking a few steps toward me and ignoring Gideon as he stood between us.

He looked around the maze clearing and placed his hands on the back of his head. He paced in a few circles until he finally let out a loud, "Fuck!" and threw his arms down before looking back to me again.

"Evangeline, I—I. Fuck. It was just sex, Love. It didn't mean anything, and I know you were having a—a hard time recently with everything going on and—"

He moved in a few steps closer, until he was only a few feet away from Gideon. Ilias scowled at him and then brought his attention back to me. "I didn't want to pressure you, you know, Love ... I—I wanted to be patient for you, but I have things that I need and you—"

His voice trailed off. He was very inebriated and doing his best to defend his actions.

I was ready to tell him off. To tell him everything I fucking hated about him. About how he made me feel and how I was so much better than he would *ever* be. That he was scum and filth and fucking dirt, and I wished to never see him again.

That was until my voice caught in my throat. It became nonexistent and futile and small. Everything I feared I was. In this moment, I perpetuated it.

I feared I was using Ilias as a crutch. As someone I could pass my blame to. I was the one who was lying. I was the dishonest one. And everything being done to me, had I not already done or ... wanted to do?

Gideon broke the line of sight between Ilias and me, keeping me in his shadow and protection.

"This again?! Do you forget who you have a contract with?! I can make you back into nothing with just the snap of my fingers. Get out of my way!"

Gideon was still unmoving. My protection against the one

who'd hurt me, who'd humiliated me. He was my shield in more ways than one.

Drops of rain started to fall and Ilias looked at me, seething as he said, "We *will* discuss this tomorrow." He stomped away.

My fists balled at my sides as I waited silently for the infernal storm of anger, rage, and complete and total despondence with my lack of confrontation with Ilias. *Why couldn't I just stand up for myself?*

"Fuck!" I screamed out, raising my fists to the sky and cursing the stars. In response, the rain fell harder.

"Why couldn't I say anything?" I said quietly to myself.

Gideon stepped closer to me and said, "Come with me." The rain was getting heavier, and the wind picked up. I hope to God he knew his way out of there or else I might have had to ride out the storm fighting through dead ends.

Luckily, Gideon led me out of the maze quickly. Not one dead end was met as I followed his steps through the confusing web of trails and tunnels in this place.

We exited and walked against the castle walls, still on the outer corners facing the garden and maze. There were small alcoves within the castle's architecture hidden below the ledges of the second floor and Gideon hurriedly made his way to one, reaching down to grasp my wrist, and pulling me to follow him. We were already soaked, but it was better than being in the direct torrential downpour.

The small space offered very little room for each of us; our bodies only a few inches apart. I took in frigid breaths, seeing the puffs of air leaving my lips, but the warmth coming from inside of me battled the cold chill I felt.

Gideon removed his helmet and pushed back the soft, dark

waves of hair away from his face at the same time a gust of wind brought a gale of blisteringly cold water onto us. Doing my best to keep my teeth from chattering, I curled in on myself and pulled my drenched cloak tight.

I glanced up, finding that his eyes were already searching over mine. Drops of water collected and trailed down his hair to drip onto his thick lashes. He took in a deep breath. His exhale was sharp and cold on my wet skin.

"It isn't my place to tell you what kind of men to keep."

He took a long pause, long enough for me to interject and say, "What if I want it to be your place?"

He gave me a dark laugh, "Did you have more Labra Laxa after I left?"

I ran my teeth over my lower lip. "No ... How about you? Still feeling the *effects*?"

"The only thing to ever *affect* me is you."

A twinge of guilt hit my gut as I thought back to the man I had kept the company of. Ilias was so parading, and forward with his affections, it made me feel like I was with someone who saw me and was proud to have me at his side. But I didn't know who he was behind it all, I was just responding to how he made me feel, how he made me feel about myself. I had grown to feel things for him, but he was a mask of a person. Not who I'd discovered him to be. But what can I expect for being half-honest my entire stay? He still called me Evangeline; he still only knew me by the facade I portrayed. How could I expect any better?

"Don't say that; I don't deserve to do *anything* to you."

He tucked a wet strand of hair behind my ear, his touch hot against my skin. His lingering fingers traveled down my jaw and wrapped around my neck. He pressed a thumb under my chin, forcing my face up. I was unable to look away from him.

"You deserve so much better than Ilias. Than me ..." He paused again, "Than what I'm about to do."

His voice was dark and heavy. It made my chest ache, and my mouth go dry. He peeked his head through the opening in the alcove just for a moment, and seemed to be contemplating what he would say next. His jaw flexed. Tension riddled his features. He looked back to me and moved millimeters closer.

"I need you to do something for me." He grabbed my hands in his.

"I don't know what—"

"You need to order me to stop," he interrupted. His eyes searched my face, and I couldn't look away from his amber eyes. From the pools of darkness in the low light looking through me.

"The moment the words leave your lips; I will be gone. I will walk to the farthest edge of the earth if you wish it. I will travel to the depths of hell, past Abaddon if you command me. If you tell me to stop. I. Will. Stop. But until then."

His face inched closer to mine, his lips barely grazing me, giving me the opportunity to order him to stop. But I knew that was the last thing I wanted in this moment.

So, I didn't say anything. I waited, the air between us shared, passing from my lungs into his, filling each other's bodies with the very thing we needed to survive, and I didn't think I could survive for much longer if he made me wait. Until finally, *fucking finally,* his lips crashed into mine. His mouth was possessive and hungry. He brought his other hand up, angling my head to deepen the kiss.

My pulse hummed in my ears, and a fiery ache built up inside of me. His lips on mine felt like a drink from an oasis. It was the very thing I had been looking for. The feeling of bliss took over and I opened my mouth slightly, wanting him to come in and explore me.

Our tongues swirled together. I wrapped my hands around both his wrists. His hold on me tightened for a moment, then he released me, pulling back from our kiss. Feeling in a daze against him, and seeing his lips, plump and swollen, I wished for more. So badly, did I want more.

He leaned forward and placed a long kiss on my forehead, just like the one in the catacombs. He breathed against my hair and pulled me tightly against him, resting his chin on my head. His hand gripped my waist and reached up to encircle me. My head fell onto his chest. The cold breastplate was welcome against my warm cheek.

"You are going to be the end of me," he said against my hair.

I wasn't sure if that was a good or bad thing, but I knew I was willing to find out. We stood there for just a moment longer. His hold on me felt like it had always been there. Like I had known his arms for a lifetime.

His voice broke the silence first. "We need to get you back."

I nodded against him. The rain was still falling heavy outside. He gave me his mantle, and I kept it over my head to run into the castle. He waited back for a bit as I made my way through the doorway ahead of him.

Twenty-Eight

I lingered behind her, allowing her to make her way inside under my watch, but I also needed a moment. The fog of the Labra Laxa had waned and the reality of tonight hit me like a fucking hammer. The kiss, the things I'd said. God, I was fucked. I licked my lips and reached for the last taste of her as a whisper on my tongue.

I inhaled sharply through my nose and centered myself, taking a few more steps towards the castle's large wooden doors. I didn't know what was going to happen if I followed her to her chambers. What I should or shouldn't do? If I fucking knew I wouldn't have told her to stop me, and I would have just stopped myself.

That's it. I had to stop this. I had to—to tell her that this needs to be it and it was a mistake. That I would be her protector and nothing more.

My chest felt like it was in my throat and the reality of ending whatever this could have been almost made me collapse onto the steps in front of me.

Pushing past the doors and taking my first steps through the castle, I walked immediately into an incoming duo of royal guards. Their faces were stern, their mouths pulled into hard lines. One halted in front of me and raised his hand, stopping my progression.

"Your presence has been requested. Follow us." They didn't give me time to respond before they turned and continued down the hall.

A feeling of dread filled me at the thought of leaving her alone with Ilias free and walking around.

That guard better not have moved a goddamned muscle.

They took me far from the apartments and into the royal quarters, where those who served the Queen would reside. Each door was shrouded in guards dressed in their fullest regalia.

We passed each door until we made it to the apex of the hall, and I stood before the expanse of rich mahogany wood. A deep huff of air escaped my lips, and my hands clenched and un-clenched. The rain had soaked through every layer in my armor; I would dare my body to remain so still that I may also rust before leaving her for this long. At least give me a good fucking reason to be here.

The two guards opened the doors to reveal the Queen's grand rooms, I stepped farther inside, and that's when I saw her, sitting with her back to me in a large chair facing the giant hearth warming the room.

"Take that helmet off. Best not to be rude." Her voice chirped through the room.

The two guards sat near the threshold of the door, leaving it open to the hall. She turned in her chair, peeking a head full of dark raven hair over the side, searching to find what was taking so long.

"Close the fucking doors!" she shouted and waved her hand at them, ensuring the privacy I would need before removing anything for her. Once we were alone, I pulled off the helmet, my hair still soaking wet and clinging to my face.

She got up from the chair to stand and face me. Her long black hair rippled down her back, a stark contrast to the bright golds and greens of her robes. The Queen was well into her fiftieth year but remained youthful with nearly no sign of aging around her almond eyes. Her pale alabaster skin was a symbol of purity, and the kingdom loved her for it. The Pure Queen of Paymon.

Her mouth picked up in the corner, and she gave me a sly smirk. "Get caught in the rain, did we?"

I tried my hardest not to roll my eyes but stand steady. Without the coverage of my helmet, I needed to control my facial expressions. If she called me in here it was for a reason, and if she had intel then it must be important.

"Gideon, you must not be so rigid." She stepped over, closing the distance between us and came to stand before me. Her hand grazed over my cheek. Her warm fingers were shockingly hot against the chill the rain had left on my skin.

Just as shockingly, I was met with a hard slap. The sting resonated for a moment.

"Was that really necessary?"

Her mouth pulled back, revealing her shiny white teeth as she barked out a laugh.

"Oh, my boy, if only you knew how necessary it was." She started to walk away and then paused mid-step, raising her right hand, the long sleeves of her robe flapping with the momentum. "And how much of a warning it will become for you?"

My brows furrowed, the only emotion I let sit against my face.

"A warning?"

She turned. "Yes, a warning, Gideon how—" She stopped mid-sentence, like she'd discovered something in her own subconscious. Her eyes darted back and forth until they once again stopped on me.

"Do you know who you've been traveling with?"

The question seemed almost rhetorical, but with the way she was looking at me, I knew she wanted a response.

"The Duke of the Midlands Nephew, Lord Ilias Terrell."

Another sharp laugh left her mouth gaping wide open, and she spun on her toes, bringing a hand to her forehead and reaching down to a table near the hearth, picking up an elaborately decorated glass.

"Oh, my dear, dear Gideon ..." She sipped from her glass, drawing out this moment for an eternity.

"Oh, this is just too good, for *you* of all people to not be aware. I just need a moment to process this. You really have no *idea* who you're traveling with?"

My mind raced, trying to understand what she could be saying. Every face of the men in the company ran through my mind and not one rung a single bell. Then ... fucking then. My memories of that night in the woods under the red moon. The body on the floor next to her was housed in armor, but I hadn't gotten a good look at what kind.

Her name. A secret. The names she wrote in the cathedral tunnel. Was I so fucking oblivious? So fucking blind? It couldn't be.

She looked at me, that same large smile brandished on her face, her teeth now freshly stained with the sips of wine. "I don't know how you hadn't figured it out before. You were always the most observant child." Her words were confirmation, but I needed to hear it.

"Who is she?"

She took a deep breath and sat down, crossing one leg over the other. She dangled the words in front of me like a starving man's next meal. "She is now known as the lost Queen of the Oriens. Queen Consort Aleda Evangeline De'Lisle of Egyn."

There it fucking was. Confirmation. Dread. Amorphous Worship. The way all I wanted to do was go to her and bow before her down on my fucking knees.

"Aleda." The name sounded more like a prayer than a name to me now. I broke from my thoughts long enough to look at the Queen before me. Her eyes bored into mine.

"So, what are you going to do now? Now that you have this —this information?"

I want to tell her that I know; I want to tell her she doesn't need to hide or be afraid. That I will do anything within my power to keep her. But that sounded crazy, even for me.

I opened my mouth to speak, but the sound of a scream echoed loud enough through the halls that we both turned to the door. My heart fucking dropped.

TWENTY-NINE

THE BUZZ IN MY HEAD HAD WANED, BUT THE CHILL within my bones was creeping in deeper. I made it to my room, laid the mantle on the bed and went to stand near the fire. My clothes were still soaked, and no heat broke through enough to warm me.

I decided to draw a warm bath; get my body back to a regular temperature. The billowing steam clouds fill the space as I settled into the hot water. The harsh temperature change stung, making me hiss through my teeth until I was fully submerged, but I knew I needed it.

I laid my head back against the tub and closed my eyes. The need for Gideon to return had turned from a minimal want to a gnawing need as the time passed. My body ached as I thought back to what he'd said. To everything. The way he'd tasted, the way his lips felt on mine. To know it wasn't just one-sided felt … felt good.

My naked body started to feel the warmth weave back into my nerve endings. I lifted out of the water, feeling the cool chill on my wet breasts, making my nipples harden. My hand grazed over them, and the feeling sent a wave of heat between my legs immediately. It was hot and heavy, and I wanted more.

I wanted so much more.

Slinking back down into the water my fingers trailed along my body, making their way down to the ache blooming deep inside of me. The point of temperance and temptation sat nestled at the summit of my sex. The soft and tender bud shot waves of pleasure through me at the most minimal of contact. My walls contracted at the sensation and the feeling of being empty was close to maddening. My fingers swirled harder around the bundle of nerves while my free hand moved back to my breast and pinched the sensitive nipple, forcing out another wave of heat.

Moving down to feel the slickness building even in the water was enough for me to easily slide my fingers just past my tight threshold. The new pressure filling me eased the ache, but I was feeling selfish, and I wanted to be filled to the fucking breaking point.

I closed my eyes and focused back to when I was in the inn with Gideon. When he fell on top of me and I felt him pressing against me. The way I could feel him grow through his pants. If all I did was grind against his bulge, I would have come undone. Just knowing he was there and wanted me just as much as I wanted him.

God, I was fucking obsessed, and I haven't even had a taste yet.

My thighs clenched, the pressure building in my lower abdomen. Just a few more soft thrusts of my fingers and I clamped down around them. Pulsing waves of pressure poured into me as I filled my chest with fresh, new air.

After drying myself, I grabbed for the few things I had with me. The one that caught my eye was the soft silk shift Gideon had gotten for me. My cheeks heated as I thought of all the things I wanted to be done to me in this.

I slipped it over my skin, and the soft fabric fell over my peaked nipples and the swells of my breast. I let a sigh out into the ether.

Lying out my wet clothes to hang on a chair, I heard shuffling in the other room. A smile grew on my lips as did a giddy feeling in my chest. I looked over myself once more. Pulling my hair back, then to the side. Back again. *It's fine, I'm fine.*

I opened the door and peeked my head out. The fire in the hearth had gone out and the only light entering the room was from the bathing chamber. I closed the door, casting everything into darkness.

My eyes searched the room and found no trace of what might have caused the noise I had just heard. I noticed a small sliver of light peeking through the door to my room. It was left slightly ajar. *That was … odd.*

A soft, strange moan came from the other side of my bed. I spun my head around. *Something was wrong.*

I searched for fucking anything to use as a weapon, my hands grasping at air as I searched the dark room. I finally settled on a large brass candlestick from the sideboard. Holding it up, I was ready to swing it at whatever the fuck was in my room. I tiptoed to the other side of my bed, stepping on something sticky and wet. My toes splayed out in whatever it was. As I rounded the side, I finally saw a slumped figure prone on the floor. The mass of black darkness moved crawling and clawing at the ground.

I screamed, swinging the candlestick. The thing flipped over onto its back, revealing the very familiar form of Ilias. I dropped the candlestick in a loud clatter and knelt. His eyes were closed and there was something dark coming from his mouth. In between low moans, it sounded like he was trying to speak.

I went to him and placed my ear near his mouth, listening for anything discernible. Choked shallow breaths sputtered from his lips.

"Ilias, Ilias wake up." I tried to shake him lightly. Turning back to the hall, I called for help, "Godrick, guards help, plea—"

Two strong hands cut off my airway and yanked me down. It felt like additional hands clawed at me, pressing my head down, forcing me to look into Ilias's red, bloodshot eyes. Foam came from his mouth and low words formed.

"I am ready for you ... I am coming for you ... you are mine." The words weren't his. The voice wasn't his.

As the last word passed Ilias's lips his hands released me, his body collapsing into a limp mass. I fell back on my elbows and slid across the floor over the sticky substance, the distance growing between us.

Gideon shoved the door open, flooding us in light from the hall.

Blood.

Blood was all over the floor, covering Ilias's face and all over my once pure white shift.

Gideon knelt and helped me to my feet.

More guards rushed in, and Gideon walked me to the back of the room, still keeping a strong hold on me. Ilias was taken away and a woman walked in. The air around her held power and elegance. She eyed me and my night shift covered in blood and fresh bruises blooming on my neck. Again. I could only imagine this was the Queen.

But her eyes only lingered on me for a second and settled

on Gideon. His posture didn't falter, but his hold on me tightened.

She gave him a nod and receded from the room, shouting at the guards to take Ilias to the infirmary.

Gideon's grip loosened. He stared down at me, grazing his fingertips along my throat, his hand forming into a fist as he pulled away. He let go of me and started to collect my things, grabbing my bag and filling it with my clothes and the few extra items I had accumulated.

We must be leaving?

I was alright with that; I didn't want to be anywhere near this room. I looked back to the blood scattered across my floor and the red handprints staining the comforter. My feet were still coated in it, turning dark and caking my skin as it dried.

I reached for my boots, not caring in this moment if I soiled them. I just needed out of this room.

Before I could slide my foot inside, Gideon was before me, my bag strung across his shoulder and his towering form blocking my way. I opened my mouth to speak, but he grabbed me under my knees and lifted me into his arms. This was wholly unnecessary.

"I can still walk, you know."

He replied with a near silent huff of air and left my room. He walked us outside of the guest apartments and down through a hallway facing opposite the one leading to the maze. We moved farther away from the rest of the castle to a small dwelling. Its exterior matched the rest of the apartments, but this one stood alone in the grounds surrounded with more fruit trees.

As he pulled the handle to the door, a screech echoed through the air as the unused hinges worked against themselves. The room was similar to the other rooms I'd seen; well-furnished but with an additional small kitchen tucked inside.

He walked in and set me on the bed, still silent even though we were clearly alone. *And still wearing his helmet.* He rifled through a dresser and pulled out a familiar garment. The type of shirt he'd loaned me before.

He handed it to me and quickly walked away, receding into the bathing chamber.

With the given privacy, I pulled the shift up and over, replacing it with the most intoxicatingly aromatic fabric. I had been surrounded by him for weeks but this— God. I took a deep inhale as I brought it to my nose. The neck was large and draped down over my shoulders slightly. I walked to the mirror above the dresser and my eyes fell on dark marks around my neck; the clear representation of Ilias's fingers pressing into my flesh.

My fingers traced over them and as I made contact, the door to the bathing chamber opened and Gideon walked back into the room, still in full armor, but carrying a bucket and a cloth.

He set it down in front of the bed and walked over to me, taking my hand in his and leading me back to sit. I did as instructed and sat on the bed, my feet high and dangling off the edge. He knelt before me, still so large he was about at my eye level.

Gideon removed his gloves and reached into the bucket, drenching a rag in sudsy water. He gently wrapped his hand behind my foot and lifted it, meeting the damp cloth to my sole.

He worked at the dry and caked blood, washing it clean from my skin. Once he had finished with both feet, he moved the bucket to the side and reached for my thighs. His grip on them was not too firm, but the tension in his body was evident. His hands slid up to my hips, and he leaned forward. Then more, and more until his helmet was seated in my lap.

He went still.

We sat like this for a moment.

I reached down and felt for the lip of the helmet. He let me lift it from his shoulders, the mess of dark waves falling over his face. He sat back onto his knees. His eyes were no longer behind a steel wall but were shrouded in something else.

They wouldn't meet my gaze. He stared like he was looking through me. After *everything* that has happened in the last few hours, I didn't want this wall back up. I wanted him. Unbridled and open. I wanted him to see me. Even though the person I presented before him was not honest, it was the most honest I had been with myself.

"Gideon ..." My voice was soft and low. Like I was worried about scaring *him* off.

More silence was all I was met with. "Gideon." I tried again, this time sterner, more questioning. I needed him to answer me; I couldn't sit with this silence between us. Not anymore.

He looked up, his eyes tracking over me, stopping and drinking in the way my throat was red and splotchy. His brows knitted together, as his jaw flexed and un-flexed. His grip tightening on my legs as his lips parted. I saw a word forming on his tongue until he bit it back and looked away.

This time I reached out. I pulled his chin to face me, placing both of my hands on his cheeks, cradling his face in my palms. Even though his eyes fought me, he accepted my pressure.

There they are.

The dark amber eyes I needed. I needed them to fill me with hope and light. Not whatever *this* was.

"Gide—"

I was barely able to get the word out before I was met with hard and fast pressure. He made the connection quick, and I fell into a frenzy of his lips on mine. I wrapped my arms around his neck and pulled into him, my fingers raking through his hair.

I felt a rush of heat move through me as his arms wrapped around me and crushed me into the hard steel. I needed the armor to be fucking gone.

My fingers searched over the armored plates and fumbled over the small straps. I didn't know what the hell I was doing, but I knew that this man, *this man,* was going to drive me perpetually insane.

He stood, pulling me up and into his arms. I eagerly wrapped my legs around his body, clinging to him with every-thing I had. His hold on me was strong, keeping me in place against him. I trailed my lips down and met the soft skin between his jaw and ear, placing soft kisses that grew into harder, more wanting ones. He let out a low rumbling moan against me and my legs grew tense, the heat building at my core ignited.

He switched places with me, and he was the one now seated on the bed, and I had my legs placed on each side of his; giving me the most wonderful pressure between my legs as I pressed into him.

I pulled apart from him, taking in gulps of air. He did the same. Pressing my forehead to his, I reached up to tug at the crest of his chest plate. "Can you take these off?"

THIRTY

Gideon

WHAT SHE WAS ASKING WOKE ME FROM MY RELIEF-
filled haze. When I'd heard the scream echo into the Queen's
chambers, I was terrified I would be too late; that she was hurt
again, or worse. When I walked in and saw her, covered in
blood on the floor; my heart had stopped.

Now she was safe in my arms and in my space. I wanted
nothing more than to lie forever with her and forget the rest of
these days. To be here, fully with her as I was and as she was.

She met my eyes with a burning desire I knew too well.
God, she wanted more, and I would love to give her more, but I
knew it wouldn't be right. Not yet. Not with everything that
had happened tonight.

I reached up and took her hands in mine, letting out a soft
chuckle, kissing along the pads of her fingers. Her ravenous
eyes searched my face for any inclination or reason as to why I
wasn't taking her right here on the floorboards.

"Does it hurt, Amri?"

She let out a low breath through her swollen lips, and I watched as her mouth twisted to one side. She was contemplating what she wanted to say, and I saw the flash of pain behind her eyes. Everything about her captivated me and I couldn't bring myself to look away. Even when she was unhappy with me.

Doubt filled me as I continued to watch her, and I knew I had to stop this. I couldn't do *this* and be who she needed. I'd already failed her. I'd failed myself. I couldn't protect her—and now all I could see were the deepening shades of vermillion as fresh bruises grew across her tender flesh. *Fucking Ilias.* I was going to hunt him down and— A delicately placed finger pressed into my chin, halting the rampage circling in my mind. Reaching to her hand, I held it loosely as I brought her palm to my lips. I pressed a kiss to her perfect skin—God—everything about her was perfect.

Her eyes settled on my lips, and I watched as her desire built. I felt her body under my fingers vibrating with anticipation. *Fuck.* My cock strained against my breeches, begging to be let free.

She bit at her lip and finally met my gaze. I raked my hand through her hair and secured my fingers along her scalp, pulling her head back and exposing her neck to me. I brought my mouth to the base of her throat and left a kiss right in the center, holding my lips there to feel her swallow against me. Then another up higher, then another just below her ear. When I was close enough to where my nose was making its way to the shell of her ear and my lips pressed against her jaw, I told her, "One thing you'll learn about me, Amri ... I am a very, very patient man."

She tried to turn to me, and I held her harder by her hair. "And" I said in a growl, "To answer your previous question, I can remove these cold plates, I can stay with you and play out every last command you have for me, and I know that with that mouth of yours, it will be many, but I won't—*we* can't."

She settled in against me and placed her hands to my chest plate and I brought her to face me. To look me in the eyes. She makes a small noise against me. I released her hair, and she turned to look away. Her face was downcast, and I watched as she swallowed hard.

"What does Amri mean?" Her voice was low.

I smiled to myself. "You're a smart girl; do some more research and I'm sure you'll come across it."

God, I wanted nothing more than to kiss her. To tell her I was lying and make the look growing on her face go away. I wanted to have her come undone beneath my fingertips instead, for her to beg me to touch her, because God fucking knows I would falter and fold the moment she asked.

She furrowed her brow and frowned at me, accepting that I wouldn't go any further. That we were destined to be separate. Who I am and who she is, we can never be. It would be shrouded in my shame, my dishonor, my vow broken. I couldn't ruin her life and bring her down with me.

"Fine, then don't tell me, if you're just going to be a tease, then I guess we're all done here."

A *tease? The gall of this girl.* She doesn't even know the levels of restraint I have in place for her.

"Fine, I suppose we are." I got up and headed into the bathing chamber.

The hot water rained down over my aching muscles. I'd left her out there and the longer I sat below the warm running water, I knew I couldn't go back. Not with what I know now. With whom she was. How was I so fucking oblivious? Or did I not want it to be true? That I'd felt this since the first moment I'd seen her. That there was something about her. Why else would I have tied her up and made sure she was safe? I was a Knight of the Crimson Cloth, but not a Saint. I didn't give charity.

I threw my head back letting the water hit me hard over my face. *God, I was fucked.* I licked my lips and reached for the last taste of her. The water didn't dull the feeling of her; she'd left a mark too strong.

I inhaled sharply, pinching the bridge of my nose, exhaling through my nostrils and centering myself. Without any restrictions, my body couldn't hold itself together anymore. My cock filled with my need for her. Its pull from deep inside magnetic on my skin.

I reached down and ran my fingers over the sensitive tip. The feeling sent a shiver through to my body. Moving down to fully fist myself, I started to move my hand up and down my shaft. The way I had touched myself to fantasies of her. I'd play out scenes of her in my head, like the one where I'd wanted to fuck her senseless in that inn. That I'd wanted to rip the rest of the shift off her and see just how beautiful she looked lying beneath me. The way her body would feel wrapped around my throbbing cock. Lips, pussy, ass. Fucking anything she would ever want to offer to me.

Just a few more strong pulls and I felt the pressure building low in my body, the finishing moment upon me and I leaned my body on the wet stone.

I couldn't take it anymore.

Shutting off the water, I wrapped myself in a towel and opened the door into the bedroom. I stopped.

She stood there, her arm raised, ready to knock. Her eyes went wide with surprise, immediately traveling down my wet body, the droplets trailing to the ever-present erection beneath the thin towel.

I closed the space like I was searching for air after being pulled underwater. I needed her. My mouth was desperate against hers. Her lips were a nectar I could live off for the rest of my days. I tugged on the hairs my fingers were wrapped around, and a soft gasp escaped her lips. She opened her mouth, and I dived deeper, exploring her. She answered me back just as eagerly. Her tongue worked against mine and a few breaths passed between us.

She pulled away first and I sucked in as much air as possible. My life-force hummed and came alive deep in my chest. An eager spark built with each connection our bodies made.

My fingers moved out of the tangles I left in her hair. She backed away from me and looked around the room, avoiding my gaze. I pulled her chin to face me, but her eyes wouldn't look into mine. The uncertainty, the shyness, the desire. She was holding back now, and I felt a faltering sputter in my heart as this interaction waned.

She bit her lip and placed her hands on my chest. I needed to say something, stop this, but before the words made it past my lips, she was pushing against me. With my lack of attention to how I was standing, she threw me off balance. I landed hard on the settee behind me and before too long, she was staring at me at eye level.

She moved in closer, her fingers tracing my lips and nose. They worked their way up until she had both of her hands in my hair, and made her way in more, bringing her lips to mine and peppering small kisses on my cheeks, working down to my neck.

My hands gripped her sides, and as she moved to a more sensitive spot. I held her harder, fingers digging into her skin and a heady moan escaped my lips. She smiled against me. I pulled her closer and she took full advantage of my guiding, bringing a knee up onto the settee, trapping my legs under her, ensuring I was locked between her thighs, just hovering over my hard cock with only a few pieces of fabric away from her skin on mine. I pulled her down to feel her heat against me. The pressure against her core made her throw her head back and a moan danced across her lips. She continued to rub herself against me and I could barely fucking hold it in.

I brought my hands under her shirt, feeling over her buttery soft body until they found her full and plump breasts. I applied the most minimal amount of pressure, and she let out a gasp into the air. As my fingers traced over her hard nipples, her hold on me tightened and she eagerly reached down to pull the shirt up and over her head, fully revealing her body to me. God, I would *never* get tired of this.

My hands traveled to her back as she arched, but I pulled her back to me. My lips connected with her collarbones, trailing down and over her breasts, inhaling deep as her scent filled my nostrils. I was taking my time as I traveled down her body, but I finally took her nipple in between my lips, flicking my tongue on the peaked flesh. The sounds of soft and patient pleasure escaped her lips. And those were nice, but I wanted carnal obsession. I wanted her to feel just how much I'd been holding back.

My teeth bit down on her sensitive nipple. A sharp gasp left her lips, and she responded by wrapping her hands behind my neck, pulling me in. I could almost feel the invisible words between us, "More. *More. MORE.*"

I pinched the other nipple between my thumb and forefinger, releasing another sharp noise from her. The ones I've been *craving* for her to make. She ground her pussy against my erection beneath the towel, and I welcomed the tinges of pain with the pleasure.

She brought her face to my ear. Her hot breath sent shivers

down my body, and my cock was fucking weeping beneath her. I could barely get even breaths out.

"What does it mean?" Her voice was low and filled with so much sex I couldn't respond. I tugged her closer, burying my face into her and letting out a deep groan against her skin. She wrapped her legs around my abdomen, and I stood, lifting her in my arms. I reached around to her ass to hold her in place and my fingers worked to her center. To her perfect wet cunt.

That's when I felt it. Just how dripping wet she was.

I led us to the bed and dropped her down, letting her body spring against the mattress, her breasts bouncing from the force. Her legs were spread, putting her on display for me. My hands found the tied fabric of my towel and her eyes were locked on me. There wasn't a single blink as I pulled the fabric away and dropped it to the floor, freeing my dick and showing her what she did to me. How fucking bad I wanted her.

Her mouth dropped open slightly and I couldn't help but smirk. I fisted my swollen cock and pumped it slowly, drawing out each movement, throwing my head back and swallowing hard. I had never been this close to heaven even when I was on the battlefield.

Looking back down at her, I said, "It's not something I can tell you."

Her brows furrowed together, and she closed her legs. *Big mistake.*

I released my dick and grabbing under her knees, and pulling her to the edge of the bed, spreading her legs back to their rightful position.

"So fucking beautiful ..." My voice trailed off, and she sat up on her elbows, brows still knitted together, and her swollen lips pressed into a hard line. I knew she was not happy with my answer. So I'd give her just a little more.

"It's something I have to show you." I dropped to my knees

in between her thighs. My hands rubbed up to her soft skin and I brought my fingers to her glistening center. She looked down at me still, watching every move I made. I saw the tension leave her face with each moment.

Inching my face closer I watched as she witnessed my first taste of her. The long languid lick from the very center of her pussy all the way up to her sensitive swollen clit.

"You taste like salvation."

A soft exhale passed her lips, and her eyes rolled back. She fell backwards onto the bed.

My body tightened and I became ravenous. I devoured her, lapping up every fucking drop she gave me. I'd thought her lips were intoxicating, but this, fucking *this*. I could have this as my final taste of this world and die happy.

I paid extra attention to her clit now, sucking and flicking it with my tongue. She moaned softly to every answering swipe. I used two fingers, exploring her, touching her and then finally working their way to her entrance.

I was caught off guard as she grabbed fistfuls of my hair, her core tightening, and the word, "Please ..." repeated on her tongue.

I did as commanded. I pressed my fingers into her, feeling her walls tighten and contract around them and fuck, she was so tight. Continuing my work on her clit, I pulled out of her and guided my fingers back in, repeating my movements. In and out, long deep thrusts with my fingers until I felt her pull on my hair grow tighter, and her thighs trembled against me.

She fell silent clenching around my fingers, her legs fighting to close around me. I kept up my thrusts and sucked harder. She struggled for a breath. I pulled away.

"Use your words." Just like that, she let out a guttural wail of emotion. She let go and I kept fucking going. She was reeling and I moved back down to her sensitive skin.

For once she was not anyone else and neither was I. She was just here with me, and I fucking loved her. My eyes went wide, this realization rattled in my skull. I stood, licking the last few drops of her on my lips. It was so fucking good. I looked down at her body on my bed, languid and limp.

She propped herself up on her elbows and I crawled over her. My body pressed into her, and my cock teased her entrance. The point of contact was close, and she rolled her eyes back, reveling in every sensation ...

I kissed her, slow and passionately, swirling my tongue in her mouth as she explored mine. Tasting herself on me. Pulling back, I looked her in the eyes and brought my fingers covered in her juices to her lips. She opened eagerly accepting them. She flicked her tongue on them, savoring the flavor like they were a delicacy. And God, she tasted like one.

After she was done, I pulled them back and moved in close to the shell of her ear and whispered, "good girl."

Just like that, she was back.

She wrapped her hands around my neck and pulled all my weight on top of her. Her legs wrapped around my torso, moving against me, wanting to coax my dick into her waiting cunt.

I reached below and moved us farther on to the bed, placing her head onto a pillow. I seated myself between her legs. Her soft skin rubbed against me, and I looked between us. At how this would change everything. How I knew I wouldn't be able to live without her. That if she changed her mind, I would simply not have the will to be on this plane.

I inhaled deeply and looked back at her. The emotion behind her eyes was familiar, a mirror filled with longing and lust and, at least for me, love.

I loved her.

She brought a hand to my cheek and traced lines from my

brow, over my eyes and down my lips but didn't stop until she placed a hand flat against my chest.

"Gideon, please."

My only answer was the slow movement forward. The head of my cock opened her and passed us into this new world.

I pushed more, still going slow. My fingers had struggled to make their way in, and the size of my dick was going to stretch her far wider, even with how wet she still was. I pressed farther, finally seating myself in her a few inches. Her face was riddled with tension, and I knew I was hurting her. But I knew she liked it. The way she reacted to my teasing bites, those weren't light, not even in the slightest.

Leaning down, I took her nipple between my teeth. She cried out and that's when I took the first full thrust. Her sharp gasp came first and then it slowly died to a string of moans and other incoherent noises. I didn't move, letting her adjust to my size.

Her fingers crawled to my back, and I moved out and in, slowly and rhythmically. Her pussy clenched in tight waves against me and she made honeyed noises that rippled their way into my chest. Her brows relaxed and she began to pant with pleasure.

Thirty-One

Gideon's weight on my body was solid and safe. He moved in slow measured strokes that drove me to the point of coming again already. The way he filled me was the most delicious type of pain I had ever felt.

My hands on his back, holding him close to me and he moved with the pattern of our breath, but I wanted more. I had him and he had me. *Didn't he?*

"More," I said pressing my lips into his neck, sucking on the tender flesh below his ear. He stilled, and then I felt the muscles in his back tense under my fingers. He answered my request willingly, thrusting deeper and harder, each one bottoming out inside of me making the tight coil build up again.

His breathing became ragged, and his grip moved down to my ass, pulling me into him at a different angle.

I gripped at his back and could hardly hold myself together as he pounded harder and deeper than before. God, I wanted to come all over him. Again. My eyes rolled back, and he hit me in the right spot, over and over again.

Emotions welled up and I didn't know what to do with them. I just knew that nothing in my life had ever felt this right. No one had made me feel so cared for, so loved.

Fuck. Like a dam breaking, all my emotions flooded me as muscles contracted and spasmed around him. Tears flooded my eyes, and I held him tighter, shoving my face in the crook of his neck. His arms wrapped around me and pulled me in as he gave a few more finishing pumps.

"Fuck." That was all I was able to choke out; the word half grumbled, and half cried.

He leaned away, and the look on his face was not one I could place in my haze. Tears clouded my vision, and I could feel him pull out of me. An ache of emptiness replaced the extreme pleasure.

Gideon moved to stand off the bed and I wiped away my tears. Looking to him, I saw his eyes wide. He stared between my legs. Bright red blood had soaked into the sheet beneath me.

I swallowed any words that might come to the surface, because what could I say?

It was clear as day and he knew it.

I was a virgin.

Was it bad that I thought the whole blood thing was a myth to keep a young girl's legs closed? Was it bad that it worked for me?

The reality of the situation filled the room in a palpable way. The emotions, the highs and lows made my mind misfire. I had been married for ten years before and not once was there even a single inclination of that type of possession in Kairos. Any tryst with a boy in the castle was short-lived and surface level. Anything with Ilias, well, fucking Ilias. I regretted any inch of my skin he'd once touched with his.

Now here I stood in the pouring warm water running down over my skin as I washed it clean. I was forever changed and still so the same. Gideon was kind and loving and strong. I felt a twinge of pain radiate through me as I thought back to everything, and I welcomed it so sweetly.

As I turned off the water, reached for a towel and dried myself, I was able to look into a partially foggy mirror. Seeing the bruises on my neck felt less shameful, less ugly when I felt so—so happy. So elated. So … safe.

I pulled on another of Gideon's shirts and welcomed the feeling on my skin, knowing that it was once on him. Letting out a deep sigh, I wrapped my arms around myself, knowing that what waited for me outside the door was good. I wasn't thinking about tomorrow, or about later.

Opening the door back into the room, I was met with an unexpected sight. Gideon was back in his full armor sans helmet but working on a buckle near his waist. My stomach dropped.

He turned to me, stepping into my space. His fingers hooked under my chin and pulled it up to look at him. His breath brushed over my cheeks and a sense of ease washed over me.

"I am still your knight, and I still have to do my presented duty." His tone was soft and sweet, like honey on his tongue. He leaned down and pulled the most languid kiss from my lips, his fingers drawing out a long caress on my cheek. Finally, he stepped away and placed his helmet over his head. Reaching for the door handle, he turned back to me. "The Queen will wish to speak to you in the morning."

And with that, he was gone.

Thirty-Two

The next morning, my head was a mess. My eyes ached and my stomach had turned inside itself. Whatever this *hangover* was, it was far worse than a standard one. I was still nursing my head when a knock sounded soon after sunrise.

"Come in."

In walked a beautiful young woman with pristine porcelain skin and long jet-black hair. The top half of her hair was pulled into an intricate knot with decorative pins cascading with small reflective jewels. "Hello, my lady. The Queen has requested a breakfast with you this morning."

"Yes." I sat up and my whole body rejected the movement. "I heard. Thank you."

"Yes, my lady. Once you're ready, I will escort you to her highness."

"Thank you. What is your name?"

"It is Avery, my lady." She turned to leave, and I called after.

"Do you by chance have anything I may wear when I meet her highness?"

Avery took a long look over me in my too big shirt and,

well, nothing else. It hung well below any private bits, and I wasn't going for a walk outside. But this was my sole option at the moment.

Her mouth pulled into a smirk. "Oh yes, let me bring you a few things."

She left and I took my time to bathe again and refresh my hair, and the moment I stepped into the room saw the red stain stark against the sheets. I pulled the blanket over the stain, but his scent wafted up, making me remember last night. My hand touched my lips. His mouth had been the most intoxicating thing I had ever tasted. My fingers craved touching him. Fuck, my entire body craved being touched by him. I could feel an addiction developing if I let myself indulge any further. And God, I would.

I felt no guilt thinking of him, no turmoil. As for Ilias, whatever we were, that was long over. I couldn't bear another moment with him. I'd sooner vomit than let him touch me again.

My hands fisted at my side. I hated that he could pull such a visceral reaction from me. He deserved nothing.

A knock at the door stirred me, breaking the spiral I was traveling down. Avery stepped in.

"I have a few options for you, my lady." She instructed me to stand and face my reflection as she held them up in front of me in the mirror. One was red, like back in the Oriens with intricate and beautiful beading. The second was the colors of the East with deep yellows and ochres with strips of green satin. The third was the northern color, black as night. It had a high neck with long sleeves and a gorgeous silk skirt that hung just above the ankles. My eyes lit up.

Avery smiled. "I think this is the one."

She helped me secure the backing. It was like it was made from my measurements.

"You look gorgeous, my lady."

"Thank you."

The neck was high enough to hide almost the entire string of bruises peppering my neck. For the rest I would wear my hair down and forward.

As I left the apartment, I saw no knight stationed outside. I was sure there was plenty of security and with my chaperone, I would be finding my way around just fine. Still, not seeing Gideon outside left an uneasy feeling in my stomach.

Avery guided us down through the palace walls and into a small tearoom. I saw a few servants posted at the entrance. One of them was the girl we'd found Ilias with.

She looked up and immediately turned her head back down, then whispered to a girl next to her, curtsied and left the room. She was more embarrassed than I was upset at her. She could fuck him however much she wanted. *She* wasn't the problem.

Avery left me near the balcony overlooking the stables, and movement down below caught my eye. I made out a glint of shiny bodies. It was armor of some sort. Leaning more in my chair, I strained my neck to see if I could spot Gideon among the people outside.

The large, elegant doors of the royal chamber slowly parted, and anticipation filled the air. The Queen had arrived. She entered, draped in intricate silks that shimmered with every step, the colors reminiscent of a sunset over the Eastern seas. Her presence was commanding, each movement deliberate.

Her eyes found me, and a soft smile built, causing little creases to form near her eyes.

"You won't find him down there," she said, gesturing to the balcony. A kind of, *oh, you caught me,* feeling hit my gut, and I stammered for a moment, little intelligence making its way past my lips. I stood to greet her, but an off-kilter curtsy was all I could make for the occasion. She was magnificent.

"Thank you for the invitation, your grace."

"The honor is mine, *your grace*."

I stammered, my tongue once again unable to create coherent words.

"Please, sit," the Queen insisted.

I did so, just as ungracious as my curtsy.

A small smile picked up on one side of her mouth. Her growing amusement was evident as she spoke; the words left her lips on the cusp of a laugh.

"Surprised that I know of who is below my roof?"

"No, not at all. I just—"

"Now, Queen Aleda. Please do not lump me with the simple group you travel with."

"I would never!" My brows raised so high, I leaned forward, bowing my head in embarrassment as my tone and outburst all but spilled out of me. "I'm sorry. I'm not the most *known*. Most, even in my kingdom, recognize very little of the Queen Consort when Kairos was the face of the Oriens."

She sipped her tea, watching me with a soft gaze. "Yes, I do quite understand. My husband, the prince, is in a similar *situation*."

"That may be so ... but I doubt you called me here to discuss titles and their significance." I took a sip of my tea wanting to uncover what she seemed so keen on revealing in these paced out proclamations; she was holding back much more if this was how she chose to arrange our introduction.

"First, I would like to offer my condolences for your late husband. May the King rest in peace. In addition, I would like to know what brought you here with the duke of the Midland's nephew. He is quite easy on the eyes, I suppose," she said with a raised brow. "But what brought you two together?"

I set my cup down on its saucer and added in two more sugar cubes before pouring more tea. "The night of the attack, Commander Bauer told me to seek out an allied company near the castle and they were able to offer me some protection. My goal was to travel home, back to the North."

"I see, and you thought going by an alias would aid on your travels if you're outside of the country?"

"It was my initial idea, yes. I didn't want to become a tool used to blackmail my already torn country, your grace." I paused, realizing that if anyone knew what had come from the attack, it would be her. "Have you heard from the west? What happened after?"

"I have." She brought a cup to her lips and took a long sip. "The night of the Crimson Moon, the demons ravaged the city. It was more than they had seen in years. They battled for over a week's time but finally it appears rebuilding has begun."

I'd run from my kingdom without any warning to them. I had always regretted that, knowing that I'd left them to fend for themselves. Guilt surfaced and tears spilled out past my lashes. The Queen handed me a soft napkin, and I dried my face.

"Thank you, I'm sorry."

She placed her hand on mine. "No, I am sorry." She took a deep sigh. "If there is anything you need, please do not hesitate to ask."

I nodded, thanking her silently.

"You said—" I coughed, clearing my throat. "You said, 'I won't find him down there.' *Who* were you implying I was searching for?"

She laughed, a real laugh, and leaned back in her chair. "Oh, my dear, do not think me blind or stupid. Please."

"No, I would never I—"

She held up her hand, stopping my progression. "You and your *knight* are very close, yes?" Her lip pulled up to one side.

I didn't know what to say, or how to respond. My jaw went slack as I watched her carefully set her cup down on its saucer. A knock came at the door, and she gestured for the guards to open it, allowing in a young boy who ran through into the chambers. He moved to grab the Queen around her shoulders, hugging her with so much unbridled affection. She let out a soft laugh and patted his hand that was locked around her. She whispered to him, and he waved to me. I waved back and he retreated just as quickly as he'd come.

I smiled, watching after him. She stood. "Would you care to join me for a walk this evening?"

"Of course, Your Grace."

"Wonderful, I will have Avery grab you when it is time."

Avery led me through the halls. In each passing corridor, my eyes strained as they searched for Gideon. I hadn't seen him since last night and—well, I felt like we had a few things to discuss.

Stop lying to yourself, you just miss him. The nagging voice in the back of my head spoke the truth. I did miss him, and I wanted to see him and know he was not anywhere that Ilias may be able to retaliate after what had transpired.

Avery's long black hair swayed left to right with each careful step as she brought me closer to the small apartment Gideon had left me in this morning. It would likely still be empty upon my arrival. I sighed deeply to myself, and Avery paused. Her stature remained as she turned to face me. Her hands neatly clasped together as she spoke.

"Is there any trouble, my lady?" she said lifting her right brow, questioning my exhalation more than I had anticipated.

"No, no trouble. Just wondering what I'm to do for the rest of the day until I am to meet the Queen in the evening."

"The castle grounds are vast, my lady. You are free to roam as you wish inside these walls." She looked around us, her eyes catching on something in the distance. I turned to see what could have caught her attention, only to be confronted with more vast emptiness in the halls.

"You are free to wander farther if you do so wish. You are not a prisoner here, my lady. Just be cautious. Please."

THIRTY-THREE

My first taste of freedom hit my tongue like rich, luscious berries. The cart stood in the bustling plaza in the city center with the deep purple berries. They were local to the area and grew in the cold weather. As I stopped in front of the cart to peek at the unfamiliar treat, the man working it held out a few in his hand. I declined, saying that I had no money to buy them. His response was a deep laugh and a few kind words, "A lovely girl deserves a lovely treat."

I reached out, bringing one of the berries to my lips. The first bite into the juicy fruit was like nothing I had ever tasted before. The flavor was rich and so sweet. I thanked the man and continued my way through the busy streets. The scent of cooked meat and deep, robust herbs filled the air. Each step I took immersed me in more and more in the culture of Paymon. From the songs of the choir, to the women in front of the garment stands, twirling silken scarves onto people passing by, hoping to pull one of them into the stalls to purchase a gift or two.

As I walked deeper through the swells of people, I finally

seemed to be reaching the end of the long hall of shops, and the sound of the city began to fade. The lights grew dim, and the air emptied of the sounds of the patrons and shoppers. It was a stale kind of feeling.

My eyes were drawn to a curtain hanging in front of an entryway. It was dark red and held the same sigil as on the mantle of the crimson cloth knights. My throat grew dry as I tried to force down a swallow. I pulled the fabric to the side finding a dark hallway hidden behind it.

The pull to go in grew stronger. All sounds of the busy city disappeared as I crossed the threshold. Walking through the darkness, my fingers reached out to graze the stone walls. They were rough and the texture stuck to the skin on my fingertips, but I didn't want to let them go. It felt like these stones were grounding me to this plane. I rounded a sharp corner, and a soft orange hue ate into the darkness. A hint of incense wafted through as I found the end of the dark tunnel.

A deep red tapestry housed the inside of the small room. At the center sat a bare wooden table filled with obscure jars and trinkets. A chair sat at either side, both vacant. I stepped farther in and looked around. There was no attendee in sight.

As I stepped closer to the table, I started to make out a carving in the center; the same carvings as the crimson cloth sigil—interlinking lines and arrows within two circles.

I reached out, the tips of my fingers wanting to trace over the carvings.

"I wouldn't do that if I were you."

Startled, I bumped into the table, spilling the contents of one of the jars. It was filled with a deep black liquid that seeped out onto the table, leaking into the carved grooves of the sigil. I looked at the person who gave the warning and was face to face with a Saint. But they were unlike any kind of Saint I had ever seen. Their veil was black, with matching robes, unlike the deep red of the Saint's in the cathedrals in the Oriens.

The face was almost discernible beneath the sheer veil layer, but in this dim light it was filled with so many shadows.

I found my voice again, able to choke out the few words, "What wouldn't you do?"

They walked closer, only a few inches away from my face. This person was about half a head taller than me and smelled of thick incense.

"I wouldn't touch a Demiurge sigil. I especially wouldn't touch a Demiurge sigil filled with demon's blood."

Demon's blood?

Thinking back to when I'd sat with Marigold as she'd cared for the rope wounds on my neck, I remembered she'd had similar jars filled with a black liquid in her pantry. She'd known much more than she let on about. And her cryptic advice about my necklace, God, I wish I'd known to ask her more about it when I'd had the chance.

I pulled my gaze away from the veiled figure and back to the table. The deep black liquid felt like it had a weighted power. I now understood the pull I'd felt coming into this place now; this dark energy guiding me.

The Saint took a seat at the table, picking up a paintbrush and dripping it into the black blood. They traced it over the sigil in slow and steady swipes, making station at the most southern point. The energy in the room built and the air within my lungs burned like I had inhaled smoke.

The *demiurge* sigil before me began to glow, a pulsating vermilion overtaking the blackness. The glow emanating seemed to move in harmony with each uncomfortable breath I took.

"Sit," the Saint said flatly. I obeyed, sitting across from them, transfixed on the glowing sigil before me. Words reached my tongue, but they didn't make it past my lips. I wanted to know more. To know what it meant.

They began to speak unintelligibly in Old Amaymon, their tongue dancing over the foreign syllables, like a song.

"Give me your hand."

My body jerked at the command, and I stretched out my hand without missing a beat, my palm floating just above the glowing sigil. Heat rose from it and met my skin in soft tingles of energy. The Saint reached out, clasping my hand in both of theirs, one above and one below. Energy prickled and built in my fingertips, a sharp sensation working through. I recoiled. The Saint reached out, locking their hands around mine so tight their fingernails dug into my skin, refusing to let me go.

They started to speak again, a breathy and hushed string of words, their voice growing louder. The room around us shook as the voice leaving the Saint became hard, and hoarse. They took a vicious breath, and the room stilled. They spoke again, this time in Old Amaymon. "Speak. Listen. Learn." The three words caught my attention. Then more and more. "For they come and go, no longer waiting for a soul to save them but a soul to set them free. A soul of both creation and passion. A soul of both death and perpetual life. A soul of never-ending desire. Never to be satisfied. Never to be extinguished. A soul for all. A soul for none."

"What is your plan from here?" The voice was known to me. I blinked away the haze over my eyes. My head felt only partially attached as I turned to face the orator beside me. My vision was slow to catch up, but they made the final station on the beaded bodice the Queen wore.

She sat neatly in her fresh gown, the hues now a deeper

tangerine and olive. Her hands vacillated between her lap or lifting a cup of tea to her lips.

I looked down at my own cup, full of well-steeped liquid unencumbered by milk or sugar.

She just asked you a question. A voice rang out in my head, startling me from this bizarre stupor.

"I'm sorry, please—please repeat that."

The Queen gave a concerned look and sipped from her cup. "What are your plans after this? Are you to travel back with Ilias, or—?"

Bile grew in the back of my throat at the thought of being stuck with Ilias for any longer. For all I knew, he would leave me stranded in the middle of the woods. *Wait, he already had.*

I inhaled, righting my posture and taking a thoughtful approach to her question. *What was my plan from here? What was I really wanting to do?* Then it dawned on me. The real pull to my journey's end was not just going back with Ilias. Not just going North. I wanted to do more. I needed to do more.

"Stop the demons." The words passed my lips, and a feeling of rightfulness filled my chest. This was what I must do.

The Queen's eyes went wide for a moment, and her mouth picked up into a toothy grin, showing off more expression than I had seen in our previous encounters.

"That is quite commendable, my dear, but to destroy the demons, you will have to destroy man itself."

"What do you mean by that?"

"Do you know why we keep the murals from before The Fall? Why our cathedral is not like yours?"

"No, I don't. I have wondered why, but I never really understood. I can't read Old Amaymon, so I never knew."

She stood, wiping away any creases made in her dress, and

extended her hand down to me. I took it in kind, standing. I still felt off center but was able to right myself.

"Come, it is better to show you."

She led me down through an unoccupied hall. Wall hangings and murals graced each side without so much as a hairsbreadth of space in-between the royal lineage portraits. Row after row of somber faces stared down at me. Their contempt filled expressions lingered within the fibers of the stretched canvases, as they resided in their finite places as this hall's silent observers.

Light filtered in above me as I followed the Queen deeper, sky lights winking through the eaves and illuminating the area. As we reached the end of the corridor, refractions of light littered the walls, and wavy washes of silver danced along the space. And an object I was not anticipating to find stood central at the final recess.

A fountain.

Its water shined like diamonds that rippled on its surface, in the flow and soft trickle of water. Beneath it was the inscription:

Thy shine by the light that fills the cosmos
Thy cup fills from the fountain of knowledge
And the grace of the ether flows in her.
For she is the made, and the maker
For she is the giver and taker of life and the
gift given to remain.
Through the seed of desperation is necessity
fruitful
By the blood of the legion, are we born
To bring back our brothers and sisters of
calamity
For calamity brings.

I read it over and over again, the words repeating on my lips.

"What does that mean?"

The Queen's brows knitted together. "Did you not say you could not read Old Amaymon? You recited the hymn of Sophia perfectly."

"I—I can't. I've picked up words here and there but that's not ..." my voice trailed off and my thoughts went off even farther. I *couldn't* read Old Amaymon.

"It is. Sophia once was a powerful God, once filling our world with wisdom and fruitful lives. She became the point of interest from another young God. He was still aged beyond our understanding but not quite as long as Sophia. She was at the beginning of our realm and long before."

We walked farther down the hall and stopped near the entrance from the day we'd arrived, in front of the large mural of the faceless God Zaphon. The same shiver worked its way down my spine as I stared up at it.

"After the young God acted out of term, he was then cast out, left immortal but with no powers inside him. He grew jealous and made a deal. He snuck back and stole the spark from Sophia. Then he turned, killed all the other Gods and took the final seat as our one God. He reigned for centuries until Sophia gathered all the broken sparks of the fallen gods and finally overpowered the God Zaphon and cursed him to Abaddon two hundred years ago. Where he is said to reside to this day."

A *God? Living in Abaddon?* The spinning feeling in my head returned and I looked to the place where the face had been painted over, my eyes trying to see past the coverage, like I was trying to pull an image from a deep memory, but it fluttered away the moment it made its way in.

"Where did the demons come from?"

"They were born of Zaphon's greed. He has a spark still in him. It is small, but it can be amplified."

"How can it be amplified?"

The Queen gestured to the mural and the item being held in his hand. My eyes went wide. How had I never noticed? At the end of the chain, hanging from his fist was a large black stone, gigantic in comparison to the one around my neck. But still. I gulped back the knot forming in my throat.

"To end the demons, that is to end Zaphon."

I laughed to myself. "How do you kill a God?"

THIRTY-FOUR

I must tell Thorian. Those were the first words that came to my mind after speaking with the Queen. As soon as we left the murals and parted ways, I all but ran to the apartment. It was empty and dark but for a single candle melted about half down its waxy column. Had Gideon come and gone while I was away? A small ache grew within my chest.

Stop, not now.

I had more pressing things to handle than a—a God I don't even know what. I needed to find something to write with. I had to get word to Thorian as soon as possible.

After all but ransacking the place, I found a few stray pages, a pen, and the wax to seal it. I scribbled the rushed words all along the page and finally sealed it away.

The door cracked open behind me and I all but jumped out of my skin. Salt and citrus hit my nostrils before I even could turn to face the door. A deep churning of dread in the pit of my stomach grew as my eyes tracked over his form. He was tall and angular and with the crawling shadows dancing menacingly over his features, he looked all the more malicious.

I gulped and stuffed the letter in a fold between my skirt and my body, *praying* he wouldn't notice.

Ilias stepped in past the threshold and the light from the candle lit him further, increasing the shadows. The smile crawling over his lips brought forth his deep dimples embedded into his cheeks. I met his eyes. They were dark and backlit with something heavy and—and evil.

His lips ticked up higher, as if he was holding back laughter. I stepped away, my backside only making it a few inches before it butted up against a wall.

As he grew closer, I could see his skin had grown grey and a tinge of red blossomed in the corner his left eye, but other than those small changes, he looked relatively unscathed from the other night.

"It's time to go." His words were short and clipped. My heart pounded as I conjured up a response.

"Go? Go where?"

"Back to the Midlands. My audience with the Queen has ended and we are due back."

"You're taking me back with you?" I was so confused. After everything that had happened, he still thought I'd be going on my merry way back with him?

"Yes. You came with me; you leave with me."

"Where is Gi—my knight."

His jaw tensed. "Outside. Grab your things and meet us. You have ten minutes." He left without waiting for a reply. I scrambled, collecting my bag and changing into clothes better suited for travel, tucking the letter into my trouser pocket.

Thoughts of staying and telling Ilias to fuck off were there, believe me. But if Gideon was heading back, then— I don't know. *God, what the fuck was happening?* I didn't ... I didn't know what to do.

The door opened again, and Avery entered, concern

furrowing her brow. She knew Ilias was bad news, but where else would I go? My home was destroyed, and this kingdom was not an ally in the slightest. Even if the Queen had been kind to me during this stay, politics were what they were.

My shaky hands pulled the letter from my pocket. I bit back the tears of fear threatening to break free.

"Avery, can you please send this out? It must—" I choked on the welling in my throat. "It must be tonight. It's urgent."

She read over the address, nodding and pulled me into a hug. I went still, surprised by the gesture. But after a few seconds, I relaxed into her and wrapped my arms around her torso, reciprocating the gesture.

"By the blood of the legion ..." My blood ran cold. She'd whispered the words against my hair, so quietly I wouldn't have known them if I had not just recited them over and over to myself. I pulled away and while her eyes were serious, we exchanged no further words.

Ilias was seated in the middle of the company. It was much smaller now since the attack by the bandits in the woods. I rode near the back, lingering as far back as I would be allowed. The only person any farther behind was Gideon. He was once again atop the midnight steed and stood out larger than life against the others.

We still had not said one word to each other since last night, and it was fucking killing me. Every spare moment I had to glance back at him, I took. And each time I was met with his helmet's cold hard steel staring back at me. Was he thinking about it, too? Was he concerned about us traveling back with Ilias?

After hours of riding through the night and following day, we made it back to Garrison Avesta. The setting sun cast shadows as we passed by the alleyway I'd been attacked in. My skin crawled as I remembered what had been so close to happening if Gideon hadn't found me.

The inn was surprisingly empty, and all rooms were vacant. I sought out a night alone and away from Ilias. There was no argument, and if there had, I would have gone to sleep in the stables.

In my solitude, I felt safe enough to empty my bag and go through its contents. I pulled out the two journals and a pair of spare clothes I had stashed from the apartment. The bag should've been empty, but I brushed against something hard and cool. My fingers closed over a hilt. It was a dagger, small and very elaborately carved with filigree all along the handle and the sheath.

Setting the unknown dagger down in line with my other things, my hands felt a pull to the journal debossed with the sigil of the crimson cloth. I held it in my hands, closing my eyes and breathing deeply through my nostrils and out my mouth. If anything had changed and I could read Old Amaymon I should be able to read this book now. Right?

Opening it to a random page near the center, I spied a language that was once lost to me and now was as clear as day.

Sangylous Sors.

Blood Magic

The left page held a depiction of a sacriment needle. The same one I had known my whole life as I made my many visits to the cathedrals for my sacrifices. The drawing showed the finger being pricked, bleeding, and placed on to the sigil. The same sigil on the right page.

I didn't have any sacriment needles—but my eyes landed

on the dagger to the right of the book. Picking it up, I moved it back and forth from each hand, feeling the weight of it. It was very light, which made sense why I hadn't noticed the extra item in my bag. Getting a good grip on the handle, I pulled it from its sheath, revealing a black blade. I held it up to the light; this wasn't blackened steel. No, it was stone, black stone. Legion Stone.

My fingers vibrated with anticipation as I held it up, almost craving the feeling of it on my skin; the sharp sting I knew would come from it. I brought it to my finger and winced as it pierced the skin. The feeling was deeper than anything I had felt when I had just merely touched the stone. This was more, stinging all the way through my body.

Watching as the red bead bubbled up to the surface, I took a deep breath and touched the bloodied finger to the center of the sigil.

The shock shot through my entire body making me feel like I was on fire and alive. The room spun around me, but I stayed seated. I closed my eyes and breathed, opening them once the spinning stopped.

I realized I wasn't in the inn any longer. I was on a battle-field, in armor and holding a sword. The demons were coming up over the ridge and I ran at them, my sword swinging and felling all who came across it. Then my sword stabbed a demon's body, and I was thrown back into darkness.

The room smelled of peppermint and I heard water dripping behind me.

"You shouldn't have done it."

I turned to face a woman, tears streaking her tawny cheeks.

"You should have just died like a man."

The words slapped me across the face. I realized I was in front of a mirror. My skin was loose, and my eyes were a dark shade of black. Hanging from my neck was a Legion Stone, its leather string dangling loosely down my chest in the opening of my shirt. Looking down at my right palm I saw a black spot. A stigma.

A loud booming knock hit my door. The room around me quaked and tumbled again until it finally fell back into place. I was back at the inn.

"Ten minutes," the voice shouted to me. The morning light shined through the curtains. My head pounded and my throat was so incredibly dry. Mental note: don't do blood magic.

After packing my things and slinging my bag over my shoulder, I opened the door to the hall and looked to my right. There he was. My knight. We hadn't had a single moment alone in days and the lack of closeness ate into my soul.

He looked down to me and reached for my bag, pulling it off my shoulder, his gloved hand lingering for just a second on my cheek. I pressed into it, not wanting the contact to end. The sound of a door down the hall creaking open made us jump apart. Gideon threw the bag over his shoulder and led the way to the horses.

There was a small breakfast served downstairs at the bar, but the flaxen-haired boy from before was nowhere to be found. And the way the men in the company violently forced down the food made me lose my appetite all together.

Out by the horses was only Gideon. He was securing saddle bags and making adjustments to the riding gear. His hands were without gloves for the more tedious tasks, and I watched as his strong fingers worked over the leather. An ache built in my chest at how badly I wanted those fingers on any part of me. I wanted more. I needed more. The fluttering in my stomach hit me as I thought back to everything he'd said.

Everything he'd done. *God, I needed this man in the most unholy of ways.* Turning away to find my horse, I put my foot in the stirrup and felt his hands grip my waist, hoisting me up into the saddle. His hands lingered on my thighs, and I tried to reach for him, but stopped as I heard footsteps approach.

I hated all of this.

THIRTY-FIVE

We rode the rest of the way to the keep in silence, past the forest where we'd been ambushed with no troubles and no demons to interrupt the momentum of the trip. The trip felt too easy. Until I began to feel flushed. I thought it was just run-of-the-mill exhaustion, but it didn't wane. This felt like I was coming down with something. Maybe it was from being caught in the storm, or just a mix of my anxious disposition and fatigue. So much had happened in the last few days and my mind and body felt run down.

Making my way up to my room I washed myself and crawled into bed, my head feeling heavy and my flush getting warmer. The maidens were very kind and brought me water and broth, telling me I was running a pretty high fever. I had a cool wet cloth on my forehead, the feeling like ice up against my burning skin. My body ached throughout the night, and I tossed and turned until I couldn't handle the puddle of sweat I was lying in.

Throwing the covers off, I felt as if I was housing a furnace inside of my rib cage and yet it didn't fight the chill in the air. It felt like my flesh was in a blizzard. I sat up and reached for a robe hanging on the side of my headboard, wrapping the thin piece of fabric around myself. I was sure I'd soak through it with sweat soon.

My steps grew steadier as I walked the room, making my way to the sideboard holding a decanter full of water. I poured the glass and brought it to my mouth, drinking down the full glass almost instantaneously. God, it tasted like the sweetest nectar. I took down another glass and wiped at any rogue drips traveling down to my chin. It seemed like the middle of the night as I walked to my balcony door, cracking it open to let in a little fresh air. But I was pushed back as a gust of air broke into the room, ripping the door from my fingers and wrenching it open.

My eyes drew over the horizon making their way lower onto the grounds. I peered into the garden below. Even in the nil light, my eyes caught onto movement. *It couldn't be?* Shock rolled through me. My stomach tightened and my breath caught. It was the man in the red bauta mask. Without a second thought or hesitation, I rushed to the stairs, keeping my hands tight to the banister. I still didn't feel fully like myself yet, the hard lacquered wood was my guide and stabilizer.

As I reached the door leading to the garden, I felt strange. Gideon hadn't been at his post again, and it made me a little uneasy. *Was he okay? Did something happen?* I shook my head, letting the negative thoughts go. I'm sure he was okay.

I pushed open the door and stepped out into the garden. There was no masked man in sight. Going in further, I made my way to the fountain. A sharp crack of twigs to my right caught my attention. And just like at the festival, the man in the red bauta mask appeared before me. He stood still; no wavering in his posture. I felt as if I had never truly assessed him before. The last meeting we were both seated, and the one before that, well, I hadn't been concerned about a random dance partner.

He was tall, probably a few inches taller than Gideon and sleeker, more angular through the shoulders, though he had a broad chest. Finally breaking the standoff, he bent into a low bow, revealing a head of jet-black hair tied in a low bun near the nape of his neck. I'd never noticed...

He stood and stretched out a hand. I held back, my fingers curling and uncurling at my side. His arm did not change position. I finally reached out and placed my hand in his. His fingers closed softly, and he brought my hand up to the mouth of the mask, holding it there for a moment. Finally, he lowered my hand, still in his, and like last time, kept a hold on it. His grip was soft, and I was sure I could remove it at any time. There was a sense of familiarity to him, more so than the last time I'd seen him.

He led me farther into the garden, and we walked beneath a covered tunnel that ended in a small stone circle surrounded by bright white moon flowers. Their sweet scent filled the area around us in a bewitching aroma.

The masked man placed his spare hand on the small of my back and brought me into a dancing pose. I placed my other hand on his shoulder, and he started to move us along to a song only he could hear. The steps were new but familiar, like I had done them a thousand times and yet never once could I remember moving this way. This was not the dance of any kingdom, but it felt good and fun. My head was still swirling from my fever and the smell of the moon flowers in the cold evening air.

The masked man, twirled and took out a small sacriment needle, pricking his hand and then immediately grabs for mine. The needle punctured me, and a bead of blood bubbled to the surface. I stopped. *What was happening?*

He brought our hands together, and before I could pull away, the magic swirled around us. Within a moment I was no longer in my robe and nightgown. Instead, I spun through a convex dimension, the world around me changing. The hidden music grew into a loud crescendo until it was no longer just inside his head.

Looking down, I saw I was in a grand white gown, its flowing skirts and tight bodice holding my tired body upright. The masked man kicked us back up into the dance and the walls around my mind melted, my vision blurred, and we were in a grand hall, surrounded by others dancing in similar attire. The music flooded my ears, and lively cheers echoed all around us.

We passed by a wall of mirrors and the person dancing with the masked man was me and yet not. There was my face staring at me, but my hair was different, glowing a bright white, like a moon beam. Long locks cascaded down my back and the top half was pulled into an intricate braid. Small pieces of hair framed my face and highlighted my cheeks. Her cheeks. They were a soft rose color.

Our chests heaved, trying to catch our breath from all the dancing. As I looked closer at my white dress, I saw the beading and embroidery and the way the lace covered my hands. Over my chest was a small amulet, hanging just above the cut of the dress. It was beautiful. It was. *It was.* Familiar. I had seen this amulet. It made me think of my mother. Of my childhood.

The masked man led me up to the thrones at the head of the room, made of midnight black stone. As I stood before them, a feeling of yearning filled my chest. My feet echoed off each step as I rose to the top of the platform. My fingers traced over the cool stone. The thrones did not give, or crumble under my touch; they were not imaginary.

I sat myself atop one and a small maiden appeared holding

a white and crystal crown, each delicate shard was casting a gorgeous refraction of light across the black stone of the throne. She stood in front of me and curtsied. I nodded, and she placed the crown on my head. It felt right. There was no other way to explain it.

I turned my attention to the throne beside me. A tall man was in my view, but he faced away from me. He had long black hair falling down his back and wore a similar but more masculine crown. Looking away, I searched the room, sensing the other man had taken his seat. I couldn't look at the man beside me, though. My head would not turn. I was frozen in place, even though I wanted to see him. He spoke, but it was muffled and inaudible.

Buzzing grew in my head again and a heavy feeling of darkness grew over the scene being played out before me.

Drip.

Looking down to my white gown, I saw a red stain.

Drip.

It grew bigger.

And bigger.

Instinctually, I brought my hand to my cheek. There was blood on my fingers. I reached up to the jeweled crown and was met with a sharp prick. The sensation of pain along my scalp grew and the stabbing of the crown's crystal shards felt like they were embedding into me.

Searching for answers, I finally turned to the man beside me. His face was not of a man. He was a demon; dark eyes sunk inside of the cracked black flesh. Twisted and broken horns rose from his head. He wore a crown of evil and darkness. His hand reached out to me, and I turned away. I tried to stand, but it was like I was glued to my seat.

The masked man knelt before me, his hand outstretched. I placed mine in his, squeezing my eyes shut, waiting for this nightmare to end. The world around me started to twist and turn.

The spinning halted, and I was back in the garden, the morning sun rising over the horizon, and I was alone. There was no masked man. No demon. Just me. I breathed in, settling a hand over my chest.

"Aleda?"

My eyes went wide at the familiar voice. *It can't be.* I turned to face him. "Thorian?"

Thirty-Six

He pulled me into one of his breathtakingly tight hugs that I knew all too well. I was in shock. There was no other way to explain it. It had been only a few days since I'd asked for the letter to be sent. Had they really gotten it to him that fast?

I pulled away, needing to make sure it wasn't just my eyes playing tricks on me. It was really him. His white-blonde hair was slightly outgrown from his usual crop, and his once youthful and bright ochre eyes were now aged and full of stress.

"What are you doing out here?" he asked as he stepped away, looking at my current outfit. My robe and bare feet were not fit for how cold it was outside. He moved in closer, placing the back of his hand on my face. "You're burning up? Are you okay?"

"Yes, I—I'm fine. It's just a cold."

"Then let's get you inside." His hand guided me through the garden and past the doors. I froze. My hand was clasped around something. I opened it just a little and my eyes went wide. It was the amulet. The same one I'd been wearing in the

—*dream?* I dropped it into my robe's pocket and walked ahead, leading us to my room.

There was once again no attendant at the door. My chest ached and the dread grew. Was he all right? I hung my robe back on the side of my headboard, just within reach, and slowly made my way back under my covers.

Thorian seated himself at the foot of the bed.

"You got my letter then?"

A crease formed between his brows.

"No, I haven't heard word from you since before the attack of—since before." His tone dropped at the end. He knew Kairos well and they would often cross paths in their pursuit against the demons.

"Then what are you doing here?"

"I could ask you the same thing. I came here on business and see my sister standing in a garden in the middle of the night."

I sat up a little straighter and reached for him. "Was I alone?"

"Yes ..." He leaned in and brought his hand back to my forehead. "You sure you're okay?"

"Yes, I'm fine. I got caught up in a storm a couple of days ago and must have ... caught something." I really couldn't escape thinking about him, could I? The same storm where everything between me and Gideon changed. God, the way he'd looked at me, just the memory was enough to make me weak. I'd never felt anything like what he did to me. *Where the fuck is he?*

"You never answered my question," I asked. "Why are you here?"

He took a deep inhale and leaned forward, his elbows resting on his knees. "I was invited by the duke's nephew."

"Ilias? What would he want you for?" He frowned at me. "I didn't mean it like *that.*"

"He has been sending me correspondents for a while, asking questions about the demons and particularly about Legion Stones." He gestured to the stone around my neck. I reached up and met the familiar bite as it stung my palm.

"What does he want to know?"

"The usual, how they work, what they do and why. Everything we don't know."

Everything we don't know.

"Thorian, have you ever heard of blood magic?"

His eyes widened and he straightened his posture, leaning back from me. "Why do you ask?"

"I found a journal in the cathedral records here. I kind of ... borrowed it. It's written by a Knight of the Crimson Cloth from before The Fall. He mentions blood magic."

He grabbed my legs and turned to look at me directly in my eyes. "Whatever you do, please don't go looking any farther. Blood magic is dark and evil. It has been long since banned. Just the mention could get you exiled. I would return that book before anyone finds it in your possession."

I bit my lip nervously. I didn't think now was a good time to tell him that I may have practiced blood magic just the other day.

"I will. I will return it in the morning."

"Good." He gave me a soft smile and squeezed my leg. "I'm sorry about Kairos. Word traveled fast about the attack. That never should have happened, the demons never should have been able to get past the gates, let alone inside." He closed his mouth into a tight line, halting any further words from leaving his sharp tongue. Thorian was never the one to hold back how he felt, but the years in the knighthood had straightened out some of his old habits.

"Thank you," I whispered.

"Word also traveled that the Queen consort was missing. Care to enlighten me?"

"After the *attack*, the Commander told me to seek asylum with an encampment to the East. I wasn't sure what would happen if they were the wrong people or just people I couldn't trust, so I withheld a little ... information. So please don't tell Ilias. I have been going by my middle name, and it's seemingly been ... fine."

"Yes, Ilias. So, are you two ...?"

"NO! I mean, we were, but things have changed." I leaned forward, grabbing his hand, "I did send word home. I'm waiting on a response from Mother to get me out of here."

"I see, well then, I will decide to keep our family-line a secret. But, with that, I should be getting on. I'll talk to you later, okay? We have a lot of catching up to do." He patted me on the head and stood, pausing at the door.

"Before I forget." He reached into his coat's inner pocket and pulled out something wrapped in a cloth. "I've been keeping this in case I ran into anyone who would be able to give it to you." Handing it to me, I slowly opened the wrapping. My eyes went wide as I saw the dagger. It was the exact copy of the one I'd found in my bag.

"It's beautiful, Thorian. Where did you get it?"

"It was Mom's. She had it for as long as I can remember. She said someone very important gave it to her. She gifted it to me when I was assigned my first scouting mission. It's yours now. Take it and keep it with you. *Always.*"

I exposed the Legion Stone blade I knew would be beneath the silver sheath. My fingers ran along the blade. I jerked slightly as it met my bare skin. Thorian reached down and resheathed it. He wrapped my fingers around the handle, forcing me to hold it tight.

"It's okay," he said in a low reassuring voice.

THIRTY-SEVEN

The next day, I woke up feeling a bit better. Still achy but hoping a bath would help wash away the last of this cold.

Letting the steam build in the room, I kept the door shut and allowed the billowing mist clouds to settle over me. The mirror was shrouded in condensation and left me in a sea of my own thoughts.

I had so much to think about after returning to the keep. I couldn't stay here for much longer, not with Ilias. Making my way North would be the next thing for me, but how? If Thorian could somehow take me with him, I could see about hiring transportation and Gideon and I could—

Gideon. Just his name ringing through my head had an immediate impact on me. My skin prickled in the cold air before I stepped into the warm water. The change in temperature stung against my bare skin but quickly turned into a welcomed heat.

I reached for the soap and started to lather myself. Bringing my hand up to wash my hair, my mind started to wander back to him. The feel of his skin on mine and his words rang out in my head almost as loud as if he were here.

The soap moved in foamy passes down my body, and I started to lather up my collar bones, over my chest and breasts. The water had started to grow cold, making my nipples become hard and sensitive. Running my soapy hand over them, I started to imagine the feeling of Gideon's rough hand come from behind me and make its way to my navel. Gently working its way up my body. My hands guided his to my breast, massaging me and pinching at my sensitive nipples. A gasp escaped my lips, and I leaned back into his hard chest behind me, bringing one of his hands down my body and over my soft curls at the apex of my thighs.

Slowly they went down, cupping me, holding all of me in his hand. I bit my lip at the pressure and coaxed my pelvis forward, wanting more. I brought my hand over his and pushed one of his fingers in just a little farther. They softly rubbed against my center, and I felt one finger slide inside of me. The pressure was good, but I wanted more.

I pushed for another. A deep moan escaped my chest. He started pumping in and out, the heel of his palm pressing into my clit. My head began to swim, the tension building until it finally crashed through me. The wave came so hard it was dizzying, like being under the water.

Centering myself and coming back from my all too vivid self-pleasuring daydream I settled deeper in the tepid water, submerging completely.

I wrapped myself in a towel and made my way back into the bedroom. The moment I passed the threshold, the door opened. In walked Gideon, dressed in his full armor. *How was that for timing?* He closed the door quietly behind him and twisted the lock. He walked to meet me, his hands coming up around my shoulders to give my arms a tight squeeze.

"What's wrong?"

He looked around my room, unsure that we were actually alone and took in a deep sigh. "I am to leave tonight."

I took a step back from him and my hand came up to my chest. "What? Why?"

He gave me a stifled laugh. "I'm sure you know why."

Ilias. He was sending Gideon away? I turned from him, pacing and trying to think on my feet. He can't just *leave.*

"But it was his uncle who hired you. Does he even have the power to send you away?"

"The specifics aren't necessary on who can or cannot relieve me of my duties. If he wants me gone, then I am gone."

"I understand that but, what can be done?"

"Right now, nothing." He leaned back against the sideboard and his head craned back to look up to the ceiling.

I went and sat on my bed across from him. His head was still leaning back his arms crossed over his chest. Was I going to stay here? I still planned on speaking to Thorian about going North. With Gideon gone I didn't want to be stuck here with Ilias. Alone.

"That's fine. We can figure something out."

"Aleda." He paused and looked to me. "There is no *we* with this. I am being sent away. As a Knight of the Crimson Cloth, I don't know what's going to happen to me. This isn't going to be a fun little side quest. This is a serious matter. I won't bring you into something I can't control and take you with me. I don't even know where I would be taking you to."

"North, let's go North. My family is up there. They can—"

God, the travel and the specifics, it was still so far away. I grew cold and detached. I needed to look into his eyes to see if he was really telling the truth. If he was really going to leave, then I didn't want to look at this version of him, the one hidden behind a mask and metal.

"Take off your helmet."

"Aleda, it's not ..."

"Take. It. Off."

He shook his head and took a deep breath. "I had a run in with the private guard last night. It was a very *combative* discussion."

I stood and walked to him. "Are you hurt?"

"Nothing that won't heal on its own."

"Show me," I demanded. I was standing directly in front of him now. He pulled off the helmet. His cloth face covering was still pulled up over his lower half, but it didn't cover the blooming black eye and cuts decorating his face.

I reached my hand up to touch the side of his face. He closed his eyes as my fingers traced down to the lip of his covering. I pulled it down and saw the line cut down from his bottom lip down the center of his chin. The line of a traitor. My eyes welled up. He grabbed my hand in his, bringing it to his lips and kissing it.

My heart felt like it had physically cracked open. *This was my fault.* People kept getting hurt because of me. I lifted my hands to my face. A sob wrecked through me. No one. No one is safe with me. Gideon was now scarred for life with that mark.

"It's fine. I've had far worse."

Wiping my face and letting out a sniffle. "You need to leave."

"Aleda, I—"

"Leave." I demanded, my voice fighting for solid ground.

"Alright." He didn't push or resist, and the small crack in my heart grew to a deep fissure. I heard him shuffle to replace his helmet and then the door opened and closed.

I was alone again.

THIRTY-EIGHT

It felt like hours had passed before I was able to pull myself together and get dressed. I chose against the dresses and wore a black long sleeve shirt with matching pants and a cloak. After the conversation with my brother, I felt like I needed to pay another visit to the cathedrals. If this book was to be of such a banned nature, then I should take it back. *Shouldn't I?*

Grabbing my bag, I threw the journal inside, along with a few other random books just in case I got asked about them. I pulled out the small dagger and placed it in the belt of my pants, along with the one gifted from Thorian. Hidden enough, I reached for my robe and grabbed the amulet out of the pocket. I didn't trust leaving anything while I was away from my room.

Opening my door, I find a different guard at Gideon's post. I wasn't surprised at his absence anymore. The new guard was a young boy, wiry and spry with a few rogue hairs growing in for a mustache. He didn't so much as notice my presence. *Not the brightest sort?*

I coughed to get his attention. "Hello, is there any way I can get an escort to the cathedral?"

He turned to face me, eyes wide and filled with surprise. "Hello, my lady, I've been given strict orders not to let you off keep grounds. With the recent change of guard, it's not the most advisable."

I quirked a brow up at him. *That's news to me.* Was Ilias punishing me and not *letting* me leave?

"Aw yes, I fully understand. But you see I am already late for my weekly sacriment. After our trip I wasn't able to make my offering. I desperately need to make a trip down. I promise, the cathedral is all I need to go to. It isn't far."

He bit his lip and shuffled in place, looking down each side of the long hall. "There's no one around; no one will know. If you are worried about getting in trouble, I can go out through the servant's entrance while you remain at your post. No one will be of the wiser."

He sucked in a small breath through his teeth. "No, I can take you. I understand the need for a sacriment. I should also tend to mine as well."

"Wonderful, can we go now?"

"Yes, let's make haste though. I don't want to be gone past dark. Demon activity is getting closer by the day."

***

We made our way into the looming cathedral, I made my sacriment and excused myself to use the washroom. Then I ran down the halls into the undercroft.

Reaching the bookshelves, I moved a few books to the side and hid the journal deep underneath, covering it back up. I don't want anyone to get in trouble if they did find it.

But my curiosity got the better of me and I wanted to do a

little more digging on the midland's history. They had stayed relatively out of all major conflicts themselves but supplying aid was a typical forte for them.

I found a few dusty scrolls and brought them over to a dimly lit table in the center of the room, bringing a light closer and unrolling the first one.

It was post-Fall by a few months. The names were written the new way and unfamiliar. Rolling it back up, I placed it to the side. The next scroll was a family tree of the hierarchy that reined over the Midlands, dated back four generations. This would be Ilias's family tree.

Stated mid-way down the page was the final recorded birth, Duke Aemon Azaraiah Ilisium. He had no siblings listed either. I turned back to see if there was another scroll that held an updated list, but the shelf was empty, and all neighboring scrolls were littered on the table before me. I opened each one, nothing. Nothing. *Nothing.*

I flipped one over, it revealed a large portrait of the duke, or it was intended to. The name listed at the bottom was the same, but the image was worn badly, scratches crisscrossing over the parchment, disfiguring it farther.

If Ilias held no relations in that manner, how would Duke Aemon Azaraiah Ilisium be his uncle? Was Ilias a blood relative or someone else entirely? Where would a seventy-something-year-old man be out to as well? All of my days at the keep and not one inkling of him around.

I looked over to where I had hidden the journal. I felt this pull come over me and I walked back to its place and removed the books I had hidden it behind. I reached my arm in and dug around until I pulled out a thin leather-bound book.

Wait a minute. This was not my journal. This book was black with a faded black ribbon pulled through the center of it, saving a page. I opened it, peeling the page apart at the ribbon.

The writing was well preserved, much more so than in the other journal.

The words *Sorsloc Cruor* scribed at the top of the page caught my attention immediately. A type of travel that allowed you to move within the realm. The sigils were similar to the ones Kairos had showed me or others I'd found in the knight's journal.

To avoid risking getting caught with the whole book I wrote down the sigil on a small scrap piece of paper and shoved it into my bag. I needed to find out more about Ilias. I put the black book back and headed into the main hall of the cathedral, looking for more information.

A Saint would know. They recalled all and were the keepers of the records. A loud scraping of wood echoed through dead space and the incense smell hung in the air, its sickly- sweet aroma had become a source of contempt more than its preceding symbol of the holy teachings. Looking through the intricate lattice window and the red of the Saint's cloak looming just beyond, I found I was once again, lost.

"How may I be of assistance my lady?

"I am in need of a revelation."

"My lady, would you like to begin with the sacrament?" they asked.

I pulled out a fresh needle and plunged the sharp tip once again into my sensitive skin. *A new finger this time.* I placed a small bead of blood into the siphon.

"We thank you for your sacrifice, my lady. What would you like in return for your offering?" asked the Saint.

"Tell me what you know of the duke's nephew, Ilias Terrell."

"Is not much to say my lady. The duke has run these lands for many years."

"Yes, but what of his nephew, Ilias?"

"You speak of the duke my lady. There is no nephew."

No nephew? Just as I assumed.

"Where is the duke?" I asked again.

"The duke is in the keep, my lady."

In the keep? Had he been there the whole time? I had yet to explore the rest of it, but I hadn't heard any word he had returned.

"One last thing."

"Yes, my lady."

"What is this?" I held out the amulet the masked man had left with me in the garden. The Saint slid the lattice back and its crimson-gloved hand reached over and grabbed my wrist. They were careful not to touch the amulet but brought it closer to the sheer fabric covering their eyes.

A soft hiss escaped their mouth. "That, that is the amulet of Lilit." Its other hand reached up and drew a long finger down my arm, starting at the crook of my elbow and down to the amulet in my palm. "You have been given a gift, my lady. A very special gift." It closed my fingers back around it and released me, closing the lattice window once more and the additional curtain behind it, casting me into full darkness.

I left the revelation and headed toward the entrance; the guard I'd stationed there looked quite flustered. We exited and found night had fallen and the stars were out once more. We needed to be back.

We passed by the tavern Gideon and I stopped into the last time I'd visited the Midlands Cathedral. I thought about sitting and listening to the patrons to see if they had anything to say about our return or the duke. *Maybe I could ask around.* I watched as the guard walked ahead of me, and as he took the turn at the end of the block I hung back and went into the tavern.

I pulled the hood of my cloak down low, hiding my face. It was particularly busy today and all the tables were full. Maybe if I waited in the back, I could keep an eye on an empty table.

Scanning over the patrons I landed on a table of two royal guards. Their helmets were off, and they sat relaxed in their seats. Neither of them was familiar to me but they were much older than I would have imagined for royal guards. One of them had hair sprinkled with salt and pepper streaks and the other's hair was nearing all grey. Their voices were deep and carried even as they spoke low.

"Odd that the duke discharged us early, isn't it?"

"I'm not complaining. He's been acting odd since he returned. Not right in the head, is he now? Been asking us to burn all incoming and outgoing correspondence for weeks. The only things to come through are marked with his returning seal."

Weeks? All my letters to my mother *burned?* No, it couldn't be. I couldn't be completely at Ilias's fucking mercy. Panic swirled in my chest, and I couldn't keep air in my lungs long enough to use the oxygen. I had to get to Thorian before he left.

I walked further into the tavern finding a hallway that led into the back of the building. I thought I was undetected until a hand gripped my shoulder and pushed me into a wall. They ripped my hood up and off and brought a small blade to my neck. To my surprise it was a girl not much younger than myself, but she loomed over me by at least a foot.

"Lose your way or something?"

I gulped and my brain went silent. "I—I"

"Yes, you. What are you doing back here? Slinking around? Trying to rob the place?"

"No! No. I'm just looking for the—the bathing chamber."

She gave me a confused look and inspected me with dark brown eyes. The same dark brown Gideon had. The longer I looked at her I realized they did share some of the same physical qualities, the deep tan skin and olive complexion. She must be from Amaymon as well.

She lowered the blade and her face softened. "You need to get out of here. It's not safe for you without a knight. Go. Home." She shoved me up and off the wall.

I took her warning and headed back toward the keep, staying close to the main roads and slinking to the alleyways to keep myself hidden from the guard I'd dodged. I knew he would not appreciate me giving him the slip.

The night sky overhead was showing some of the most well-lit constellations I had seen in a long time: Cassiopeia, Cepheus, and Ursa Major. The twinkling lights danced across the inky black sky.

The cloak's hood slipped back and a fresh layer of fog rolled in to the streets. The lamps now looked like floating orbs, their posts hidden out of sight. Being out alone in the foggy streets began to feel more eerie by the second.

Walking past a dark alley, I heard a clatter and voices. I began to sprint, turning around the next building and taking a right towards the keep. I could see the lights settled into the high windows.

I'm close, it'll be fine. I slowed back to a normal walking pace, letting out a slow exhale and as if my own breath reached out and extinguished them, all the lanterns lighting the streets were snuffed out. A chill crept up my spine and I turned around, looking at all of my surroundings. The air was silent. My heartbeat felt like it was in my throat. I cursed myself for giving the guard the slip. Something didn't feel right. The guards being released early and the concern from the girl. What did she know?

Finally, I took the last few steps and approached the keep grounds. I turned to face the darkness while I reached for the Legion Stone around my neck, taking a deep steadying breath. Something was off.

THIRTY-NINE

Getting back to my room, I hung my cloak on a hook near my sideboard and took a deep breath. I needed to get to Thorian before he left. A hand snaked out of the shadows and grabbed me over my mouth while another hand wrapped around my abdomen. The intruder yanked me into them and I shoved my body back, forcing us into a wall. Their grip loosened enough so I could reach for the daggers in my belt. I spun and held one up to the intruder's throat. Just a warning amount of pressure and a soft choke of surprise followed by a chuckle vibrates down my body. Hot breath washed over my cheek and a voice whispered, "I have been waiting to play rough with you for some time now. I'm happy to see you make the first move."

Gideon.

His grip loosened but I kept my dagger pressed into his throat. He wore a large hood over his face and was no longer in his armor. Instead, he wore all black clothes and a cloak. I took a deep sigh and lowered the blade. As I did so, he took my wrist, holding the knife in his hands and forced the blade back into his throat. He pushed in deeper than I had, and a small bead of blood trickled down to his collar. I pulled it away quickly and got my hand free from his.

"Why would you do that?" I exclaimed, putting the knife down on the sideboard and pulling his hood back. His face looked just as puffy and bruised as before.

"I guess you can say I'm a glutton for punishment when it comes to you."

My heart picked up. "I told you to leave."

"I did, and I don't remember there being a time limit on my return."

I tried to take a step away from him, but he pulled me back into his hard chest. His arms ensnared mine. His warm breath came close to the shell of my ear again and he said in a deep breathy tone. "Don't be so hasty. I have other things planned."

I became all too aware of where his hand was moving to. One was splayed across my lower stomach and the other one just below my breast. His touch felt warm, and I wanted to lean into it. I relaxed and pushed into him. His hands grabbed at my shirt and pulled me harder. A low rumble grew in his chest and my breathing increased.

His face nuzzled in closer to my ear and his lips touched where my jaw and neck met. They traveled down to the crook of my neck and bit down. Shock hit me and I turned in his arms.

He gave me a small smile and pulled my mouth into his. His hand came to my chin and angled me to deepen the kiss. Both hands explored my backside, cupping my ass. I moaned and felt him smile into the kiss. I reached my hands up around his neck and he lifted me up on the sideboard.

Our faces were now level, and he took full advantage, his tongue exploring my mouth, his hands doing the same to the tops of my thighs, his fingers digging into the soft flesh. I bit his lip, toying with him and he pulled me in, pressing himself hard between my legs.

I felt his need for me between all the layers of our clothes. I wrapped both my legs around his waist, wanting as much pressure as I could get. I could feel the tightening in my lower stomach grow. My body reacted so much to his touch.

He broke the kiss and leaned his forehead against mine, taking in large gulps of air. With a wink, he leaned over and pulled off my boots, setting them near the door. Coming back up he pulled me into another deep kiss and reached for the clasp to my breeches.

"I need these off. Now," he said, his mouth pressed to mine, the words muffled and heavy. He undid the clasps, and I lifted myself up to pull them down and off. Not stopping there, he pulled my top up and over my head, dropping it onto the now growing pile of my clothes, leaving me in just my underwear.

He took my breasts into his hands, massaging them and pinching the sensitive skin of my nipples in-between his thumb and forefingers. I let out another gasp and felt myself flood with arousal. He lowered and took one nipple into his mouth. I reached up and grabbed hold of his shoulders, throwing my head back and reveling in the sensations.

He traveled back up to kiss me again. His mouth was ravenous against mine and my arms wrapped tight around his neck. His hand traveled between my legs, his fingers grazing me over my underwear. There was just a slim piece of fabric between us being skin to skin. He applied a soft pressure. I tightened at just the slightest touch of him there. I was already so wet, they had to be completely soaked by now. His fingers traced circles over my center, sending what felt like bolts of lightning through me.

I pulled away from the kiss to stare at him. I wanted so

much more than this one night. I reached up and touched his stubble-lined cheeks and he pushed into my palm, closing his eyes. I pushed a small piece of hair behind his ear, bringing my hand back to settle on his chest.

"Take me with you." It came out as more of whisper than I'd wanted.

His mouth pulled into a sad smile. "Aleda, I ..."

My heart stuttered as his face grew more grave. All the heat building in my body ran cold. I can't do this, not if I can't get more.

I unhooked my legs from around him and pushed myself off the sideboard. My feet were back on solid ground, and I didn't want to look at him and his—his gorgeous face. Even riddled in bruises and the cut newly gracing his chin, he was nothing less than a God. A God I would gladly worship. I would beg on my fucking knees for him but not if he didn't want that from me. If he wouldn't accept my idolization, he could find it elsewhere, with someone he deemed more worthy.

He took his hand to my chin and forced it to face him. His aura was darker, and he felt more powerful.

"Don't dismiss me." He placed a hard kiss on my lips, his mouth working against mine. His arms crushed me once again to him. "I want you ... I want to take you with me. I just have to finalize a few things first."

I looked him in the eyes, holding his gaze. "You promise?"

His hand reached up and cradled my neck as his thumb glided over my mouth. He pulled both hands into my hair and angled my head down, placing a small kiss on my forehead. His lips still resting there he said, "I promise."

He reached back down and pulled my underwear to the side, exploring my smooth skin, still slick with desire for him. Very gently he slid a finger inside of me. Then another. I clenched around them, reveling in their entrance. He slowly started to stroke and plunge them in deeper, then pulling them out entirely. A soft whimper left my mouth.

He brought me over to a chair in my room. When he took off his shirt, I noted more fresh cuts marking over his skin. He pushed me back to sit in the chair, grabbing my throat. He placed a hard kiss on my lips and turned me to face away from him and pressed onto my shoulders to lower me down, keeping my rear in the air. He grabbed both sides of my ass and pulled me apart, revealing everything to him.

His hands left circles on my skin and his mouth placed a soft kiss that quickly turned into a bite. I gasped and his mouth was back on me, consuming me whole. His tongue flicked at my sensitive clit. Nerves shot up my body and the tightening in my lower stomach was unbelievable.

He turned me to sit back in the chair his mouth and tongue continuing, lapping me up. I writhed under his touch, my body lighting up. He sunk his fingers into me once more and I fully came undone, covering my mouth with my hand to muffle my screams of pleasure. He watched me tremble removing his fingers and sucking them clean. "God you always taste so good."

My head was still spinning from the orgasm, and I sat up in the chair. Leaning down once more he grabbed my cheeks in his hands, pinching them together, forcing me to look up into his eyes.

The bell tower across the courtyard rang out the sign of the twelfth hour. His breath on me was exasperated but he knelt before me, grabbing my hand. He pulled a Legion Stone from his pocket and gave it to me, closing my hand around it. The sting was stronger than ever. "Stop! That hurts," I all but screamed.

He said nothing. I tried to pull my arm from him, but Gideon kept it clasped in his, his head hanging lower. He licked his lips and looked at me with dark eyes. He let my hand open. The flesh around the stone had turned black, but the stone was white. My body felt like it was vibrating both on fire and frozen. Pure energy filled me in the most horrific way I could imagine.

"What did you do?" I gasped, barely able to breathe. I knew exactly what this mark was. A stigma.

Tears welled up. He plucked the stone from my hand and put it in his pocket. He leaned forward and before I could stop him and kissed the blackened flesh. My head spun and I gasped for breath, unable to get any air.

Gideon stood and started laughing, a low strange laugh. Unlike anything I've ever heard from him before. His shoulders shook violently. He began to change, the hair falling from his head and his stature shifting. He turned, his face not his own.

It was pale and smooth and those fucking dimples. He was ... Ilias, but different. his skin was sallow and his cheekbones standing out and his eyes were the most unnatural color, a deep orange.

He came to me again, forcibly grabbing my wrists as he held up his hand, brandishing his own stigma, rubbing it into mine. Fiery pain burned my skin, and I screamed. I tried to pull away, but my vision went blurry. I stumbled to the ground and a black figure walked in and threw a sheet over me and picked me up, carrying me out of the room. Blackness surrounded me.

Forty

MY VISION WAS CLOUDED AND MY BODY FELT weightless, like I was floating among the clouds. Little by little I could see the light leaking in past my eyelids. Blinking back the heaviness in my lids I made out the large dark form carrying me.

Its horns, black as night reached up and twisted to the ceiling. The flesh looked charred and burned, the color of coal. I reached toward the horns. My fingers lazily floated up and above my face, feeling heavy and light all at the same time.

The demon faced me, his deep black eyes penetrating my soul. A deep burn ignited in my body like a torch. My chest tightened, and air felt too light to grasp onto. My lungs burned as a silent scream found me. Unfathomable pain rose inside of me. I turned my head, breaking the bridge of his gaze, and the burning stopped.

My arms, once light and reaching, were now anvils on my chest. My eyes felt heavy, wanting to close. If they did, maybe this dream would be over when they opened again.

The farther down the halls we got I heard distant

screaming and the smell of fire and smoke coming in from the outside. They were ravaging the keep, taking its people. We had to do something. *We.*

The weight of Gideon not being here stirred me, my eyes searched the hall for any sign of life, for any sign of him. But I was alone.

My heart remembered to sing one last silent prayer, to a God above or a God deep in Abaddon. *Alone.*

A tear fell; the once welcomed cool salty sting now felt like a personification of my mortality. The cold bitter ending I was going to face.

I came into this world alone, and I would die alone. But I would not die in this demon's arms. I found my strength and twisted in the demon's grasp, trying to free myself. It responded by digging its claws into the exposed flesh of my thighs, hard enough to draw blood. Panic set in immediately and I remembered the man who was scratched by the demon. The man who changed. *Caenum.* Was that now my future if I didn't die here tonight? Was I destined to rot and whither as a cursed woman? After everything ...

I cried out and struggled in his arms even more, flailing and fighting against it but it only dug its claws in deeper. A shrill scream passed my lips, until my throat felt raw. Blood seeped onto the white sheet my naked body was wrapped in.

We finally reached the throne room, the demon slamming and locking the heavy doors behind us. I was swiftly deposited onto the floor, lying in my mess of blood and now ripped sheets. Ilias on the throne. At the sight of him, disgust filled my stomach. He had pretended to be Gideon. He took advantage of me. I couldn't believe I'd ever let that fucking asshole touch me.

He was leaning in it with the most carefree expression. I

scanned the room, searching for help, any help, and my heart stopped.

Thorian sat at a large table to the right of the thrones. His arms were tied to his side. His eyes widened once they saw me. He was terrified, I could feel it. *What was going on?*

Ilias adjusted his posture and came to lean his elbows on his knees, resting his chin in his hands.

"Well, *Evangeline.* Isn't this a fun site? And also, a bit of a family reunion."

He knew. Of course, he fucking knew.

"Isn't this quite fun? He really has been the most helpful young man. Now haven't you Thorian?" Ilias said, gesturing to my brother.

Thorian's eyes dropped to the floor in front of him.

"Thorian?" My words felt muffled in my ears. He turned to me, and the look of helplessness grew stronger, and any beacon of hope died in my heart.

Ilias continued his rant of insanity. "You see, your brother was quite knowledgeable in the most obscure ways. He *had* traveled all over the four kingdoms in search of answers to the demons and yet, never thought to look into the eyes of the brethren beside him. He never looked into the souls of the men he trusted or fought for with each sweep of his sword. He never looked within himself."

"Thorian is no monster!" I bit out, using up the last of my energy. I was fading fast.

"You know so little about who is before you I almost feel a sense of remorse for you as I keep it all to myself."

Tired of Ilias's word games I finally sought answers unencumbered by his devious tongue. "Ilias, where is the duke? I know he's in the keep. Where are you hiding him?!"

He sat up. His face was elated, and a laugh built from him,

growing louder and more fucking insane with each passing moment.

"Oh, my dear, I thought you'd be smarter than that."

A figure similar to the Saints, but dressed all in white walked in, their head cast down. It placed an arm on Ilias's shoulder and stood behind him. A feeling of dread came over me. I instinctually reached for the stone around my neck.

"That won't help you here ..." The voice from the being came out as breathy long-drawn-out syllables.

Ilias let out another laugh and came forward more.

"You really are fucking stupid. There's no uncle, or I should say, there is no nephew. This here is Asmodei, we've grown quite ... *close.*"

Ilias opened his shirt to reveal dark and decaying flesh. The demon ran a claw down its chest, drawing blood. It rubbed the blood into Ilias's chest, the flesh decaying even more. Ilias moaned.

"You see, my dearest *Evangeline,* I *am* the duke. I'm the ruler of these lands. And I have found the fountain of everlasting life." He closed his shirt. "And you, you are going to help me finalize my payment."

He climbed off the throne, staring down at me. Then he reached down and gripped my wrist bringing my hand with the mark to meet his lips, licking the stigma. It burned.

"I haven't made a deal with anyone. This stigma doesn't belong to *me.*" The words passed through gritted teeth as I pulled my hand back. "You did this, I am not your payment, I am not yours to give Ilias. Fuck off."

He let out a laugh and went back to his throne, spinning the tip of a knife along his index finger. He watched me as I tried to stand and scanned the room again, searching for any help. For Gideon. My hands gripped the sheet so hard my knuckles turned white.

"If you're looking for your *knight,* he's been, *disposed* of." A smile crawled across Ilias's face, showing his too-sparkly teeth.

He was lying. I didn't believe for a second that he so easily killed Gideon. He couldn't have. My breathing came out ragged and rough. I hunched over and grabbed my abdomen. I was going to be sick. My eyes welled up with tears and I faced away from Ilias.

"Tsk, tsk, tsk, no need to cry, *my love,*" he said, stepping back down from the throne and walking over to me. I turned away, not wanting to look at him. All I felt was hate and disgust and shame. He wrenched his hand into my hair, grabbing a handful and forcing me to face him.

"If it's his body you wish for, you know I can help with that." His eyes changed to Gideon's amber.

"You did get so wet for me when you thought I was him. You writhed under his touch. I bet your pretty cunt feels so good wrapped around his cock, doesn't it?"

I spat in his face.

He paused. Venom might as well have spilled from his eyes as he lifted a hand to wipe his face. His grip on my hair tightened, and I screamed. He pulled me to him, and I lost my balance, slipping on the sheet and falling to the floor. His grip on my hair never faltered—he crouched—caging me in with his body, bringing his face too close to mine.

"You think I didn't know that you were *fucking* him? That a whore wouldn't do what a whore does best? You got into my bed quick enough, didn't you?"

He dragged me across the floor by my hair. I screamed and kicked, thrashing my body but it did nothing to hinder him. He sat me before the demon covered in the white robes. Its face was hidden to me, but I felt his gaze burn, like the others. A searing pain washed over my flesh as I sat back on my toes and stared up at it, tears flooding down my face. Ilias yanked back the demon's hood. A flash of light came first and then once my eyes adjusted, I saw it. Saw him; a creature of the underworld with midnight skin and eyes white and shining like stars. But his face wasn't a black shadow with black eyes. It was ... human with strong masculine features and long black hair rippling down his back.

I felt drawn to him. Just like I had reached to try and touch the other demon's horns, I felt the pull to touch him as well.

His dark eyes were hypnotizing. Drawing me in closer. I stood, holding the white sheet around me as I looked up at him. He stood at least four feet over my head. My heart raced.

A loud clatter ripped my attention away and I saw that Thorian had loosened his bindings. He stood, and threw the chair back and screamed, "ALEDA RUN! Get away from here!"

In a flash Ilias was on him, slamming Thorian's body forward onto the table. My brother fought him, but Ilias was too strong. The demon blood must be enhancing his strength. He grabbed Thorian's hair and wrenched his head up.

"Now, now, let's not be too hasty. They were just getting acquainted."

Thorian's panic-filled eyes found me. "Aleda, get North. You have to find Mother." he threw his head back, hitting Ilias in the chest. Ilias regained control as he dug his fingers into my brother's hair, squishing Thorian's face into the table with a bruising amount of pressure. Thorian took in a ragged wet breath, releasing the last words I would ever hear from my brother. "By the blood of the legion."

Ilias's eyes grew to the size of saucers, their yellow-orange hue shining against his sallow skin. He reached down and squeezed Thorian's cheeks, reaching inside his mouth.

"Let's avoid any more unwanted distractions, shall we?"

Ilias grabbed Thorian's tongue and raised the small knife he'd been toying with and sliced through it like it was butter.

My screams were trapped in my mouth. My eyes wide with horror, I forced my body to move; to go over to them.

Ilias threw Thorian's tongue across the tile. The bleeding pile of flesh skittered across the hard floor of the throne room. Ilias pulled Thorian back up, his hand still fisted in his hair. Blood poured from Thorian's mouth. The sounds of choking and gagging were all I could hear as he sputtered blood onto the table.

I was only a few steps away and Ilias stared into my eyes, his orange irises holding my gaze. With a sick grin, he turned back to my brother and dragged the knife across his throat. A final sputter of air escaped Thorian's lips as Ilias thrusts his head back from the table. The dead weight of his body following, and the loud crack as his skull collided with the stone floor. Deep, red blood pooled around him.

I couldn't ... I couldn't believe he was gone. Thorian was gone. Numbness filled my veins. I couldn't blink. I couldn't swallow. I watched as Ilias set the knife onto the table and walked to me, grabbing me roughly by my shoulders, his fingers digging into me.

"I do hate when guests try to spoil a good time, don't you?"

He took me by one arm and dragged me back to the demon, slamming me to the floor in front of him again. Ilias grabbed a new knife from his side and sliced down his palm. Droplets of blood littered the floor, and the demon leaned down, using the blood to draw a sigil.

The blood changed, glowed, and the floor where the blood was, fell away. The demon stepped over it and through. *Sorsloc Cruor.* He'd made a portal.

Ilias came back to me, pulling my face up to meet his. His

eyes searched mine, his face shifted, and he looked like the old Ilias. The Ilias that had called me love and fed me sweet bread and danced with me.

A tear fell down my face, "Ilias ... why?" I whispered. His eyes flashed, changing again. He grabbed my hand with the stigma, holding it up and bringing it to hold his cheek.

"When will you finally understand, my love? You are mine and will always be mine." His voice was not his own; it was the same voice as when I'd found him on the floor of his room.

I pulled my hand from his face. "I will *never* be yours."

He seethed, slapping me and throwing me to the ground. He ran his hand over his head, whispering to himself. "I told you; she is *difficult.* —I know, I know, yes, it will be done."

He was pacing now, and I crawled to my brother's body. I grabbed the knife Ilias had left on the table, hiding it in the folds of the sheet barely clinging to my body as I sat next to Thorian.

My brother's face was cold and losing color. His strong friendly face. I lifted his head carefully into my lap, sitting in his blood, soaking it in the sheet below me.

I'm sorry brother. I'm so sorry you were led here. You did not deserve this. Kairos didn't deserve this.

Ilias kept pacing the throne room in a deep discussion with himself. This was my last chance. I took a steadying breath, gripping the knife in my hand. I ran for Ilias. I just had to hit one vital thing, an organ, artery, one, and he would be down.

Raising my arms, ready to strike, I closed the distance. In a flash Ilias turned. His hand caught my wrist midair, halting me and knocking the blade from my grip. He pulled me to him, smashing his mouth into mine, hard and aggressive against my lips. I bit down, feeling my teeth tear into the soft flesh of his mouth as I drew blood. He pulled away and spat onto the floor. The blood was dark and inky. His teeth were coated and black dripped down his chin.

"I forgot, you like to play rough. Just like earlier," he growled, wiping his mouth. Staring at the black covering his wrist he began to laugh. He closed the space between us and punched me in the gut. Air rushed out of my lungs, and I toppled over, gasping, trying to force air back into my chest.

"You're making me hard again, looking at you on the floor below me. So small, so weak. I don't know how *he* ever saw you more than a hot wet hole." He grabbed the small knife from his pocket again and held me by my hair, forcing my face up. He brought the knife to the base of my bottom lip, splitting my flesh and traveling it down my chin. A traitor's mark.

He pulled me roughly up by my bicep, grabbing the tattered sheet and throwing it to the floor. I stood naked, trying to cover myself. He reached down and grabbed my exposed center. I yelped and tried to pull away.

"Oh, this pretty little thing is going to feel so nice against my cock. I'll finally get to see what our little knight friend saw in you."

A loud explosion sounded outside the room and the doors swung open. A huge demon stood before us. We froze and the demon let out a choked cough, spewing black blood over the floor. Its body fell forward, smashing into the ground, exposing the doorway.

A Knight.

My Knight.

Gideon was larger than life. His stature was strong, and he held his sword covered in black demon blood out and ready for any strike.

"Fuck," Ilias said under his breath. He kissed me hard one more time, covering my mouth in his blood, mixing it with my split skin along my chin. It burned and I clawed at it in pain.

He pulled out a new knife and cut his hand, dropping a few black droplets, squatting and drawing a quick sigil onto the floor. He stepped through a portal and was gone.

I kept clawing at my chin; his blood felt like acid and like it was traveling inside my body. Gideon stopped before me and threw off his helmet.

"What's wrong?" he demanded, shaking me, but the burning was eating into me.

"It's burning," I choked out. He grabbed a decanter of water off a nearby table and poured it down my face. It helped to sooth the burn, but the ache was still there. Gideon grabbed my face, his eyes searching over me, falling over the deep cuts in my legs and finally settling on my chin. His brow furrowed. Then his eyes met mine. They were filled concern and fear and — God, those beautiful amber eyes. I'd missed them so much. And he was here, he was alive. Ilias either lied or was mistaken, and I didn't give a fuck about either or where he went. I was looking into my savior's eyes again and I—I.

Screams came from the open door as more demons flooded the keep.

Gideon pulled me to him, kissing me gently so as not to hurt my wounded chin further. "You have to get out of here. Get somewhere safe."

I shook my head in defiance. I wasn't leaving his side *ever* again. "No, I won't ... please don't leave me, Gideon. Not again ..."

"I'll find you. I'll always find you." He caressed my cheek and placed a kiss on my forehead. He pulled his red mantle from his shoulder and wrapped it around my naked body. I nodded. He was right—I needed to get out of here.

FORTY-ONE

The cathedral was the safest place I could think of. I didn't know if the sacred ground would keep them out, but I would be putting it to the test. I made my way down to the stairs in the front of the keep and saw a fire blazing from inside. A loud explosion rang out, and I started running, not looking back. My feet slapped against the stone steps and finally hit some flat ground. The dirt and rocks cut into my skin, but I pushed forward, arms holding the red fabric tight around my shoulders.

I didn't know what to think about right now. I couldn't think about Ilias, or my brother, or what the demon blood might have done to me. I just needed to get away. Just breathe and run. That was it.

Making my way to the cathedral doors, I pushed them in, using all my strength. They only moved a fraction of the usual opening, yet it was big enough for me to slip through. I closed it securely once I was inside.

The smell of incense was almost overwhelming. I gasped, big gulps of hurried breaths that nearly choked me.

There was nothing to barricade the door. They never locked it; the cathedrals were open at all hours so I would be testing just how far the demons would venture. I walked through the main hall through the pews, down to the apse and empty altar. It was far into the night but typically the Saints were seen moving about perpetually.

My bare feet were cool against the stone floor as I stood before the chancel, under the empty altar. The great emptiness elevated it to a dark corner below the biggest rose window in the cathedral. Beneath it sat nothing. No God. No hope.

And still, I knelt. And still, I prayed.

For something, for *someone* to come and save me.

The candles were lit. The incense was burning. But I was alone.

I stood, taking a step up, then another, until I stood in the center of the thing we believe would grant us solace. I stretched out my arms and the red fabric fell to the floor, my naked body on the most holy pedestal, and there was no one to see it. No one to deny me my irreverence.

I stepped down, wrapped myself once more in the mantle, and searched for the Saints. I started at the black Box. There was no one. The hallways were bare; even the stairway down into the records was empty. The courtyard at the back of the cathedral was the only place left I could look.

Going through the back door I noticed how unnerving the outside felt. The cool air was brisk on my cheeks and by now my blood had cooled and pulse slowed. The early morning light was beginning to make its way over the mountain ridge, cresting over the cathedral's high walls. The courtyard was paved with weathered stone that extended to the farthest two pillars holding us in a deep rectangle. It had lush rose bushes lining the gates and a central fountain topped with a small morning star.

I felt a change in pressure around me; a kind of buzzing feeling traveled up my arms. In my peripheral vision, a sea of red started to envelope the courtyard. Saint after Saint flowed around me, filling in all the spaces, their faces hidden to me under their long red robes and veils. A sense of relief came at first. I walked towards one, words hanging on my lips. I wanted to ask for help, to tell them about what just happened, where I came from. But before I could get a word out, they piled in, close to a hundred red bodies surrounding me. Something was wrong. I felt like a cornered animal that just walked into a trap.

Walking forward to one standing slightly farther in, I reached out my hand. "Please, can you help me I—"

The Saint raised its hand, silencing me. It turned the hand into a point and gestured behind me.

Turning around, I was confronted with a Saint a few inches from my face. Fear wracked through me, and I stumbled back a few steps. The circle of Saints parted, and I kept stepping farther and farther back, never taking my eyes off the one before me.

The Saint lifted their hand, palm flat and held outstretched towards me. A spark ignited and a ball of shining light sat hovering just above their skin. It was pure white and rippled in the early morning light.

"Please,"

The light rushed at me, throwing me off my feet and sending me flying back. I didn't remember falling. I didn't remember landing either.

Epilogue

Gideon

THERE SHE WAS. STRUNG UP LIKE A FUCKING ANIMAL. What will she ever think of me now? Will she think I let them take her down here? The Saints caught her, dressed her in black robes and brought her down here. Black was for those who were to be sentenced. They'd looked at the stigma on her palm and knew a pact had been made. Holding her here was supposed to be for her own good while they decided what to do with her, but I knew with that color, their minds were made up.

I snuck down after a week of stalking a single Saint in particular. The little husk sang like a songbird when I pulled that sheer piece of shit over their face. I bet they thought they were untouchable in that red trash. They knew who she was and still, this level of treatment was barbaric for the Queen Consort of the Oriens. She was princess to the Northern Throne. She was mine.

I would not let her out of my sight again. She called to me

in my sleep, in my dreams. Attempting to leave her was a mistake. I could have avoided all of this if I just listened to her.

As a Knight of the Crimson Cloth, I'd made an oath to the Saints, I'd made a deal with the Queen, and I'd made a vow to my mother.

But I'd made her a promise.

A soft noise came from her lips as she stirred, her head swaying from side to side until her eyes fluttered open. My heart swelled with more emotions than I had ever felt. This woman made me question everything I have ever fought for. Everything I had ever believed.

She was my atonement.

Acknowledgments

If you read my dedication, flipped through every page until you made it here, then I want to first say thank you to you, my reader.

I'd also like to thank a dear friend, she has read every version of this story imaginable, even when it was a slough of unintelligible mass texts because my ideas were spewing out faster than my thumbs could keep up. Thank you, Marley. You inspired me to read and engaged in many a debate on Faye vs Vampire stories over your kitchen island as we ate soup near midnight. My favorite nights.

I'd like to thank my Chapters & Chains girls for your endless support and love you've shared for me and my story. You are my very own found family!

Last, but definitely not least, I'd like to thank my husband, Adam. You have shown me endless support, kept me grounded, and talked me through every breakdown and never let me quit. Thank you, my love, for everything.

www.ingramcontent.com/pod-product-compliance
Lightning Source LLC
Chambersburg PA
CBHW030343120726
47901CB00007B/1899